CRY FOR ME

ARGENTINA

INSPIRED BY A TRUE STORY

PHYLLIS GOODWIN

CRY FOR ME ARGENTINA

Copyright

Phyllis Goodwin

goodwinmaydene@aol.com

www.maydene.co.uk

DEDICATION

FOR LESLIE AND GUY

CRY FOR ME ARGENTINA

CRY FOR ME ARGENTINA

CONTENTS

ACKNOWLEDGMENTS

•

To my friends at Wight Writers thank you for your help and encouragement.

•

A special thank you to Pam Houltram who edited each chapter and made helpful suggestions.

•

CRY FOR ME ARGENTINA

PART I
1956

1

An unwilling passenger, that's what I am on this flight to Buenos Aires, forced to undertake a journey of torment. How could I have been married for all those years without knowing or even having a suspicion that William was leading a secret life?

•••

'We'll all have wine', called William to the Stewardess. 'We must be in the spirit of things!' The others didn't answer and Sybil drank her small bottle of Chardonnay hoping that it would dull her senses and help her to fall asleep. Flying was not really her thing. She preferred the old ocean liners with their open spaces and tranquil atmosphere.

'I'm really thrilled about this trip. I was only twelve when we came home to England and that was seven years ago. There is so much I want to see. Charlie feels the same. We just wish you were happier, Mummy.' Sybil smiled at her daughter 'I'm not feeling too bad, darling. Perhaps Daddy is right – everything will sort itself out in time. And you know how pleased I'll be to see Auntie Ethel again.'

Sybil was torn between her own feelings of impending sorrow and Nancy's enthusiasm for new adventures. William looked anxiously across at Sybil. He was sitting by the window with Nancy in the middle. Charlie was in the row behind.

'Would you like to change places for a while, Sybil? They're bringing tea round soon.'

'No thanks, I'm all right here.' Sybil felt anger welling

up. William could be so charming when he wished but he just didn't understand her anguish. She twisted round so that she was facing away from him. She must have dozed off when the lights were lowered and was suddenly awakened by the voice of the pilot: 'the temperature in Buenos Aires is twenty-eight degrees centigrade, eighty-two Fahrenheit. An ideal spring morning to start your holiday!' Passengers hurried to their seats in readiness for landing. Sybil began to feel anxious, but William was his usual self, giving everyone a running commentary as the plane flew low over the city.

His excitement was contagious – Sybil and Nancy leaned over to catch a glimpse of the sun sparkling on the muddy waters of the River Plate. The skyscrapers stood proudly in clumps and Sybil assumed that the patches of green were parks. In no time the plane was screeching to a halt and they had arrived in Buenos Aires.

A young man, smartly dressed, met them at the airport and escorted them to a nearby hotel. Sybil felt content surrounded by people chattering away in Spanish. It brought back pleasant memories. Their hotel was small and comfortable and Nancy ordered a light meal but Sybil hardly touched hers. She could see that Charlie was angry with his father.

'How can he just go on as if nothing has happened? There he is - just sitting in the bar with a beer, eating ham sandwiches, just as if he were at home.' Sybil was tired of arguments and decided to retire to her room. At two in the afternoon they were collected and driven to their destination. Here they waited patiently. The drone of the large wooden fans could be heard above the muted sound of the audience. Visitors were assembled in one of the splendid halls of the British Embassy.

The warm scent of jasmine wafted through the open windows and an air of expectation filled the room. Sybil sat with the invited guests. Those being awarded honours for services to King and country were seated nearer to the stage. She could see William's head near the front. Her gaze remained fixed on his small bald patch. His remaining curls were harnessed and flattened with brilliantine. It was just as well she remembered to pack the jar. William had been too distracted to think of such trivial matters.

Nancy was sitting at Sybil's side and every now and again she patted her mother's arm. 'Are you all right, Mummy?' she asked anxiously. Sybil merely nodded. On her other side was her son, Charlie, looking smart in his pinstriped suit. He'll be nineteen this year, she reminded herself, so handsome with his blond hair and light blue eyes. He just sat silently staring ahead. Nancy, on the other hand, was fidgeting. Her curly hair framed a pretty young face.

Sybil sensed that they were all finding it difficult to come to terms with the present situation. It was a nightmare and she fully expected to wake up and find herself back in England in her cosy house surrounded by favourite bits and pieces. Her thoughts drifted back to log fires and happy days since their retirement. Suddenly everything changed when the letter with the official coat of arms arrived. It was then that all the trouble had started. William was still in bed when Sybil took the letter to the bedroom and handed it to him with his morning cup of tea.

'It looks as if it's from the Queen and addressed to you.' William slowly opened the letter and read the contents.

'Well, what does it say?' Sybil was curious. There was no answer. The colour had drained from her husband's face and his hand holding the letter trembled.

'Is it a tax thing?' It could be, she thought. William was always trying to find loopholes in his tax return. He objected to paying twice on his pension from Argentina.

'No, it's not a tax thing,' he sighed, mopping his brow with the sleeve of his pyjamas. 'Come and sit here and I'll tell you.'

Sybil perched on the side of the bed and William began to recount an incredible story of his life during the war. Her discomfort steadily increased as the tale unfolded. It was endless. At first she felt elated and then her emotions changed to disbelief. She had spent over thirty years in Argentina with William as her husband. Now she was learning that for nearly five of those years he had been involved in all kinds of intrigue and espionage. She felt overwhelmed by a feeling of betrayal. William tried to take her hand but she pulled away.

'Why didn't you tell me? Or did you forget that I was living right next to you during the war?'

'No, of course, I didn't. Please calm down. It was difficult for me at the time and I did want to confide in you but you were busy with the babies and then we had the scare with the blackout. You were stressed sewing all the curtains and I was warned about keeping things to myself.' He paused for a while. 'I was so disappointed when I was refused permission to return to England. I wanted to join the Air Force. Officials interrogated me at the Embassy.

They knew all about my work in designing planes with A.V. Roe and my time with the Royal Flying Corps. Later that same week I was summoned to their office and this time I was offered undercover work with a qualified agent in the secret service. I felt it was a great honour to have been chosen. For four and a half years I carried out highly sensitive duties. It would not have been secret if I'd told you . . .or anyone else.'

Sybil refused to be consoled. The war had ended over ten years ago and she couldn't understand why he had kept quiet all that time. William slid out of bed and made his way to the bathroom. She heard him close the door but she remained seated on the bed, completely stunned by the news in the letter. William was to receive an award of some sort. She had no idea of why he deserved an honour. As far as she could see, William had been living a double life and at no stage had he confided in her. Why didn't she know about it? Had he told the children? Questions filled her mind and her sadness began to give way to anger.

●●●

A resounding fanfare announced the arrival of the Queen's representative. It was not the Prince of Wales as people were expecting and Sybil didn't recognise the tall, distinguished-looking individual. The audience stood for the National Anthem as the dignitaries, led by the Ambassador, moved to the dais. It was a long, drawn-out ceremony and Sybil sat in a trance as one person after the other climbed the steps to the stage. She didn't clap, not even when it was William's turn, but she couldn't help noticing his straight back and svelte like figure. It was hard to believe that he was over sixty.

After talking intimately to each person, the Lord presented what appeared to be a box tied with a red ribbon to each of the men and women. He then addressed the audience to explain the lateness in acknowledging these brave people for their work in the war.'

'They were all volunteers,' whispered Nancy. 'Dad was one of the six undercover agents.'

As they strolled into the adjacent banqueting room, Sybil realised that Nancy was deeply impressed by her father's award. Although she was reluctant to admit it, Sybil also felt proud of him. If only he had given her some inclination of what was happening and not suppressed it after the war.

Refreshments were laid out on pure white damask cloths with pink floral arrangements adorning each table. People were helping themselves to dainty sandwiches and pastries from silver dishes. William was a changed person. Men unknown to Sybil came up and congratulated him. He became animated by the chat of his former colleagues. Arrangements were made for a trip to San Juan and several of them were to travel together. 'I shall bring Charlie, so book two tickets for me please, Harry. Are you sure we can't go by train?'

'It's faster by air and more convenient for the lads,' was the reply. Sybil and Nancy stood together . . . locked in a sense of isolation.

'They don't even notice we're here,' insisted Nancy. 'Why can't we go?' she demanded. It was to be an all-male journey and Nancy was showing her mounting frustration. Sybil felt uneasy about the whole thing.

'Come and have something to eat, Mum. Just have a dessert if you don't fancy anything else.' They moved to the far table where an array of delightful puddings was on display: there on a long narrow silver dish was a selection of pastry cones filled with the local '*dulce de leche*'. Sybil could not resist one of Argentina's favourite delicacies.

'You loved this when you were a child,' she told Nancy. 'I used to let you and Charlie have a spoonful out of the jar as a special treat.'

'Yummy, they're lovely,' Nancy mumbled with her mouth full. Mother and daughter strayed into the garden to sit on one of the ornamental seats. A little later, William and Charlie followed, strolling down to the pond deep in conversation.

'I think we're invisible,' whispered Nancy as she watched her Dad and brother disappear. 'I don't know why Daddy has to leave us alone in Buenos Aires, I want to visit places like Charlie. I'm determined to see some of the country after coming so far. I wish you felt well, Mum, then we could travel somewhere together. Perhaps Auntie Ethel could come with us.'

Sybil smiled when she thought of Ethel, her dear friend. She knew her before she met William. Their friendship endured for all those years and it was a wrench to leave her when they returned to England after the war. Nancy was right, a trip with Ethel would give Sybil a chance to confide in her. 'When we know how long the men are going to be away, we could book a trip to Patagonia. You said you wanted to see the glaciers.'

On their return to the hotel, William and Charlie were engrossed in their plans, preparing for the journey. Sybil helped William to pack a small case. To her annoyance he refused to discuss his journey. 'You must understand that I have a lot of things to put right. I've already upset you and I'm sorry.' Sybil kept quiet and just made sure he had everything he needed. I've always been like this, she thought, tending to his every whim, feeling it was my duty. Bitterness was beginning to ferment in her mind. What was to become of them?

She was pleased when Charlie came to kiss her goodnight. 'Dad says if we have time we may drive up to see Puente del Inca,' he declared. 'Some of the high peaks are in that region.'

'Mum and I may go down to Patagonia,' Nancy chipped in. Charlie frowned.

'It's a shame we can't all go together', he replied. Sybil closed her eyes when the children left the room. She was utterly dismayed to hear her son whisper to Nancy:

'I hate to tell you this, but I think our parents are hiding other skeletons. I'm probably going to find out more on this strange journey to San Juan.'

2

The family was up early and breakfasted together in the small dining room. Nancy pressed her father for more information about the trip to San Juan.

'How long are you going for Dad?' she asked.

'Just a few days - Harry and I want to look up some old pals,' William explained. 'You'll have a chance to go later, dear. We'll probably have a family trip before we go home – just look after your mother, please.' Suddenly the dining room door opened and Harry came breezing in.

'Are you ready? The car's waiting.'

'We just need our bags,' replied Charlie. As father and son left the room Harry came over and sat down at the table.

'I've heard so much about you Sybil and at last we've met, though I do wish the circumstances were different. William has been knocked sideways by all these revelations. He genuinely believed his secret service work was buried in the past. I'm here to help with Charlie. I think you know what I mean. I owe Billy one you see.' He leaned across the table and gently patted her hand before leaving.

Sybil and Nancy stared at each other in complete bewilderment. A few minutes later Charlie and William waved to them from the door. 'Goodbye then, behave yourselves you two!'

Nancy poured some more coffee. Sybil nervously held the cup to her lips.

'We don't want to sit and brood,' Nancy tried to distract her Mother.

'You're right; brooding will not help matters. The trouble is that I feel my life is in a large box and my world has been turned upside down. The lid of the box is open and parts of my life are falling out. I am not sure if these parts are crumbling before my very eyes. It's a frightening vision. And what about this Harry Baker: who is he? I've never heard of him before and what does he mean that he owes Daddy one?'

'Oh, Mother, everything is so mixed up. I don't know what to say to help you'. Sybil knew she had to pull herself together. The events of the last few weeks were extremely puzzling, especially for her daughter and, in spite of all the difficulties, she understood that Nancy wished to take full advantage of her visit. Argentina had played such an important part in their lives.

'Daddy never stops talking about this place. No wonder Charlie and I want to see as much as possible. I feel it is part of my heritage.'

•••

Nancy came back from reception looking rather dejected. 'Auntie Ethel doesn't return from Cordoba until the end of the week. It's part of their holiday.'

'They didn't know we were coming to B.A.,' explained Sybil. She felt deflated because she so wanted to see Ethel again. What's that you have dear?'

'It's a leaflet I picked up in the hall.' Nancy slid it across the table. 'It's a three-day, two nights excursion to the Perito Moreno glacier. It's only a two hour flight and we could enjoy some good meals in the hotel and have plenty of time to talk about everything.' Sybil studied the leaflet. She was not over keen, but she agreed. Nancy smiled widely and Sybil could see the relief on her daughter's face as she went to reception to make the reservations.

The flight was at midday. 'We need something warm to wear. Mr. Alberto said to be prepared for the Antarctic winds.' In the quiet of her room, Sybil threw a few things in her case and then slumped on the side of the bed, her head on the pillow. 'What a mess I'm in,' she thought. 'At least Nancy didn't pick up the bit about Charlie – all that was going to come out! That was why William was taking Charlie with him and she was left to tell Nancy. I just can't do it!' Tears were streaming down her face and she felt like a traitor and - worst of all - she was William's accomplice. Her relationship with her daughter had always been close.

'Were you happy as a child?' Nancy asked her.

'Yes and no', she replied. 'Losing my Dad at fourteen was a terrible shock and I felt put upon when I had to leave school and help mother with the other kids. I felt, somehow, let down by my Dad. He was my hero and I adored him. Why did he die and leave me? He was the first man in my life.

'Then there was David. I've told you about him.' She twisted the ring on her finger and bowed her head. She refused to remove it - even on her wedding day. 'Then I had my escapade in Switzerland with Gustav and nothing came of that. It was when I met your Father that I fell in love.'

As they queued at the check-in, even Sybil was beginning to feel a flutter of excitement. After their passports had been seen, they wandered into the departure lounge. 'I'm going to look at the magazines.' Sybil followed and began to browse through the bookshelves.

'Here's a copy of Gerald Durrell's 'The Whispering Land' - I have read it before but I think I'll try reading it in Spanish. It covers his adventures in Patagonia. You may like to read it after.'

'That's the book in which Peggy's husband is mentioned. David Jones, do you remember I told you about it when I first bought my copy?' He was one of the drivers for the expedition. You've written to Peggy, haven't you?'

'Look, our flight's up on the board, we must hurry,'

Nancy took her mother's arm.

They settled comfortably on the aeroplane with Nancy by the window. The Aerolinas Argentina flight left on time. It was a fine day and the views were clear and distinct. Sybil stared at the changing scenes below. There were few buildings once they left Buenos Aires and the green started to merge into brown as they flew over the central areas. There were large circular water holes that appeared to be man-made.

Sybil noticed that Nancy was deep in thought; the magazine lay unopened on her lap. The affair that had brought them back to Argentina was probably on her mind. Sybil wished she could hide her feelings. Nancy and Charlie had probably discussed the revelations over and over again and had decided to stand by both of them equally, but they were finding it difficult to keep this balance. How could her children support both parents?

The voice of the pilot interrupted her thoughts – the plane would soon be landing at the first stop: Bariloche. It was obvious from the buzz of conversation that many of those disembarking were going on holiday. Sybil and Nancy looked out of the window and caught their first sight of the mighty Andes with their pine-covered slopes, bright blue lakes and snow-capped peaks.

'This part is known as the Argentinean Switzerland.'

'I wish I could join the crowd leaving the plane here.' Nancy told her mother.

'I've read all about this area with the fields of wild blue lupines and prehistoric monkey puzzle trees and beautiful lakes and valleys. I could even buy one of those ponchos made by the Indians on the reservations and visit that place called El Bolson where the hippies are supposed to be gathering.'

'I expect you'll come back one day, darling. 'The Cholila valley is somewhere near here. Butch Cassidy and the Sundance Kid sheltered in this region when they were on the run from the American agents. In the end they were ambushed and killed by the police.'

'Did you and Dad ever come to this district?'

'No dear, we could only afford long journeys when Daddy obtained a special pass for us on the train. Railways were our main means of travel in those days.'

It was snowing in El Calafate and the temperature was below freezing. They were pleased to be able to wrap up in their warm clothes and delighted to see a guide holding a placard with their surname printed in bold letters. The hotel was compact with a log fire burning cheerily in the lounge. After a rest, Sybil changed and joined her daughter. Nancy ordered an aperitif for the two of them and they settled down to study the menu.

'In Argentina, beef takes pride of place in every restaurant. The delights of a first class *bife!*'

'I don't know what to choose?' Nancy sighed. A middle-aged couple sitting in the corner ambled over to join them. The woman was neatly dressed in a royal blue suit and the man looked distinguished with his greying hair.

'Please excuse us, we heard you speaking in Spanish and hoped that you would be able to help us with the menu. We only know a few words.'

They moved into the dining room and the man invited them to share their table. He introduced himself as Frederic Schroder and his wife Carol. Even though their Spanish was limited, Frederic had spent time studying the wine scene in Argentina. Sybil thought he was a bit of a bore when he droned on about the wines as if he was the only connoisseur in the world.

'We're going to visit Mendoza and the San Juan districts. Hopefully we can taste those great wines made from the Cabernet Sauvignon grape,' he said haughtily.

'My Dad and brother are in San Juan looking up some old friends.' The waiter came to take their wine order. They had all chosen steak. Frederic ordered two bottles of red wine to drink with the meal.

'*Saludos*!' he said, clinking his glass against Nancy's.

For a brief moment Sybil was reminded of William and wondered how he and Charlie were faring but the worries in her mind were soon dulled by the wine and convivial conversation. Carol was a pleasant woman and Nancy found their travel tales quite entrancing. Sybil was pleased to see her happy for a change. It was past midnight when they retired to bed and all four were on the same excursion in the morning. The guide, Chichita, had asked them to be ready at eight. Sybil was awake early and went down for breakfast. She asked for tea and toast. Nancy came down a little later looking rather tired, but she soon revived after a strong cup of *coffee*. There was no sign of Frederic and Carol.

'Tour 240 for Perito Moreno, your coach is here,' announced Chichita. 'Please join us now.' The Guide was a friendly person and her English was excellent. People moved towards the door carrying their coats and bags. Sybil and Nancy were near the back of the queue but they need not have worried about getting a good seat because Frederic and Carol were at the front of the coach and two *seats* had been reserved for them.

'Come and sit with Carol!' boomed Frederic officiously, 'Nancy can stay with me.'

'We can always change later,' Carol informed Sybil. When they were settled, Carol whispered, 'Please don't mind Frederic, he's very bossy and just can't help it!' Sybil smiled and nodded. She looked towards Nancy who seemed happy enough with Chichita close at hand to answer questions. Sybil felt relaxed and was even pleased to be sitting *with* Carol.

There was a buzz of excitement and cries of delight when the guide pointed out the first condors gliding high across the valley. The coach slowed down and the mighty birds came closer. Sybil could even see the white ruffle round their necks. There were two adults and two youngsters.

'You're very lucky to see a whole family together. Usually we only see one baby but it looks as if this couple have reared two.' Frederic passed his binoculars to them for a more detailed look. The young ones were following and imitating their parents.

'Condors have been known to live for fifty years,' Chichita told them before sitting down again. Sybil sank back in her seat wondering if the birds mated for life? The coach picked up speed again.

'Are you on holiday?' Sybil enquired.

'Yes, Frederic is supposed to be doing some detective work. He's trying to trace one of his relatives, a cousin who lived in San Juan before the war. The old couple returned to Germany but the children remained here. The boy eventually joined the navy and was on the Graf Spe. He was taken prisoner but they never heard what happened to the girl. The Graf Spe was a German ship that was scuttled in the river Plate during the Second World War.'

There was a lull in their conversation as Chichita explained about the milky blue turquoise of the Lago Argentina. Sybil began to think about William and his hatred of the Germans. That was before they met their friends in San Juan.

'You wait and see,' he used to say. 'Germany will control Europe and the French will be on their side.' He was like that sometimes, arrogant in his opinions and convinced that he was right about everything. Sybil couldn't help smiling to herself when she remembered the arguments they used to have as a family. Charlie and Nancy were, like most of their generation, keen to forget the past and look to the future. 'Just you remember,' William would roar, 'Leopards never change their spots!'

'What about you Sybil, are you on a family holiday?' Carol enquired.

'Not really - we came back to Argentina because William has been awarded a belated honour for his work during the war. There was a big celebration at the Embassy.'

'Why was it so long after the war?' asked Carol.

'I suppose circumstances had a lot to do with the delay. What with the sale of the railways and then the Peron and Evita era, it must have been very difficult to arrange things, especially as most of the honours went to men and women who fought on our side and were born in Argentina.' Chichita's voice broke into their thoughts:

'When we reach the next bend you will catch your first glimpse of Perito Moreno on the left.' The passengers reached for their cameras and sat up eagerly in their seats.

The coach turned the corner and there, nestling in the distance, between the mountains was a craggy mass of ice. Sybil was amazed to see that the glacier was not white but instead a delicate shade of turquoise blue. It showed up clearly because the snow on the peaks on either side was pure white. The coach zigzagged round bends with the glacier disappearing from view and then reappearing nearer and larger. The ragged edges and large black cavities impressed Sybil.

'Why was William awarded an honour? Did he fight in the war?' probed Carol. Sybil felt uncomfortable. 'No', she replied reluctantly. 'He worked as an undercover agent.'

That night Sybil could not sleep. She tossed and turned thinking about her conversation with Carol. She had not told her the whole story and to her amazement she felt a stirring of pride at the thought of William as a secret agent. It didn't change the fact that he never confided in her and she still felt wounded at his lack of understanding. Sybil always made allowances for William's unusual ways. He'd told her so much about his unhappy childhood. She felt that his mother's 'bouts of madness', as he called them, had affected him in his adult life. Suddenly she pictured her own father on his deathbed with her mother and her young siblings standing in utter silence and despair . . . Tears crept down her cheeks and onto her pillow.

PART II
1906-1918

3

'Be careful with the skewer, Jason. I'll help you in a minute when I've finished reading to Sybil'.

'You're always reading to and playing with the girls,' grumbled Jason.

I cuddled up to my Dad just in case he decided to put me down and give Jason a cuff round the ears. Every evening he reads a chapter of 'Alice in Wonderland' to me. I feel warm and content when I'm on his lap and I love every sweet moment. My brother Jason is fidgeting on the floor trying to make a hole in a conker.

'That's all for tonight darling. Run along to help Mummy.' I gave him a big hug. 'We'll read some more tomorrow.'

Dad is in great demand when he comes home from work. First of all Mum sits him down to have a cup of tea with a slice of home-baked cake or, on special occasions, she gives him his favourite, a piece of bread pudding covered in sugar.

Millie, just four, and Jerry two, lean against Dad's knee staring up at his handsome face. They are allowed to dip their fingers in the sugar if Mum isn't looking.

'You grow more beautiful every day, Millie,' he chortled gently pinching her rosy cheek. As soon as Mother collects the empty tea things, Dad begins playing.

'Throw me up to the ceiling, Daddy!' Millie shrieks.

'Me! Me!' Jerry screams, stretching out his chubby arms and jumping for joy.

I would like to romp on the floor with the others, but I'm nearly seven and I'm the eldest girl so I have to be more grown up like Jason. I wait for my turn. Listening to Dad read is the highlight of my day. Jason is five years older than me and it's different for him. He likes making things with bits of wood and Dad helps him. They often disappear into the workshop at the bottom of the garden. Sometimes Jason shows off when Dad is reading to me, like tonight. He's trying to make holes in conkers ready to take to school tomorrow and he has a rag bandage on one of his thumbs where the skewer cut the skin.

Go on Sybil, see if you can help Mummy,' Dad urged, pushing me off his knee. I prefer to stay on his lap but Mum says that it's difficult to argue with someone you love. Sometimes I feel cross.

'I'm sure Dad spends more times with the others than with me,' I complain. She laughs and responds: 'Don't be silly dear – you always want him to read to you and time goes quickly when you're involved in a story. Daddy does his best to share time fairly with all of you.' Even though Mummy says this, I still feel as if I'm the in between one in the family. After every birthday, I'm expected to do extra chores and spend increasing time helping my Mother with the young ones.

Millie has blue eyes like me but my Auntie Meg says they look brighter than mine: 'Her eyes shine out of a perfectly round face framed by delicate black ringlets. She is a pretty child!' Dad says beauty is not the only thing in life and that intelligence and kindness are the two things that should be aimed for. On one occasion when Auntie Meg was visiting I heard her say: 'Sybil looks more like Henry every day. She has the same pale skin, almost translucent.'

'Yes,' agreed Mother, 'though her best asset is her golden hair. It's very thick and that's why I tie it back in a bunch.'

'Sybil, will you comb Millie's hair please?' I start by

trying to get the knots out and sometimes I'm mean to my sister. I pull so hard that I make her squeal.

'Ow!' she yells, 'you're hurting me.'

'Will you run your bath tonight Sybil?' I'm only six but I can run my own bath. I struggle a bit with the taps but I keep on trying until I manage to run enough water. I undress carefully. It's hard to push my long pinafore over my head but I concentrate and get it done. Then I copy Mother and fold my clothes neatly and put them on the chair. Last of all I clamber in and wallow in the water like a baby hippopotamus. I love pretending to be an animal of some sort.

'You are a good girl, Sybil,' Mum says when she comes in. 'I'll just sponge your back for you.' Then she helps me out of the bath and makes sure that I'm properly dry. When I'm fresh and clean in my warm nightdress she gives me a big hug.

'Can I stay up a bit later tonight? I have been good!'

'Not tonight, love. I know Jason stays up but he's much older than you.'

There was nothing for it - I had to go to bed straight after my bath at the same time as the others. 'It's not fair,' I decided.

My parents come in every night to kiss me. The other two are often asleep. On this particular night Dad was smiling and he whispered to me: 'Mummy and I are going to let you into our secret, Sybil.'

'What is it then?' I asked excitedly. 'I love secrets.'

'Next month we're moving into a new house and you'll be able to have your own room and, not only that, you're having a new brother or sister at the beginning of the year.' I feel so happy and important. How wonderful to have a room of my own. I shall be able to have a shelf with my books, high enough so the others can't reach. Also I shall have space for my sewing basket. I'm determined to finish my cross-stitch mat for Mum's dressing table.

I try not to think about the second thing that Dad

mentioned – the new baby. It means more work for Mummy and me. I don't know if I was dreaming but I thought I could hear Mummy crying downstairs. Then Jason slammed his bedroom door and soon after I must have fallen asleep.

'Breakfast is ready, hurry up everyone!' called Mother cheerfully. I help Millie to put her socks and shoes on – she still can't tie her laces. I comb my own hair and look at myself in the long mirror to see if I'm dressed decently for school. We run down the stairs and take our places at the large wooden table. The air is warm with the delicious smell of bacon and eggs.

'Good morning, girls,' Dad says. He and Jason are tucking into their cooked breakfast and Mum is dishing up bacon and eggs for Millie and me. Jerry was sitting in his high chair, still dressed in his nightgown with a large bib covering his front. He wants to feed himself now and he gets egg all round his mouth. He is disgusting because he screws up his dippers and tries to plaster some of the bread into the screw holes of his chair. No one else seems to notice.

Mother believes that it's essential for everyone in the family to start the day with a good hot breakfast. When the weather gets cold, porridge is on the menu, either with milk and sugar or sometimes honey. I'm going to be like Mother when I grow up and cook for my family.

Every morning Mother kisses each of us goodbye and waves from the doorstep. 'Make sure you hang on to Sybil, Jason!' she calls. Dad meets his workmates at the end of the road and Jason grabs my hand. He is rough because he doesn't want his friends to see him with me in tow.

'Don't pull me so!' I cry. 'My satchel will fall off.' It's a relief when we reach the school gates and he pushes me into the playground and I see my friends. I like it at school because I'm learning to read and write and I enjoy sewing and knitting.

'Sybil's report is good this time', Mum said.

'She's making good progress,' Dad agreed. 'Perhaps she can go to the Blue Coat School later on if she goes on like this.' The idea thrills me because I've seen the older girls coming home in their smart uniforms.

As the time drew near to the great move, Dad and his friends came home with large tea chests and my brother and I helped with the packing.

'Here you are Sybil, you're good at wrapping things.' Dad handed me the spare cutlery, eggcups, gravy boats and other small items. I take care wrapping each piece separately and then pass them to Dad so he can place them in the box. Jason soon becomes fed up and runs into the garden to play with Millie. I am never tired of helping Dad so I stick to everything he asks me to do. I'm pleased when I receive a big hug after filling the chest. He picks me up and kisses me on the cheek.

On the day of the move Father hired a horse and cart to help with the larger pieces of furniture. My Uncles and Aunts came round to help. Moving house is a happy occasion with all the family taking part. Mother is in the kitchen of the new house. The great black range has heated the room and the kettle remained on the boil for most of the day. At intervals, Mum provided the helpers with thick slices of bread covered in dripping accompanied by hot cups of tea. For the rest of the time Mum was chief supervisor telling everyone where to place the different items.

At the old house Auntie Meg is in charge and she makes sure that all the crates leave the house at the right time and in order. Jason and I have to move the linen, pillows, cushions, towels and even small doormats. We use the baby's pram as a vehicle and have great fun pushing it between the houses. Jason, as usual, wants to run faster and faster when we're going down the hill. 'Jason, stop! I cry. 'I'll fall over.' He takes no notice and I let go of the handle and he charges on without me. When I reach the corner, the pram is on its side in the middle of the road.

Jason was trying desperately to lift it upright without any success. Some of the towels and other stuff had fallen to the ground.

I loved the horse called Jake and I asked if I could give him a sugar lump. 'Just one,' the owner replied. 'We can't have Jake getting fat, he's lazy as it is. Hold your hand out flat, girlie, if you don't want your fingers bitten off!' I did as I was told but I squealed when the horse tickled my hand as he took the sugar lump. 'Oh I do love Jake, Daddy – isn't he grand? May I have a ride in the cart, please?'

'We still have a lot of things to move, darling, but perhaps later Griffiths may let you have a special treat. 'From the road the new house looks narrow and tall. It's built on five levels. The front door opens onto the wide pavement. The room at the back overlooks the garden and stretches across the width of the house. The other room is smaller and this is to be Dad's study and library. 'I've always wanted a library and there's plenty of room for others to share the space.' I didn't say anything. I want my books on a shelf in my bedroom.

The basement is large and stretches someway under the pavement. At the back it is level with the garden. Dad says that the basement will become the communal centre for the family. Mum loves the kitchen because it's large and there's a decent pantry. A corridor leads to the back door. It surprised me to see the bath with a curtain round it and at the far end of the room a large mound of coal stood in a heap. During one of the breaks when I was sitting with my cousins, Dad gave us a lecture about the coal. 'You've all seen the coal out there next to the bath? Well that's the Lewisham coal mine and it's out of bounds for children.' He said this in a serious voice. 'Coalmines are dangerous, especially this one. When the coalmen deliver the coal, they empty the sacks through a hole in the pavement. Mum and I don't want any crushed children!'

'Jason is going to help me build a partition round the bath with a door. Eventually it will be a proper bathroom.

Who wants a ride on the horse cart before it gets dark?' There was a mad scramble up the stairs. The older cousins climbed on the back of the cart and us four were allowed to sit with the driver and his sheep dog. I'll never forget that day. It was a fantastic adventure. From then onwards I started to love all animals, especially horses and dogs. I have this secret wish that when I grow up, I shall one day own my own animals.

'It is idyllic here', Mother said to Dad. 'The children are healthy and have plenty of room to play and you have the garden to grow vegetables. The only problem is that they're all growing up too quickly!' I love having my own bedroom but Chris was born in 1905 and the following year Mum had another baby. This time a girl called Polly. Our idyllic life became a thing of the past. I knew that I would have to share my room with Millie again. I didn't mind because we're friends now. By 1909 we had two more babies, Gary and Grace. I'm grown up but I have very little time to myself.

Jason left school and joined the navy. He's training and earns a small amount but he is able to pay Mother his wages and this is his contribution to the family. Jason moans about this arrangement because Mother just gives him pocket money as if he were still a child and he thinks he should keep more of his own earnings. The other boys help Dad to collect wood and dig in the vegetable patch. We are never short of fresh vegetables and fruit.

I suppose we need extra money with such a large family so Mother has taken a part time job as a nurse's assistant. Being the eldest girl means that some of my clothes are new but most of the time we have things passed down from other relatives. We wear every item until it becomes threadbare and has to be thrown away. Millie and I spend hours darning socks and patching aprons and dresses.

'Life is stark!' says Mother. 'But Dad and I love you all!' At weekends it's great because we are together. 'Let's go for a picnic!' is the usual cry when it's a fine day. Mother makes us sandwiches and jam tarts and we pack the food into baskets for the boys to carry. The hills around Bath are beautiful and we all have our favourite walks. I like climbing Little Solsbury, especially at blackberry time. Jason prefers Bannerdown. 'I can have a go at the rabbits up there and you all like rabbit stew' he says.

'You're horrible Jason, you always want to kill things' I answer.

One day Dad came home with a furry creature. It was a stoat. The boys called him Sam and they were taught by Dad to catch and shoot rabbits. Sam's job is to flush the animals out of their holes. Mother makes stews and pies with the meat and rabbit is everyone's favourite food. I never go on the shoots but I do forget the cruel bits when I'm eating the delicious pies. Jason calls me a hypocrite, but I can't help it because I don't like seeing animals being killed.

I like being at the Blue Coat School. I don't like to boast but I usually achieve top marks for my essays and I love poetry. Mum and Dad say that they're proud of me. My English teacher thinks I'm a suitable candidate for University if I work hard at all my subjects. Sadly, this was never to be because one day in 1912 when I was just fourteen, my brother Jason, dressed in his naval uniform, came to collect me from school.

'Dad's very ill, Sybil', he said quietly. 'I think he's dying – Mum wants us at home straight away.' My brothers and sisters were waiting at the gate and as we hurried home, Chris and Polly began to cry as they hung on to Jason. I felt like crying too but I took Millie's arm as we walked home as fast as we could. Auntie Meg was at the door to meet us. 'You poor dears!' she cried as she tried to hold us all in her arms. Jason pushed past and ran up the stairs to Mum and Dad's bedroom. A few minutes later he came slowly down the stairs looking pale and frightened.

'Our Daddy is dead,' he announced, slumping down on the bottom step. I felt a big lump in my throat and I began to shake. Millie tried to push past Jason.

'You can't go up yet,' he said pulling Millie and me into his arms. Auntie Meg was holding the younger ones. I felt it was the end of my world but I pulled Polly towards me so that I could try to console her. Eventually Dr. Parker came down the stairs. His sleeves were rolled up and he walked slowly. He sat on the bottom step next to Jason.

'I'm so sorry I couldn't save your Daddy,' he faltered. 'He had a massive heart attack. Your Mummy is very sad and you children will have to be as kind as you can. Jason is now the head man of the family.' He gently put his arm around the young shoulders. Jason is only nineteen. 'Now you can quietly go up to the bedroom.' Jason took my hand and we walked up together. I had never seen a dead person before. I ran straight to my Mother who was sitting upright in a chair next to the body. Her eyes were red and swollen where she had cried so much.

'Come here, darlings. We have to say goodbye to Daddy,' she sobbed choking over her words. 'He is still here in spirit and will go on caring for us from afar.'

I stared at my Father. He looked as if he was just asleep with his lovely golden hair combed back from his face. His strong hands folded above the sheets and I so wanted to hold one, like he had held mine on so many occasions. Polly stretched out her hand to touch him and Mother said: 'You can kiss Daddy goodbye.' Then go down with Auntie Meg. Jason, you stay here for a while with me dear.'

4

'Come away from the window, William, you'll knock the candle over.'

'He's only six, Rosie, you can't expect him to sit still.' I ran to my dad and clambered on to his knee.

'He'll be seven next birthday and he needs to learn,' my mother insisted. 'You let him get away with everything, Henry.' My mum and dad are always bickering and it's usually about me. On this occasion the three of us are sitting in our front room and there's a candle burning on the windowsill. I'm dressed in my best clothes that I wear on a Sunday. Dad was up early to light the fire. It had snowed in the night and he guessed that Mother would want to sit reverently in her best room.

It's bleak in here and I hate the musty smell. Dad says that the pungent mustiness of the room will clear after a while. I couldn't see why we had to dress up in our best clothes. I prefer to sit in the parlour where it's warm and cosy. Dad went to shovel some more coal on the fire and Mother jumped up quickly. 'Don't make the fire too big, the heat will damage the piano.' She walked over to the instrument and opened the lid to reveal its shining keys.

'Ivory and ebony,' she said to me once. That was the first exciting moment when she allowed me to put my hands on the glistening keyboard. 'This is middle C,' my mother pointed out. 'Remember, William, you must never bang the keys and don't dare touch the piano when I'm not in the room.' I'm frightened of my mother. She looks like a witch or a gypsy with her staring black eyes and long dark hair. Sometimes I see tears trickling down her face.

'Leave your Mother alone when she's in a bad mood,' Dad told me in a low voice. It's a different story when my mother sits down to play her beloved piano. It's like a magic world where I imagine demons and angels locked in battle. At times there is a sweet calm in the middle and, occasionally, joy at the end but mostly it finishes with a feeling of sorrow. I can tell when the end is happy by the expression on my mother's face. She allows herself a gentle smile. But when it's a sad ending she sobs and the tears stream down her cheeks. Sometimes she hides her face in her hands and her whole body trembles. I am afraid but also obsessed by her playing and I adore her when she reads the stories of the operas.

At ordinary times Mother wears black for practicing but when she plays in concert (as she calls it) she wears royal red. I know when I'm in for a treat because she comes down the stairs in her long dress with her thick black hair coiled up on the top of her head. Showing above the hair is a large jewelled comb. Dad says it's her tiara. I think she looks beautiful, like a princess!

Today, Mother is dressed in black and Father is wearing his sombre funeral suit. It's a sad day for everyone – our beloved Queen Victoria has died, far away on that small island, somewhere near the south coast. 'It's the Isle of Wight,' said mother. She always knows everything. On the way to the corner shop I said to dad: 'Why is the Queen dead?'

'The Queen was very old and we all have to die sometime,' he answered. Groups of people were huddled together, whispering and looking grey and sad.

'You won't die Dad, will you?' I started to wonder what would happen to me if I were left alone with my mother.

'I will one day dear, but you'll be grown up by then,' he said squeezing my hand.

In the shop people were talking about the funeral. 'It's

always in London and we never get the chance to see the coffin and pay our respects,' said one old lady in the queue. 'She was our Queen too, even though we only saw her in photographs.' I suddenly remembered that Aunt Emily lived in London. 'Could we go and see the coffin? We could stay with your relations.'

'No lad, your Mother hates London and we can't leave her on her own, can we?' I live in a row of terraced houses and according to my mother we are the Queen's loyal subjects and this is why we are gathered in our front room. We have been to buy candles to burn in the window. 'It's a vigil,' Dad says, 'in honour of our dear Queen who has reigned over us for so long.' No one in our road ever thought about going to London.

●●●

It was to be a long year of sadness for the Lawson family because Mother's idol, Guiseppe Verdi, died in January. 'Why does Mother keep crying?' I asked.

'It's because that idiot Verdi has died,' Dad replied with an angry sigh. He showed me the photograph in the paper. 'Anyone would think he's family by the way your Mother goes on.'

'Does she want to see the coffin then?'

'No William,' he replied. 'She's just sad and don't keep asking silly questions.'

The truth is that my Mother is fanatical about Verdi. He's her idol. She knows all his operas and can play many of the famous arias on the piano. A photograph in a gold frame hangs in our front room near to the piano. I gaze at the picture when my Mother is playing. According to her, he is a distinguished looking man. I can see that he has a long beard and bushy eyebrows and I quite like him. I wish that I could grow up and write beautiful music. He doesn't look a bit like my Dad.

'Do you know William, Verdi played the organ in public when he was only ten years old? And look at you – you can't play a note yet.' I blushed and felt sad at my

Mother's words. 'I want to learn, Mother,' I said. My dad told me once that: 'Mother has uncontrollable mood swings. One minute she's on top of the world with dark sparkling eyes and full of fun, then for no apparent reason she descends into deep despair.' Playing the piano is part of her existence but she feels that she never reaches her potential in music or anything else in her life. I feel sorry for my Mother but I do wish she loved me a bit more.

Mother told me once that she would like to go to Milan and attend a performance of one of Verdi's great operas. Ernani is her favourite. 'It isn't just the music, it's the story,' she explained. 'Ernani has all the qualities that I admire. He is handsome, noble and has a commanding presence. He shows courage, faithfulness and above all he is an honourable man.' I just listen because I can't understand everything she says and she doesn't like me to interrupt. In this story of love, betrayal, vengeance and final tragedy I think of my Mother playing the part of Elvira. She cries out in woe as Ernani stabs himself with his dagger and falls, dying, at her feet!

•••

My Dad is quite different. He tells me that he loves me and he's gentle and kind. He craves law and order in his home and garden, and keeps detailed records of the family's accounts, including my pocket money. If I receive a new present it has to be added to the alphabetical lists of all our possessions. We only have a small garden and Dad works there in all kinds of weather. In summer we have bright coloured marigolds and in autumn Dad pulls them out and plants bulbs to bloom in the spring.

There is a small shed at the bottom of the garden and Dad and I sometimes sit in there. 'It's a kind of refuge,' he explained. It is my favourite place. We sit there chewing shortbreads from his biscuit tin and drinking lemonade.

'Can I carry the bucket with the weeds?' I ask because I desperately want to play a part in my Dad's world. He has lists pinned to the walls and all the tools have their proper place. I do the same as Dad. I have lists in my notebooks - lists of my books, toys, friends and relations. My mother says 'It's a trait in the family.' I'm used to being on my own and I always manage to keep myself amused and though I say it myself, I am good at numbers and dad says that I may become a statistician when I grow up.

One day my mother was intrigued by what I was doing. 'Why are you looking at those rows of figures?' she asked.

'I'm working out the odds of horses winning in a race and sometimes I do it for greyhound racing.' I spend hours with a cup and dice recording and deducing the probability of a six coming up. This irritates my mother. 'Stop rattling that cup William, find something worthwhile to do.' But she was pleased when I told her which horse was likely to win. She even kissed me when she won five pounds on a bet.

On special occasions when my Mother is feeling happy, we plan visits to the park. She loves listening to the band. 'You sit here, Rosie in the shade and I'll take the boy on the boating lake.' I find it difficult to stop jumping in glee when Dad comes up with this proposal.

'Take care, Henry, you know what a fidget he is. And don't lose your hat this time'. Dad dresses for these occasions in grey flannels and navy blue blazer. He wears a boater at a rakish angle. My Mother dresses me all the time in grey, the only variation being in the tones and shades of this dismal colour, pale to dark.

●●●

I find it difficult at school because I'm used to being on my own and now I have to play with other boys. At first I liked the strict rules and regulations but now that I'm growing up I feel hemmed in and Mother says: 'I'm losing my confidence.' My favourite subject is mathematics but I have my own way of working out problems and my schoolmaster wants me to conform. He says I must follow the same procedures as everyone else in Algebra and Geometry.

'Just do it this way Lawson – don't keep going off on a tangent.' I sulk when I'm criticised and I'm getting angry with everyone.

'There are more ways than one to solve a problem!' I yell at my friends. My reports began mentioning my stubbornness and my parents were worried. My Mother blamed my choice of friends. 'He's always with those Persians! Every night he goes round there and comes home smelling of herbs and spices. He told me that they hang carpets on the wall,' she moaned, throwing her arms dramatically in the air. 'Why can't he have English friends like everyone else?'

I was cross when my mother said this because I really like my friends. Their mother is kind to me. I'm very unhappy and I want to run away. Dad tells me he keeps finding empty gin bottles in the house and he thinks Mother is a secret drinker. They quarrel more than ever.

'You'll be going up to London for a few weeks in the summer. Your Aunts have invited you there for a holiday. You're a lucky boy, Will. Not many people go to London.' I tried to feel brave but I am anxious and a little afraid.

'I've never been away from home before; how will I get there?'

'You're going by train and Aunt Emily is meeting you at the station.' I became excited and fearful at the same time but Dad's gentleness calmed me down. Mother made me a cardboard placard with a string to hang round my neck. On it she wrote my name and address and she told me to wear it when the train reached London.

On the day of my journey Dad arranged for the Guard to keep an eye on me.

'He'll be fine in this compartment with old Mr. Watson.'

There was so much to see that after waving to my parents, I soon forgot about being afraid. The old gentleman kept me amused with a pack of cards. He taught me some tricks and I practised them over and over again. The man laughed at me. Then I must have fallen asleep for the rest of the journey. Aunt Emily was there to meet me. 'Hello Will,' she kissed me on both cheeks. 'Where's your luggage?' she asked. I felt myself blushing. 'I haven't any Auntie, just this paper bag. The old man on the train gave me the pack of cards.' She took the bag from me.

'Keep close in this crowd, we've got to catch a tram.' I held on to her skirt, overwhelmed by the noise and the number of people. I remembered meeting my Aunt once when she came to Manchester. It was a long walk from the tram and I was surprised to see trees growing from holes in the pavement. It was leafy and cool in the shade and I wanted to stop and rest. 'We're nearly there now.'

My Aunts live in a bungalow. I have never seen a home like this before. There are no stairs and it looks so pretty from the outside. 'Hello dear,' Auntie Beattie was standing at the front door. 'Come on in, your cousin Hilda is out in the garden.' I felt embarrassed – I am not used to girls. Hilda is older than me and she likes reading and telling stories. She enjoys playing cards. It didn't take me long to get used to my cousin. In fact she soon became my best friend.

I really like it in London. Aunt Emily takes me on excursions to see the famous sites including Big Ben and the Tower of London. Hilda comes with us sometimes and we take a picnic to eat in the park. In the evenings we play Shove Halfpenny and Bagatelle. As a special treat I am allowed to help Aunt Beattie with her stamp collection. She's always looking for Penny Blacks. 'I think they'll be valuable one day. If you like, William, I'll buy you an album so you can start your own collection.' Everyone was kind to me but I worried about my Mum and Dad. They didn't answer my letters and I sent them a note every week. My Aunts say that they're busy decorating and putting up new shelves. But I know we don't need any shelves. I've decided to sulk because I know my Mother is ill and it's being kept a secret.

'What's the matter Will? Why don't you want to play?'

'I'm going home soon and I need to think about packing my case.'

'You're not going home yet until your Mother has recovered.'

'My Mother isn't ill!' I shouted.

'Yes she is!' Hilda shouted back. I ran to my room and threw myself on the bed. Later I learned that my Mother was having a nervous breakdown. I'd been sent to London to be out of the way. It's difficult for me to understand all the secrecy and I felt betrayed by my parents and my aunts. Even Hilda knew about it.

My Dad and Aunts have cooked up a scheme between them. They've agreed to educate me in London at a private school and I'm to start there in the autumn. 'Next week, we shall buy your uniform and Beattie is knitting you a jumper and socks to match.' I reacted badly to this news. It isn't the school so much because I really hated the old one. It's because I've been deceived and I want to see my Mum and Dad.

I raced out of the house and slammed the door behind me. I didn't know what to do so I climbed high into the apple tree. I'm sitting on a comfortable branch and I'm not coming down. I feel like crying but they've sent Hilda out to coax me.

'Come down, William. I'm getting the blame for telling you.'

'Go away or I'll throw apples at you.' I hurled several small apples at her and one hit her leg. She called out in pain and my aunts came running out.

'Come down, William,' said Aunt Emily.

'I can't understand this aggressive behaviour, it's quite bizarre,' Aunt Beattie looked up at me.

'I'll come down if I can go home,' I was close to tears.

'You can't go home yet, dear, but we'll write to your Father.' I decided to come down but I refused to cooperate. I cried myself to sleep that night.

'He's lost his appetite. I'm anxious for him.' I heard my Aunts talking about me.

Nothing changed. As a last straw, I decided to climb up the lamppost outside the bungalow. By time Aunt Beattie came home a small crowd had gathered looking up at me. The children were laughing and pointing but I didn't care.

'Come down at once, you naughty boy,' Aunt Beattie cried. I stared at her for sometime but I was furious with everyone so I decided to swear.

'Not bloody likely,' was my shocking reply. A gasp came from the crowd and Auntie Beattie went in to call Emily. They both looked up at me, pink and flustered.

Then suddenly a neighbour appeared. He was large and looked like a boxer.

'I'll get the lad down, whip his hide and wash his mouth out.' I began to scream and yell.

'I want to go home, I hate it here!' But to tell the truth I felt afraid. I didn't want to be whipped so I slid down the post when I saw the man coming with a ladder. I dodged everyone and ran for the house. I knew the stubbornness would pay off, though I did feel a twinge of guilt for upsetting my Aunts and Hilda. They had been so kind to me. Everyone was relieved when I was bundled onto a train back to Manchester.

5

Everything changed for me when Father died. Without his wages our family began to feel the pinch. My Mother took on full time work to support us. As the eldest girl, I left full time education to look after the younger children. Leaving school was an event that I regretted for the rest of my life. Not only did I enjoy studying but also I felt that my potential for an interesting career was disappearing before my eyes. Millie, in contrast, hated being at school and couldn't wait to leave. She wanted to work at Jollys, the large department store in the centre of Bath, but she had to wait two more years before she could do so. When she did start as a junior assistant, Mother took all her wages and only gave her pocket money like the rest of the children. Needless to say, Millie felt that this was unfair and I agreed with her.

•••

'I shall get married as soon as I can,' Millie confided in Sybil. 'I don't know how you can put up with being at home all the time. You're just like a charwoman,' she taunted. Sybil winced.

'I'm needed here. Grace is only three and someone has to look after her.' She paused and thought about her mother. 'Gary is just four and Polly is starting school next term. Someone has to be here when they come home.'

'I suppose you're capable,' Millie said tossing her head. 'I'm just glad it's not me left in charge.'

Sybil noticed the change in her mother. She aged suddenly after Dad's death. Her hair was nearly white. 'Of course, I'll look after my brothers and sisters, please don't worry Mother.' Jason decided to bring Grandma home to stay for a few weeks. The old lady had fallen awkwardly, spraining her ankle. It was meant to be a short stay but the weeks turned into years and Grandma eventually became a full time resident.

'I love hearing Grandma's stories about Dad when he was a little boy,' Sybil told the others but she realised that the old lady was relying on her too much. Her demands increased and she found there was less time for visits or going out with friends.

'Don't forget you've got to brush Grandma's hair before she goes to bed,' Mother reminded Sybil when she was about to leave.

'All right, Mother I'll be back at nine.'

'Better make it by eight thirty if you can dear, you know how she dozes off.'

In time Sybil became frustrated with her routine and was desperately trying to think of ways of bringing a little pleasure into her life. She remembered that her father once mentioned that he wanted to buy a dog to help with the hunting. So one day Sybil said: 'I've gone off that stoat of yours Jason, he just lives in his cage all the time and you're away so much. He's not much of a pet. Do you think we could have a dog? Dad did say that terriers are useful for hunting rabbits. A dog joining us on our walks would be fun.'

'Don't you have enough work to do Sybil?' Jason asked.

'I thought it would get me out of the house if I had to take a dog for a walk.'

'I'm not sure, I shall have to think about it,' Mother replied.

Rags, a smooth haired Fox terrier, became a member of the family. Everyone loved him but he had one bad fault: he liked to fight with a dog that lived in the same road. Whenever he did this, Mother insisted that he should be given a dose of salts. Rags soon cottoned on and hid at the back of his kennel. The only person who could persuade him out was Gary, Sybil's youngest brother. Gary had an affinity with animals, a talent that he shared with his sister. 'Come out you devil!' he shouted and even though Rags was growling, he put his head and arms into the kennel and pulled him out by the scruff of his neck. He forced open the dog's mouth and poured the liquid down his throat. The poor animal crept back into his kennel and they all waited for the medicine to work. Very soon the dog shot out and rushed up the garden to be sick.

Whenever Jason came home on leave, Millie pleaded with him to take her out to the local dances or to the cinema. 'Please take Sybil and me, we never go anywhere!' she cried.

'Do you want to come Syb?' Jason asked kindly. Before she had a chance to answer Mother butted in:

'Sybil has to help with Grandma,' she pointed out.

'I think Sybil deserves a break.' Jason replied with authority. 'I want her to come. I have a mate who wants to meet her.' Sybil blushed and Mother was quiet for a moment.

'Perhaps I am too strict with the girls,' she murmured. 'You take them Jason, I'm sure you'll look after them.'

Sybil and Millie were thrilled. They rushed upstairs to decide what they were going to wear. Most of the money saved by Millie was spent on clothes. Her collection of dresses included the pretty mauve one that she took from the wardrobe. 'It's real silk', she told Sybil. 'What are you going to wear?' Sybil rummaged on her side of the cupboard and pulled out a homemade cotton dress.

'You can't wear that thing,' Millie insisted. Instead she checked the wardrobe and held out one of her dresses. It was pink and decorated with white lace. The lace had been made and sewn on by their younger sister Polly who was becoming an expert seamstress.

'That's one of your favourite dresses', Sybil said, holding the dress up to herself and looking in the mirror.

'Yes, I know, but I think it will suit you'. Sybil took the dress from her sister and tried it on. Millie was right. She admired herself in the mirror and felt good in the pale pink with the white lace round her neck and the beautiful frill at the bottom.

'My word, what a picture,' Jason said proudly, as the girls came down the stairs on the night of their outing. Sybil thought Millie looked beautiful, but then she always did. Her black ringlets were natural and her skin was perfect, with just a faint rosy glow on her cheeks.

'You look lovely this evening, Sybil,' Jason crept up behind her. 'That dress really suits you with your golden hair.'

'Keep your eye on them, Jason. They look so grown up.'

Millie had a string of male admirers. Sybil felt shy in company, she couldn't help being a home bird. This evening was different. Millie was soon whisked away on to the dance floor and Sybil, rather overawed by the noise, kept close to her brother. Jason had a variety of friends, some from the Forces like him and others who worked in Bath. Sybil glanced at her brother. He is so handsome, she thought. In fact he looks more like Dad every day. She loved him dearly.

'Come and meet my friend David,' Jason whispered. He took her to the other side of the hall where a young man was standing with a glass in his hand. Sybil blushed when Jason introduced them.

'This is my sister Sybil. Will you keep her amused for a while? I need to talk to Cathy.' Sybil felt embarrassed as her brother rushed off.

'Let me get you a drink?' David asked. He was tall and slim with dark hair. She particularly noticed his hands. The fingers were extremely long and thin, perhaps he's a musician, she thought. He took her arm and guided her to the bar.

'What would you like?'

'A ginger beer, please', Sybil replied. This and lemonade were her favourite drinks. She had tasted alcohol once, when her Uncle had given her a small sherry at Christmas time. David was drinking beer and when Sybil's drink arrived he carried the glasses over to one of the empty tables.

'Do you like dancing Sybil? Your sister certainly does'. They looked over towards Millie. She was whirling around the dance floor tossing her curls and smiling at everyone. It was a special evening. Sybil liked David. They danced together for most of the night. She felt enveloped by a warm glow and was sure that she was falling in love. Later a group of them walked home at the end of the evening and she was thrilled when David held her hand and whispered that he would like to meet her again. It was the beginning of a happy relationship.

David was made welcome at the Lewisham's home. He was able to get round Sybil's mother and even Gran liked him. His parents welcomed Sybil to their home and Mrs. Moore, who only had sons, made a great fuss when Sybil arrived for tea. The two of them did the washing up together and chatted about sewing and knitting and the younger Lewisham children. Polly was often invited to come along with Sybil for tea because David's mother admired her embroidery and sewing skills.

There was an upright piano in the front room. David was extremely talented. He had reached high grades in his piano lessons. 'I've written a special tune for you Sybil. It's called 'Moonsprite.' The words were like poetry. After each encounter, David walked her home, holding her hand or sometimes with his arm around her waist. Often he would draw her close and kiss her on the cheek and then one evening he turned her right round and kissed her gently on the lips. Sybil wanted the kiss to last forever and she put her arms round his neck nuzzling her head to his chest.

'I think, I love you Sybil,' he whispered tenderly. This was Sybil's first love and she adored him. He was kind and considerate. 'I like being with your family,' he told her.

'Having a rough and tumble with the young ones. It's great fun.'

'You do get them overexcited,' Sybil laughed.

•••

The happiness that Sybil enjoyed was short lived. In June 1914, the Archduke Franz Ferdinand was assassinated. In August, the Germans marched into Belgium and soon after, Britain declared war on Germany. Young men all over the country rushed to the recruitment centres and volunteered to fight. Sybil pleaded with David to stay at home but to no avail.

'You don't want me to be a coward do you?'

'No I don't!' she cried 'but I do want you to be safe.' Jason was already in the navy and he was called back to his ship. He had no idea where he was going. Sybil with her Mother and sisters wept when he left.

On the day of David's departure, the young couple sat in the garden. David took a small box out of his pocket. 'This was my grandmother's ring. She told me that it's called an'eternity' ring. I want you to have it Sybil,' he said taking her hand and putting it on her finger. 'When I come home, I'll buy you a real engagement ring. That's if you still love me then.' Sybil threw her arms around him.

'I wish you didn't have to go,' she sighed. 'Please write to me and I'll write to you every week,' she promised. He kissed her and stood up. 'Please stay here, I will write as often as I can. Goodbye, darling.' Sybil remained on the seat and watched him as he walked away down the path and out of the garden gate. Rags came and jumped up beside her. He licked her hand as if in sympathy and she cuddled him in return. She looked at the ring on her finger - three small diamonds embedded in the gold. It was so fine looking and beautiful that she vowed to wear it forever.

During the following years, Sybil, like everyone else, was caught up in the war effort. The Royal family vowed to give up alcohol as an example to the people. The gesture was mainly aimed at the workers in the shipyards and armament factories in the hope that their productivity would increase. Lloyd George, who was Chancellor, thought Britain's enemies were Germany, Austria and drink. 'Sybil, will you turn out that cupboard in the library where Jason keeps his bottles of beer and whisky,' her Mother asked. 'There's going to be a fine of one hundred pounds for anyone buying a round of drinks and I don't want Jason getting into trouble when he comes home.'

'That silly law won't last for long. We could put the bottles up in the loft', Millie suggested.

'All right then, but we must keep it a secret. Don't tell the youngsters.'

'I'm glad you managed to persuade Mother, I don't think Jason would like us destroying the contents of his drinks cabinet.' After stacking the bottles in the loft and covering them with an old sheet, the girls returned to the sitting room.

'Look at this in the paper. Over a thousand suffragettes are going to France.'

'What for?' asked Sybil.

'It just says war work,' Millie explained.

'I wish we could go. It's so boring just waiting for the war to end.'

'Can we go and do some war service, Mother?'

'I suppose the children are less demanding now - perhaps you and Sybil could do some part time farm work. I'll talk to Mr. Tarrant when I see him in the lane.' It wasn't quite what Sybil envisaged.

'I suppose it is something,' Millie said sarcastically.

•••

Mother managed to arrange part time work at the farm for the two girls. It was to be in the summer months from about four in the afternoon until eight at night. The young ones came up to help on occasions. Sybil helped them to collect the potatoes and if they were very good Mr. Tarrant allowed them to search for duck eggs and help put the chickens in for the night. When it grew dark the family wandered home. Sybil helped Grandma to bed and then crept into the library to read or write to her beloved David.

Often she reread his letters. She treasured them and kept them safely in a wooden box that Jason made for her. The key to the box was tied round her neck on a pink velvet ribbon. There was one letter that she read over and over again. It was the first she received and she could hardly believe the contents. The families expected the war to be over by Christmas. It was supposed to be a short war but the forces remained on the battlefields. So they sent Christmas parcels with basic foods and special home made treats to cheer them up. David thanked them for the parcel and it was the following part that amazed Sybil and the rest of the family:

It was Christmas Eve, and we were sitting with the others in the trench, trying desperately not to put our feet down in the muddy water. Suddenly we heard voices singing a carol – 'Silent Night'. We all joined in. Then we sang, 'Hark the Herald Angels' and 'Good King Wenceslas'. It was heartbreaking. There we were, singing carols with the enemy instead of being home with our loved ones.' The letter went on: *'The Germans lit fires and some of our soldiers went back to collect wood and we did the same – it was lovely to feel the warmth. Some of the lads tried to dry off their clothes. Then we could see figures approaching from the enemy's line. We quickly reached for our rifles, but they kept coming, singing as they walked slowly towards us. Some were carrying branches lit with small candles. 'They're just lads like us!' someone shouted and we crept carefully out of our disgusting trench and met them in no-man's-land. I shook hands with a lad called Karl. It was difficult to communicate but he managed to tell me that he was seventeen and then showed me a picture of his Mum and Dad. I showed him my photo of you, Sybil, and I think he was envious. We seemed to stay up all night, singing, trying to dance and sharing our food parcels. Christmas day was not so happy, we spent most of it digging graves. The Germans collected the bodies of their soldiers and buried them with a short service. We did the same and it was very sad. Several lads from our trench had to be buried. I was so pleased to be alive, Sybil dearest. Yours for ever, David xxx'*

Sybil gently held the letter up to her lips and kissed the signature.

6

During my absence, which must have been almost two months, my mother's health improved. She was amused by my behaviour in London. It made her laugh! She was genuinely pleased to have me back home. On returning to school I settled well. My parents seemed to be happier together and the atmosphere at home helped me to recover my confidence. My relationship with mother improved and I became braver in every way.

The front door opened and his Dad came in carrying a newspaper. 'Just look at this Will!' his father called. 'Some chap called Bleriot has flown across the Channel!'

'Let's see, Dad?' He and his mother peered at the newspaper. On the front page a man dressed in leather was standing by an aeroplane. 'A French man has flown across the English Channel.' The event became the main topic of conversation. William sat with his Dad in the shed looking at the paper.

'That's what I want to do Dad – not just fly them but help to design and draw them.'

'You'll have to learn to be a draughtsman.'

'Do you think I can do that?' asked William who was inspired by Bleriot's story.

'Of course, you can son!' From then on William worked hard at school. He talked to Mr. Cox, his Maths teacher.

'One day I want to become a designer of aeroplanes that can fly all over the world. Just imagine flying to

America!' William became carried away by his enthusiasm.

'I have a friend who is a draughtsman at Lynotype & Machinery Ltd. I think he did an apprenticeship there. I'll find out for you, Lawson,' suggested Mr. Cox.

It was not just at school that his behaviour changed. At home he developed an interest in card tricks. Ever since he met the old gentleman on the train he became fascinated with playing cards. He practised the few tricks he knew and tried them out on his mother. 'How did you do that?' She was amazed at his speed of hand and enjoyed trying to work out how the tricks were done. William was delighted that his mother took so much interest in his hobby.

At Christmas the three of them went to the local pantomime in the church hall and William saw his first Conjuror. Birds, rabbits and flags came popping out of this man's sleeves and top hat. His assistant put a rabbit in a box and the magician covered it with a red cloth and then tapped it with his wand – hey presto! The rabbit disappeared. He and his mother clapped loudly at the end of the act.

'I know that man,' his Dad said in the interval, 'I think he works in the office at the station.'

A few weeks later his Dad came home beaming. 'I've met Mr. Magic,' he said cheerfully. 'He wants to meet you, Will, and watch you doing your card tricks. He's invited us to his house on Sunday afternoon. That's if you would like to go?'

'What about me?' said his mother who wanted to join in the fun.

'We're all invited for tea,' Dad replied. William practised hard in every spare moment. 'Just look at how he shuffles the cards, Rosie, he's a natural.'

On Sunday they dressed in their best clothes and walked briskly to a detached house that was about a mile away. 'Come on in,' said the cheerful voice of Stan Webster. 'Here's my wife Daisy. Is the tea ready, love?' They sat down in the parlour and William relaxed in the friendly atmosphere.

'Let's have a look at your performance, young man.' William felt confident as he moved a table to the centre of the room and began shuffling the cards. 'We have four aces and two kings. I'm placing them face downwards on the table. Your job is to remember their position. Please Madame, will you pick one of the cards?' And so he went on until his repertoire came to an end.

'Well done!' were the cries. Everyone clapped after each trick. William was elated with his performance. He even received a hug from his mother.

'Your son has talent.' Mr. Webster said as they were leaving.

•••

In his sixteenth year William became an employee at Lynotype and Machinery Ltd. 'You're going to be here for five years if you're suitable.' said the manager to the 1909 recruits. 'You'll get the chance to work in each department of the company and let me remind you, it's an honour to be accepted here.' The ten young men, including William, stood in awe listening to every word.

'The whole idea of this scheme is to offer you plenty of experience in the kind of work we do. We're hear to guide you in the right direction.'

William knew what he wanted to do. His ambition was to be an aircraft designer. He needed to learn how to draw.

'We do not tolerate laziness and we expect everyone to check in on time whichever department you're in. Do I make myself clear?'

'Yes Sir!' they replied in unison. William waited anxiously for his name to be called out. He wished he could go straight into the drawing office. To learn technical drawing was what he wanted to do more than anything.

'Lawson, W.H., you will start in the Tool Room. Please join Mr. Lofhouse's group.' William's heart sank. He tried unsuccessfully to hide his disappointment. Mr Lofthouse noticed his expression. 'What's the matter Lawson?' he asked in a brusque voice.

'I really wanted to go into the drawing office Sir,' William said meekly.

'You will, you will,' roared Lofthouse. 'You need to learn the basics.'

•••

William regularly practised his conjuring tricks on his mates at work. 'Pick a card, Bob,' he held out a pack of cards. They were standing in the small courtyard during their tea break.

'Don't you know any other tricks? You always use cards.'

'Here's something new.' William took a jar of jam out of his pocket and proceeded to take a teaspoon from behind his friend's ear and a plate from inside his jacket. Bob laughed and some of the other lads came to watch.

'Someone put a spoonful of jam on the saucer please.' Bob took the jar and tried to unscrew the lid.

'It's just going round and round,' he said passing the jar to someone else.

'You're a load of weaklings,' William took the jar back and placed it firmly on the floor. The crowd gathered round gazing down at the jar. William tapped it with his wand and suddenly a loud hiss came from the jar. Before they could move, a long green snake-like creature sprang out, splattering the onlookers with slimy goo.

'What the hell!' they shrieked moving back. 'Look at my shirt!'

'That's not funny,' fumed Bob.

William moved quickly. He started producing coloured napkins from the top of his coat. 'There you are, you can mop up now. There's only one minute left.'

William chuckled as he ran back to the office. He could hear the laughter of his mates as they rushed after him.

'That was a bit close to the mark,' whispered Bob as he strolled near to his bench. William saw the glimmer of a smile on his friend's face. He was not pleased when Bob placed a slimy hand on his coat sleeve. When they finished work that evening Bob, a keen rugby player, grabbed William by the lapels of his coat.

'You're a little magic elf aren't you? Why don't you give us a magic show at the Christmas party?'

'I haven't been asked,' mumbled William. The following Christmas he was invited to perform. He went round to Webster's house and they started to plan William's first appearance in public. 'You'll be O.K. Will, you're my star pupil.' He patted him on the shoulder.

William's CV began to look impressive for such a young man: 'Good timekeeper, attentive to his duties, industrious, keen and anxious to do well. An above average student and should do well in the Flying Corps.'

'We're so proud of you Will,' glowed his Mother. William was delighted that at last he was pleasing his parents. He wanted so much to join the Royal Flying Corps. When war broke out in 1914, the Manager asked to see him. 'Lawson, we know you want to join the Flying Corps but we've trained you to be an excellent draughtsman and your country needs you. A.V. Roe is searching for designers. You really ought to apply; you can always join the Corps later.'

That same year William joined A.V. Roe & Co. Ltd. and that was the beginning of a long love affair, an obsession with his favourite aeroplane, the Avro 504. 'Do you know Mother, A.V. Roe designed and built one of the first British planes to fly?' William noticed that his Father was listening quietly to him with a worried look on his face. Later, when his Mother went into the kitchen to put the vegetables on, he whispered: 'Why in heaven's name don't you join the forces and do your duty Will? I know your Mother doesn't want you to go away but all the young men round here have joined up. My work mates keep asking about you. I don't know what they think?'

William felt stunned. His father knew about the

importance of his work. Now it suddenly dawned on him that he and the people in the neighbourhood were beginning to suspect that he was scared to fight.

'Dad, do you think I'm pretending or something?' William felt angry. 'I'll show you the card Mr. Roe gave me, that ought to shut your mates up!' William ran upstairs to his room and unlocked the black metal box where he kept his private papers. He picked out the card and took it with him to the parlour. His Mother was busy laying the table as he put the card down in front of his Father.

'What's that dear?' Mother asked.

'It's a card given to me at work. Dad can read it out to you,' William was still fuming at his Father's lack of faith.

'Mr. W. Lawson is employed in Aeroplane design. In the opinion of the Lord Commissioners of the Admiralty, so long as he is employed, he is doing his duty for his King and Country equally with those who have joined H.M. Forces to active service afloat or ashore'.

'There you are Dad, you can copy that and show it to your mates!'

After an awkward lunch William retired to his room. He sat thinking. 'I've had enough of this. Next week I'll look for a room and move out.' He tried hard to please his parents but lately, he yearned to be free and independent. He wanted to go out more with the lads without being quizzed by his Mother after each outing. His Father's latest outburst tipped the balance. He felt he had to break away and live his own life without interference.

Orders were coming in from the Admiralty for a hundred machines at the time and, as there were only a handful of technical staff, there was no time to worry or even think about anything else but work. It was not unusual for the great man himself, A.V. Roe, to spend days and nights in the office.

'What do you think he's doing here?' William asked.

'He's working on an Airship. It's called 'Astra', said one of the seven or so Draughtsmen working in the office.' No one complained about the long hours.

There was change in the air.

'Look Will,' said a friend, giving a whistle under his breath. 'Girls, lots of them and guess what? They're going to work in the factory.' William and the other Draughtsmen looked out of the window. Some were joking and pushing each other. Even the Office boy was smiling at the sight.

'Back to work men!' called the Chief Designer. 'We can't afford to waste time. The Avro 504s will soon be bombarding the enemy'. And so it was that in October 1914 the first aerial bombardment of the war took place.

There was great excitement when an officer arrived to break the news: 'It's my pleasure to inform you that a party of Avro 504s have raided Cologne. Despite heavy German firing our planes descended to 600 feet and destroyed part of the Cologne military railway. They also managed to take some impressive photographs for use on future runs.'

'How did they manage the bombs?' asked one young man.

'It was not an easy manoeuvre, they were dropped by hand over the side.' The men, including William, were overcome by excitement. Most of them wanted to be released so that they could join the R.F.C. and become involved in the action.

'Have you heard about the latest stunt? Some chap called Bigsworth has managed to fly his plane over the top of a German Zeppelin and drop a bomb on it.'

'Oh yes', said one man sceptically 'tell us another!'

'It's true. The bomb went right through the airship without exploding. It was damaged so much that it soon crashed to the ground and burst into flames.'

In May 1916 William and three of his friends were released from the company to join the Flying Corps. 'At long last,' sighed William. 'Thought we'd never make it. Even A.V. Roe has resigned and enlisted in the R.F.C. By the time William joined the service, everything seemed to be going wrong.

Problems surfaced in the organisation of the country's air power. 'I just can't understand the mess up,' said one trainee. 'How can we have two bosses?' William could see the difficulty – the responsibility of air defence was divided between the Admiralty and the Home Office and these organisations blamed each other when things went wrong. The young men tried to get on with their flying even though the quarrels higher up in the ranks affected their training. 'At least we're going up in the 504s,' William told his parents.

Secretly he was extremely disappointed because he was not chosen to become a pilot. He never told his parents the whole story. During this time the Germans began to bomb London from their airships. 'What's the matter Will? Why can't you stop the buggers?' yelled his Dad in despair.

'They'll be bombing Manchester next', added his mother.

'I can't tell them what to do' William answered angrily. He wrote:

'Dear Mum & Dad, You'll be pleased to hear that the Naval planes are joining forces with us. It's about time because we are so hard-pressed. Our main task, when we've finished our training, is to support the troops on the Western Front. The German air crews will be forced to scurry back to the front and the bombing of England should *come to an end.'*

This was the turning point of the war. William missed out on the action. He flew planes as a trainee on reconnaissance flights over France photographing strategic landmarks. With a heavy heart, he decided to leave the force in 1918 when the war was coming to an end. It was not long after, that a long-range bomber force was set up and the joining of the naval air groups with the Flying Corps was complete. The new unit became known as the Royal Air Force.

•••

William felt uncertain about his future. It was hard for

him to hide his disappointment when he was not chosen to train as a pilot. Returning home was not an option. He couldn't face the thought of living in his old house with his parents and it depressed him to think of searching for a job in the dreary part of Manchester where he once lived. He wanted to join the young crowd moving south. 'London is where I want to be!'.

7

The favourite part of the day for Sybil was to be out in the fresh air up at the farm. Millie was often out with her new boyfriend. Sybil didn't mind because she became friendly with Mrs. Tarrant and if it rained, she helped with pickling and jam making in the farm kitchen. 'We sell this produce at the church hall and people without gardens can buy treats at reasonable prices. It's all part of the war effort.'

Early one morning, Sybil woke up to see her Mother standing by her bed. Tears were streaming down her cheeks. All semblance of her usual composure had disappeared. 'Oh Sybil!' she cried. 'Jason's ship is lost - somewhere off Jutland. I can't bear it.' She sank down on the bed, covering her face with her hands. Her whole body was shaking with emotion. 'No news of survivors'. Sybil felt sick. She was shocked and confused but in a few seconds her thoughts turned to her Mother. She moved close and automatically put her arms round the shaking figure. She meant to console her but as the news sunk in she could feel the tears starting to run down her own cheeks. Fear and anger overwhelmed her feelings.

'What are we to do? First Daddy dies and now Jason is missing. Why does this always happen to us? Jason was supposed to look after us.'

Millie, lying in the other bed woke up suddenly. She got up and moved towards Sybil. 'What's happened?' she cried.

'We've lost Jason. His ship's gone down,' Sybil shrieked

almost hysterically. She could feel her sister's warm arm round her neck.

'Stop it, stop it,' Millie yelled. Sybil shivered with fear as she clung to her mother and sister.

'It just isn't fair,' said Millie pulling away. Mother was trying to regain control as she turned to embrace them both.

'Jason's a strong man - he may survive. We must pray for him.' After a while she walked over to the marble washstand, poured some water from the jug into the blue matching bowl and started to dab her eyes. She straightened her clothes and tied her hair up in a bun. 'We must have faith and hope that he's still alive and we don't want to frighten the children, so let's try to go on as normal.'

Sybil helped Millie and the two of them dressed slowly. Millie's eyes were red and swollen like hers and every now and again Millie clung to Sybil as if she were a child. 'I'm not going to work,' she said. 'I just can't face people.' Sybil began making the beds and tidying the room.

'That's what you always do!' cried her sister. 'Just go on as if nothing has happened.' Later in the morning Sybil dressed the young ones ready for church and the family walked through the village to St.Saviour's. Other families joined them and the rector said special prayers for the young men who were missing. Several lads from the village were on the same ship as Jason. Times were bleak. Sybil's thoughts and prayers were for her dear brother but she couldn't help thinking about David. It was a long time without hearing from him.

The Moores received terrible news about Alf, David's brother. He was killed in action during a retreat. Sybil went round to their house but Mrs. Moore refused to see visitors. The sadness and devastation all around played heavily on Sybil's mind and she couldn't help thinking that she was losing everyone she loved.

The two sisters tried to keep the children's spirits up.

Sybil took over the kitchen and managed to prepare meals for the young ones.

'Why is Mummy in the study all the time?' Polly asked when they were gathered round the dining table.

'She has a headache', explained Millie. 'She likes having her meal on a tray and it's quieter in the study.'

'I like Sybil's dinners', Chris announced. 'She doesn't keep telling me to keep my elbows off the table.' Grace, the baby of the family, was missing her Mother and Sybil found it difficult to console the child. It became obvious that the anxiety felt by the adults was beginning to affect the younger members of the family.

Mrs. Tarrant from the farm was a frequent visitor and Sybil appreciated her support, especially when it came to talking to her Mother.

'No news is supposed to be good news, but heaven knows what will happen next in this war.' She addressed Sybil and Millie: 'You're such good girls and I hope your brother survives his ordeal.' They watched her trudging back up the hill to the farm.

In the next week a letter arrived from Portsmouth. Jason was alive but in hospital. Sybil and Millie hugged each other with joy and the youngsters were jumping about and throwing themselves on the floor. It seemed as if an enormous weight had been lifted from their shoulders.

' Why are you so quiet Mother?' Millie asked.

'Because I haven't finished reading the letter,' she sighed. 'This is what it says: *'It is with pride that we inform you that your son Able Seaman Lewisham has not only survived the sinking of his ship but has also saved the life of a fellow crewman. Sadly, however, the length of time in the water and his experience of seeing others drowning around him has affected his mental state. He has not uttered one word since he arrived at the hospital. We recommend that he remains here for at* least *two more weeks.'*

'Oh Mother, what can we do?' Millie cried. 'Poor Jason, he can't stay there on his own.'

'He's not on his own – the ward is probably full of sailors and soldiers wounded or dying. It's terrible,' Sybil added.

'I'm not leaving my son there.' Mother looked determined and marched to the front door.

'Where are you going?' called Sybil. The young ones started to cry and everything became chaotic. Mother turned back.

'Just keep them quiet' she yelled. 'I'm going up to see Mr. Tarrant – he will take me to the hospital and I'm bringing Jason home. I'm a nurse and I shall look after him myself.'

Mr. Tarrant agreed to take them to the south coast to collect Jason. It was a long way and they were not sure if they could complete the journey in one day. Sybil packed some supplies for them and Millie joined her Mother on the journey. That night Sybil managed with difficulty to persuade her brothers and sisters to go to bed. They all wanted to sleep in Sybil's room. Polly helped move Grace's cot and then stayed with the boys until they were asleep. Sybil found her there curled up on the carpet.

'Come on, Polly, you can sleep in Millie's bed tonight. Thank you for helping with the boys.' She put her arm round her sister and they walked together to the bedroom just as the clock struck twelve. Sybil was exhausted but she couldn't sleep. Jason was alive but she feared for him. How ill was he? And what about David? There was still no news.

●●●

Mr. Moore brought the telegram round and showed it to Sybil's mother. He was stunned and speechless by the news and Mother walked him straight back home. Sybil stared at the ring on her finger. David is not coming back - she felt it in her bones. He was posted as missing after one of the fierce battles on the western front. She felt numb and helpless. The Moores had lost both their sons. How could anyone recover from such a tragedy? Sybil was persuaded by her mother to visit the grieving couple but she was reluctant to go.

'No one seems to care about me losing David!' she cried. 'We were going to have a future together and he loved me,' she gasped. Sybil was close to tears again.

'There is a difference. You are a young woman and you'll find it easier to recover. The Moores have lost their children – both of their babies! Boys stubbed out of existence in this evil war. No more happy family reunions for those two. No dreams of weddings or looking forward to grandchildren like most of us.'

'Alright, I'll come,' Sybil whispered to her mother. 'I know I'm being selfish.'

The house where Sybil had spent so many happy times with David and his family looked deserted. The curtains were drawn and there was no sign of life. They went through the back gate and could see David's dad in his garden shed. He came out to meet them and Sybil hardly recognised him because he looked so pale and drawn. His eyes were red and empty. Mother went forward. He was trembling.

'Please help Cynthia! ' he cried. 'She hasn't eaten since the telegram arrived and she just wants to die.'

'I'll take Sybil back and then I'll return' promised Mother. Sybil was out of control. She was crying and, as her Mother turned towards her, she ran on ahead.

'You don't care about me' she insisted when her Mother caught up.

'Come here, darling.' Sybil buried her head in her mother's shawl.

'How can God be so cruel?' she sobbed.

'I don't know, dear, there is no answer to that question. At least he showed our family some mercy when he sent Jason back to us.'

'But, I've lost David!' cried Sybil. 'And look at Jason, he's changed completely. He'll never be the same again after his ordeal.' Mother took her arm and guided her back home.

PART III
1918 – 1936

8

When the war came to an end in 1918, not everyone rushed out to celebrate. Sybil was pleased to see the younger members of her family happy with their lives, but she hated them trying to cheer her up. Millie often came home with the local newspaper under her arm.

'There's an interesting ad in here Sybil. I've ringed it round in pencil.'

'You know I'm not interested,' Sybil snapped. 'Just leave me alone.'

'Well, I'll put it here on the table just in case you change your mind. A holiday by the sea in Wareham sounds good to me, and you could also earn some money.'

Sybil ignored her. She was fed up with her sister and younger brothers telling her what to do. Jason was her mentor and she always talked to him when she was unhappy. After his experiences in the war, he became a recluse staying in his room. She tried to talk to him, but instead of his kindness, he turned into a mad thing .

'Don't keep coming into my room. Bloody well grow up and get on with your life.' Losing David was bad enough for Sybil. The trauma and the lack of sympathy from her family confused and hurt her. Just when she needed her brother most of all, she found that he had changed so much that he was like a stranger to her. Sybil always counted on him to help solve her problems and now she was frightened even to enter his room. She never heard Jason swear like that before or lose his temper. In her heart she wanted so much to be able to comfort him, and somehow assist with his recovery but a solution evaded her. After his outburst Sybil felt devastated and lonely.

Millie is only trying to be helpful, Sybil thought, and before leaving the room she glanced furtively at the newspaper. 'Wanted urgently – young Nanny to care for two children aged seven and three. Must be willing to travel with the family between Bath and Wareham.' Sybil paused and re-read the advertisement. Perhaps Millie was right. She needed to emerge from her depression.

In the kitchen, her Mother was busy preparing the vegetables for the evening meal. Sybil sat down beside her. 'Millie saw this advert in the paper,' she passed the newspaper to her Mother. 'Do you think I should apply?' she asked in a hesitant manner.

'I don't see why not,' her mother replied. 'I'll miss you if you go away but it may do you good. The children are growing up and even Grace can dress herself. The boys are out every day and Polly loves helping with the chores – she even likes looking after Grandma'.

'I could send you some money from my wages.' Sybil was beginning to warm to the idea of going away.

'Of course you can darling. I really want you to move on with your life - you're much too young to be weighed down with such sorrow.'

Sybil admired her mother. ' I don't know how Mother does it,' she confided in Millie that evening. 'She's been round to the Moore's house every day and David's mother is now eating normally. She even goes down to help at the Red Cross whenever she can.'

'I know,' said Millie. 'And Mum's so worried about Jason. Dr. Waring says that it will take months or years for him to recover from his shock. All that time in the water and seeing his friends drown or blown to pieces – it's horrific!' Millie paused for a while. 'I'm so lucky to have Frank, even though he lives in London and can only come across at week ends.' Sybil turned away hiding her distress. Her control was all on the surface and any little thing started her off again.

'It's good for you to go away, Syb. It will help Mother and Jason if they can see you trying something new. As Mother says 'time will heal' and this job looks really interesting.' Sybil was not too sure. Since leaving school she felt secure and wanted at home. She came to enjoy looking after the children. Leaving all this behind and venturing out on her own was a bit of a risk, she concluded. In this uncertain frame of mind she sat at her Father's desk and ran her hands over the smooth inlaid leather.

There was a kind of warmth in the study that Sybil loved. The cosiness of the walls covered in books reminded her of her Father. When they first moved into this house he announced that this room was to be his library and study. She so wished he were still here to guide her. After a while she dipped the nib of her pen in the ink and began writing her letter of application. After all, she thought to herself, if I am offered the post I have the option to decline. Millie popped her head round the door.

'I'll post the letter for you on my way to work,' she offered.

'Thanks Millie - if it hadn't been for you I wouldn't have seen the ad'. It was a long week of waiting. Then on the Friday Polly came running in from the hall with a letter addressed to Sybil.

'Dear Miss Lewisham,

Thank you for your application. My wife and I should like to meet you on Sunday next at 10.30 am in the reception area of the Empire Hotel. The hotel is situated near to the river in the centre of Bath. We look forward to meeting you. Yours sincerely,

Samuel F. Crawford.'

Sybil felt elated and somewhat worried at the same time. The prospect of telling her Mother about the interview sent a shiver of apprehension down her spine.

When she walked into the kitchen, her mother was smiling. Sybil smiled back, even though she was finding it hard to control her emotion. On Sunday morning she decided to get up early so that she could wash her hair and have plenty of time to allow it to dry. Luckily her Mother was there to help.

'Your hair is so long dear,' she said as she took small bunches of the golden locks and rubbed them as dry as possible in a warm towel.

'Thanks Mother - I'm feeling quite nervous you know. What do you think they'll ask me?'

'Just be yourself, darling, and don't be nervous. There's not much you don't know about children - not only that, but you can cook, sew and certainly read a good story. You'll be an asset to any family.'

These generous words from her Mother and the support from her sisters gave Sybil encouragement and she was able to compose herself in readiness for the interview. To her delight, just as she was leaving, Jason appeared from his room.

'Good luck, Sybil' he whispered in a gruff voice. He kissed her hastily on her forehead and before she had a chance to speak he turned and climbed the stairs back to his room.

•••

Sybil walked into the lobby of the hotel and was overawed by the splendour of the place. Her polished shoes sank into the deep pile of the magnificent carpet and as she moved forward she was even more impressed by the flower arrangements in the cut glass vases around the room. The scent of carnations and roses filled the air.

'May I help you Madam?' enquired a young man dressed in a smart uniform.

'Thank you, I'm meeting someone here,' Sybil replied in a quiet voice.

'They'll probably help you over there at reception.' He pointed.

Sybil walked gingerly towards the desk but a tall gentleman strode up to her. 'Are you Miss Lewisham? ' he asked.

'Yes, I am sir.'

'How do you do, I'm Samuel Crawford,' he smiled. He offered Sybil his hand. She took it timidly. His strong grasp made her wince as she tried to smile back at him. 'Come this way and meet my wife Sophie. She's just ordered pastries and coffee. You may prefer tea, Miss Lewisham. My wife was born in the French part of Switzerland and she thinks everyone likes *café au lait.'* Sybil followed the tall elegant form of Mr. Crawford to a corner table where a diminutive figure was sitting.

'Meet Miss Lewisham, dear.' Sybil could not help staring at the woman who looked even younger than her.

'How do you do?' she said in a quaint accent, standing up to shake hands with Sybil. She was dressed in a pale grey gown and her dark hair was pinned up in two thick plats that joined in the centre of her head. A fringe lay in fine wisps on her forehead. 'She's quite beautiful,' Sybil thought, 'and so delicate.'

'Would you like some coffee? Please sit here with us.' She poured the drinks and passed Sybil a white porcelain cup and saucer. She pointed to the milk and sugar.

'May we call you by your first name, dear?'

'Yes, of course, my name is Sybil.'

'You seem very young. Have you been a Nanny before? Have you had any experience with children?' Mr Crawford demanded.

'Please let her have a drink first, darling. Then you can bombard her with questions,' suggested Mrs. Crawford.

'I've never been a paid Nanny. My Father died when I was fourteen and I help my Mother to look after my seven brothers and sisters. Now the children are older, she is allowing me to leave home. That is why I applied for this position. My mother says you are welcome to come to our house to meet the family if you so wish.'

'That's very kind,' said Mrs. Crawford. 'Would you like to meet the children now?'

'Yes please,' agreed Sybil enthusiastically.

They finished their drinks and moved towards the lifts. The Crawford's suite was on the first floor and as they entered the room the children ran to their Mother's side.

'This is Esme, she is seven years old and this little chap is Mervyn. He is only three.'

'How do you do?' asked Esme, in a grown up way. 'We've been playing a game. Come on Mervyn let's pick the pieces up off the floor.' Mrs. Crawford bent down to help them.

'Sybil has seven brothers and sisters,' she informed the children, 'and she's invited us to her house to meet them.'

'How lovely, Maman, can we go today?' Esme asked. She ran over to Sybil. 'Do you live in the countryside?' she queried bubbling over with delight.

'I live in a village called Larkhall, it's close to country lanes and we can go for lovely walks.'

'Sheep?' enquired Mervyn in a sweet voice.

'Yes, there are sheep in the fields near bye and cows and horses,' confirmed Sybil taking the little boy's hand.

'Will you show me your toys please Mervyn?' There was quite an age gap between the two children and it showed in their behaviour. Mervyn pushed the toys at Sybil and made sure he was the centre of attention. Esme, on the other hand, stood back holding a book in her hand. She was rather a plain child compared to the little boy who resembled his mother with her good looks.

'Now we must let Sybil go,' said Mr. Crawford. 'She's going to ask if we can visit this afternoon.'

'I want to show Sybil how I can read,' pleaded Esme.

'Later dear,' insisted her Mother. Mr. Crawford accompanied Sybil to the entrance of the hotel.

'See you later,' he smiled.

When she arrived home and announced that the Crawford family were calling that same afternoon, chaos ensued. 'The place is in such a mess,' said Mother. 'Millie, Polly, please help to tidy up. I'm going to bake a cake. Why didn't you let us know before Sybil?'

'You've got some cake left in the larder,' replied Millie

'I expect they only want to meet you Mother and ask you a few questions.' Sybil felt mortified at the commotion caused by her announcement.

After all the excitement the Crawford's visit went very smoothly. Polly took charge of Esme and they disappeared upstairs where they dressed dolls and read books. Mervyn played with Gerry out in the garden on the homemade slide. At teatime they sat round the pine table in the kitchen and ate sandwiches and some of Mother's delicious coconut cake. All the right questions were asked and answered. Eventually, the children had to be dragged away by their parents.

'Can we come again?' called Esme as they were leaving.

That evening Sybil sat quietly with her Mother in the kitchen. The others were busy preparing for work or school in the morning. 'They are a pleasant family. They do so many exciting things. I like Mrs. Crawford and her French ways.'

'You'll have to wait and see, dear,' was the reply. 'Mr. Crawford told me that three others have applied for the job. You're the youngest. You never know they may prefer to have an older Nanny, with perhaps more experience.' Sybil picked up her embroidery and sat there glumly checking the pattern. For the first time in her life she felt in a competitive mood.

'Mind you,' added her Mother, 'if I was choosing I'd certainly employ you straight away – but then I am biased.' Sybil smiled affectionately.

'As you say, I shall have to wait and see what happens.'

Once in bed that night, Sybil tossed and turned from side to side. In her mind she went through the events of the day. Moving from one luxurious hotel to another was a captivating thought and perhaps there was a house in Wareham near the beach. Apparently, Mr. Crawford's parents live there and there was talk of a business in Dorchester - something to do with land and estates. London was also mentioned. A trip to the capital was a regular occurrence. Mrs. Crawford liked joining her husband on these occasions.

'I love shopping in London' she informed Sybil. 'Though it is only second best to Paris!' she laughed. It seemed like a far off world to Sybil and she began suddenly to descend into uncertainty – she was so unsure of herself and lacked confidence in her abilities despite all her Mother's efforts. She drowned herself in the sorrows of the recent past – David and Alf had gone forever and poor Jason's mind was shattered. How could she forget all this and just go off to enjoy herself? Eventually she cried herself to sleep.

9

The turning point of the war arrived and William had missed out on the action. He flew in planes as a trainee on reconnaissance flights over France photographing strategic landmarks but he never became a pilot. With a heavy heart, he decided to leave the force in 1918 when the war was coming to an end.

'Why don't you stay on, Lawson, after all the fuss you made about joining?'

'Because I wanted to be a pilot,' William replied. 'I enjoyed the photography but I wanted to fly my own 504 and I wasn't chosen.' He turned away. 'All those disputes held our group back and now they're forming the long-range bomber force. It's going to be called 'The Royal Air Force. We shall never get a look in - we've lost our chance!'

William felt uncertain about his future. It was hard for him to hide his disappointment. Returning home was not an option. He couldn't face the thought of living in his old house with his parents again and it depressed him to think of searching for a job in the dreary part of Manchester where he once lived. He wanted to join the young crowd moving south. London, he thought to himself, is where I want to be. On the spur of the moment, William allowed himself to follow the flow of the young men making their way to the metropolis.

After the first excitement had worn off, he decided to call on his aunts, Beattie and Emily. William remembered his last visit with trepidation. It was not a happy time so he was pleased and frankly amazed at the joyous welcome he received. 'Beattie, come quick, look who's here! Emily cried. His aunt looked much smaller than he remembered but he could still see that twinkle in her eye. William bent down to kiss her and was amused to see her blush and become quite flustered. 'Oh, Will, you're so grown up, you look just like your Dad with your brown curly hair and you're nearly as handsome.'

'So what's all the fuss about?' Aunt Beattie popped her head round the door.

'Why are you standing there? Come on in, Will.' He followed his Aunts into the bungalow, leaving his kitbag in the hall and going through the open door to the sitting room. It was just as he remembered, a quiet oasis far away from the hustle and bustle of the London streets. The armchairs were covered with brightly coloured rugs and cushions and the walls were lined with books and paintings. An aroma of freshly baked cakes wafted in from the kitchen. It's such a homely room he thought as he bent down to kiss Aunt Beattie. He noticed that she was more round and chubby compared to Emily who had become thin with a pale, rather pasty complexion.

'Make some tea, Emily and then we can find out what this young man has been up to.'

'Alright Beattie, but I don't want to miss anything.'

'I'll help you,' offered William.

'No dear, you sit down, you look tired.' He moved over to his favourite chair.

'How are Mum and Dad?' Beattie enquired.

'They seem O.K. They probably would like me to go back home and find a job in Manchester.'

'And what do you want to do, dear?' Emily came back carrying a tray with all the tea things and a plate of freshly baked cheese scones.

'I cooked these this morning – I must have known you were coming Will.'

He took a scone and some butter from the delicate silver dish.

'I'd like to work in London, if I can find a job. Most of my friends want to go abroad. We've all been so fed up with the war. India seems to be the favourite place. They're crying out for people to work on the railways out there. Mind you, I've got to find a room first, somewhere central before I tell Mum and Dad. How about Hilda, what is she doing?'

'Hilda's at College' said Beattie, 'she's doing a secretarial course. Her mother wanted her to try for University, but you know Hilda – she likes it at home too much. She'll probably pop in on her way home.'

'Could we ask William to stay here for a while until he finds work?' suggested Emily.

'I don't want to be a nuisance,' insisted William, blushing as he remembered his last visit.

'You can stay as long as you promise not to climb up any lamp-posts,' Beattie smiled. 'The bed is made up in your old room, dear.'

William was pleased and relieved. He felt so much at home here and he was tired after his long train journey. He only had a week's money in his pocket and a few pounds saved in the bottom of his kit bag. William needed to find a job quickly before telling his parents that he was not returning to Manchester. He knew they would be upset. A new life, a new beginning: that's what he wanted.

That evening his aunts invited Hilda and her family over for a grand reunion. He and Hilda chatted non-stop. 'What are you going to do when you leave college?' William asked.

'Look for a secretarial job, I suppose. My shorthand speeds are very good so I may apply for a job at the B.B.C.'

'Don't you want to travel to new places?'

'Not really,' she replied. 'But I tell you what, there are new companies starting up in the travel business. Also shipping lines with interesting jobs for women. There is one company called Thomas Cook and they are organising trips for people. You never know, I may become a courier or something like that.'

'I want to change course and do something completely different. I don't want to go back home.'

'They're looking for people on the railways, that would make a change from aeroplanes. I saw an advertisement in *'The Times'* and they even have notices at Waterloo station. Why don't you come with me tomorrow morning and you can have a look around in central London?' William agreed to meet Hilda at the bus stop and next morning they travelled together.

'I'll walk with you to college,' offered William. There were groups of girls standing outside the buildings and, as they approached, a pretty red head called out 'Are you going to introduce us Hilda?'

'This is my cousin William', explained Hilda, blushing slightly. 'He's looking for a job in London.'

'What fun! ' William returned their greetings and thought, 'yes, this is the place I want to be.' As the bell rang, the students moved towards the door.

'Good luck! ' Hilda called. 'See you this evening.'

●●●

Stephen and William met each other at the railway's head office in London. They were both there for interviews. He was seeking promotion and hoped to be selected as a group leader. They chatted about their careers. William tried to explain what it was like living with his parents in Manchester.

'I don't know if it's being an only child or what but my Mother is so clingy – she cries at the least upset and makes me feel terrible.'

'I think all Mothers are like that with their sons,' Stephen replied. 'I've got three sisters and they're always complaining about Mother. They say she spoils me and allows me to get away with murder.'

'I suppose the most exciting thing I've done so far is to fly in an Avro 504 plane.' William said.

'Well, I've never done that. I'm a navy man,' he stated with pride. Stephen was a year older than William. His parents moved to Argentina and he lived with them until he joined the merchant navy and played a part in transporting food to England from South America. He then joined his father working for the British Railways.

•••

'Your credentials are excellent, Mr. Lawson,' the Manager beamed. 'If you're interested in working in Argentina we can offer you a job as a draughtsman. Later, you may have the opportunity to branch out and train as a surveyor. We're laying new tracks up in the Andes. It's all unknown terrain for us so there's plenty of adventure for a young man like you.' William was overjoyed with the offer. He wanted to work in the open air as opposed to sitting in a large drawing office. It would be an extra bonus if he were to be chosen to work on the new frontier up in the Andes. He agreed straight away.

'Thank you Sir, I'll take the job. When do I start?' he was full of enthusiasm.

'The next group goes out in November. We'll write to you with the date and all the details. You'll have to find your own accommodation. I expect you'll be able to double up with one of the other lads.' Stephen was waiting for William when he came out of the Manager's office. 'Thought I'd wait and see how you got on,' he said kindly. 'I'm going to be in charge of one of the surveying groups and I like you Lawson, perhaps you can be in my team. I've been working nearly two years for the railways. I love living in Argentina. The weather's great, the company is good and if we're lucky we shall arrive in early summer. It will be the start of the outdoor picnic season or *Asado* time. Wait till you see and taste the Argentine beef,' he enthused, licking his lips.

The two men exchanged addresses and promised to

meet in Southampton the night before they sailed. I'll book us somewhere to stay near the station. It won't be far to walk to the docks. The ship usually sails in the late afternoon,' Stephen explained.

'I'll let you know what train I'm catching, I'll probably have to change at Paddington and go over to Waterloo.' William was pleased to meet Stephen. He'd flown in planes over France during the war but he still felt insecure about travelling over the sea. The thought of sailing away from his country to the other side of the globe was a daunting prospect. He felt happier at the thought of having a companion. And what a companion Stephen turned out to be.

●●●

'We're going to have a great time,' he said when he met William at the station. 'I think we're sharing a cabin – just check your number Will'.

'Twenty three.' William assumed he was having his own cabin.

'Yes, that's the same as me,' he confirmed. 'You can sleep on the top bunk.' They dropped William's luggage off at the hostel and decided to go out for a pint. 'I know a good place that does homemade steak & kidney pies. Are you hungry, Will?'

'Yes, I could do with something hot.' He didn't mention that his Mother had supplied him with two different types of sandwiches and a homemade cake.

Stephen carried a torch as they made their way along a narrow path, dwarfed by the high ruins of the city wall. It seemed an unsavoury area to William, but it was near to the docks and they wouldn't have far to go tomorrow afternoon when the ship sailed They met quite a few undesirable characters on the way. Some were drunk and others begging. It was a relief when they reached the main road and walked up to the Bargate. The inn had a log fire burning at one end of the room. It was warm and cosy. People were sitting at tables tucking into delicious looking pies. They found themselves a table. 'Pie and chips do for you, Will?'

'Yes thanks, I'll pay for mine.'

'You can get the drinks in, I'll have a pint of bitter please.'

It didn't take long for William to fall asleep that night. They planned their shopping for the morning. Stephen wanted last minute things, such as soap and toothpaste. 'I do like a decent bar of soap and you can't buy it abroad. The soap is so coarse over there. It's only good for washing clothes.' William ended up buying all kinds of toiletries, including Brylcream, which he wanted to try on his curly hair. He admired Stephen's straight glossy locks. 'I use Brylcream on my hair,' he told William.

The next evening they made their way to the docks and through the Customs. A Railway representative was there to check on the recruits. There were several other young men travelling to Argentina and Brazil. South America seemed to be the 'in' place. William soon learned that life on board was hectic, to say the least. There was a round of parties, one after the other starting on the first night. The only problem was that William was seasick so he missed the first three nights. Stephen let him sleep on the bottom bunk.

'I don't want you spewing all over me,' he laughed. 'Haven't you ever been to sea?'

'No,' replied William. I've only been on a rowing boat on a lake and I feel weary tonight. Stephen's cheerfulness was beginning to grate. 'Buzz off Stephen, leave me alone.'

'O.K. old chap, you'll get your sea legs in a day or two.'

●●●

William was not a heavy drinker. He often had a beer or two with his friends at the pub and when he was in the Flying Corps he was too far away from pubs and other drinking holes. His Father wanted him to join the Temperance Society and he did become a member for a time. He wasn't going to tell Stephen that bit of information. He would never hear the end of it. The Captain and Officers of the ship joined the passengers in the bar after meals. They often started on beer when they were trying to be polite and chivalrous but as the evening wore on they changed their drinking patterns to something stronger such as whisky, brandy or rum.

'Come on old chap,' William grabbed Stephen before he collapsed in a heap on the floor. Most nights he ended up carrying Stephen back to the cabin and on these occasions he was glad to be back on the top bunk. The sea journey was an initiation for William. His friends from Manchester and even the student pilots were not like these people on the ship. The crewmembers were mainly ex. Royal Navy and it soon became apparent that they considered themselves superior to members of the Army and Air force. The Flying Corps was considered to be a fledgling force by the Captain and Officers and as for the new Royal Air Force that was just a laugh to them. Stephen was of the same opinion.

'What did they do in the war?' he asked jokingly. 'All we heard was that they spent their time squabbling amongst themselves and drawing a few maps.' William cringed at this assault, but he knew that some of it was true.

'We did drop a bomb or two over Germany and we managed to destroy some of their Air Ships,' he retorted defensively. 'You wait and see, The Air Force will become the main contributor in the future – especially with all our knowledge about building planes and flying them. Didn't you read in June about Alcock and Brown flying non-stop across the Atlantic? It only took them sixteen hours. Passenger ships like this one will become extinct; people will prefer to fly everywhere. It's so much quicker.' Stephen smiled at William's outburst.

'Didn't those two chaps end up in an Irish bog?' Stephen teased. 'They were brave though, and I suppose it was quite a feat. But whether you like it or not, the Navy is the senior force and as far as I am concerned it will remain so.'

'We shall have to agree to differ on this one,' concluded William who believed implicitly that air travel would take over in the future.

10

William felt himself sinking in the green slimy water. He kept his mouth closed because he knew about the detritus in the pool. He didn't want to swallow. Some must be entering my nostrils, he thought as he dropped down and down. He was blindfolded and he struggled to release himself. The scarf fell away but he kept his eyes closed. His second instinct was to hold his arms high above his head. He didn't want to crash on to the bottom. One of the previous prisoners managed to twist his neck and he was carried off to the infirmary. Suddenly his hands were bent back by the force of his descent and he pushed himself upwards. He was on his way to the surface to face the King again.

When he spluttered out of the water he gasped for air. What a relief! He could breathe again and open his eyes. Grinning faces stared down at him. The crew and passengers were clapping as he was dragged out of the pool by two powerful sailors dressed as monsters of the deep. He was marched along the deck to stand before the mighty King Neptune.

'Step forward my son.' The two sailors pushed William to his knees.

'Kneel,' they hissed. William looked up at the King who was dressed in silvery robes, with various ropes coiled around his head. The odour tickled William's nostrils and he noticed that the King had garlands of seaweed and shells round his waist.

'Come forth, William Henry Lawson, you have this day been initiated into the ancient order of the Brotherhood of the Deep. You are now free to enter and pass through my domain at all times without any hindrance whatsoever given unto hand this 20th day of November in the year of Our Lord 1919.' He handed William a certificate signed Neptune Rex, Ruler of the Raging Deep.'

William got to his feet, smiling. He looked round at the crowd and he could see boys and girls hiding behind their parents fearing that it may be their turn next. It was quite frightening, even for a grown man. Being tied up on a high chair, covered in shaving cream and forced to drink a salty concoction was not very pleasant. Then to be blindfolded and thrown backwards head first into the pool was not William's idea of fun. Crossing the Equator for the first time was a miserable ordeal.

'Well done Will,' said Stephen. 'You passed that with honours.'

'What was that terrible drink? I can still taste it in my mouth.'

'Scotch and seawater,' he replied grinning. He pulled a small flask from his pocket and gave William the cap. 'Just have a nip of the real stuff, that will make you feel better.' He was right, the warmth of the golden liquid soon revived him and he felt more like himself again. The children lost their fear when they realised that King Neptune was kinder to children. They stood quietly in line waiting to meet the King. He didn't shout and rave and none of them were ducked. Instead they were sprinkled with salt water from a font and each one received a small packet of seaweed fudge – it looked green from where William was standing.

Life was so different on board the ship. William was impressed by the behaviour and attitude of the women passengers. They didn't sit meekly with their husbands. Most of them were ready to join in discussions. The topics were diverse and William could not recall talking about these things back in his hometown. Politics, perhaps, but it was usually local stuff. The adventures in South America were quite new to him. One chap climbed in the Andes and several had trekked across Patagonia. But the hot subject on everyone's lips this year was birth control and that book entitled 'Married Love' by Dr. Marie Stopes. It was published in 1918. The conversation at dinnertime became quite heated.

'I'm all for it,' declared Stephen in his brash way. 'It may stop people having such large families and not being able to look after them.'

'I agree.' William surprised himself when he joined in the debate. 'Nearly every family in my part of Manchester has seven or eight children and that's a lot to feed and clothe. The houses are small and the children are squashed into bedrooms where they share beds, if they're lucky. If not they just sleep on mattresses on the floor.'

'It all depends on how rich you are,' said a girl called Fiona. 'If you can afford it you can choose to have as many children as you like.'

'The trouble is that poorer women think it's their duty to have children and they always give in to their husbands.' William quite liked this girl called Penny – she was down to earth and talked a lot of sense. She even tried to see both sides of the story.

'Well, I suppose birth control could help the poor.'

'You are a snob, Fiona.' Stephen liked to stir things up. 'I think it's a good idea for everyone. Just imagine, we needn't get married at all. We can just have one affair after the other and no children to spoil our fun.'

'Trust you to come up with that idea.' William grinned at his friend.

What he liked most of all was the intensity of the discussions. His parents were not religious, but William enjoyed Bible studies at school. He was only aware of the Church of England and Catholicism. That seemed to be complicated enough with all the smaller factions that existed in Britain.

'The Pope will never allow birth control - it's against the teachings of St. Paul. For all we know it may be morally wrong to tempt fate in that way. How can a wife be sure that she will become pregnant when she does want to have babies?'

'What are we doing tonight?' William asked. He wanted to change the subject because Stephen was becoming too controversial and spoiling the evening.

'There's horse racing tonight. Let's go to that, we may win a buck or two.'

The ladies impressed William. In the evening their casual clothes were replaced by elegant evening gowns. He thought about his Mother – she would have loved the glamour of it all! The dresses and hairstyles were fantastic and the younger women looked so graceful when they danced to the latest tunes. Dancing took place in the intimate ballroom. The polished floor was oval in shape. Only a few couples knew the latest dances. Stephen danced well and the girls all wanted him as a partner. William was rather clumsy on his feet. His friend was always trying to fix him up with one of the unmarried girls.

'The girls like you Will. I suppose you are quite good looking with your mass of curly hair – I think they want to mother you!' He laughed. William ignored him. Stephen made an effort to teach him to dance and he could manage a waltz if he danced with Penny. She tried to help him and he did improve slightly. He preferred to talk. The girl was so knowledgeable. One of her favourite subjects was 'communism' and she was always going on about Trotsky and his Red Brigade.

'I think the Reds are infiltrating our Unions. They're behind all the strikes in England and in European countries.'

'I just thought the men were fighting for a fair share – after all some of the bosses earn a fortune and the workers are left behind on the bread line.' William replied.

'Yes, I know that, but I just can't believe that people can be forced to be equal.'

'Well, it's going to be interesting to see what it is like living in a country ruled by a dictator.'

The journey was coming to an end. William stood on the deck of the ship that had carried him for almost thirty days. He looked down at the murky brown water.

'It's called Rio de la Plata; that means river of silver.' Stephen winked at William.

'It looks like mud to me! You can't even see the other side – it's more like a sea than a river.'

'The nearest seaside place is called Mar del Plata and down there the sea is blue. Rio de la Plata, Mar del Plata - the early explorers were mad about silver.'

'You don't need to show off your accent. I'll never be able to learn the language.' For a second, William looked gloomy. 'At least the technical terms are in English, so I suppose I'll manage somehow.'

He frowned and tried to focus on the far horizon. England was in a mess when they sailed away, with strikes and disputes everywhere. In September, the national rail strike had caused chaos and in Liverpool the police went on strike and the troops had to be called out to stop the looters. William felt somewhat guilty at leaving his parents. His mother had clung to him as she kissed him goodbye.

'You will write to us son?' said his Father. 'If things go on like this for long, we may decide to join you.' His two aunts came to see him off and they looked frail and cold on that misty November morning. Hilda kissed him goodbye. 'Good luck, Will, we shall miss you.' Was he doing the right thing, he wondered?

'I can see some of the buildings,' Stephen pointed as they sailed closer to the coast. 'You're very quiet Will,' he observed nudging him with his elbow.

'You'll love it in Buenos Aires – we call it B.A. There are plenty of girls.

Wine is so cheap that the locals drink it with every

meal. Come on Will, let's go and collect our cases.' He grabbed William's arm.

'What happens about the trunks?' asked William anxiously.

'We don't need to worry about those. The office boy will meet us and he'll take the luggage to my flat.' William was pleased that he was staying with Stephen.

The ship docked amidst a loud clatter of trolleys and shrill voices. People were swarming everywhere. 'Hold on to your wallet, Will. This lot will pinch the coat off your back if they get the chance.' William clung on to his large leather case. He wished he had not packed so much – it was so heavy. His wallet was safe inside his jacket. He only had a few pesos in it anyway. The rest of his money was in a belt round his waist.

'I've got Fiona's address,' Stephen told William. 'She lives near Penny.' They slowly made their way down the gangway. It was packed with people on the shore. He tried to keep up with Stephen.

'Ola, Senor Stephen!' yelled a dark haired lad, who was running on the other side of the barrier waving frantically. He looked like a teenager.

'Ola, Ricardo, there are two trunks this time – one for Senor Lawson, and the other is mine.'

'O.K., Senor,' he quipped giving them an exaggerated salute.

The men found themselves pushed along by the crowd. William became hot and nervous. He hated being jammed in like this and he could feel someone pushing him in the small of his back. William attempted to turn round but couldn't see Stephen anywhere. His arm was grabbed and he was drawn along and pushed into a small windowless room. It was like a prison cell. He felt threatened by the two burly men dressed from head to toe in black. Their hair was greasy, plastered down flat. They had long bushy sideboards. The silky black material of their suits sparkled in the bright light. Even their faces looked oily and their skin was a yellow olive colour.

They kept asking him questions in Spanish and when he didn't reply they attempted to speak in English. That wasn't any better and William began to feel sick. The smell in the room was disgusting. It was worse every time one of the men opened his mouth. He was forced to raise his arms high above his head whilst the smelly one searched him. He had to turn round several times. The two yelled at each other in high-pitched voices, especially when William tried to avoid the man's breath. They left the room for a while, locking the door behind them.

William felt completely lost. He had no idea of what was happening and he wished he knew what to do. Tackling two men was out of the question. If only he knew the language. Where was Stephen? Was he in small room like this somewhere? The men looked at his passport and opened his case but did not search through his belongings. He could feel dryness in his mouth and found it difficult to swallow. He was so thirsty. The men returned with a third man who could speak English.

'Is this your first visit to Argentina?' he asked.

'Yes,' spluttered William. It seemed hotter than ever in the room.

'What is your business here? '

'I have a new job on the railways,' William tried to explain. 'Why am I being held here? I'm travelling with Stephen Andrews and I'm staying with him in his flat until I can find my own accommodation. Will you please let me go?'

'All in good time, young man, we need to check with your company before we can let you come into Argentina. We have to be careful.'

The two other men were talking loudly, waving their hands about in desperation. William was told to sit down again facing the bright light. He sat on the stool as he was told, but the heat and smell were oppressing him. 'May I have some water, please?' He was starting to feel weak and began gasping for air. Faintness came over him and slowly everything became dark. He was slipping down into the cold ground.

11

Sybil glanced at the clock on the mantelpiece. It was ten past eight. The sun was streaming in through a gap in the curtains. She climbed out of bed and looked at herself in the mirror. Her eyes were still red and swollen from the previous night and she splashed them with water and held a cold flannel over her face. The lavender water that Polly gave her was on the dressing table and she carefully shook some on the back of her neck. The coolness and sweet fragrance made her feel better. Dressing quickly in yesterday's clothes she pulled a clean pinafore out of the cupboard and hastily tied the straps as she went down the stairs.

Her mother was in the scullery with the washing boiler full on. She was pushing the white clothes in with some wooden tongs.

'Come on dear, just sort out the boys' shirts before you have your breakfast. The collars will need an extra scrub. I don't know if your brothers ever wash their necks,' she grumbled. Sybil walked across to tackle the heap of shirts.

'This one of Jason's needs a new button.' Deep in thought, she held the shirt up to her cheek. The softness of the material and the familiar scent made her shiver. She was close to tears again.

'There's lots of work to do – moping around won't solve anything. Make some toast for yourself and then help me with the washing.'

Sybil did as she was told. The drudgery of washing day

progressed. It would be wonderful to leave all this behind!

'My arms are aching now, can we stop for something to eat?' She guided the last white sheet through the old mangle. The pinafores and damask table clothes had been starched and were hanging on the clothesline.

'Have we finished the whites?' her mother asked stretching her arms above her head. 'The coloured stuff won't take so long.' It was time for a break. Sybil sat with her mother on the garden seat. They ate bread and dripping, washed down by a large mug of tea.

'You may be saying goodbye to all this. Mr. Crawford told me that the children would be your sole responsibility. There will be no cleaning, washing or cooking. They have maids and cooks for all that sort of work. You'll be a lady of leisure!'

' But I won't have my family around me.' Sybil was feeling a pang of indecision. 'Mother, do you mind if I just pop down to the shops? I want to buy that magazine that Millie suggested. It gives tips about applying for jobs – it may come in handy.'

'All right dear but don't be long. We must finish the washing. 'Sybil slipped her apron off, picked up her purse and strolled down the road to the general store. She found the magazine on the shelf, bought it and was hurrying out of the shop, when she heard a child's voice.

'Hello Miss Lewisham.' It was Esme. Mrs. Crawford and the two children were just behind her. 'Mummy has some news for you.' The little girl ran to Sybil's side.

Mrs. Crawford, looking as elegant as ever, was holding Mervyn's hand. 'We're just going for a walk up to Chalcombe Church. I believe it's very beautiful up that way, the children wanted to come. You mentioned the walk at your interview.

'Tell her, tell her!' Esme skipped in her excitement.

'You are not supposed to know this yet and you'll receive a formal letter from Mr. Crawford probably tomorrow. He and I have decided that we want to offer you the position as Nanny. As you can see, the children want you to accept.' The girl and boy ran to Sybil.

'Please say yes! ' Esme pleaded. Mervyn tugged at her skirt, his face beaming with pleasure. Sybil bent and picked the small boy up. Her other arm went round Esme's shoulder.

'I'd love to be your Nanny,' she smiled down at them. A tingle of pleasure crept up her spine. It was great to feel wanted again. Mrs. Crawford came over and kissed her briefly on the cheek and Sybil at last felt a glimmer of hope for the future. After saying goodbye, she hurried back to tell her Mother the good news.

A few days later the official letter arrived with the details of Sybil's first appointment. From the moment she wrote accepting the post her life seemed to lift to a new plane. There was no time for depression or feeling sorry. The whole atmosphere in the house changed from the morose to one of optimism for the future. Laughter was heard once more. Even her mother took on a new look.

'I'm having my hair trimmed and dressed by the hairdresser. I want to look smart when Sybil goes off on the train with the Crawfords.' A new form of vitality crept into the home. Each person began to do his or her own thing again, except for Jason who still stayed closeted in his bedroom.

One afternoon Sybil was summoned to the hotel and Mrs Crawford handed her an envelope. 'Sam asked me to give you this. I've made you a list of the clothes you need. I expect your sisters will help you with the shopping.' Sybil stared at the sheet of paper. Three plain everyday dresses, one special dress for parties, four skirts, blouses, underclothes and footwear, including boots.

'I do have some clothes,' Sybil muttered. 'This will be so costly.'

'The money to pay for it is in the envelope,' she replied. Sybil found it hard to believe that this was happening to her. It seemed like a dream.

'You lucky thing, I'm green with envy!' Millie hugged Sybil.

'Will you come shopping with me, then? You know what I'm like choosing clothes.'

'Can I come?' Polly asked. 'I don't want to miss this shopping spree.'

As the day drew nearer to her departure, Sybil tried to spend more evenings with Jason. She approached the task with some trepidation because her brother was still isolating himself from the rest of the family and she didn't want to alienate him. A preset plan was in her mind and she discussed it with Millie. Now she wanted to start putting it into action. Millie agreed to help. The aim was to try to persuade Jason to leave his room and involve himself with family life once more.

'Can I come in Jason?' She tapped gently on her brother's door.

'Are you on your own, Syb?'

'Yes.'

'Come in then.'

'I've brought this milk jelly for you to try. Mother has been teaching me how to make special puddings for children. She says I need to have surprises up my sleeve in case of emergencies.' Sybil walked over to the chair where Jason was sitting staring out of the window. Whenever she saw him her heart sank. He looked so thin and gaunt. Even his hair was starting to turn grey. He's not even thirty!

'Thank you Syb,' he sighed. 'You want to listen to Mother. She knows a thing or two about survival.' Sybil handed him the glass dish and a spoon.

'Tell me what you think? It's made with tinned milk, strawberry flavouring, gelatine and fresh raspberries from the garden.'

'Yes, it's very nice, though I think it could be a bit sweeter.' Sybil was pleased to see him tuck into the pudding and he even scraped the sides of the dish.

‘ I thought I’d let you know that your brothers are doing their best in the garden. I did hear them saying that they haven’t the faintest idea how to prune the raspberry canes or the blackcurrants. Jerry assured Chris that he knew how to do it. “It’s easy, I’ve seen Jason pruning the bushes. As far as I can see you just chop them down.” I thought I ought to warn you Jason about their conversation.’

‘Don’t worry Sybil, Mother will teach them,’ he assured her.

‘Mother tries to do so much!’

It wasn’t long before Sybil’s strategy began to work. After a day or two Jason waylaid his brothers and gave them a lesson in pruning.

‘Why don’t you help us Jason?’ Jerry grumbled.

‘Shut up Jerry,’ snapped Chris. ‘I want to learn to prune bushes, especially the raspberries. They’re my favourite fruit.’ Millie managed to persuade Jennifer, one of Jason’s girlfriends, to visit in the evenings. That was also a success. Jason and her sat together in the garden.

‘Jennifer is so sweet.’ Millie observed.

‘She’s gentle and considerate, I’m sure Jason loves her.’ Sybil watched with pleasure as her ‘one step at a time’ plan began to work. Little by little her brother began to return to normal life after the terrible war that caused him so much pain and shattered him so badly.

It was nearly one year to the day that the news about David’s death had arrived. He was one of the many who died in action on the Western Front. Sybil was still wearing his ring. She tried to give it back to his mother, but Mrs. Moore would not hear of it.

‘He loved you Sybil, and I’m sure he wants you to keep it. He told me many times that he wanted to marry you.’ She put her arms round Sybil and whispered: ‘I would have loved you as my daughter in law, but it was not to be. Now, dear, I’m very pleased that you’re starting your first job and I wish you all the best for the future. ’

Two days before their departure for Wareham, Sybil moved into the hotel with the family. Mr. Crawford was not travelling with them.

'Why aren't you coming with us, Daddy?'

'I've got some work to do in London dear. Granddad will be at the station to meet you. I may have some really exciting news to tell you later.' The children were easy to keep amused. Sybil knew some good walks in Sydney Gardens and along the canal paths near the hotel. She also enjoyed playing games and loved reading to them. The long-awaited day came at last.

'You keep hold of the bag with the cards and books in, and I'll call for a porter when we arrive at the station. Esme, you stay with Sybil and I'll hold on to Mervyn.' Mrs. Crawford was flustered so it was a relief for her and a surprise for Sybil to see the whole Lewisham family standing in a group on the platform. They were dressed in their best clothes and looking rather awkward but Sybil was delighted to see them.

Even Jason was there with Jennifer. Sybil felt a lump in her throat as she kissed her mother. Polly was holding Esme's hand and Mrs. Crawford couldn't thank them enough for coming to help. The younger boys were fooling about and Jason castigated them brusquely. Sybil smiled. In the distance they could hear the train's whistle and the clunking of the wheels coming closer. Sybil moved over to say goodbye to each of her siblings. When she reached her Mother she clung to her for a second.

'Good luck, darling,' her mother whispered in her ear. 'Look after yourself.'

The four of them climbed on to the train and found a first class compartment. Doors were slamming and the train was moving slowly away. Sybil stood waving out of the window for as long as she could see her family standing there, huddled together, with her dear mother in the middle.

'I shall miss them so much,' she murmured. Then

quietly she turned to face her new employer and the two children who were to be part of her new life.

12

Mr. Crawford Senior was at the station to meet them with a small entourage of servants. Two lads took the cases and carried them out of the building, one climbed on to an open cart and the other boy passed the cases up to him. Sybil watched as he carefully stacked the luggage. A girl with ginger hair helped Mrs. Crawford with her belongings. Near to the wooden cart stood a black shiny carriage drawn by two elegant horses. An older man jumped down to open the door for the passengers. The children were very excited.

'Come here you beautiful girl!' Mr. Crawford whisked Esme up in his arms.

'And look at you little fellow.' He pinched one of Mervyn's cheeks.

'Hello, Sophie dear, you're looking well. Motherhood suits you.' He smiled broadly at his daughter-in-law.

'This is Sybil, our Nanny.' She gently pushed Sybil towards him.

'How do you do.' He politely shook her hand. As he turned away, he whispered to Sophie: 'She looks rather young.'

'She's just twenty and very capable,' replied Sophie as they moved away towards the carriage. Sybil felt herself blushing.

'I'm Rosie, we're travelling in the cart.' One of the boys, the cheeky-looking one, bowed to Sybil and helped her climb up the steps. There were seats on either side and she sat herself down awkwardly between the cases. She felt embarrassed. To make things worse, the boy kept eyeing her up and down.

'How old are you then?' he asked.

'Mind your own business,' Rosie answered. 'Don't take any notice of him, Miss.'

The ride was bumpy and noisy but Sybil tried to enjoy the drive. It was wonderful to see the Dorset countryside for the first time and she was thrilled when she caught a glimpse of the sea. After a while the cart swung round into a tree lined drive and a majestic looking house appeared in the distance. It was square-shaped, built of stone with an impressive porch. There were columns on either side. As the horse trotted forward, Sybil could see that the carriage was at the front door. The passengers were climbing out to be met by a group of family members. They could hear the laughter as they drew nearer.

'Madam will be pleased to see the children.' Rosie hesitated and, re- considered her statement. 'She'll be pleased to see Esme. She doesn't have much time for the little one and I think that's why they haven't been here for ages.'

'It's because he's married to that French woman,' the cheeky one giggled. 'She's quite a dish,' he added, giving Sybil a knowing wink. 'You'd better look out, Miss, the young master likes ladies of a certain age.'

'Don't be so disrespectful,' Rosie said in a stern voice. The cart travelled on to the back of the house and came to a halt at the rear entrance. The two girls climbed down and walked into the lobby. 'This way Miss.' Sybil caught hold of her arm.

'Please call me Sybil.' Rosie smiled as they walked into the large kitchen. An older woman was rolling out some pastry on a marble slab. 'Sybil, the new nanny,' Rosie announced.

'Hello dear, I'm Mrs. Oliver, the family cook and Rosie is the housemaid.'

Mrs. Oliver reminded Sybil of her Mother and she

began to feel more relaxed. The two girls helped themselves to a drink and sat at the table. Sybil savoured the taste of the sweet tea. She felt tired and anxious about her new job. It had been a long day, in fact a long week all together. The warmth and aroma of cooking in the kitchen calmed her nerves. Suddenly the door opened and a slim, rather austere woman entered. She was dressed from head to toe in black and there was no sign of a smile on her ghostly white face.

'I suppose you're the new nanny? Why she needs one with just two children I really don't know. The previous Mrs. Crawford managed without such luxuries!'

Before Sybil or anyone else could answer, she picked up the silver tray and swept out through the same door.

'Don't fret Sybil. Miss Yardley is always severe. She's the housekeeper and companion.'

Sybil was confused by the banter between the servants. It was obvious to her now that Mrs. Crawford was her employer's second wife. What happened to the first one?' she wondered. When the door opened for a second time, a cheerful Mrs. Crawford appeared.

'Hello Cook, you look busy – probably creating something delicious for supper,' she smiled at Mrs. Oliver. 'I see you've met Sybil.'

'I've been looked after by Rosie.' Sybil told her.

'The children are playing in the nursery, I'll show you the way in a moment.' She turned back to look at Cook.

'Will you arrange for the children's tea to be sent up to the nursery, please? Sybil will supervise. I'll show you to your room, Sybil.' She followed Mrs. Crawford up several flights of stairs. The nursery was on the third floor at the top of the house. As they entered Sybil detected an air of mustiness as if the room had not been aired for a long time. 'I've opened the windows, but the air is stale.' The windows were pulled inwards to accommodate the thick iron bars on the outside. Sybil could see that there was no escape from this room!

'This was Daddy's nursery,' Esme explained. 'Look at his magnificent horse! Mervyn and I have been riding, haven't we, Mummy?'

'Yes, dear but Mervyn's tired now and I think you need to calm down. Sybil will read to you from one of Daddy's old books in a minute, when I've shown her where the bedroom is. You choose one Esme.' There was a loud knock on the door and Sybil went over to open it. An elderly lady was standing there leaning heavily on two walking sticks. Sybil assumed it was Mrs. Crawford senior. She instinctively took a step forward but the old lady pushed her aside and moved towards an upright chair. The children ran to their mother as the old lady sat down. She completely ignored Sybil.

'I hope you don't mind Mother, I've arranged for the children to have tea up here with Sybil. They are both tired and I want them to go to bed early this evening. It's been a hectic day and we all want to be fit so that we can go to the seaside tomorrow.'

'The nanny can sleep in the servants' quarters - Rosie has a spare bed in her room.'

'I've asked her to sleep next door to the nursery,' the younger woman insisted.

The old lady continued to ignore Sybil. She could feel the tension in the air.

'She can keep an eye on the children if she's close by. It's such a big house.

I don't want them wandering about on their own.'

The young Mrs. Crawford was flustered and annoyed. Her eyes had a certain glint in them and she was blushing slightly. Sybil thought it politic to leave the room. The atmosphere between the two women made her feel uncomfortable. She was happy to retire to her room where she unpacked a few things. The dispute continued for a while. Sybil could hear the raised voices and finally the door slammed. Soon after there was a faint knock on her door and she went over to open it. The two children stood there holding hands. Sybil opened her arms and they ran to her.

'Mummy's crying. Grandma always makes her cry when we come here. We like Granddad best, he plays with both of us.'

Yes,' Mervyn whimpered,' his bottom lip pursing up as he tried not to burst into tears. Esme was holding a book in her hand and Sybil decided to let them climb on the bed whilst she read to them. All three were engrossed in the story of Rapunzel when Mrs. Crawford called: 'Tea is ready, Rosie has just brought it up and laid the table.'

When they entered the nursery Mrs. Crawford left by the other door and the children moved slowly to the table. Sybil settled them down to have their tea. When Rosie appeared later to clear the table, Sybil thought that she ought to start preparing the children for bed. 'I'll help you if you like? The bathroom is just along the corridor and there's plenty of hot water.' Sybil was pleased at the offer because she didn't know her way around yet.

'Mervyn can play with the boats and ducks.' The children enjoyed splashing about in the water. Sybil put their bedclothes in the airing cupboard. Rosie helped to dry Mervyn whilst Sybil dealt with Esme's long hair. Soon they were snuggled up in bed.

'They'll soon be asleep. Then you can come down to the kitchen to have something to eat with us.' Sybil felt unsure and decided to stay with the children until Mrs. Crawford came back to say goodnight.

'You can go down and have your supper now, dear. I'll stay here with the children for a while.'

Sybil hurried down the stairs. She was intrigued by the mystery surrounding the first Mrs. Crawford. She was too shy to ask direct questions but she felt that she needed to know some of the details. When she reached the kitchen the others were already eating.

'I've put yours in the oven to keep warm. You haven't met Larry, have you?' Rosie asked. 'He's head Groom and in charge of the two rascals.' Larry stood up to pull the chair out for Sybil and she thanked him nervously. He was tall and very good-looking: quite a heartthrob, she thought as she tucked into her dinner.

When they all sat back to relax, Sybil summoned up her courage: 'Esme and her grandmother seem to be close. Mervyn is left out of things and he clings to his mother all the time since we arrived.'

'Things are edgy here,' Cook explained. 'My mistress has never recovered from losing Pamela. She was Esme's mother. They looked after the child for several years when Crawford Junior moved back to London.'

'Pam was only twenty five,' Larry said. 'She was very popular and everyone liked her.' There was silence for a while and Sybil felt awkward.

'I'm sorry, I didn't mean to pry and distress you all.'

'It's all right Sybil. It was such a tragedy and the old lady has never been the same since. She thinks she is to blame, poor soul!' Sybil still felt in the dark.

'What happened then?'

'The Crawfords gave Pamela a horse on her birthday so that she could learn dressage. She was mad about horses. It was during one of her competitions that she had a fatal accident. She was thrown to the ground, hitting her head on a low wall. They rushed her to hospital but sadly she died soon after. The place has never been the same since.'

'What about Esme? She lost her mother; how very sad.' Mrs. Oliver paused for a while before she resumed.

'Crawford Junior was devastated as you can imagine. He went off to live in London. Esme remained here with her grandparents and in time she got used to her loss.'

'That was until her father turned up with a beautiful girl one day,' Larry continued. 'His mother did not approve. To make matters worse for old Mrs. Crawford, Esme adored her father's new companion. The engagement was announced but the Mistress remained hostile to her son's new sweetheart. Only Mr. Crawford went to the wedding in London and Esme was the bridesmaid. They didn't return here for a long time and the mistress never forgave them for taking Esme away.'

'Then three years ago Mervyn was born and again only Mr. Crawford went to the christening.' Cook took up the story again. 'It's all very sad and we think Mrs. Crawford blames herself for the accident because it was her idea to give Pamela the horse. We don't know the reason for this visit but we suspect there's an ulterior motive. Sybil was astonished at the revelations. Her first instinct when she was on her own was to write home to her family. What would her Mother think about poor Esme?

It took Sybil ages to get to sleep that night. Her mind was in a whirl as she endeavoured to fathom out the reason for their present visit. Why had Mr. Crawford sent them here whilst he himself remained in London?

13

Sybil woke the next morning to the sound of squabbling in the nursery. The sun was shining through the light-coloured curtains. She walked through to the adjoining room. Esme and Mevyn were both trying to climb onto the horse.

'He wants to be up there all the time! It isn't fair.'

'Come on now, we've got a lot to do this morning. Have you forgotten that we're going to the seaside?' Sybil took Mervyn away from the horse and led him to the table where a jug of milk and biscuits had been laid for the children.

'Sit down both of you and no more arguing. I'm going back to my room to get dressed. I'm leaving this door open and I don't want to hear a sound. After you've finished your snack we'll look in the case for your beach clothes – you can have your shorts on today.'

When Mrs. Crawford came in later, there were no signs of the strain from the night before. She kissed the children.

'I like your shorts Esme. I forgot you had those.'

'Daddy bought them for me in London,' she boasted.

'Guess what? Grandad is taking us to the beach. He told me he has a special plan for today.' Esme took Mervyn's hand and they clapped together. Even Sybil felt excited. The atmosphere in the nursery became filled with anticipation.

The next few weeks were packed with one adventure after the other. Mr. Crawford arranged outings for every day. Sybil was enthralled by it all and surprised to find that

Wareham was so steeped in history.

'Now this is what we're going to do: first thing we shall visit a place of interest, then we shall have a break on the beach for paddling and making castles.'

'My bucket and spade,' interrupted Mervyn pointing at the bag.

'Yes, later,' whispered Sybil pulling the boy towards her.

'Then we shall have our lunch,' the old man continued. 'Cook makes excellent picnics.' Sybil was beginning to like Mr. Crawford. It was all fun with him and she could tell that he was knowledgeable, especially about the local history.

'I love it on the beach,' Esme confided as Sybil was towelling her dry. Mervyn paddled for a while but was rather nervous of the waves. He preferred to fill his bucket and pour the water on his mother's feet.

'That's cold!' yelled Mrs. Crawford as she pretended to chase her son who ran screaming to Sybil. Mr. Crawford just laughed and enjoyed the rumpus.

After their first outing he introduced Sybil to the family library. 'Those books are for children and you can borrow them at any time. The books on the middle shelf are all about Wareham and the surrounding area.'

'My father had a small library and I loved sitting there, reading or just searching through the volumes.'

'Use the library whenever you like.' He smiled at Sybil. 'It's a treat to have young people in the house again.'

Each day Sybil learned something new about Wareham. The expeditions were short so as not to bore the children. Esme loved the stories about King Alfred and the Vikings. The great earth walls fascinated them all and then there was the Roman period with the pictures of soldiers in helmets and armour. Mr. Crawford was an excellent raconteur and even Sophie became interested in the ups and downs of the town. She particularly liked to read about John Churchill.

'He was so brave and a local hero!' In one of his exploits he led the King's forces into battle with only pitchforks as weapons. They visited both churches Saint Martin's and Saint Mary's and, somehow, Mr. Crawford managed to make each occasion into an enchanted journey of discovery. The children always giggled whenever Granddad mentioned the River Piddle or Peasedown St. John where Grandma's sister lived. Sybil couldn't help smiling at them.

Old Mrs. Crawford never joined them. Most of the time she remained in her room and on occasions she visited her sister and sometimes stayed for a day or two. Miss Yardley accompanied her wherever she went.

'I wish Mother would come with us sometimes,' Mr Crawford said to Sophie.

'She is missing so much and the children are delightful.' Sophie placed her hand on his arm.

'It must be so difficult for you, Father.' She paused.

'At least Esme is joining her most evenings to read and chat.'

'Yes, that's something. She's such a good child and seems so happy.'

'That's since Sybil started working for us, she has a knack with children, especially my two with the age gap between them.' Sybil felt a warm glow on hearing these words and she smiled at Sophie.

'Here's Daddy. Here's Daddy! ' Esme yelled. Mervyn tried his hardest to reach up to the window. Sybil picked him up and looked out to see the coach drawing up to the front door. Young Mr. Crawford climbed out and waved to the children. All the members of the family, including Sybil, were summoned to the library. Old Mrs. Crawford was there, sitting by the window with Miss Yardley. The children ran over to sit on the sofa with their granddad and there was great excitement when Mr. Crawford came in and produced a large bag full of presents. He handed them round including a small gift for Sybil.

'It's like Christmas,' Esme laughed at her brother who was struggling with a large box. 'What do you have, Sybil? Shall I help you open it?'

'No Esme,' said her Father. 'You concentrate on your own presents.'

Sybil was delighted to find a small bottle of perfume in her parcel. The writing on the label was in French. She unscrewed the top and with her finger, gently put a small dot behind each ear. The aroma was delicate. She thought it was lily of the valley.

When things were calm again, Mr. Crawford put his arm round his wife.

'Just a minute everyone,' he said in a loud voice. 'I've got an announcement to make.' All heads turned toward him and the room fell silent.

'In fact, Sophie and I have two announcements, haven't we darling?' Sophie smiled up at her husband and held on to his arm nervously.

'First of all, the most important piece of news is that we are to have a new baby in the family – a little brother or sister for Esme and Mervyn.' There were squeals of delight from the children. Then before anyone else could speak, Mr. Crawford continued: 'And I have a new position in a far off country called Argentina. We shall move there and live in a big house and at long last we can have our own animals, dogs, cats and horses.' This time the silence was different. Anxiety showed on the faces of those present as they tried to absorb the information.

'I like it here with Granddad.' Esme whispered. 'And what about Sybil?' she continued. I want her to stay with us. I don't even know where that place is. Why do we have to go there?' Tears started trickling down her cheeks. Mr. Crawford senior took Esme on his lap to console her. Sybil noticed that the old man looked pale and tired. It was not good news for him either. Miss Yardley moved to put her arm round old Mrs. Crawford's shoulders and they both stared quietly out of the window.

Sophie came over to Sybil.

'Don't worry dear, we shall ask your Mother if you can come with us. We're going to Switzerland first to see my parents. Please take the children up to the nursery. I'll be up soon to explain things in more detail.' Sybil did as she was told. But, as they climbed the stairs, she couldn't help thinking that Mr. Crawford's news was to change their lives forever.

•••

The young Crawfords spent several days working on their plans for the future.

Sybil was left to look after the children. Esme was still distraught about the move and she showed her anxiety by doing everything possible to upset her brother. Sybil even caught her pinching his legs under the table. The only answer in Sybil's mind was to be stricter than usual with the girl and she found herself excluding Esme from some of her favourite games. This tactic failed because the child just broke into tears or threw herself on the ground in desperation. In each case Sybil ended up with a sobbing bundle on her lap and a guilty feeling for being so cruel to her defenceless charge.

•••

'We're going up to Bath to ask your mother if we can take you with us to Switzerland.' Mrs Crawford announced. 'The baby is due in five months time,' she confided. 'I really need you to help me with the other children. Esme is such a sensitive child and you seem to be able to do wonders with her. Please say you want to come with us!' she pleaded. Sybil didn't answer. She thought about the last few days and the difficulties with Esme. Mr. Crawford's news had left the whole family in shock. Sybil felt apprehensive. Wareham was the furthest she had ever travelled from Bath. She was not too sure about crossing the sea to a new country. When Sybil didn't answer Mrs. Crawford began talking about her home in Switzerland.

'My parents live on the outskirts of Lausanne and

our garden goes right down to the lake. It is so beautiful, especially in the winter when the snow covers the mountains and the air is crisp and cool.' She sighed and turned her head away, but not before Sybil saw tears glistening in her pale blue eyes.

'Where will you have the baby?' Sybil asked.

'I shall go to the same sanatorium where Mervyn was born. Sam may have to leave for Argentina but my Mother will be there and the rest of the family and you, of course dear Sybil, if your Mother will allow you to come.' She closed her eyes and turned away.

It didn't matter because Sybil had plenty of thoughts of her own. Though she was old enough to make decisions, she couldn't help wondering what her reaction would be if her mother showed strong reservations about her leaving the country. Switzerland was familiar to Sybil because she had read many books about the Alps. She particularly remembered an article that Millie read to her when she was at home. It was about two suffragettes travelling alone to Switzerland with the intention of climbing one of the highest mountains. She smiled to herself when she remembered Millie's enthusiasm.'

Switzerland looked quite small on the map in old Mr. Crawford's library and it didn't look too far away. Argentina was a different proposition. It was on the other side of the globe and Sybil didn't feel too comfortable about that idea. It was a delight to see her family again. Jason was on the road to recovery and appeared to be well and happy. 'Jennifer and I are engaged,' he told Sybil, 'and Millie has been going out with this chap from London who's in the music trade. I think they'll get engaged soon.'

The two boys were doing well with their apprenticeships and Polly and the others were still at school.

'I hope to be a teacher, when I leave,' Polly told Sybil.

'You look well, Mother.'

'I'm still working but just part time. We have more money coming in now and the boys make me rest regularly.'

'And you have Polly,' said Sybil looking over at her sister.

'Yes, I don't know what I would do without her.'

'So what's all this Sybil, are you going to leave us for good?' Jason asked.

'You lucky thing,' said Millie. 'I wish I could go to Switzerland.'

There was a family discussion that evening and they all seemed to be in favour.

'It's a great opportunity. You ought to go, Sybil.' Strangely enough it was Polly who held back with her comments.

'I shall miss you so much and if you go to Argentina we may never see you again.'

'Don't be silly Polly. I shall always come home to Bath.'

'Sybil has to make her own decision. She loves the children and there's a baby on the way. Mrs. Crawford will need help'.

Sybil listened carefully, but deep inside she knew she wanted to stay with the Crawfords. It was not that long ago that she left for Wareham and somehow things were not the same here, she didn't feel needed as she was in the past. Perhaps leaving home inspired the rest of the family. It was different when she was fourteen and was obliged to leave school to help Mother with the younger children.

'You don't need to worry about us, dear. We're all managing our lives in our own way and we want you to feel free to make your own decision.'

'Look at the time, I'm off to bed.' Millie stood up and made for the door.

'Come on, Sybil. You're sleeping in our room tonight.' Sybil took Polly's arm and they walked up the stairs together. She kissed her sisters goodnight.

'Don't worry about me Polly, I shall always come back

home and we can go on writing to each other.'

Sybil made her decision but she didn't tell her family until the morning when they were all sitting down for breakfast. 'I'm going to Switzerland,' she announced. 'I'll think again when the time comes about going to Argentina.' Sybil felt sad about leaving Polly who had clung to her, very nearly in tears. But as soon as the train was on its way her thoughts turned to the two children who were part of her life.

'I do hope Esme is behaving.' The train rumbled on. 'She was being so difficult with Mervyn.'

'Yes, I know, she doesn't like change. When I come to think of it, not many children do like change. They seem to be happiest when they live under a strict routine. That is why parents are so bored with it all and that's why I need a nanny like you.' She rested her head on the back of the seat.

Sybil was surprised at this sudden outburst. I suppose Mrs. Crawford is very young to be tied down with a stepdaughter, young son and a baby on the way. It does rather limit one's choices in life and Sybil felt pleased that she was not attached to anyone. It was a relief when the train pulled in at Wareham station. It was hot and claustrophobic in the compartment.

'Fresh air at last.' Sybil stepped on to the platform and took Mrs. Crawford's bag.

The next few months were a shambles in more ways than one. Sam Crawford disappeared again to London and the rest of the family organised the purchase of trunks, cases and other travelling necessities.

'We shall need at least three trunks plus one for Sybil. Shall we go to Dorchester or Weymouth? Really it would be better to go to Harrods but Sam doesn't want me to go to London. He thinks I need to rest.' There were arguments and tears over nearly everything culminating in a mighty row over the rocking horse and whether it should go to Argentina or not. The children's father had to sort that one out.

'You'll both be able to have your own horse when we move there. In the meantime you can learn to ride in Switzerland That includes you as well Sybil. Sophie's brothers are always out riding.'

'I've never been on a horse. But I'd love to learn to ride.'

Esme slowly came out of her tantrum mainly because she was delighted at the idea of learning to ride. 'My Mother was an excellent horsewoman. Her horse was called Hero. I shall call my horse Hero. But I want a white horse not brown.'

The preparations were over and the trunks sent ahead. Sybil and the family were on the station waiting for the London train. Saying goodbye was not easy. The old folk stood together and Sybil thought how small and fragile they looked. The children were over-excited at the thought of the train journey.

'Goodbye Granddad,' Esme called as she ran over to kiss him. She did this several times before the train even came into view. Mervyn copied his sister. He even kissed his Grandmother and to everyone's amazement the old lady put her arms round him and kissed him back. There was no coldness left - only regrets! It's a bit late now thought Sybil. She could have been pleasant to the child before and enjoyed all the fun. In contrast Sybil felt sorry for the old man. He loved his grandchildren and here they were going to the other side of the world. She felt like giving him a kiss and a hug but knew she couldn't do that. Instead she shook hands with the old gentleman and thanked him for being so kind to her.

●●●

The journey to Lausanne was long and tedious. The best part was on the ferry. They sailed across the Channel at night and Sybil was in a cabin with the children. When breakfast was served, they tucked in to their croissants. Sybil managed to eat two with a large cup of café au lait.

'Let's pack and when we're dressed we can go up on deck. We may be able to see France.' The children didn't need to be told twice and soon they were looking out across the water to the coastline.

'This is my first trip abroad.'

'I've been before and Mervyn was born in Switzerland'. Sybil watched as the ferry drew nearer.

'I can see the harbour walls and there are people on the top. I think they're fishing.' She felt herself shiver in the morning breeze. I'm just twenty-one, she thought and this is a new beginning.

14

It was dark when they arrived in Lausanne. Mervyn was fast asleep and didn't stir with all the noise. Mr. Crawford carried him gently through the station buildings. Mrs Crawford's brothers were there to meet the family. Sybil watched in amazement as her employer threw herself into the arms of her brother. He was the taller of the two and after a few minutes she turned to the other one and embraced him. She was laughing, completely unaware of everything else around her. Esme clung on to Sybil's hand. She was strangely quiet and solemn.

'Are you alright dear?' Sybil bent down to the child.

'I'm not sure if they like me,' she whispered. A frown appeared on her face as she watched her Mother talking away in French.

'They're my step uncles and that is my stepmother, not my real mother.'

'I know that dear,' Sybil cuddled the girl. 'I'm sure Mrs. Crawford loves you.' She continued trying to diffuse the tension even though she felt a pang of sympathy for the girl whose small face looked troubled.

'She likes Mervyn better than me because I'm not her real daughter.' The child disengaged herself from Sybil. She looked angry and the colour was mounting in her cheeks. Sybil thought one of Esme's tantrums was about to start. This would spoil their arrival and probably the whole evening!

'And where is our Esme?' A voice behind made them jump. It was the tall brother. He picked Esme up and held her high above his head. The girl began to smile and then to giggle.

'Throw me again,' she cried. Sybil sighed in relief. Mrs. Crawford joined them.

'These are my brothers - Anton is the one with Esme and this is my baby brother, Gustav.'

The two men came over and shook hands with Sybil. She tried not to blush but she could feel her face burning. Why is it that I become so agitated when I'm introduced to people, Sybil pondered? She hated looking foolish yet it happened every time. The reason on this occasion was the nearness of two young men, both handsome and charming in Sybil's view. They had striking pale blue eyes like their sister. She felt that now she was twenty-one she ought to be more casual and grown up. It was not the only thing that she worried about, she needed to keep her distance, after all, she thought - I am just the Nanny!

●●●

For sometime now Sybil noticed that the Crawfords treated her as part of the family. She liked this arrangement because she was fond of them. They were as Mr. Crawford said: *avant garde!* Sybil felt that she was still influenced by her Mother and she remembered her words: 'Never try to act above your station in life; it will only end in tears.' Her sister Millie just laughed at this advice. 'Don't take any notice Sybil, you marry someone with money if you can.'

'Sophie told us all about you. She says you're a wizard with children.' It was Gustav standing next to her. He took her arm, as they walked towards the carriages. Mr. Crawford was sitting in the first one with Mervyn on his lap. Sybil was relieved when he called out: 'Esme and Sybil, you come with us. Sophie can go with her brothers. I know those three have plenty to talk about.'

When they reached the house all the lights were glowing. Madame and Monsieur Ricard greeted them on the doorstep.

'Hello! *Bienvenue!*' they chanted. Mervyn was wide-awake by now and it didn't take long for him to become the centre of attention. His Grandfather carried him. They greeted the other members of the family who were standing just inside the doorway. Esme held back, but Anton soon appeared to take charge of her.

'We can't leave Esme out, she's very special.' Before entering, Sybil glanced up at the building - a magnificent chateau! She turned to find Gustav by her side again.

'I'll introduce you to Maman. Sam tells me you want to learn to ride? We'll go down to see the horses tomorrow.' Sybil was overawed by the splendour of the great hall. Columns stood framing each doorway. In contrast the solid wooden doors were a dark mahogany colour. The tiled floor was a patchwork of cream and brown.

'What lovely colours, Gustav! So welcoming and restful.' He gently squeezed her arm.

'I'm so glad you like it. Your room is upstairs on the first floor next to the nursery,' He pointed to the wide staircase that lead to the bedrooms. It was built in the same creamy white marble matching the columns.

'The children should go to bed, Sybil.'

'Not yet *Maman*! We want to play with Uncle Gustav.'

'Can I stay up?' pleaded Esme. 'I'm older than Mervyn'. Their Grandmother came to the rescue.

'There are toys in your bedroom and your Uncles can come up to say goodnight. Amelie will make you sandwiches and a cup of milk. You'll need to be fresh in the morning when you go down to see the ponies.'

Sybil was awake early. She dressed quickly before the children began to demand her attention and she quietly opened the wooden shutters. She stood, mesmerised by the beauty of the scene. Her eyes were drawn down through the magnificent gardens to the shimmering lake below. The sun was just appearing on the horizon.

'What a sight! It's like a fairy tale.' There was a knock on the door and a maid appeared. She was carrying a large jug of fresh orange juice.

'Le petit dejeuner est a huit heures.'

'That means breakfast at eight, Sybil.' Mrs. Crawford was standing in the doorway looking fresh and beautiful. She was wearing a simple jade green dress. Her hair was loose and hung in ringlets on her shoulders.

'Are those two still asleep?' she enquired moving over to the beds.

She was carrying a bag that she placed on a chair.

'Here's some riding clothes for the children and some jodhpurs and blouses for you Sybil.'

'I thought this skirt would do for riding,' she answered. Mrs. Crawford laughed.

'You'll have to ride side-saddle in that.' She had a mischievous grin on her face when she said: 'Gustav is taking you today so you'll have to wear trousers. He's a devil with the girls and I think he likes you.'

'Isn't Anton coming with us?' Sybil asked.

'No, he has to work. Only Gustav is a man of leisure.'

Sybil turned away looking out of the window. She wondered what was in store for her on this first day in Switzerland. The arrangements were made at the breakfast table.

'We shall leave at ten o'clock. Two of the Grooms are getting the ponies ready and they've offered to help with the children.'

'May I have a white pony please?' asked Esme.

'Not this time *ma petite,* both are brown. Giselle is a little bit lighter in colour, so you could ride her, Esme.' There were no arguments. Esme was full of enthusiasm. Mervyn, on the other hand, was rather withdrawn.

'I want to get on a horse with Sybil.' This remark was greeted by laughter from those sitting at the breakfast table. He ran to his Mother who lifted him on her lap.

'You'll be safe darling, Sybil will be there and Uncle Gustav will look after you.'

'Your pony is called Pom Pom and he loves little boys. Sybil has to ride a bigger horse because she's grown up.'

He smiled broadly at Sybil.

'You're going to have Apollo. He's my very special one and it's a shame I can't ride him at the moment. But just you wait, as soon as the baby arrives I shall be down there at the stables again.' Sybil moved her hands on her lap. They felt hot and sticky. The skin on the back of her neck felt the same. 'I'm scared like Mervyn,' she thought, or was it because Gustav kept looking at her across the table?

'I want everyone to learn to ride. When we arrive in Argentina we shall be living on an Estancia. The distances are great and most people travel on horseback.' Mr. Crawford showed his determination.

●●●

It did not take long for Sybil and the children to become confident riders.

'Just look at Apollo, I think he recognises me.' Sybil strolled towards his stable. 'He's pricking his ears up and nodding his head.'

'Giselle loves me and I love her, even though she isn't white.'

Mervyn, with Gustav's help, began to enjoy his lessons. But as usual he was impatient and somewhat stubborn.

'I want Pom Pom to go round in circles like Giselle does with Esme,' he told Gustav.

'You can't do that yet you need to grow a little taller.' He turned to Sybil.

'That boy is a handful. His legs are not long enough for his feet to fit properly in the stirrups. If he wriggles too much he will fall off and he certainly can't go round like Esme.'

'Perhaps now you've done all the groundwork, it may be better if Esme and Mervyn had their lessons on different days. Mervyn is so competitive that he aims to do everything his sister does, even though he's younger.'

'That's a good idea. One could ride in the morning and the other in the afternoon or on different days. But you must promise to come each time Sybil. I never know what to say when they cry.' Sybil laughed at him.

'What will you do when you have children of your own?' she asked still smiling.

'God forbid,' he said coming closer. 'I shall have to marry someone like you.' and before she could react, he kissed her on the cheek.

15

The family soon settled into their new routine. Mrs Crawford attended the Sanatorium each week for her check up and spent the rest of the time with her mother. They walked in the gardens and went shopping for baby clothes.

'I'm catching up with my reading,' she told Sybil. 'And it's lovely to be with *Maman*, especially now Sam has gone.' Mr Crawford had left for Argentina to take up his new position.

'Sam says he'll be back to collect us. He may even return before the baby arrives. How are you getting on with your riding Sybil? The children love it. Is Gustav behaving himself?'

'It's much better now the children have their separate riding times. Mervyn behaves when he's on his own. I'm doing very well as I'm having double lessons and I'm very fond of Apollo. He is so kind and gentle. You must miss riding him.'

Sybil did not mention 'the kiss' because she noticed that the Swiss people were always kissing each other when they met. They usually kissed both cheeks and, to tell the truth, Sybil liked the custom. It's so friendly compared to just shaking hands she thought. Nevertheless she kept her eye on Gustav. He tried to be familiar on odd occasions.

'Have you lots of boyfriends back home?' he asked one afternoon.

'No I haven't!' Sybil answered in a brusque manner. She decided to be sharp with him when he became too friendly, even though she rather liked him. Often they rode out into the countryside and Sybil loved it. The views of the snow-capped mountains in the distance, the delightful chalet homes and the friendly people rendered the place enchanting. In addition, the gentle sounds of cowbells from the fields and the colourful wild flowers made every journey special.

'I expect you've left at least one broken-hearted fellow in your hometown. I've noticed that ring you're wearing,' he whispered.

'That ring was given to me by David, the boy I was going to marry.' Sybil didn't know how to tell him the whole story and she hoped that he would keep quiet now. The memories came rushing back and she wanted to hide away. She turned Apollo round and started to make her way back.

'Hey, Sybil, I didn't mean to pry . . . please forgive me.'

When they were back at the stables they were too busy to talk. Gustav taught them how to take off the saddles, bridles and then rub down the horses, feed them, make them comfortable and put them back in their stalls. Esme loved this bit.

'I'm really grown up now because Uncle lets me do all this work,' she boasted. Then, the three of them would sit round the boiler in the tack room to drink hot tea or coffee. Esme was still attending to Giselle and Sybil was checking if the water was hot enough for the tea when Gustav came into the tack room.

'I didn't mean to upset you. Sometimes it's better to talk about things, you know?'

'Yes it is . . . David was killed in the war and talking about it brings back so many memories. I have decided that I shall never get married.'

'*Ma cherie*! Does Sophie know about your past?' He came close to Sybil, put his arms round her and just cuddled her for a short while. Sybil didn't try to escape. She felt warm and protected. They drew apart when they heard Esme approaching.

That evening as she watched Gustav sitting on the other side of the room, she wondered if he really liked her. She admitted to herself that she liked him holding her close. Cuddling the children was the only physical contact she had. It seemed such a long time ago that she went dancing with David.

After two months in Switzerland, Mrs. Crawford's baby arrived. It would soon be time for Sybil to make a decision about Argentina. Either way she would be leaving Lausanne and Gustav behind. When she looked up he was walking towards her. She smiled at him and secretly decided that she would let him kiss her if he tried again.

•••

That night there was a great commotion and when Sybil opened her bedroom door, the servants were rushing about, carrying items of clothing and looking very serious.

'What's happening?' Sybil asked.

'It's Madame, she thinks the baby is arriving. It's too early and Madame Ricard is very worried. They are taking her straight to the sanatorium.' Sybil quickly put her dressing gown on and went down stairs.

'Can I help at all?' She was too late because Mrs. Crawford was walking slowly to the front door supported by her father.

'Just look after the children please, Sybil,' she asked as she left the house. Sybil turned to find Madame Ricard in tears.

'I told her not to search for the photographs. But Sophie climbed on the ladder to reach the top shelf. The servants could have done it for her.'

'Did she fall then? Sybil asked

'She didn't fall right down, she just slipped and twisted herself. It's all my fault. I do hope the baby is safe.' Sybil tried to comfort the elderly lady. She asked Amelie to bring tea. She poured a cup, making sure to put in two teaspoons of sugar.

'Come on Madame, have a sip of this sweet tea. I'm sure your daughter will be well looked after at the hospital.'

Anton and Gustav came rushing down the stairs to be with their mother. Their rooms were at the other side of the house and one of the maids had woken them with the news.

'Please go to the hospital, Anton. You know what your father is like. He probably needs support.' She was calmer after the tea. Anton went off as asked and Sybil remained with the family, awaiting news. The hours dragged by.

'I feel so helpless,' Gustav announced.

'We all feel like that dear,' Madame agreed.

It was just after two in the morning when a dishevelled Anton returned to the house. 'You have another grandson, Maman', he looked weary. 'He's very small and in an incubator, but they think he'll be alright.'

'What about Sophie?' cried Madame.

'She's rather weak because the birth was complicated.'

'What does that mean and why is the baby in an incubator? Gustav asked in an anxious voice. 'I thought farmers used incubators to hatch eggs!'

'Not now, Gustav please,' Madame was impatient with him. 'Is your father staying with her?'

'Yes, I want to send a cable to Sam. He must be told about the birth.'

'I think everyone should retreat to their beds and make an effort to sleep.' Madame was taking control again. Sybil felt sorry for Gustav. His mother never seemed to answer his questions. 'Gustav . . . one of my sisters was very small when she was born and she was placed in an incubator. I remember my mother telling me that a French doctor experimented using different boxes. At first they were known as incubator cribs. They consisted of a box with double walls and hot water was circulated between the panels to heat the inside of the crib. A vulnerable baby was kept warm in that way. Now the design is more advanced but the use is the same. The whole idea is to keep the baby warm and isolated from possible germs.'

'Thank you Sybil, you're so kind to give Gustav an explanation. Please remember that you have the children to deal with tomorrow so you must rest.' Sybil went back to her room, popping in to see Esme and Mervyn. They slept like angels! Sybil felt a lump in her throat. She knelt down and said a prayer: 'Please let Mrs. Crawford and the baby survive. They are part of my family,' she said aloud.

•••

The next few weeks were touch and go for the premature baby. He came into the world nearly two months early and the Doctors were doing everything in their power to keep him alive.

'He's a fighter like the rest of his family. We must try to keep the children in some kind of routine.' Sybil looked towards Gustav.

'We can continue with their riding lessons. Esme and Mervyn need to keep their minds occupied.'

'I do wish Sophie would come home,' Gustav said to Sybil.

'She can't leave her baby, Gustav. It's important for her to be close to him.

Mrs Crawford regained her strength but refused to leave her new born. The baby was moved from the sanatorium to the main hospital in Lausanne where the equipment was more up to date and suitable for the intensive care that he needed.

'What's the baby called?' asked Esme. 'I really wanted a sister.'

'I'm glad I've got a brother. You're still the only girl!' Mervyn mocked Esme, sticking his tongue out at his sister. She reacted by pushing him over.

'That's enough.' Sybil bent down to help the boy to his feet.

Later when they were sitting on their own in the tack room, Gustav confided in Sybil. 'This family is obsessed with girls. We always seem to have boys and I'm sure

Sophie is just as upset as Esme. She wanted a girl, she told me, and so did Sam. The baby hasn't a name because they've probably only thought of girls' names.'

'I expect they have thought of names for boys. Mrs Crawford is probably just waiting for her husband to return before they decide.'

'Sophie even asked me if I like the name Nicole. I do, but I told her that I preferred Josette.' Sybil found it difficult to cope with Gustav's sudden depressed state.

'Why are you so upset Gustav? They've said at the hospital that the baby is doing well. He just needs time to become stronger.'

'Yes, I know . . . the trouble is that I keep thinking about my childhood. My mother wanted a baby girl and she had me instead. Anton told me that she dressed me like a girl when I was a baby. All through my life I have felt that I was second best.'

Sybil tried desperately to keep a straight face.

'I expect she used the clothes that she'd bought. Bet you looked sweet in pink!'

'It's not funny, Sybil. Sophie has bought lots of pink baby clothes. I know, because she showed me.'

'Well, she can keep them in case she has a girl later on. Everyone has something in their childhood that upsets them. I'm the eldest girl in my family and I hated leaving school when my Father died. And to make it worse my mother was very strict and I resented looking after my seven brothers and sisters.'

'I expect you were always loved though.' Sybil gave up trying to cheer him up. As far as she could see he was determined to descend into a deep melancholy. She didn't see Gustav for the next few days.

'He has a terrible headache. It only goes when he stays in a darkened room.' Madame explained. Instead of riding, Sybil took the children out for long walks and they played games indoors and in the garden. They enjoyed having stories read to them and their grandparents took them out occasionally in the coach.

'You'll be able to go and see the baby soon. He's putting on weight and I have some other news.' Madame announced. 'Your father will be back at the weekend.'

When Mr Crawford arrived in Lausanne, he went straight to the hospital to see Sophie and the baby. Later, when it was lunchtime, he walked in full of smiles. The children ran to him. 'I'm taking you in to see your brother Richard, this afternoon,' he announced. 'The Doctor says he can come home next week.' Esme ran to Sybil.

'We need to change out of these play things.' The children could hardly contain themselves. They still had their dessert to eat and Mr. Crawford sat at the table with them sipping his coffee. He talked seriously to his mother and father-in-law about his plans.

'I can't be away too long. There is so much to do. It's just fabulous in Argentina. You'll have to come and visit when we're settled.'

'Sophie and the baby won't be able to go yet.' Madam looked worried.

'Well no, not straight away, but in a week or two we shall be able to return to England. There's a liner leaving Southampton at the end of the month. I want my parents to see the new baby and Sybil needs to go back to Bath. There is a lot to organise.'

The older couple looked surprised and rather gloomy but didn't say anything. Mr Crawford took control of the proceedings and Sybil was pleased, but apprehensive, about the speed of things. She was required to make a decision sooner than she thought. Their whole routine was disrupted when the baby arrived home. Esme was delighted with her brother and Mrs Crawford allowed her to help whenever she could. She particularly liked brushing his black hair with the small pink brush and, she made sure that the baby basket was neat and tidy after every bath and feeding session.

'She is so helpful - I can hardly believe she's the same

girl.'

Mervyn was not as keen! 'I want to go riding with Uncle,' he demanded. But this was out of the question.

'Uncle Gustav has a meeting in Geneva. He'll probably be away for a week or two.' Sybil thought that it was strange that Gustav left without saying goodbye to her or the children. Later she learned that he often disappeared for short periods in order to help himself recover from his bouts of depression.

Sybil found herself packing trunks and cases again and soon they would be on their way back to England. Mr Crawford painted a magnificent picture of Argentina and the house in the country or *'en el campo'* as he described it.

'*El campo* sounds good,' Esme agreed. 'Daddy says that there's a white pony for me to ride. She's called 'Porota' and that means 'bean' in English.' Mervyn giggled.

'Do you think that name is better than Giselle? I really like Pom Pom and we have to leave him behind.' The children went on discussing their feelings about their imminent departure.

Sybil's thoughts dwelt on home – did she really want to live in Bath again? In a way she thought her love was torn between two families. Or was her indecision due to her new wanderlust and desire to see new places? The picture of her mother and siblings was becoming faint in her mind. What was she going to do if she did return? Polly kept her in touch with all the news in her letters. Everyone seemed to have a career and even Mother was involved in full time charity work. The house was in constant turmoil with everyone rushing about. Was there really room for her? Not only that, Sybil was beginning to feel that life back home was rather bland and lacking in that certain sparkle. In comparison, a trip to Argentina appeared to offer a great adventure and not many girls of her age were given that opportunity.

'I do hope you will decide to come with us Sybil,' pleaded Mr Crawford. 'Sophie relies on you and the children will be devastated if you decide to stay in England.'

'I like being with you. It's the distance that frightens me. The ship takes nearly a month before it arrives in Buenos Aires. I worry about my Mother and her health.'

'You do have brothers and sisters at home, and if they're anything like you, your Mother won't have much to worry about,' was the honest reply.

Sybil thought deeply about these words. She decided to look forward and not back at the past sacrifices she had made for her family. The only circumstance, she thought, that was likely to change her mind was if her Mother begged her to stay. But she knew in her heart that this would never happen. Yes! She would go to Argentina with the Crawfords.

16

It was rough on the cross-channel ferry and the children were sick and miserable. Sybil felt unwell and shaky on her legs but she managed to eat a sandwich and drink a cup of tea with Mr. Crawford. He was not affected by the unsteadiness of the ship.

'Sophie's staying in the cabin with the children. She's rather gloomy and hopes it'll be calmer than this when we sail to Argentina.'

'I'm not very keen on rough seas either.' Sybil tried to keep her cup and saucer in one place.

'It always takes time for novices to acquire their sea legs.'

England was shrouded in mist and rain as they sailed into Dover. The car journey was difficult in the bad weather. Sybil wished she could go directly to Bath but instead she returned to Wareham with the family. Looking out of the window, she thought Dorset looked like a model county with minute hills and bleak cold towns with grey looking people. It was so different to Switzerland. When they left Lausanne, it was bright and sunny and the mighty Alps with snow on the peaks looked majestic. The lake was shimmering as they drove along the drive.

'You really like Switzerland? Mrs. Crawford noticed.

Mr. Crawford planned a schedule for everyone to follow - so on the following morning Sybil found herself on the first train to Bath. The Crawfords knew of her decision to join them on the trip to Argentina but they insisted that she should tell her mother in person.

The Georgian buildings in Bath looked impressive. But the continuous rain made things look bleak and gave it a chilliness that Sybil disliked. She was pleased to see her brother Jason at the station.

'It always seems to be raining in England,' she told him.

'You know that isn't true,' he hugged his sister and smiled fondly.

When they arrived home, Sybil sat with her family round the kitchen table. It reminded her so much of the happy times before the war when her father was still alive. Those days would never return.

'You look younger than ever Mother!'

'We're pleased that you're enjoying life, dear.' Sybil could see that the members of her family were trudging along in a contented manner. They seemed reasonably happy. Parting with them was not as hard as she thought it would be. They guessed that she wanted to go to Argentina. The only one she felt guilty about leaving was Polly. Her younger sister was different from the others. She didn't appear to have many friends and she had this deep sense of loyalty towards her family. In a way Polly had taken over from Sybil. She now organised the meals, did the mending and darning and was at Mother's beck and call.

I'll keep writing to you Sybil. You'll get all the news.'

●●●

Mr. Crawford was determined that the family would sail for Argentina in September as planned. 'We don't want to be here for the winter,' he explained. 'It'll be Spring in Argentina when we arrive and, hopefully, we shall be settled in our new home before the midsummer heat reaches the high peaks.'

The Bay of Biscay was calm, though the skies were grey when Sybil, wrapped in her warm overcoat, ventured out on the deck for some fresh air. The children were having a great time being spoilt by the crew. Antonio, the cabin boy whom Sybil thought was only about fourteen, bribed the children with sweets and chocolates.

'I've never had those yellow sweets that taste like lemon and go fizzy in your mouth. Have you Mervyn?'

The small swimming pool for the children was constructed as soon as the weather became warmer. As well as swimming every day, the children loved looking for unusual sights.

'I saw a mermaid. It was half lady and half fish and it was on the deck and talked to me.' Mervyn shrugged his shoulders as if it was a normal occurrence.

'Are you sure, darling?' asked Mrs Crawford drawing her son close to her.

Sybil was thrilled to see flying fish in large groups. They shimmered silver in the sun before plunging back into the frothy sea. They even saw a whale close up, spouting water high in the air.

•••

'We're arriving in Tenerife, today. If we're good Daddy said he would take us to the top of the volcano.' A buzz of excitement spread through the passenger lounges and people rushed on deck to see the ship docking. Sybil waved to the hundreds of faces looking up at the ship. Soon people were moving. Mr. Crawford carried Mervyn and Sybil held on tightly to Esme's hand as they walked down the gangway. They turned and waved to their mother who was staying on board with Richard.

The islanders were trying to sell their merchandise. The hustle and bustle was extreme and the children looked worried and clung to the adults.

'Hello Sam,' said a young man coming up to them.

'Are you going to the top? Do you want to join us, there's probably a space in our taxi!'

'Yes please, I was hoping you'd invite me.'

'This is Robert. He speaks the lingo – he may come in useful if we lose our way on the mountain.'

A row of taxis were parked on the roadside and the drivers were rushing up touting for business and loudly announcing the cost of a fare to the peak and back. Sybil and Esme stayed close to Mr. Crawford whilst Robert bartered for a cheap fare.

'This one looks genuine.' He held the door for Sybil and the children. Mr. Crawford joined them in the back and Robert took the front seat next to the driver.

'He wanted half the fare before we leave. I think that's normal.' It was a squash in the back and as they started to ascend, the road became narrower and the bends sharper.

'I keep falling over.' Esme giggled. Mervyn squealed in delight when his sister landed on top of him. The scenery was changing dramatically and soon they were out in the wilds.

'What a mad driver!' Robert turned to check if they were comfortable. Every now and again, Sybil held her breath as tyres screeched round a bend and she could see the precipitous cliffs hanging down to the sea.

'I'm looking for those dragon trees Sybil told us about.' Esme told her brother above the roar of the engine.

'I don't want to see the dragon with a hundred heads.' Mervyn, hid his eyes. Esme continued to recount the drama: 'His name was Ladon. Poor thing was only guarding the special gardens and Atlas came along and killed him. The drops of blood that fell to the ground became dragon trees.' Sybil smiled at Esme.

'Montana Blanca.' The driver pulled into a large flat area.

'This isn't the summit!' Robert turned to speak to the driver.

The children were pleased to stretch their legs. It was barren except for a few thorny bushes, and something that looked like broom.

'Let's look for lizards.' Mervyn found a twig to scratch round the rocks.

'We can't go up any further. It is possible to reach the peak by walking up that track. It takes about six hours.'

Robert explained.

'Well that is out of the question . . . we could walk up the track for a short distance.' As they turned a corner, Sybil gasped at the view before her. It seemed as if she could see all the islands of the archipelago!

'I can see six.' Mervyn pointed. They gazed in wonder. Then, as they ascended, the track became narrower and suddenly the wind started to pick up and a thick mist was coming in from the sea. The blue sky began to be replaced by dark threatening clouds. The driver came running up behind them.

'*Vamos, tenemos que ir!*' he was waving his arms dramatically.

'We've got to get back to the car,' Robert instructed. 'The driver thinks we may be caught in a violent storm!' They were pushed back into the car. 'It must be urgent,' thought Sybil as she and the children climbed in quickly.

'That's better,' she shivered. 'I was beginning to feel cold.' In reality she was anxious and slightly afraid because Mr. Crawford and Robert remained outside talking to the driver. The conversation became heated. The man, a short fattish fellow, was shouting and gesticulating. All the other cars were leaving and their taxi was the only one left.

Over by a small corrugated iron shack stood two burly youths with their hands dug deeply into their trouser pockets. They were staring at the lone taxi driver and his passengers. Sybil trembled and drew the children close to her. She could see that Esme was on the verge of tears and Mervyn tried hiding his face in Sybil's lap.

'Why is Daddy so cross?' asked Esme, her voice quivering with fear.

'I hate it when Daddy shouts,' cried Mervyn.

'He's having an argument with the driver. Robert will sort it out. He can speak Spanish.' Sybil was trying to keep calm.

'What is he saying?' demanded Mr. Crawford.

'The crook's gone back on his word,' Robert's face was

flushed with anger. 'He wants double money for the return journey.'

'Look here, young man,' Mr Crawford threatened as he moved close. Sybil thought a fight was going to break out but Robert intervened.

'It's no good losing your temper, Crawford. We're the only ones left up here and we need this chap's car to get us back to the ship. He says that the change in the weather makes it more difficult to drive – hence the increase in price.'

'Let's jump the crook. We are two against one.'

'That's not on, old chap. Look over there - he's got local back up. And in any case we've got the children and Sybil with us.' The two men who were standing by the shed, whistled and waved to the driver.

'So what do you suggest then? Just cough up the money, I suppose, but I'm going to kick up a fuss when I get back. If we'd been on our own we could have flattened them.' Sybil had never seen him so angry. He was red in the face and kept tut, tutting when he climbed into the car. The children were terrified – perhaps they'd never seen their father like that before. The journey back was a nightmare. Mr. Crawford kept checking his watch as they descended through swathes of fog. The screeching of the brakes, and what Sybil thought was the swearing of the driver was enough to scare anyone.

'Close your eyes! We'll be seeing your Mama soon.'

After what seemed hours the car emerged from the clouds. It was sunny now and Sybil could see the vines growing on the lower slopes and as they descended further the atmosphere changed.

'Look at the bananas growing over there,' Sybil pointed trying to distract the children. Mr. Crawford regained his composure and began joining in the conversation.

'There's the ship. There's smoke coming out of the funnel. She must be ready to sail. I'll tell the driver to hurry.' In about ten minutes or so they were driving into the docks. Sybil sighed with relief. She could see Mrs Crawford waving from the deck.

'There's Mama! Let's tell her about the volcano, Mervyn.' Mr Crawford made a note of the driver's number plate and he proceeded to give the dock policeman all the details of their unpleasant experience. The driver made a quick exit and was nowhere to be seen.

Later that evening when they were safely sailing south, Sybil met Robert on the deck. 'What happened to that horrible little man?' she asked.

'He got away with it,' he replied. 'They can't catch the scoundrels, so the police say – they just change number plates when it suits them. I wouldn't be surprised if that policeman received a backhander as part of the deal. I expect we were chosen as suckers because we had the children with us. Poor Sam! He has a lot to learn about Latin ways.'

17

There was great excitement at breakfast when the Captain announced that King Neptune was coming aboard.

'He'll hold a court because he has to decide whether we can pass through his kingdom or not. Some people will have to be ducked in the swimming pool.'

'Not me, I shall hide.' Esme looked aghast.

'He doesn't usually duck children, only if they're misbehaving during the ceremony.'

In the morning Esme and Mervyn stayed close to Sybil as they climbed the stairs to the main deck.

'Look at his throne.' Esme pointed, half hiding behind Sybil. 'It's covered in seaweed and shells.'

'What are the small stools for?' Mervyn asked.

'He must have helpers.' Sybil smiled, feeling as excited as the children.

'I've never crossed the Equator.' She moved over to a notice attached to a nearby pole and read: 'Mortals are expected to come before the King at exactly ten o'clock this morning. You must not be late.'

The deck became crowded and Mr Crawford picked Mervyn up so that he could see the proceedings.

'There's my mermaid,' he cried, 'I told you I saw one.'

'There are two mermaids. They're sitting on those stools. They've got long golden hair.' Suddenly a loud voice came from the bridge.

'Ladies and Gentlemen, Girls and Boys we are here to welcome King Neptune and his beautiful daughters. Your majesty, we plead for you to allow us safe passage through your kingdom. If you so wish, you can meet every mortal sailing on this ship. My chief officer will call the names of the people that you specifically asked to meet. Ladies and children first.' Mervyn held on to his Mama and Esme walked confidently beside Sybil.

'You're very brave,' Sybil whispered to her as they walked towards the throne. It was quite nerve racking even for Sybil. The King shook her hand and placed a colourful garland over her head. 'The colours match your lovely hair,' he winked as he handed her an important looking certificate. The children received a bag of seaweed toffee each.

'I'm not sure if I like that,' said Mervyn in a faint whisper.

'You'll love it, young man.' The king boomed.

Esme took hers without a word.

'Say thank you,' Sybil said quietly.

'Thank you, your Majesty.' She moved quickly towards her father.

The family climbed the stairs to the upper deck where they had a good view of the scene below. One by one the crew were called before the king. There was no reprieve for the officers.

'Chief Engineer, Henry Watson you are charged with putting too much grease on the pistons . . . Three duckings for you, Sir!'

'He's got all his clothes on!' Esme was not sure whether to laugh or cry. The poor man was dragged to the pool and thrown in without ceremony. The children began to join in the fun, laughing whenever a victim was ducked and spluttered to the surface.

'Senor Antonio Costas – you are charged with damaging children's teeth.'

'No, No not me, I love children,' he pleaded.

'You give them too many sweets!' the king roared. 'Three duckings for you Senor.'

'But, I can't swim, I can't swim,' Antonio cried.

The audience fell silent. It seemed real even to Sybil and she felt uncomfortable. 'Was Antonio being bullied? Esme and Mervyn shrank down to the ground, fearing for their friend. It was only a minute or two but it seemed much longer.

Antonio was about to be thrown into the pool when suddenly the king yelled:

'Halt, we must ask the jury. Girls and Boys, is the prisoner guilty or not guilty?

'Not guilty!' roared the crowd.

When the court hearings came to an end, the King stood up and, waving his spear said: 'I, as King of the deep, take pleasure in granting this ship and all who sail in her, free safe passage through my domain in this year one thousand nine hundred and twenty.' With a great flurry, he walked towards the stern of the ship. Two members of the crew carried the mermaids behind him. They passed through the barriers and out of sight. The passengers stood silently watching the stern of the ship until they heard a mighty splash followed by two smaller ones. The Captain and officers were seen waving. King Neptune had returned to his home beneath the waves.

The ship had two more stops to make . . . Rio de Janeiro in Brazil, and Montevideo in Uruguay. 'I don't think we'll risk going up the Sugar Loaf.' Mr Crawford said to Sybil. The jewellery and other items for sale in the shops fascinated Sybil. They were embedded with the wings of butterflies.

'What a delicate blue!' Mr Crawford decided to buy souvenirs. Mervyn chose a small box that opened with tiny hinges. It was covered in yellow and white butterfly wings.

'It's to keep my treasures in!' He told his Father. Esme preferred the yellow wings. She chose a pendant on a silver chain. Sybil and Mrs. Crawford chose the shimmering blue.

●●●

'We're very near to Buenos Aires. You'll have to pack your cases tonight and put them outside your door. We arrive in the morning.' Mr. Crawford was giving instructions. Sybil was feeling excited and a little apprehensive. This is where she may live for months or even years. She only knew a few Spanish words and she found those difficult to pronounce. What if she didn't like the place?

Early in the morning Sybil peeped out of the door and found that the trunks and cases had been taken. Her clothes were laid out neatly on the chair. As she could hear sounds from the adjoining cabin, she was obliged to rinse her face, comb her hair and dress in haste. When she opened the door she was surprised to see Esme fully clothed. She was trying to help Mervyn to do up his shirt buttons.

'We're having our photos taken this morning before we go ashore.' Sybil took the children along to the cabin. Mrs Crawford was fussing with the baby and she handed him over to Esme.

'We'll see you later, Sybil.'

The main staircase was quite near so Sybil decided to go up on deck. Quite a few people were leaning on the ship's rail and she saw Robert in a small group. He was looking through his binoculars. She walked towards him gazing out at sea. It was slightly misty but she could make out a dark thin line on the horizon.

'That's Argentina, at last. It's such a long journey. I can't wait to be back with my friends. He laughed, turning to Sybil. 'It's all new to you, but the boat journey is boring when you've done it several times.' Sybil could hear music and singing coming from the rear of the ship.

'What's that?' she asked

'That's the immigrants - they're excited about reaching their *promised land.* Most Spaniards own a guitar - it's part of their culture. Some can play better than others.'

'I rather like guitar music, sometimes it's sad and then

suddenly it bursts into a happy song. Why are they kept at the back of the ship?' she asked.

'Poor souls can't afford to pay for cabins. For a nominal sum they are fed and watered and that's about all. They camp out on the open decks and if by chance there are any empty third class cabins, the women and children are allowed to use them.' Robert looked glum. 'It's desperation and lack of opportunity that makes them leave friends and family.

I remember my mother telling me about people emigrating to Australia and Canada. In fact my granddad went off to Canada and just disappeared. My poor Gran never heard from him again. She thought the old fool probably found himself a young wife over there.' Robert smiled at Sybil.

'What are you going to do with yourself when you live in Argentina? You can't look after the kids all the time. You need to have some fun whilst you're young. Once you go out into the camp you'll be isolated. You must have time off. A weekend, or preferably a week when you can come back to the capital.'

'I don't worry about that. I can always find something to do.'

'If you're going to a cattle ranch, all you'll see is flat land for miles and miles. You'll meet *peones* who work and ride on the land and native girls who work in the kitchens

'You make it sound awful. I shall have the children and we can go riding and I believe there is a swimming pool.'

'I really don't know how Sophie is going to put up with it. That's probably why they're going to look for a flat in the city,' he announced. 'You'll be spending a week or two in Buenos Aires, so perhaps you would like to come out to my club. I can introduce you to some of my friends.

'That's kind of you, I do miss chatting to people of my own age.' As they sailed nearer to the land Sybil could see buildings in rows and flags flying in the breeze. She rather liked the pale blue and white of the Argentine flag. The docks reminded her of Tenerife. There were masses of people just standing and staring, others were milling around. There were horses, carts and the occasional automobile moving in and out of massive iron gates.

'I'd better go back to the cabin,' Sybil said to Robert. 'I have to collect my hand luggage and then join the family in the lounge.'

'Yes, we must go. I know where you're staying, so I'll ask Sam if you can come out with us. I want you to meet Evelyn when you come to the club. We're engaged to be married.' Sybil was taken aback by this information.

As the family stood waiting to disembark, Sybil could see the immigrants going down their own gangway at the rear of the ship. There were men in white coats at the top and bottom of the plank inspecting papers and counting the passengers. Sybil felt sorry for the children holding on to their mother's skirts and being dragged along. They looked thin and grubby and the women were carrying enormous bundles of clothes and bedding. The men heaved heavy-looking open boxes onto their shoulders. Sybil could see, saucepans and other everyday chattels. The men in white were directing them across the road to an impressive building. *'Hotel de los Inmigrantes'* was on the large sign.

'A lot of those people will stay at the hotel for a while until they can find work. The whole country is crying out for workers in the city and out in the provinces.' As Mr. Crawford spoke a large lorry with wooden wheels trundled along carrying some of the heavier luggage on its way to the hotel.

'We're off! All stick together now.' Sybil was pleased that he was in charge and ushering them along. She felt safe, even though she knew from experience that he could lose his temper if things went wrong. Soon they were climbing into an open carriage whilst Mr. Crawford supervised the stacking of their hand luggage. Sybil felt a surge of excitement as the coach driver climbed into his seat and took the horsewhip in his hand. She was about to embark on her first journey down the streets of Buenos Aires.

18

The horse and carriage moved slowly through the gates and out into the busy main road. Sybil didn't know where to look first. It was so noisy with loaded carts going one way and empty ones returning to the docks.

'I think this is *Calle Belgrano*?' Mr Crawford was shouting above the clatter of the traffic. He was sitting upright with a somewhat superior smile on his face. 'I know this place'.

'Yes, dear.' Mrs Crawford answered automatically. Sybil noticed that nearly all the buildings were decorated with wrought iron. Her impression of the place was one of style and brightness. In particular she liked the trees that lined the pavements with the sun filtering through the spring leaves.

'Look over there, small birds in cages on the balconies!' Esme wriggled round to see the view. The new sights and the buzz of activity kept the family mesmerized during the short journey to the hotel.

'We'll be here for about a week.' Sybil's room was at the back of the hotel and looked out on a small park. It's quieter here than at the front with all the noisy traffic, she thought to herself.

'We can go sightseeing in the afternoons.' Sam has to search for a suitable apartment. He thinks we ought to have a base in the capital. Robert put that idea in his head. You can start looking after Richard, Sybil. Sam wants to go out in the evenings when we're here. I shall be pleased to socialise once more after all the trauma with the baby.'

Sybil thought it strange that she was not allowed to help with the baby. She assumed that the reason was mainly because Richard was rather a sickly child when he was born. He was progressing well now and Sybil was looking forward to caring for him with the other two children. In the morning they strolled along to the group of local shops and peered in the windows.

'Sam told me not to go too far from the hotel. He's given me a few pesos to spend, but I'm not too keen. I don't really want to enter the shops. They speak too quickly and I can't understand a word.' Sybil was surprised because Mrs Crawford was the star when they were having their Spanish lessons on the ship.

'Can we buy one of those windmills?' asked Esme.

'Yes, Mama, can I have one too?' cried Mervyn.

'You'll have to ask Sybil to do the talking.' The children tugged at Sybil's hand.

The windmills stood in a tin bucket. They were made of coloured cardboard with feathers on each paddle. Most of them were whizzing round in the light breeze. The assistant, dressed in a white overall, emerged from the shop and a torrent of musical words flowed from her bright red lips. Sybil felt awkward as she pointed at the toys. It was just as well she knew her numbers and colours, because she was just about to make her first purchase in Spanish.

'Dos por favor,' she stuttered feeling quite hot under the collar.

'She wants to know the colour!' Mrs Crawford was gaining in confidence.

'May I have red, please,' Esme blushed . . . I think that's *'rojo'*!

'Muy bien senorita', the assistant smiled and turned towards Mervyn. He was feeling shy holding on to his Mama.

'Green,' he whispered.

'Verde por favor,' Sybil translated. The assistant walked

with them to the door.

'*Muchas gracias y adios,*' she waved to them from the shop entrance.

They turned back towards the hotel. The smell of ground coffee wafted across the road from the local café. They walked slowly, enjoying the warmth from the sun and admiring the caged birds. The canaries were singing as they jumped from perch to perch. 'I think those beige birds are finches. Their beaks are quite different.' Sybil pointed out.

•••

The baby was no trouble in the evenings when the Crawfords went out. He loved watching his bother playing with Esme. When Richard became tired, Esme came to the rescue.

'I'll wind the musical box up - that usually makes him go to sleep.' Their afternoon excursions became a treat. Even Mrs Crawford, who was used to Paris was impressed by the width of the avenues and delightful parks. Plaza de Congreso with the unique buildings became a favourite place. The children loved the Central Park where they could run and chase each other safely away from the noise and dangers of trams and cars.

Sybil was pleased that there were so many places to visit where the children could run free and enjoy themselves. It meant that when it came to bedtime there was plenty to talk about and it wasn't long before all three were sound asleep. There was a surprise in store for Sybil towards the end of the week. Mr Crawford announced that there was an invitation from Robert and Evelyn for Friday.

'It's for you Sybil. If you want to go they will pick you up at seven. There's also a crowd going on a picnic on Saturday and you're invited.'

'It's good for you to make new friends.' Sybil detected a sad tone in her mistress's voice that was quickly picked up by her husband.

'You'll be going out Sophie. I've arranged visits to the

Opera and the Ballet and we'll go to some of the Club evenings. There's one on Saturday night that sounds good.'

Sybil couldn't wait for Friday to come. She searched through her case wondering what to wear. Skirts and blouses formed most of her wardrobe, but she remembered one dress that Mrs. Crawford had handed down to her. It was a fine silk shift dress in a light turquoise. She tried it on several times and admired herself in the mirror but so far an opportunity to wear it had not materialised. When Friday arrived, Sybil took special care with her hair. It was long and she noticed that young girls here and on the ship had their hair cut short in a modern stylish bob. She remembered her dear Father saying 'Your hair is your crowning glory, Sybil, let it grow for ever!' She knew that other girls envied the colour: even Mrs. Crawford had paid her a compliment.

'You're hair is like pure cold, Sybil. I hope it never darkens.' She gave Sybil a pair of white silk stockings. They were extremely fine, looked opaque on her legs and complimented the light turquoise of her dress. When her hair was dry she pulled it all round to one side and made a thick plat. She interlaced white and pink satin ribbon and allowed a couple of strands to hang down on the upper section of her dress. There was a knock at the door.

'Can I come in?' Mrs Crawford entered carrying a box of velvet and organdie flowers. 'Thought you may like a flower on your dress.' She circled round checking everything was in place. Sybil was surprised at her enthusiasm. She was acting more like a sister than her employer. She isn't much older than me and perhaps that's why she likes talking and planning with someone of her own age. Her husband is ten years older than her and rather conservative in outlook.

'All his friends are old!' she told Sybil. 'Perhaps this one would look nice in your hair.' She held a delicate dark turquoise flower made of velvet against the gold of Sybil's hair.

'That's perfect! Just a bit more powder on your nose and you're ready, Sybil.'

When she reached the lobby, Robert and Evelyn were chatting to Mr Crawford. Robert spotted her and came over.

'Wow! You don't look like a nanny tonight,' he was grinning broadly. 'Come and meet Evelyn . . .' Sybil shook hands with Robert's fiancée. Her crimson dress was elegant and went perfectly with her black hair that was trimmed in the latest style with a full fringe covering most of her forehead. Lacking in confidence, Sybil began to feel old fashioned with her long hair and flowers, but she didn't have time to think about it because Evelyn took her by the arm.

'Come on Sybil!' She was whisked out of the hotel and into a waiting automobile. 'We'll sit in the back. Hold on tightly. This is Robert's new toy.'

They chugged along the brightly lit streets with Evelyn giving a full commentary. She kept on about Gath and Chaves. 'We'll have to take you there. You've never seen anything like it. A fairy palace is a good description.'

'Sybil's only here for a week, so she can't fit everything in.' Robert interrupted. 'I expect she'll have time when they come back to B.A. for breaks and holidays. We'll treat you to tea on the terrace! waiting.

'Oh blow! We only have the gramophone tonight. The Jazz band is here tomorrow.' They moved across the hall and into a large rectangular room with a stage down one end and a bar to the right. The Friday cocktails were set out on trays and Robert passed one to each of the girls.

'There's Ethel and Jack over there, let's join them.' Evelyn whispered to Sybil as they walked along. 'Beware of the Church boys, Sybil. They're mad about English girls.'

'This is Sybil, will you look after her please Ethel? Evelyn wants to dance this one. It's the Tiger Rag, one of her favourites.' Sybil felt flustered and unsure of herself. Her head was spinning with the sounds of voices and the fast music.

'Hello, Sybil . . .' Ethel's soothing voice calmed her. 'I'm Ethel and this is Jack. Come and sit with us, we'll find a table over there.' Sybil followed them.

'Evelyn's a keen dancer and Robert has to keep up to date with all the new steps. I'm glad Ethel is not like that. You do like a whirl now and again, don't you darling?' Jack looked fondly at Ethel.

'I'm not used to this sort of thing. It's quite a long time since I went out with a young crowd.'

'You're the same as me,' replied Ethel. 'It took me ages to adapt to this life. It was so dull back home, especially during the war. My parents were strict and I didn't go out much. You'll soon learn to enjoy yourself here.'

'Are you both from England?' Sybil enquired.

'I'm from Winchester. Jack was born here in Buenos Aires. All the Church children were born here.'

'We're moving out to the Pampas soon. Mr. Crawford has bought an estancia and he's looking for a suitable flat here in the city. Everyone says you need to visit the city for a break if you live in the wilds.'

'That's the same as the railway people. Some have to work way up in the Andes constructing new lines. Soon the railway will reach Santiago in Chile. It is exciting at first but the work is hard. Some live in San Juan and Mendoza but they always seem pleased to return to the capital.'

'Just look at Billy! He's such a clown. Ethel pointed towards the stage. The young man in charge of the gramophone was dancing and mimicking the singer, Al Jolson. Billy was wearing oversized white gloves, waving them by his face and gliding along the stage. 'Swanee, Swanee, how I love you, how I love you.' The dancers on the floor turned towards the stage and copied the actions. There was laughter and stamping until the tune ended. Then calls for encore, encore! Sybil found herself joining in, clapping and stamping.

'You'll have to meet Billy. He's great fun – comes from

Manchester. That's his own collection of records and he takes requests for favourite tunes.' Sybil looked towards Billy who was now picking out the next record. He chose a gentle song this time 'I wonder who's kissing her now?'

'May I have this dance?' came a deep voice from behind her.

'Really Harold, you haven't even been introduced.' Ethel moved closer to Sybil.

'You introduce me then?' The pompous fellow was not much taller than Sybil and she noticed he limped slightly as he moved towards her. His face was pleasant and he was smiling broadly.

'Meet Harold Church, he's one of Jack's brothers and quite harmless. This is Sybil Lewisham. Robert met her on the ship coming back from England.' By the time they started dancing the song was nearly over but they managed to dance their way to the other end of the room. Harold chatted all the way telling Sybil about his family.

'You'll have to meet mater. She loves girls - especially English ones! Geoff and Paul are my brothers. They're always in trouble and Jack is the goody, studious one. Jack is mater's blue- eyed boy, even though we all have brown eyes. She's always trying to marry us off.' Sybil couldn't help laughing at Harold.

'Hey Harold, who is that?' A cheerful voice from the stage interrupted them.

Sybil looked up and found she was gazing into the hazel eyes of a charming young man. He was beaming down at her with a cheeky grin. Sun-tanned and noble, his face was framed with a mass of black tight curls. Unique was the word she was looking for. He reminded her of a Roman nobleman or perhaps he was Romeo in Shakespeare's play. He jumped down from the stage.

'I'm William Latham,' he offered Sybil his hand. She took it shyly.

'Sybil Lewisham, just arrived from England,' Harold introduced her. Sybil gazed at William's bow tie and smart waistcoat over his shirt. He had his sleeves rolled up and looked relaxed and simply debonair!

'Look, I have to choose the next record. Do you want to come up and help me, Sybil?'

'I am with Harry,' she started to say.

'Oh he won't mind. Come on, let me show you the way up.' He took her hand to help her up the steps to the stage and before long she was sitting beside him at the table.

'Pass me the duster please, Sybil . . .' He wiped the record making sure he went round the grooves carefully. Sybil noticed the shape of his hands. The fingers were long and slender. He must play the piano like David, she thought to herself.

'The Sunshine of your Smile,' he announced placing the record on the turntable.

•••

The light from the lamppost flickered when the branches swayed in the breeze. Sybil lay on her bed staring out of the window. She could not sleep. Her mind was saturated by present emotions and thoughts of the past. Her evening at the club turned out to be pure delight. She turned over and faced the bare wall. William, (she was not going to call him Billy like everyone else,) had kept her by his side all evening.

'Do you like this tune? Al Jolson is one of my favourite singers. I have the records organised in alphabetical order, according to the singer's name. All his songs come under J. One day when I have more time and my collection starts to grow, I shall cross- reference everything so you can look up the name of the songwriter.'

'My favourite song is 'Roses of Picardy.'

'That's under Richard McCormack. He sings it beautifully, but it's a sad song. I just play it on patriotic occasions. I have to collect "happy tappy" songs for dancing and "lovey dovey" ones for the slow dances.' Sybil helped him all evening: dusting, looking for records and returning them to their correct place. In between they chatted about England and their home- towns.

'We do have other friends for you to meet, Sybil, and it's nearly ten o'clock.' Evelyn climbed on to the stage and grabbed Sybil's arm.

'I've had a lovely time helping William,' Sybil turned to wave to him.

As they walked back to where Jack and his brothers were sitting, Ethel whispered to her: 'Did Billy let you touch the records? I thought I saw you putting some away.'

'Yes he did – he's very particular about putting them in the right place.'

'Well, you're honoured, I've never known him to allow anyone to touch his precious records. He's a bit of a control freak!'

'I didn't think so.' Sybil felt put out by Ethel's comments.

Her thoughts turned to David, dear David: why did he have to die in the war? She twisted the ring on her finger. It reminded her of that terrible day when he kissed her goodbye. Then there was Gustav – he kissed her that time when she was waiting for Esme. She knew all about his sad childhood. She loved riding with him when they were in Switzerland. He knew so much about horses. But he was Mrs Crawford's brother and her mother warned her about falling for someone above her station.

She turned over on to her back. Slowly and deliberately she pulled David's ring from her engagement finger and gingerly changed it to her right hand. She vowed to wear it there forever.

19

'Mama's ordered a picnic lunch for you because you're going out again!' Esme grumbled in a peeved voice. On the dot of half past ten, Evelyn appeared.

'Are you ready Sybil? We're meeting Ethel at the Church's house. Ma Church invited us there for Coffee – and that means lemon drizzle cake. Wait till you taste it.' Sybil followed with her picnic basket.

'You can sit in the back with Billy.' Sybil was taken aback to find that William was in the car. Robert was holding the door for her. William reached across to take her basket. He was smiling broadly.

'Hello again!' When they arrived at the house there was a buzz of excitement. Everyone called Mrs. Church "Mater". Harold ushered Sybil forward to meet his mother.

'Here's Sybil!' He yelled above the noise. 'What do you think of those eyes, Mater?'

'Hello dear! Welcome to the mad house. Have you met everyone? My daughter Roberta, we call her Bob. You've met Harold and Jack and those two are Geoff and Paul my youngest, they're twins, not identical as you can see. Over in the corner reading the newspaper is my old man, or Dad to everyone.' Sybil went over to shake hands with Mr. Church.

'Welcome sweetheart,' he smiled cheerfully. 'Harold has it right for once - you are a good looker!' Mrs. Church was bringing the coffee pot in and Bob carried the large rectangular lemon drizzle cake. It was still warm and Sybil felt her slice melting in her mouth. She sat at the large wooden table with Harold on one side and William on the other. It reminded her of what it was like to be part of a large family again. Mrs. Church sat at one end of the table and her husband at the other. Both were trying to control the argument about where to have an ideal picnic. The younger members of the family wanted to go to Vicente Lopez on the river beach and possibly have a swim. Others wanted to go to Palermo, the famous park.

'I think Palermo,' Harold suggested. 'Poor Sybil has seen enough water for a while and the park is better for a picnic. We don't want sand in our food.' So Palermo it was. They found an ideal spot with plenty of shade. Large rugs were spread out on the grass. The Church boys surrounded Sybil. Harold, in particular, was very attentive. 'Hope you can come over for Sunday lunch, Mater's an excellent cook.'

'Yes, I know she is, I've just eaten two slices of her cake. The trouble is I have to help with the packing tomorrow. We're leaving on Monday for the *estancia*.' A voice behind her joined in the conversation and Sybil was relieved to find that it was William.

'Do you fancy a walk, Sybil?' She looked up at him - his hand outstretched to help her up.

'I'd love to,' she answered taking his hand. She felt awkward leaving the other men, though she was pleased to escape their constant attention. The two of them strolled towards a large pond with fountains playing in the sun.

'I thought you looked over crowded by Church men,' he chuckled.

'I told them that I'm leaving Buenos Aires on Monday and travelling south, well I think it is south?'

'How sad . . . we haven't much time together! I'm heading up country in the opposite direction to you. I'm working near a place called Mendoza, high up in the Andes. You'd love it there, it's so majestic and the only sound you here is the echo of the wind. We live under canvas and it's quite primitive. But we do miss the buzz of the city and the company. How sad . . .' he murmured again. Sybil looked at him closely - she thought that he meant every word.

'We'll meet again.' She was trying to cheer him up.

'We don't even know if we shall have leave at the same time and those Church boys will be there waiting to pounce whenever you come back to the city.

'I like you, Sybil. We must keep in touch. Shall we write to each other?'

On the way back to the hotel, William wrote his address on a page of his diary, tore it out and handed it to Sybil. She went to put it in her purse, but William held on to her hand. He held it gently for the rest of the journey.

•••

The next day was long and boring for the children and uncomfortable for the adults. When the others dozed off Sybil tried to stand and stretch her legs but this was difficult. The train was packed, it was hot and every now and again a fine dust blew in through the open windows and settled in her hair. Her eyes felt sore. It was hard to relax.

'This journey's terrible,' Mrs. Crawford, coughed and spluttered. 'Are we nearly there, Sam?'

'Not yet my love, we're travelling through the province of La Pampa and soon we'll reach the capital called Santa Rosa. You'll be interested in that place, Sophie: the town was named Santa Rosa in homage to the Governor's wife.'

'I'm only interested in getting there, Sam. We're all hot and tired and the history of some place is the last thing I want to hear.'

'We shall be changing at Santa Rosa because Alfonso was not sure if the train went through to Guatrache.' It was a relief when they reached the station and Mr. Crawford called out: 'We're here!' He proceeded to usher everyone off the train and across the yard to the waiting carriage. 'There's Alfonso, he's come to meet us.'

The sun was low on the horizon and there was still more travelling ahead. But it was cooler now as they set off across country. Looking out Sybil could see for miles, flat grassland fenced with wire. There were groups of cattle and the occasional small home with a thatched roof. Suddenly the sun disappeared and it became dark almost immediately. There was no twilight here.

'The horses know their way home and we're nearly there.' Mr. Crawford tried hard to raise some kind of enthusiasm. But no one wanted to talk. Sybil felt exhausted and she imagined everyone else felt the same. The housekeeper met them at the door. She smiled, dimples showing on her round chubby face.

'Welcome Madam, welcome *Ninos,*' she called.

'We're here at last Barbara, everyone's tired and hungry and not in a very good mood. I think we'll just have a light meal in the kitchen tonight.'

A young servant girl showed Sybil to her room. A washing bowl and jug was ready for her to use. A pure white flannel and towel hung on the side rail of the marble washstand. Sybil looked over at her bed. It looked so pretty and inviting covered by a pale pink and blue floral bedspread. But she was hungry so she washed quickly, unpacked a few things, changed her blouse and skirt before going downstairs.

The kitchen was large and busy. Esme and Mervyn were sitting quietly waiting for their parents. A cold supper was laid out on the table. 'Sit with us tonight Sybil. Do you feel better now? That dust seemed to get everywhere.' The water on the table was cool and fresh from the well and the food was plain and wholesome. Soon everyone was feeling better and relaxed. It was time to explore the new house.

•••

The first few months at the estancia were filled with excitement and a sense of adventure. There was so much to do. Alfonso was in charge of the stables and the children were dying to see their ponies. Esme fell in love with Porota.

'She's so handsome and white like Daddy promised.' The pony was standing placidly by her new mistress nuzzling her hand.

'This is Caballo, a pony just for you senor Mervyn.'

'He's a beaut,' said the boy taking the reins of the black pony. 'He looks great against Porota doesn't he Esme?' The children were delighted and then it was Mrs Crawford's turn to choose a horse with Alfonso's help.

'Now you Sybil - what about this grey?'

'Am I to have my own horse?' asked Sybil feeling rather nervous. 'He's quite handsome and regal!'

'Sam wants to have riding and hunting parties so he can invite friends from the capital to stay with us. It should be fun if he invites the young crowd as well as his older friends,' Sophie sounded optimistic at this stage. 'Apparently there is a game reserve near Guatrache with wild boar and deer.'

The family were shown round the milking and cattle sheds where the special calves were born. There was one orphaned baby bull. He was fed by the cattlemen with a large bottle. His mother died giving birth to him. Every morning he was weighed and fed a special porridge. He was not strong on his legs and fell over when he tried to run. Esme took special interest in Solo and asked if she could help look after him.

'Alfonso says he needs vitamins mixed with his food and he's short of calcium,' she explained in a serious voice. 'He says I can help if I'm up early.'

Sybil enjoyed working with the animals. She often fed the chickens, ducks and geese.

At mealtimes, Sybil sat with Barbara, Cook and the servant girls in a parlour next to the kitchen. She liked this arrangement because she was able to practise her Spanish. Mr. Crawford was away on many occasions. He was either in B.A. at the markets or ordering equipment for the estancia. When he was home he rode out with the men and returned late or even stayed out all night.

The children were used to their father being away and soon fell into a daily routine: riding, swimming in the pool and helping Alfonso with the horses. Mrs. Crawford enjoyed her riding and that was about all. Cook objected to her interfering in the kitchen but she was allowed to discuss the menu for each meal.

'Cook tells me that Madam cannot tell when water is boiling.' Barbara told Sybil. Robert warned that Sophie would soon be bored being isolated in the camp. The trouble was that her employer was never allowed to do any menial tasks or to join in everyday events.

'I don't want my children to grow up like me. I want them to try new things and to be able to look after themselves. I'm so pleased, Sybil that you have taught them to dress themselves and wash their cups out when they've had a drink. I don't want them to rely on servants all the time. Do you think you can persuade Cook to allow us to work in the kitchen occasionally?

'Yes, Mama, I like cooking. Mervyn may become a famous chef!'

'I want to be a Gaucho, like Alfonso,' was the reply

Although Mrs. Crawford had the authority to arrange a cooking morning, Sybil knew she hated confrontations. She always relied on Mr. Crawford to make decisions and put them into practice. Sybil talked to Cook and persuaded her to allow them to make a few cakes and jam tarts on Cook's morning off.

'Everything will be left tidy.' Their first morning in the kitchen was a success. Mrs. Crawford was happy rolling out pastry and mixing cake ingredients.

'These are the best jam tarts I've ever tasted,' she said wiping flour from her sleeves. She even had a blotch on her nose but she didn't mind.

Later that evening when the children were asleep Sophie invited Sybil to sit with her on the veranda. It looked out on the swimming pool and beyond to the formal garden.

'Will you call me Sophie when Sam's not here?' She lowered her head and murmured, 'which seems to be all the time! I want you to join me when we eat in the kitchen or in the dining room. I need someone, other than the children. Sam's away so much that it isn't fair that I have to see you eating and laughing with the servants and I'm on my own with the children.'

'Well, thank you Mrs. Crawford . . .'

'Sophie, please dear'.

'Sophie', Sybil whispered. 'My Spanish has improved but sometimes the girls gabled away and I lose the trend of the conversation. What about Mr. Crawford?' Sybil realised that the situation may become difficult. Mr. Crawford was such a stickler for protocol.

'He'll have to get used to it,' was Sophie's sharp reply.

In the morning Sophie came in when Sybil was plaiting Esme's hair. Mervyn was helping to dress Richard and tickling him under his arms. The baby was laughing.

'What a happy scene! May I brush your hair Sybil? Sophie moved towards her. Sybil's hair was already dressed in a bun. She started taking the pins out and brushed her long hair from top to bottom very gently. Sybil blushed with embarrassment but couldn't help enjoying a moment of pampering. She tried to remember the last time her hair had been brushed by someone else. It must have been when I was at home with Millie.

'Leave your hair loose today, dear. We're only going to the chapel for prayers.' Sophie put her arm round Sybil's waist.

The next few weeks were unusual, to say the least. Sybil always felt welcome and needed by the family, but now she became much closer to Sophie who treated her as her confidante, or even as a sister. They walked together arm in arm round the grounds and most evenings they sat side by side in the comfortable basket chairs on the veranda.

Sophie even persuaded Sybil to partake of a glass of sweet wine. Barbara noticed what was happening.

'You take care Sybil, the master won't put up with that behaviour,' she warned.

'She's just lonely and starved of adult conversation. She's left on her own too much!' Sybil felt uncomfortable because in truth she liked all the attention. She found Sophie to be intelligent and most attractive. When she brushed against Sybil she was soft and sweet. The aroma of her expensive perfume wafted round her, intoxicating her thoughts.

'Try some of this perfume?' she said approaching Sybil's side, turning her head and dabbing the liquid on the back of her ears. They were so close that Sybil felt a shiver down her spine.

'Are you cold, dear? Here, let me put my shawl round your shoulders.' She arranged the garment carefully so that the goose pimples on Sybil's arms were covered.

•••

Sophie's pregnancy began to show. Mr. Crawford fussed round her in a false way. 'I don't want any accidents this time,' he warned. 'I shall have to spend more time at home to keep an eye on you. Sybil, you must stop her climbing and doing foolish things. No more riding for you dear!' Although he appeared to show concern, Sybil thought him pathetic because he still stayed away for long periods. The cosy evenings on the veranda with Sophie continued without hindrance.

'Men don't have any idea of how we feel. This will be my third child and I'm only twenty-five. We don't have much fun out here in the wilds. I shall be glad when we move back to the city. I think Sam's made all the arrangements for the hospital.'

'Shall I put a record on?' Sybil tried to raise Sophie's mood. 'It may cheer you up!'

'Dear Sybil, let's have some music! I don't know what I would do without you,' she smiled. Sybil wound the gramophone up and reached for one of the records. It was an Al Jolson number and the sound of his voice brought back the memory of that evening with William. She stayed standing by the gramophone lost in her thoughts.

'Can we have a dance to the next record?' Sophie asked. Sybil felt disquiet when she thought about her relationship with Sophie. At first she liked all the attention and affection that was coming her way but now she wondered where it was going to lead. Every evening, Sophie wanted her to sit close to her, often holding her hand and some of the revelations about Sam and their private life she found tricky and burdensome. She began to make excuses to leave and go to bed and she felt so pathetic when she even decided to lock her door at night.

'Let's have 'Tiger Rag'?' Sophie made her way towards the pile of records. The strong beat of the tune blared out. It was just as well the children were asleep in the far wing of the house. Sybil couldn't help laughing as she held on to Sophie's hands. They twisted and turned trying out different steps. They particularly liked striding across the room one behind the other pretending to be chorus girls. Out of the blue came a sudden bang and the music stopped.

'What is happening? What do you think you're doing, Sophie?' An angry Mr Crawford stood by the gramophone. He stormed into the middle of the room, agitated, with his face red and convulsed. He nearly choked when he saw the glasses and the bottle of wine. 'You've been drinking!' he said in disgust. 'Go to your room Sybil, I'll talk to you later.' Sybil rushed out of the room and up stairs to her bedroom. She could hear Sophie pleading: 'We were just having a bit of fun, Sam.'

The door was slammed and Sybil was pleased to hide in the safety of her room. She knew what Mr. Crawford was like when angry. The experience was not a pleasant one.

20

In the quietness of her room, Sybil reached for the box that contained William's letters. She needed comfort and feared the consequences of her recent friendship with Sophie. Mr. Crawford was so angry that she expected him to appear at any moment and tell her to pack her bags and leave. There were many letters, one nearly every week. She wrote back mainly about her family. News from Polly was passed on to him. His letters were about his work up in the mountains, surveying and supervising the laying of new lines near Mendoza and San Juan. There were some horror stories of floods and landslides. Sometimes the lines were damaged by the ferocity of the floodwaters. Other times he talked about his aunts and his cousin Hilda. He appeared to be very fond of this side of his family. He very seldom mentioned his parents.

Next day Sybil was back eating with the servants. Nothing was said about the previous evening. 'Sam's gone out with the men and I think it would be sensible for you to eat with Barbara and the others again.' Sophie seemed cheerful enough and on the way down to the stables Sybil learned why. 'We're having friends down from the city and Sam's invited the young crowd. There's to be an *asado* including beef and lamb. Not a small joint but a whole carcass. Then we shall have baked potatoes, including the sweet ones and Cook is going to make a variety of salads and crusty bread. I'm lending her my recipe book of French salads and I offered to help with the homemade mayonnaise. I think she was pleased and accepted my offer. Robert, Evelyn and Billy are coming plus the Church boys with their girls. Did you know that Billy is a conjurer?'

'No, he hasn't told me that,' Sybil managed to say. 'He's a clever young man and he seems to like you, Sybil, if the number of letters you receive from him is anything to go by. He's promised to do a show for us.' Sybil was happy to hear that William was invited but she felt perplexed at the thought of bumping into Mr Crawford.

'Sam's made all the arrangements for us to move back to the city after the party. Esme and Mervyn are going to start at one of the English schools. You will only have Richard to care for until the baby arrives. We've been talking about sending Esme to a boarding school in Switzerland, but don't say anything to her yet. The schools in B.A. are near to the flat so the children need to be dropped off in the morning and collected at teatime. I can't wait to be back in the city.'

Sybil smiled at her enthusiasm but felt dubious about the other plans. She wondered where she stood in this grand re-organisation. There was even talk of a special nanny for the new baby. After the drama of the other night Sybil still felt vulnerable. The party guests started arriving and Sybil was pleased to see Ethel again.

'Thanks for your letters, Sybil. You've certainly kept yourself amused out here in the wilds. It would drive me mad!'

William and Jack were down early for breakfast. The men were planning a shooting party. They were starting on the artificial lakes and then moving on to more difficult terrain. Jack admitted that he was not a gunman.

'You have to be a good shot to catch anything,' William pointed out. 'My experience is pathetic, using toy shot guns at fairs and carnivals. I won a doll for my mother once. She still has it in her glass cabinet.'

Mr Crawford supervised the lighting of the fires before he joined the others. Sybil was to take Esme and Mervyn for their morning ride and she was surprised when Ethel appeared.

'I didn't know you could ride,' laughed Sybil when she saw Ethel in her riding clothes, hat and all.

'I learned to ride at home. My parents were keen and often joined the local hunt for the season.'

The women were sitting round the pool when they returned from their ride.

'Sam is going to arrange for some of us to have riding lessons before we leave.' Evelyn explained.

'How long are you staying then?'

'About a week, I think,' she smiled at Sybil. A whole week! Plenty of time to spend with William . . . Sybil found it strange during the first few days because William showed his extrovert side most of the time but, when he was alone with her, he was awkward and shy. He came alive with his music for the dances and he asked Sybil to help again with the records.

'You're the only one who understands my system.' He even asked her to find John Mc Cormack's record so he could play her favourite tune. He sang to her:

'Roses are shining in Picardy
In the hush of the silvery dew
Roses are flowering in Picardy
But there's never a rose like you'.

William knew all the words by heart and Sybil felt herself melting with the sweetness of it all. But then the mood changed instantly.

'Make sure you dust it before you put the record back in the jacket,' came the unromantic demand. The big surprise was the conjuring show. The children loved William. 'Can we help Billy?' pleaded Esme.

'You can be my assistant.' He looked solemn. Esme took her post very seriously. The old trick with the jam jar and the snake jumping out was popular. There were shrieks and screams that turned into laughter when the snake turned out to be a large spring covered in green and brown material.

The show culminated with William asking Evelyn to step into a large wooden box. She was blindfolded and her hands tied together. 'Are you going to saw her in half?' squealed Mervyn.

'No young man, you wait and see.' William tied a rope round the trunk and padlocked it securely. He then jumped on top holding a small black wand in his right hand. 'I need to concentrate, please be quiet.' The audience fell silent. William closed his eyes and held the wand high above his head. Then he tapped the box several times. 'Are you there, Miss Evelyn?'

'Yes' came a muffled voice from within. The procedure was repeated several times. The voice faded until there was silence. The audience was entranced as William started to undo the ropes and asked Esme for the key to undo the padlock. The suspense was overwhelming as he cautiously opened the lid.

'She's gone,' shouted Esme. The children moved forward to check inside the trunk. But William put it on its side so everyone could see that the box was empty. Evelyn had disappeared.

'Where is she?' everyone was asking. William closed the trunk and jumped on it again pointing both arms towards the swimming pool. Suddenly a figure emerged from the pool. It was Evelyn and the audience clapped and cheered in pleasure and perhaps relief. How did he do that? William was a very popular man.

•••

Throughout the week Sybil waited patiently for William to walk with her in the gardens. He became the centre of attention and the children followed him everywhere demanding new tricks and games to play.

'Sybil, I really want to spend more time with you but I'm overwhelmed by everyone's attention. Even Mr Crawford wants to know how I made Evelyn disappear.'

'It's difficult when you're famous isn't it?' she joked.

'I'm not famous - the tricks are simple and stop laughing at me. I'm trying to be serious.' He took her hand and they strolled towards the pond. Sybil loved the touch of his fingers on hers and she smiled up at him. Esme and Mervyn ran ahead.

'We're moving back to B.A. after the party. Sophie can't wait. She hates living here.'

'What about you Sybil, will you be pleased to go back?'

'Yes, I think I will, though I shall miss certain aspects. Seeing you more often will compensate for that.' William frowned.

'The trouble is that I'm still up country for most of the time. I suppose I can try to arrange more weekends in B.A. Then we could be together.'

The children ran out of sight and William put his arms round her and pulled her towards him. She didn't resist when he kissed her lips and she rested her head on his shoulder. He reached across and pulled the ribbon that was holding her hair and as it fell loose, he stroked it gently. Sybil felt engulfed by a sensation of warmth. I'm falling in love, she thought. They broke away when Mervyn came running back.

'I'm in love with you Sybil,' he whispered as they drew apart.

'Esme won't let me climb on the gate,' the boy whimpered. 'She says I'm wearing my best clothes.' William picked him up and lifted him high on his shoulder.

'She's right, young man, and very smart you look.' Sybil tried to regain her composure, she felt herself blushing and her heart was still racing. William kept smiling and blowing kisses when no one was looking. She just laughed and smiled back.

As they walked to the house, she suddenly remembered the problem with Sophie. I really must tell William when I have the chance. The opportunity came sooner than she thought because that evening William was waiting for her at the bottom of the stairs in the nursery wing. He took her in his arms and kissed her passionately. Sybil was overwhelmed by the sudden change and allowed herself to savour the moment. But the difficulties of the last month flashed before her eyes and she found herself pushing him away.

'What's the matter darling? You do love me don't you?'

'Yes, Yes, I do', she said moving close again. 'But I have something on my mind and I need to tell you.' She faltered and held back.

'What is it?' Sybil stared into his anxious brown eyes.

'I've been in trouble with the Crawfords.' She began her story about Sophie and their recent liaison when Mr. Crawford was away from home.

'He caught us dancing together and when he saw the glasses of wine he was furious. He sent me to my room and yelled at Sophie. I locked my door in case either of them tried to come in. I thought he would tell me to clear off – but nothing happened. Now I feel awkward, especially when I meet him anywhere.'

'Why did you do it Sybil? You know you're just an employee.' He looked perturbed as he drew his hand across his forehead.

'It was all very innocent, though when I think back, I realise how foolish I've been. The point is that I feel sorry for Sophie. She is so lonely and goes days without seeing Sam. She was just looking for company and a bit of fun. The wine was a mistake because it dulled reality and made us both act irresponsibly. The thought of being restricted in a flat in the city does worry me. I suppose I should look for a different job, but I hate to leave Sophie in the lurch. The baby is due in a few weeks.'

'You have to think of yourself sometimes.' William looked solemn for a second or two and then a broad smile lit up his face.

'You could always marry me and live in the wilds.'

'Is that a proposal or just one of your jokes?' Sybil blushed and looked down at her feet. She couldn't look at him because she cringed at the matter of fact way he was treating her. Proposals of marriage, in Sybil's opinion, should be romantic.

'I love you Sybil . . . I could kneel before you if that is what you're expecting? It is rather sudden and I don't have a ring. We haven't known each other that long and I was planning to ask you to marry me when I've finished my project in San Juan. It doesn't sound very romantic does it?'

'No, it doesn't', she replied. 'I decided long ago never to marry but now I've met you I feel differently. You are a bit of a clown and odd on occasions. I'm far from perfect. Flowery descriptions and promises are not for me I'd rather have a straightforward conversation. I know I'm in this mess at the moment with the Crawfords but I don't want to rush into anything either.'

'Let's have this pact then. We can be secretly engaged and when you move to B.A. and I'm in town we can find out if we feel the same. Then we can go and choose a ring together. What do you think?'

'Yes, let's give it a go,' she looked at him in amazement. Was this really happening to her? He stepped forward, wrapped her in his arms and kissed her. He kissed her lips her eyes her cheeks and her hair and she nestled closely against his body. 'I love you so very much', he whispered. 'Do we really need to wait?'

Sybil could feel the force of his passion and knew that he was trying hard to keep in control. She pulled away.

'I must go,' he murmured.

'Goodnight, my love.' She watched him walking away and as he half turned to wave and opened the door, the moonlight flooded in and lit his smiling face.

21

Looking back at the house Sybil saw Cook and the other servants waving goodbye. She wondered if she would ever return to the estancia? Now that she was leaving she realised how much she would miss the animals, especially the horses. She loved the freedom of trotting round the unmade roads in the grounds of the estancia.

'I'm not waving,' declared Sophie in an arrogant manner. 'I just can't wait to be back in the city. Stop sniffling you two!' Esme and Mervyn were crying at the loss of their beloved Porota and Caballo.

'You'll see them in the holidays and you know Alfonso will care for them.' They boarded the train and Mr. Crawford soon found an excuse to leave them.

'Our neighbour Laborda is in the next carriage. We haven't solved that dispute about the fence yet. He's on his own so I must take the opportunity.' He picked up his hat and walked away. Sybil felt embarrassed because his disappearing act was becoming the norm whenever the family was together and she was beginning to think that it was her fault. After a while the children fell asleep and Sophie searched for her book and began reading. Sybil was pleased to relax without any demands. She watched the miles and miles of flat pampas from her window. The occasional group of gauchos waving to the train broke the monotony. The journey didn't seem so bad this time.

When they reached the new apartment Sybil soon discovered that her fears were beginning to materialise.

'You're in this room next to the children. It's only small

but I think you can make it cosy. The important thing is that you're near to Richard. He does have terrible nightmares. He dislikes Sam for some reason. The baby will be over there in the nursery and Sam's engaged a nanny to take charge. She will sleep in the adjoining room.'

'Why isn't Sybil looking after the new baby?' Esme asked.

'Because Daddy wants a new Nanny and Sybil will look after you three.'

'Richard's the only small child,' she continued. 'Mervyn and I can look after ourselves, can't we Sybil?'

'Yes, of course you can dear. But this is what your Father wants.' Sybil was feeling rather despondent and wounded at the obvious rejection of her services. Even Esme could not understand the turn of events.

When Sybil looked at Sophie, she was surprised to see tears in her eyes and when the children raced off to explore the flat she tried to explain. 'Sam has set his mind on having a new nanny to look after the baby. I wanted you Sybil but he's never forgiven me for that night when he caught us enjoying ourselves. He is so old fashioned that I can't believe it.'

'Don't worry Sophie, we shall just have to wait and see what happens.' Her voice faltered at the awkwardness of the moment. She thought about William and his recent proposal. It was difficult but she needed to keep it secret.

'It's not only that, Sybil, Sam has made his mind up to send Esme to boarding school.'

'Oh no,' sighed Sybil.

'I love her dearly and shall miss her company. She's become such a kind and helpful child. I can't understand why he wants to send her away.'

•••

Letters from William arrived regularly and helped to sustain Sybil's spirits.

She wrote back explaining what had happened and finished her letter pleading that he should try to arrange some leave. She was feeling lonely and needed someone to talk to in confidence. Sybil told Ethel about her demotion. She felt herself lucky to have such an understanding friend and they met as often as possible. Sometimes she took Esme and Mervyn with her when they met in the park. They enjoyed having sticky buns and lemonade and when they went to play on the swings, Sybil could update Ethel with all the news.

Mr. Crawford spent most of his time at his office but he did come home for evening meals. If there were arguments he just retired to his study. Life for Sophie was just as boring but she had one spark of hope on the horizon. Her brother Gustav was coming to Buenos Aires and he might even stay.

'Listen to this Sybil,' Sophie held a letter in her hand. 'It's from Gustav – *I've decided to seek my fortune in South America,* he wrote. *I'm starting in Argentina because you, my sister, can point me in the right direction. My health has improved and I want to stand on my own feet. You keep telling me about the opportunities in Buenos Aires so that's where I shall begin. Also I want to be around when the baby arrives. Is the lovely Sybil still with you? You're lucky to have her – she's so good with the children.*

Sophie stopped reading and folded the letter. She put it carefully back in the envelope.

'It'll be great to see him again. He always makes me laugh.' Her lip quivered and she turned away. The days passed slowly and Sybil ticked them off on her calendar. William was away for a whole month because he was supervising the building of a new bridge. Gustav was arriving next week when the baby was due.

'I'd like to go and meet him at the airport,' said Sophie, ' but Sam wants me to stay here. He's arranged for me to be taken to the hospital at the first signs and he doesn't want any complications. He's going himself to meet my brother.'

Gustav's arrival cheered everyone. Esme and Mervyn were delighted to see their uncle again and Sophie was all smiles. He was so handsome and his accent when he spoke in English was delightfully sensuous. He addressed Sybil as one of the family and Mr Crawford showed his annoyance.

'I thought you were helping Angelique to sort the clothes for the baby,' he said brusquely.

'Yes, I'll go and do that, Sir.' Gustav smiled at her as she left the room.

'I'll see you later, Sybil'.

It wasn't until the next morning that she saw Gustav again. Sam left for the office early and Sybil was about to take the children for their walk in the park.

'Do you mind if I join you?' he asked.

'Yes please,' said Mervyn catching hold of his hand.

'I was asking Sybil, not you young man.'

'Yes, of course you can come. We're meeting my friend Ethel this morning. You'll like her Gustav, she's engaged to be married, so none of your flirting.'

'As if I would,' he chuckled. 'I hear you have a boyfriend. Sophie says he's a magician.'

'Well, he does a bit of conjuring, that's all.' She blushed.

'Perhaps he needs to make Sam disappear. Sophie is far from happy at the moment.'

'She'll be fine now that you're here.'

Ethel was waiting for them at the coffee shop. 'I was just going to ask for coffee but I saw you had a friend with you.'

'This is Sophie's brother, Gustav. He's joining us for our morning walk.

'I'll buy the drinks,' Gustav said in a husky voice. Will you help Esme?'

'I'm surprised you haven't mentioned him before, he's gorgeous,' Ethel watched him going across to the counter. 'William will be jealous if he sees you walking about with him.'

They sat round the table talking about Buenos Aires.

'We go dancing, riding, playing tennis, you name it and we do it. It's a good crowd isn't it Sybil?'

'Yes, we do have fun, but you and Jack live in the city. Poor William is way out in the country and he can't be here every weekend.'

'Perhaps, you would allow me to escort you?' Gustav asked.

'I don't know if that will be allowed. Sam's very strict at present.'

'I can please myself, I'm a free agent.' He sounded irritated by the suggestion in Sybil's voice.

She enjoyed the following weekends with Gustav. He was better and less anxious. The Chuch boys made him feel part of the gang. The girls were impressed by his good looks and he soon became a firm favourite. Sybil danced several times with Harold and when Gustav managed to catch her eye and ask for a dance, he teased her about her suitors.

'You have quite a few admirers here Sybil. This William chap must have something, if you've fallen for him!' Later when they were sitting alone, he took her hand.

'Is there no chance for me?' he pleaded. 'The reason for my visit is to see you again. Sophie warned me about William.'

'Gustav, you never kept in touch and you didn't even say goodbye when we left Lausanne! You now expect to pick up the threads and carry on as if time has stood still.'

'I think you are in love with this chap, aren't you? I'm too late to sweep you off your feet. What a pity . . .' he looked glum.

'I'm very fond of you Gustav and I hope we can continue to be friends. I've promised to stay until the baby is born but I feel that I shall have to move on after that. Please don't say anything yet to Sophie or the children. I don't want to cause any more upsets.'

Sybil kept thinking about Gustav. It was so strange that he suddenly decided to come to Argentina. She did feel at ease with him and loved the way he smiled at her.

'You'll have to make your mind up,' Ethel declared

when they were talking together. 'He's good looking and rich. Billy's O.K. but he doesn't have an inheritance like Gustav.'

'Money, isn't everything,' Sybil replied. 'I've learned that living with the Crawfords.' Even so, there was a twinge of uncertainty and she wished William were here and not miles away in the Andes. When he did arrive back in Buenos Aires, she was up to her eyes looking after the three children. The baby arrived safely. It was a boy again and disappointment showed on Sam's face.

'Sophie has asked to see you tomorrow Sybil.' Mr Crawford stared out of the window. 'I'll take you and the children to see the baby, if that is what makes her happy.' The new nanny was busy giving the nursery the final touches. Gustav saw his sister regularly and he promised to stay in the capital and look for employment. He had completed a design course in Switzerland and he was hoping to work in the fashion world. Evelyn and Robert were helping him with introductions.

'There you are at last,' Sybil was desperate for William to take her in his arms when she saw him. He obliged by holding her tightly and kissing her urgently.

'I've missed you so much,' he whispered. It didn't take long for Sybil to realise that this was the man she wanted to marry. How could she have doubted her feelings?

'Please marry me Sybil – we can't wait till I've finished my contract. They want me to stay up there for two more years. They're looking out for suitable houses for married couples and I could put my name down for one. It's out in the wilds, but we'd be together.'

'I'm used to being isolated on the estancia. It would be a change living close to the mountains. I enjoyed the scenery in Switzerland when we were there.'

'This is a bit different, love, and when I'm out surveying I may have to leave you on your own for a few nights or more.'

'I think I'll get used to it,' she said nuzzling up to him. I hope you realise I love you. I don't want you to think I'm marrying you on the rebound.'

'Shall we get engaged then? He was serious, looking deeply into her eyes.

'Yes, darling, yes . . .' William told Sybil that he was anxious about her fragile situation with the Crawfords.

'I share a pad with one of my workmates when we're in the city. There's a spare room if you have to leave in a hurry.'

'I have to tell my family back in England. Polly may have guessed but I still need to write to Mother.'

'I'm allowed three weeks off if I get married.' William was enthusiastic. 'Do you want to marry in Bath? They may let me have longer if we want to go back to England.'

'St. Saviours is a lovely church. My mother and father were married there. I think you'll like it William!' The next day they bought the engagement ring. William put it gently on her finger and kissed her tenderly. Sybil could feel David's ring on the other hand. It was similar but his had three diamonds instead of one. William didn't ask her to remove it because she'd told him all about David and his tragic death. Now was the difficult part; she had to break the news to Sophie and the children.

•••

The right moment to tell Sophie about her engagement didn't occur immediately. She knew William was planning a home in San Juan and their journey arrangements back to England, but it was not a simple matter.

'I have to tell them that I'm leaving. What about Esme going to Switzerland and the others having to get used to Angelique?' Sybil felt distressed as she told William about her fears. 'Sam has been treating me better just lately. I don't think he's so keen on the new nanny.'

'You always worry about other people. Just put your ring on and tell them.'

'I know you're right,' she mumbled. 'We do have a new life before us, but I worry about the children and Sophie is just a shadow of what she used to be.'

'We'll have our own children one day,' William looked so serious that he made Sybil laugh.

'Well, I hope we do,' she replied smiling at him. 'Sophie's about the same age as me and I don't want four kids in such a hurry.'

'That's why we have to plan,' he retorted.

Sybil decided to impart her secret that evening when Sophie, Gustav and the children were playing cards.

'I've got some news,' she tried to keep the tremble out of her voice. 'I'm so excited about it – William has asked me to marry him and I've accepted.' There was complete silence. Then Gustav came over.

'Congratulations! He put his arm round her shoulder. 'Come and look at the ring.' The children ran over to Sybil.

'Does that mean you're leaving us?' Esme gasped.

'You can't do that,' Mervyn cried. 'We don't like Angelique and Esme is going away.' He began to cry and Richard joined in. Sybil held the two boys close to her. She felt tears in her eyes.

'Now, now, you want Sybil to be happy don't you?' Gustav pleaded. 'She'll still be living in Argentina and Angelique is not that bad. When you know her better, you'll like her just like Sybil.'

'No I won't!' Mervyn yelled between sobs and hitting his uncle.

Sophie stood at the other side of the room still holding the cards in her hand. Sybil thought she looked like a ghost, she was so pale. Gustave went over and guided her to see the ring.

'Congratulations, Sybil dear, I hope you'll be happy.' She kissed Sybil gently on the cheek, turned and collapsed into Gustav's arms.

22

The atmosphere in the flat was strained and far from happy. Angelique tried her best to win the children over. Esme became withdrawn and only smiled at Gustav. Sophie spent most afternoons in her bedroom. 'I feel guilty about leaving.' Sybil told Gustav. 'It's good you're here to support your sister. You'll come back after taking Esme to school, I hope?'

'Yes, I think I'm needed here. Don't you worry Sybil. This is the start of a new life for you. I like William he's a decent chap. You should be happy together. I do worry about Sophie, though. She is so fragile.'

•••

The sea journey back to England was a luxury for Sybil with darling William by her side. What more could she ever want? Their friends Robert and Evelyn travelled on the same ship, so the four of them danced the nights away and gazed in wonder at the moon and stars. They enjoyed the sun and swam in the pool and they talked non- stop about the future. Evelyn was taking Ethel's place as maid of honour at the wedding. Robert was to be William's best man.

The family loved William instantly and Sybil was delighted when her mother treated him as a son. He in turn revelled in being part of such a large family.

'You must take good care of Sybil!'

'Of course I will. She's the love of my life,' William responded by putting his arm round his future mother in law.

'You can call me Mother if you wish.' She directed her smile over to Sybil.

William spent hours with Chris and Jerry out in the back yard.

'What are you doing out there?' asked Sybil when he came in with his hands covered in black grease.

'I'm helping them with their motorbikes. Chris has a side-car on his so you can come for a ride with us if you like?' Sybil declined the invitation.

'I'm helping mother at the moment. And what about going up to Manchester to see your parents? She asked.

'Must go now, see you later.' He vanished out of the back door.

'Where's William? He said he would play with us!' Sybil noticed how he teased the two younger girls and he even flirted with Millie when Frank was absent. William did not invite his parents to the wedding and Sybil told her mother about her misgivings.

'Perhaps they're in prison,' Jason joked. 'Just tell him you want to go and meet his mother and father.'

'Shall we go up to Manchester?' Sybil asked that evening when they were sitting together. 'Then we can invite your Mum and Dad to the wedding.'

'I've told them I'm getting married,' he snapped.

'Mother thinks we ought to go,' she said tentatively.

'I don't think they'll come,' he answered with a slight tremor in his voice. Sybil drew near to him looking at his troubled face. 'We did agree to talk to each other about problems. What is the matter?'

'I've told you about my mother. She is not like yours, kind and cuddly. She could be nasty to you!'

'Whether she's kind or not, I think you'll regret it if you don't ask them. And what about your Dad? Why should he suffer because of her?'

'He's suffered all his married life,' he retorted with a grim look on his face.

If your mother thinks we should go, let's do the trip on

Tuesday. Shall we take Polly? She likes music and we may have to sit through a concert.'

•••

Mr. Lawson opened the door of the small terraced house where William had spent his childhood.

'William,' he smiled, wrapping his arms round his son.

'This is Sybil,' said William pushing her forward.

'Welcome dear,' he said offering her his hand. Sybil took it, leaned forward and kissed him on the cheek. He smiled broadly.

'Charming.' He turned to show them into the house.

'Where's Mother?' William asked. Sybil could see the anxiety on his face.

'We're supposed to wait in the front room – I expect your mother is going to make an entrance.'

The fire was burning and the flames were dancing in the small grate. The tiles on the fireplace were a warm bronze colour but even so the room felt cold. Sybil shivered. She suddenly felt apprehensive.

'Look at the piano,' said Polly. William moved across and opened the lid to show the gleaming keys. Polly moved forward and was just about to touch one when the door burst open. Mrs. Latham appeared in one of her long concert robes. She moved straight across to the piano and closed the lid.

'Hello Mother,' said William crossing over and kissing her on the cheek. 'This is Sybil and her younger sister, Polly. We've had a long journey.'

Polly retreated just behind Sybil who bravely advanced towards her future mother-in-law. She was amazed to see her smooth skin with only a few lines round her eyes and over the bridge of her nose. She was wearing rouge on her cheeks and bright red lipstick. Her dress was black, high necked with a cream lace collar. A formidable character . . . Sybil stretched out her hand. Mrs. Latham took it limply. Her hand felt cold in Sybil's warm grasp.

'How do you do?' she recited in a formal way. Sybil was

stunned by her coldness.

'Who is that hiding behind you?' she asked.

'It's Polly, my sister.'

'Where did you buy your dress, Polly? I like the stripes.'

'I made it', whispered Polly. 'I copied it from a magazine and my sister Millie helped me with the sewing.'

'You're both clever then.' She paused for a moment. 'I need to go shopping this afternoon,' she announced. 'Henry will look after you.'

They sat down awkwardly. Polly was staring at the large portrait of the bearded man on the wall behind the piano.

'That's Verdi! He is mother's favourite composer,' William explained.

'Will you play for us, please Mrs. Latham?' asked Polly. 'William says you play beautifully.'

'I only play for guests in the evenings,' she answered. 'And I must go now.'

She left the room with a flourish and a few minutes later the front door slammed and Sybil noticed that she had changed her clothes and was walking purposefully down the street.

'I'm sorry about that, I thought Rosie had done all the shopping.' Mr. Latham was embarrassed.

'That's just like mother. Let's go into the parlour and see if we can find something to eat.' It was warm and cosy in the back room. Sybil and Polly relaxed in the lighter atmosphere as they sat round the small table to eat and drink. That evening they found themselves waiting patiently in the front room again. Mrs. Latham was dressing for the evening concert. Sybil and Polly sat together on the sofa. William sat on the edge with his arm round Sybil. There was complete silence when she swept into the room followed by gasps of amazement. William's mother was wearing an identical dress to the one worn by the fifteen-year-old Polly. Sybil grasped William's arm as he went to get up.

'Leave her,' she whispered. 'Polly will take it as a

compliment.' At long last, Sybil began to understand William's frustration and his reluctance to visit his parents.

What a peculiar thing to do, thought Sybil. She looked at Polly. Her sister was mesmerised by Mrs. Latham's playing. When she stopped, Polly rose to her feet clapping loudly.

'Please play some more,' she begged.

'What a delightful child', said the concert pianist standing and bowing directly to Polly as if she were the only person in the room.

Sybil felt relief when the visit was over and the wedding invitation was handed to Mr. Latham. She liked the old man who showed her his small garden and was impressed by his well-organised shed. The labels on the drawers and tidiness reminded her of William's gramophone collection. She felt comforted by the fact that her husband to be was more like his father than his mother. William could play the piano, she suddenly remembered.

•••

The wedding was a time of joy for Sybil. She appreciated the love that emanated from every member of her family and friends. She felt herself to be lucky indeed. Her sisters excelled themselves saving their pounds, even Grace gave her pocket money, and they purchased a Bruxelles lace veil for Sybil to wear with her cream brocade dress.

'It's just exquisite, the tiny flowers and sprays of leaves are so delicate – it must have taken hours, days, or even weeks, to complete. It goes perfectly with my dress. Thank you darlings.'

St. Saviour's Church was near to the house but Jason arranged for a special wedding car to convey the bride and bridesmaids to the church. He took his post very seriously. As the eldest brother he was giving his sister away! Thinking about poor Jason's trauma when he left the navy, Sybil was so pleased to see him well and happy.

'You are a big tease,' said Sybil. 'Just because you're

married you think you know everything!'

'Well, I do know more than you about weddings and honeymoons,' he answered.

'Come now, that's enough you two,' Mother ushered the young ones out of the way. Jason came over and hugged Sybil.

'You'll be a wonderful wife, Syb. Will's very lucky.'

Sybil felt like a queen going up the aisle. Flickering sunlight shone on the intricately carved backdrop of the altar. Aunts and Uncles from both sides of her family filled the pews. William's parents were sitting together on the other side and there were two old ladies and a younger one smiling sweetly at Sybil.

The familiar kind face and twinkling eyes of Rev. Baker met her as they reached the steps to the altar. William and Robert stood together gazing at Sybil as she approached.

'Smile and say something, William,' Robert nudged him.

'You look beautiful!' Sybil smiled because he was flushed and worried. But as soon as they were holding hands, he beamed and came alive again. As they said their vows Sybil felt his seriousness. The grasp on her hand tightened. Later when the register was signed, it was time to walk down the aisle and out of the church.

'That's my cousin Hilda and my two aunts from London.' William pointed. The reception was held in a nearby hotel. Sybil and William mingled with the guests.

'I shall never remember everyone's name.' William moved from aunts to cousins, uncles and great aunts and more uncles. 'It is bewildering,' he whispered.

'You seem to be doing all right, especially with my sisters and girl cousins. They appear to be infatuated by you. I hope it doesn't go to your head.' Sybil felt proud of him. Robert made a witty speech as best man including some Spanish words that impressed the guests.

'What does that mean? You are showing off,' called Millie.

'That's not for young ears,' he retorted giving her a big grin. There was a surprise when Mr. Latham had a bit of a knees up with Sybil's mother.

'Look at those two,' said Sybil

'I can't believe it,' answered William. 'Look at my mother's face, she's furious!' William introduced Sybil to his aunts and cousin. 'They're charming, it's a pity we can't stay longer and chat to them.' Mr. Latham was mingling happily with the guests but her mother-in-law was sitting on her own at one of the tables. She made no effort to mix and frankly looked bored and tired. When she yawned Sybil decided to go over to cheer her up.

'I think I'll say hello to your mother,' she told William.

'Be it on your own head then,' he replied wandering off with Polly. The younger children were trying to persuade William to do some card tricks and he was refusing their requests and teasing them at the same time.

'Are you all right mother-in-law? Can I bring you something, a drink perhaps?'

'Don't call me that Sybil,' she interrupted. 'I hate weddings and this one in particular.'

'I was hoping that you would like me,' Sybil whispered.

'I didn't want William to get married. He's flinging his life away because he'll be tied down by your apron strings. William has married beneath his status. Goodness knows what damage you'll do to his life.' Sybil felt her self-esteem plummeting and this angry old woman had shaken her happiness. 'Just look at your relations putting on a show of happy families – not an ounce of ambition among the lot of them,' she continued. Sybil was lost for words. It was such an outburst from William's mother. She felt angry.

'How dare you criticise my family? I've only met you once and I find you weird and disagreeable. I love William and I would never do anything to hurt him and I'm glad we're sailing back to Argentina at the end of the month.' Sybil was pleased when she saw William coming over.

'Hurry up Sybil, you need to change your clothes. Jason is bringing the car to take us to the station. Soon I shall have you all to myself,' he said winking at her. He did notice that she was flushed with anger. 'What's the matter, has my mother upset you?'

'No, I'm just getting a bit tired.' She decided to keep quiet about his mother's raving. After all he had warned about her peculiar temperament. How awful to have a mother like that, she thought. Sybil's younger brothers were not to be outdone by Jason. All three climbed on to their motorbikes and followed the car with its clanging cans attached to the bumper. Even Polly rode pillion on Chris's bike. The young crowd cheered when the train drew out of the station. Sybil and William waved for as long as they could and then collapsed on the seats. They were on their own at last with only the clicking of the train as it wended its way to London. William drew her close and gently kissed her. The rhythm and clattering of the wheels on the rails made Sybil feel content as she slumbered in William's arms. But as she woke she couldn't help thinking of the words expressed so angrily by Mrs. Lawson. Doubts emerged. Perhaps she wasn't good enough for William? She stared at his relaxed face. He did attend a Grammar School and he was in the Royal Flying Corps and what about me – I left school at fourteen and just became a Nanny!

23

Ethel and Jack were at the port to meet them when they sailed back to Buenos Aires. 'Mother says you can stay with us until you leave for San Juan,' Jack informed them.

'It's lovely to be back,' Sybil linked arms with Ethel.

'How did everything go? I want to hear all your news. We've decided on a day for our wedding,' Ethel confided. 'There is so much to arrange. I don't know whether I'm coming or going. I'm so glad you're here Sybil!

'I hope we can come to the wedding. William is keen to leave for San Juan as soon as possible.'

'It isn't that far away. You can always come for the weekend.'

William was up early the next morning to go into the main office and at midday he was back. 'Where's Sybil?' he asked. 'I hope she hasn't unpacked anything. We're off tomorrow on the overnight train.' Mrs. Church sighed.

'What a pity, I was looking forward to having Sybil's company for a few days. You're a lucky young man, William. She's out in the garden with Ethel.' Some of the luggage was going ahead on the morning train so they changed all the labels on the cases and trunks. William held a bunch of keys in front of Sybil's face. 'The keys to our first home!' He announced with a broad smile.

'What's it like?' Sybil was almost jumping in her excitement.

'I don't know – I think he said two bedrooms, a kitchen and a sitting room.'

'What about a garden?' asked Sybil who was banking on a small plot where she could grow things and perhaps have a few chickens.

'Yes, it has a garden but he didn't mention the size. We're allowed to decorate the place and make alterations with permission from the local landlord.' Sybil was delighted. 'What fun! I have so many ideas.'

The next evening Mrs. Church kissed Sybil goodbye. 'Good luck dear, William's a great fellow and I hope you'll be happy together.' She hesitated for a second or two. 'I do wish you'd chosen one of my boys. I don't think Harold will ever marry now.' Sybil was about to answer but William appeared. 'We'll be back for Jack and Ethel's wedding at the end of the month,' William put a protective arm round Sybil's shoulder.

At San Juan station, William's junior gang leader was there to meet them.

'Senor Lawson, *para qui,*' he grabbed two of the suitcases and marched off towards a battered old vehicle. It was high off the ground and William helped Sybil climb up into the cab before he joined her on the worn out seat. Miguel took the wheel, completely ignoring Sybil. He started chatting to William about work.

'Miguel you've been eating garlic,' said William in disgust. He turned to Sybil: 'These people chew it all the time.' She did wonder about the pungent aroma, but to tell the truth she didn't find it that bad.

'It's awful in B.A. I don't go in the lifts. I'd rather walk up the stairs especially first thing in the morning. Please don't put it in our food Sybil. I can't stand the stuff.' They rattled along on an unmade road. There were puddles that Miguel tried to avoid. Occasionally one or more of the wheels sank into the mud with a mighty clatter. Sybil held on to William in case she was jerked off the seat. They slowed down as they came to a short parade of buildings. Miguel waved and called out to his friends. There were people sitting outside at rustic tables. Some raised their glasses as the truck passed along.

'That's our local bar, so Miguel says. There's a general store, butcher and haberdashery. They sell some clothes, but not quite up to Paris standards.' William joked. Sybil stared out of the open window trying to distinguish one shop from the other. They had blinds on the windows and on the doors there were walk through beaded curtains in bright colours, billowing slightly in the breeze. The scent of freshly baked bread wafted in through the open windows of the truck.

They continued along the road and turned suddenly into a narrower lane. There were homes of some sort on either side. It was difficult to see into the properties because high hedges formed barriers, only a glimpse now and then was possible. Sybil noticed that to gain access it was necessary to cross a deep ditch so there were bridges of all shapes and sizes. They varied from two planks of wood to elaborate constructions with banisters. Some were decorated with pretty pots of hanging geraniums. They stopped suddenly and Sybil's heart sank. William helped her to balance on the narrow planks.

'I'll soon build us a decent bridge,' he said catching hold of Sybil's hand. He opened the rickety gate and Sybil couldn't help gasping. The path was covered in knee-high vegetation and to her dismay their new home looked like a shack with a corrugated roof. Miguel was following with the cases and even William looked disappointed. 'It looks bleak, I thought it would be better than this.'

'The Railway has purchased quite a few properties but they haven't allowed enough time to modernise them. I expect they think people like you will do it for them. Don't worry, Senora Lawson, my sister Catarina has cleaned inside and the range is on in the kitchen. We'll soon scythe down the weeds in the garden.' Sybil and William moved slowly towards the front door.

'It's alright darling,' she tried to lift his spirits. 'It will be a special home when we've finished. Are you going to carry me across the threshold?' Sybil was surprised at the flimsiness of the structure. It was a wooden building painted a dull brown. On the inside the walls were lined with strips of plywood and stained the same colour, perhaps a slightly lighter brown. 'I suppose it won't show the dirt', she thought to herself. The only bright colour was in the wool rug in the middle of the floor.

The main bedroom was a decent size with a double bed that was made up with fresh white linen. There was plenty of room for other pieces of furniture. The second bedroom was smaller and empty. Everywhere looked clean and the glass in the windows sparkled with the rays of the sun. In the kitchen a kettle was boiling on the range and in a corner stood a young woman, holding a teapot in her hand.

'This is my young sister, Catarina. She doesn't speak English but she wants to learn. She's cleaned the whole house and the bed linen belongs to my parents. Catarina would like to be your maid?' Miguel spoke in a slightly humble manner.

The girl stood smiling and shyly said 'ello'. Sybil noticed the silent 'h'. She herself had found the pronunciation or lack of it difficult when she was learning Spanish. 'The girl's charming,' she thought.

'I don't think we need a maid,' William began complaining but he caught Sybil's expression and added: 'I suppose she would be good company for you when I'm away.'

Catarina poured the tea. Sybil saw William staring at his so she nudged him and said: 'Thank you Catarina,' then she turned to William and whispered, 'I'll soon teach her to make English tea, or I should say northern tea, just put some more sugar in it William.'

'Miguel and I can go shopping, now that we have a maid. I'll buy a few basic food things and find out where we can buy paint and wood for the bridge.' When they left, Sybil went to pour herself another cup of tea, but Catarina stepped in and took the cup and filled it for her.

'You have some tea, Catarina,' Sybil pointed at a spare cup.

'No' she answered picking up a gourd, '*mate para mi*!' Sybil remembered seeing the *peones* drinking *mate* on the estancia. They used a *bombilla*, a silver metal straw that filtered the green tea as they drank. Ethel liked *mate* and she told Sybil that it's very refreshing when the weather is hot. She made a mental note that she would try it one day on her own. Somehow the picture of William sipping *mate* was difficult to visualize. She was beginning to realise that her husband was, to say the least, stuck in his ways.

He returned with some items of food. 'I just bought some essentials,' he unpacked a crusty loaf, butter, cheese and a bottle of wine. 'They had some fresh ham. The girl in the shop cut a piece for me to try, so I bought some. We can have ham sandwiches tonight.' Miguel struggled in with pots of paint and whitewash. 'I've left the wood outside, Senor.'

'He's going to help me tomorrow so you and Catarina can explore the shops. The brother and sister stood at the door, smiling.

'We're going home now. We shall be here at eight, as the Senor requested.'

That evening they sat together on the sofa munching their ham sandwiches and made a plan or strategy, as William called it. 'I think the best idea is to paint everything white then later we can add amounts of colour to our own taste.' Sybil agreed to everything that William said but she also had her own ideas. 'This sofa is not too bad. Loose covers would freshen it up, with matching curtains,' she thought. She cuddled up to William as they sipped a glass of local *vino rojo*. 'Things are not too bad,' she murmured. 'At least we're together and we have some sort of roof over our heads.'

●●●

In the morning Sybil wrapped a coat round her

shoulders. She was still in her nightdress as she went out of the kitchen door and strode down the gravel path trying to avoid the high weeds. She reached a small building that looked recently whitewashed. She suspected that Miguel had painted the place before their arrival. Last night, she and William had collapsed with laughter when they opened the door to the new outside toilet. There was a shelf across the back of the shed with a perfectly round hole in the middle. The wood looked scrubbed and a strong smell of disinfectant was in the air. Sybil sat giggling on the throne.

'Wait till I tell Polly about this and she tells Mother.' William saw the funny side.

'We're like the early pioneers,' he joined in the laughter. It did seem funny last night when it was warm, but Sybil couldn't help wondering what it would be like in the winter when it became frosty.

'At least we've got chamber pots under our bed if we need to go in the night!'

'Do you know Sybil, I think I can make an extension on this building and install a posh shower,' he was full of enthusiasm.

'You and your ideas,' Sybil smiled as she came out into the garden. 'There is so much to do that you won't have time to go to work.' On her way back Sybil tried to imagine a picture of the future garden and where she could put the chickens. 'It's big enough to have a pond – I may be able to have ducks!'

Sybil and Catarina helped each other to cross the ditch. The girl was carrying two shopping baskets and was walking about four paces behind Sybil. This was awkward because every time she stopped and looked round the girl also came to a halt and smiled. In the end Sybil walked back, took one of the baskets from her and held onto the girl's arm. 'You can walk next to me,' Sybil said in Spanish. 'We are going to be friends, *amigas*!' The girl blushed but did as she was told. Sybil wanted to be free to do things on her own, she certainly didn't want a slave or a shadow. It's best to be clear from the start. She remembered her difficulties with the Crawford family. It was not going to be easy to teach the girl English but Sybil was determined to have a go.

The owners of the *almacen*, grocery shop welcomed them cheerfully. They knew Catarina and congratulated her on her new employment. They shook hands with Sybil and tried to tell her something about the district. She appreciated their friendliness. There was a small larder in the kitchen and Sybil thought it was a good idea to collect a supply of tinned vegetables and fruit. She wasn't too sure about sugar and flour because she was warned about ants. She really needed a box that could be sealed. William said he would try to devise something. Catarina took the items from the shelves and as she put them on the counter, Sybil called out the name in English. The girl soon caught on and tried to mimic the words. It was a good beginning.

When they arrived back at the house all the windows were open and Miguel had given the walls a coat of paint. William was busy sawing wood.

'It will need several coats to cover that dark colour, but we have made a start. I'm almost ready to assemble the bridge. It's not going to be as grand as some of the others but it will be safe and strong.' Sybil came over and kissed him on the cheek.

'I'm going to make us a bite to eat, we'll have lunch at about one.'

The following days were hectic. They wanted to do as much as possible before William returned to work. Sybil was pleased with the progress. The bed for the small room arrived and Catarina, with her brother's help, transformed it into a pleasant second bedroom. William arranged for the girl to sleep at the house when he was away from home. She didn't mind this arrangement. There was no street lighting and when Sybil looked out of the windows at night it was pitch black. The exception was when the moon was shining and the stars were out. But even so it looked deserted and creepy with the sound of croaking frogs and toads that lived in the ditch.

The gardener's first job was to cut all the grass down. This revealed a larger plot than they thought. Sybil was to start planning the garden and William thought it was a good idea to have a pond and some ducks.

'I expect your friends from the ditch will move in and spawn and then we'll have tadpoles.' he grinned at Sybil. In her heart Sybil had to admit a twinge of fear when William announced his first trip. He and Miguel were to travel up country to supervise the construction of a holding wall alongside the track. She was surprised to find that William was nervous about going.

'I'm worried about leaving you; are you sure you'll be all right?'

'I've got plenty to do when you're away. I want to make the covers for the sofa and the armchair and I haven't bought the material yet.'

'Come in the bedroom a minute I want to show you something,' He was extremely serious. Sybil followed.

'I like the new furniture especially my modern dressing table. I've put my silver hairbrush and mirror set on the top. Chris and Jerry gave me those for my wedding present.' William ignored her and walked to the wardrobe and produced a wooden box that he placed on the bed.

'I want you to learn to use this before I go. He opened the box and to Sybil's horror he pulled a revolver out and calmly inserted the bullets.

24

She gasped, 'I don't know how to use a gun!'

'Sybil, you have to learn. You need to protect yourself when I'm away.'

She was desperate for him to take her in his arms, to console and reassure her that everything would be all right. But instead he just put his arm round her shoulder and led her out into the garden.

'Come and see our shooting range.' Sybil followed him to the far corner of the garden and stared in disbelief.

'How can you call that a shooting range? It's just a corner of the garden with a large tree trunk and you've nailed some fruit tins on it at different heights. And that scarecrow just makes me laugh.'

'I know, but if people hear the shots and we talk about it, they'll believe we're serious about protecting ourselves and our property.' In order to please William she agreed to practise even though she found it difficult and frightening to use the revolver.

'I don't think I can kill anything, animal or human being.'

'You're getting on well Sybil - just aim for the legs as I showed you.'

●●●

On the day of departure, Catarina arrived early with Miguel. Her belongings were tied up in a sheet and he helped her to carry the bundle through to the spare room. William's bag was packed the night before. He was dressed in substantial overalls and high leather boots and was carrying a thick waterproof cape. Sybil tried to put on a brave face.

'I'll be fine. Catarina's father has promised to check on us every day.' She waited for William to take her in his arms.

'Keep your boots on in case you meet any snakes or horrible spiders.'

'You're wonderful, Sybil. I love you. Don't forget Jack and Ethel's wedding. We need a present and we ought to send a telegram.' Sybil watched him as he climbed into the cab of the truck and sat next to Miguel. She and Catarina waved until the two men were out of sight. Returning to the house Sybil felt deflated. It was a kind of anti-climax. She wondered how to cope with her feeling of desolation.

'Nice cup of tea?' Catarina came to the rescue and Sybil couldn't help smiling. The young girl soon learned that English people solve their problems with the help of their favourite beverage. Miguel fenced off an area for a chicken run and his father was coming round to build a house for the birds. He also promised to take Sybil to the market to look at hens with their chicks. William left money in the small safe in the wardrobe and as soon as she was on her own she hid the gun. She didn't like seeing it on the sideboard. Rosario turned up as promised and Sybil could hear the banging and sawing. She went out several times to inspect his work.

'*Muy bien*,' she said when he was nearly finished. She could easily walk inside without stooping. Along the left there were nesting boxes and perches and lower down a separate compartment for the mother hen and her chicks.

'You've made a good job of this Rosario. I can put the straw in the boxes later.'

'Senora there is one essential bit I need to do and that is to dig a trench all round the runs and house. Then I can nail on some rabbit wire bringing it down and burying it into the trench. It's to keep the rats out.' he explained.

Sybil shuddered; she hated rats ever since Jason held a

dead one up in front of her. It looked so mean and she saw its evil teeth and scraggy tail. Ugh, she thought. Jason explained that rats have families to feed just like any other animals but she felt no sympathy. Her brother killed the rat with his shotgun and she wondered what he would think if he learned that she was becoming efficient with a revolver.

Next morning Rosario arrived dressed smartly in his best suit.

'Are you ready Senora? It's market day.' Sybil quickly brushed her hair and tied it back with a ribbon. Rosario's donkey and cart awaited them on the other side of William's new bridge. Sybil admired his work, after all he wasn't a trained carpenter and the structure was strong and looked impressive. It was much better than the previous planks. The handrail was a bonus. She clambered up on the seat next to Rosario and she made sure to hold on tightly as they trundled along the uneven surface.

The market was a revelation. She was glad she remembered to bring a couple of baskets. They were soon filled with brightly coloured fresh vegetables and fruit. The fish stalls were tempting with trout from the mountain streams and other strange-looking creatures.

'What are those?' Sybil enquired.

'Those black-looking fish are from the lakes. Some are like eels.'

As they walked on, the contents of the stalls changed from food to live creatures.

'What a selection!' Sybil was spoilt for choice.

'I don't recognise these vendors. It is best for us to buy a hen from someone I know. There he is: my friend Paolo and his wife.'

Sybil followed and to her delight she caught sight of a beautiful white hen with her babies. 'That one,' she pointed.

'That's a good choice Senora,' said Paolo. 'I'll bring them to the cart when you've finished your shopping.'

'I think we've finished' said Sybil. As she turned round someone tapped her on the shoulder.

'Are you Mrs. Lawson?' Sybil found herself staring at the kindly face of a middle-aged lady.

'Yes,' she replied.

'Hello, I've been meaning to come round to see you. We've been waiting for you to settle in your new home. You probably were busy like we were when we first moved up here. I'm Iris Browning. I don't think my husband is in the same gang as yours but I think they know each other.'

'We have been up to our eyes trying to decorate our home. As you say there is a lot to do. I'm here to purchase some chickens. William left this week on his first mission since we arrived. It's taking me time to adjust to being on my own.'

'Would you join me for a coffee, there's a place just along here?'

'That sounds lovely. I'll just tell Rosario.'

'They can always find someone to talk to,' said Mrs Browning as Sybil came to join her. They made their way through the busiest part of the market.

'Look at those piglets in that pen! They look too small to be away from their mother. Oh my word look at the puppies.' Sybil gazed in wonder.

'That's what I need – a guard dog for when William's away.'

'You have to be careful buying a puppy. It's best to buy one from a reputable breeder or from someone you know. Dogs catch rabies here and if the disease is passed on to humans, there is no cure. Having said all that; I do have a small dog of my own. She's called Gypsy and she's great company when Bert's away. She makes a lot of noise when anyone comes to the door.'

'Where do you come from Mrs Browning?' Sybil asked.

'Please call me Iris. I came originally from Hammersmith but my parents have retired to north Devon. Where are you from?'

'I'm Sybil and I come from Bath.'

'The beautiful Georgian city, it always reminds me of Jane Austen. You'll have to come and join us on Thursdays. We have an unofficial ladies club and we meet once a week. The programme is varied; book discussions, sewing and embroidery, cooking: especially jam-making, gardening. It all changes with the seasons. This is the address for the next session, please try to come.' Sybil took the card and studied it carefully.

'I don't know my way around yet but I'd like to join you.'

'That's settled then. I'll call round for you at about quarter past ten. You'll soon learn your way around. We start off with a talk or demonstration, then we stop for lunch and in the afternoon, we knit, sew or just chat. Some of our members have swimming pools and if weather permits those who feel like it can have a swim. The rest of us sit round the pool under the parasols.

'It sounds great. I shall be ready when you call on Thursday.'

It was the evenings that dragged for Sybil. She missed sitting down to a meal with William, telling him about her day and listening to him recounting his trials and tribulations. I suppose I shall learn to cope, especially sleeping with the revolver on my bedside table. On the Thursday, Iris arrived as promised. Sybil looked forward to a change of scenery. It was a luxury to wear a decent frock for a change.

'The meeting this week is at Beryl's bungalow. It's quite near and looks a bit like your place. They've been there nearly a year and worked wonders. She's a very keen plants woman. Beryl and her husband go searching for new species. They often send seeds back to Kew Gardens and he writes botanical papers and has them published. They are devoted to their hobbies.'

'Do they have children? Sybil asked.

'Not yet – I think they met in England and moved out

here when he started on the railways.'

Sybil enjoyed her day with the wives and their guests. She found them friendly and full of vitality. The older ladies tended to mother the younger ones and Sybil liked this because it made her feel less lonely.

'You can call on any of our ladies for advice or help. The older ones are home most of the time but some of the youngsters have part time jobs and one or two work full time and can only come occasionally. Helga is one of these. She is a full time Nurse at the hospital and came to us first as a guest. She was born in San Juan - her parents are German. They've been here a long time, well before the war. They own a large vineyard on the way to Mendoza. I think you'll like her, she's about your age.'

Iris was right. Sybil liked Helga right from the start. She reminded her of Sophie when they first met in Bath – only in looks though, the same delicate features and light blue eyes but not the same hair. Sybil found it difficult to describe the colour of her new friend's hair. I suppose it could be silver, she thought. It was certainly not grey.

'Would you like to come over to meet my parents, I've got a whole day off next week? I have a brother called Carl. He's home on holiday from Buenos Aires where he's studying engineering and maths.'

'I'd love to come, thank you.' Sybil was pleased that she had bumped into Iris at the market and was now making new friends. Her spirits rose even more when William came back earlier than scheduled.

'Just thought I'd check on you!' He breezed in. 'I'm really impressed by the improvements. Is that a new sofa or did you make the covers? I'll need to change my clothes before I sit on that.'

'It is washable you know and stop teasing.' She ran towards him and as he took her in his arms she nestled contentedly against his body. Late afternoon they strolled down to feed the chickens. The mother hen was scratching the ground and the chicks were rushing in to find the odd delicacy. Sybil threw handfuls of crushed corn into the run and the ensuing stampede made William laugh.

'Our next job ought to be the pond. Even I'm becoming interested in livestock and I love roast duck.' Sybil winced – she hadn't thought about killing her own birds for the table. She didn't say anything.

'I've met interesting people at the club and been invited to join. They're mainly railway wives and some are just friends. Helga has invited me to meet her parents next week. I didn't know you were coming home early.'

'Helga sounds a German name to me,' William said, with a disapproving note in his voice.'

'She was born here in San Juan and her parents emigrated long before the war started. They have their own vineyard and the son is studying in Buenos Aires.'

'Germans are Germans wherever they are,' was the sharp reply.

'I've accepted the invitation and she's coming round to pick me up early next Friday.' Sybil was irritated by William's attitude. She had never met any Germans before and, as far as she knew, neither had William. Cartoons from the war years depicted German girls with gross bodies. The shadow of the war was always present.

'It's a shame that you've made those arrangements because my boss wants me to take some drawings back to head office and that means we can spend nearly a week in B.A. for the wedding. I thought you would be pleased to be there early to help Ethel with preparations.'

'I didn't know all that did I?' Sybil felt frustrated. Of course she wanted to spend more time with Ethel and her old friends. She may even have the chance to pop round to see Sophie.

'I'll just have to cancel my trip with Helga. She'll understand when I tell her about the wedding.'

'Of course she will and I expect she'll invite you some other time.' Sybil felt William was being smug about her having to change her plans. She didn't want to quarrel with him so she changed the subject.

'My Spanish is improving,' she told him. 'Catarina enjoys her English lessons, but I think she misses her family and is fed up stuck here with me.'

'I suppose that's natural. I was away for a long time. Did you miss me? In future it will only be a few days and at most a week at a time.'

'Of course I missed you – the days do drag.' Sybil knew this wasn't quite true because she enjoyed herself with the railway wives.

'I'm not exactly sure but I have a feeling that Catarina is up to something. She doesn't always tell the truth. Rosario told me that she's often late for meals.'

'Perhaps she has a boyfriend. She is attractive. May be they meet on her way home. Don't worry about it.' He put his arm round Sybil and they strolled back to the house together.

On Thursday morning, Sybil was preparing to go out to the meeting. She recently bought a swimming suit so that she could join the younger ones in the pool. As William was at home she decided to leave just before lunch so she could return in time to prepare the evening meal. There was a knock on the door and she heard William going to open it.

'Hello, you must be William. I'm Helga, Sybil's new friend.' Sybil rushed out of the bedroom.

'I'm here,' Sybil called. She felt agitated because she wasn't sure what William was about to say.' She needn't have worried because her husband was shaking hands with her new friend. He looked sheepish and startled at the same time. He was obviously mesmerized by her beauty. Helga was dressed in her nurse's uniform with a few strands of her silver hair showing from under her pure white cap. The freckles on her sweet face seemed to dance as she smiled.

'Come in, please,' he stuttered, but tried to be gallant. 'Would you like coffee or tea? Here's Sybil.'

'Thank you, but I can't stay. I've just come to apologise to Sybil. I'm sorry but I have to postpone our trip next Friday because my Mother will be away in Buenos Aires. But she insists that I make another date and this time I can invite you William to come with Sybil. I'm sure my brother Carl would love to meet you. He's studying maths and engineering and hopes to join one of the railways. We can make up a four and play tennis' Sybil held her breath as she stared at William. What was he going to say?

'That's wonderful, thank you. Sybil and I need to practice our tennis. We haven't played for a while, have we darling?'

'No dear, I don't know where the tennis rackets are,' she moved closer and took William's hand.

'That's settled then. I'll let you have some dates when mother returns.'

'I'll walk you to the bridge,' William opened the door for Helga. Sybil felt like sitting down. Surprised and pleased at William's reaction she hoped that they would become friends. When he returned William was still smiling.

'Why didn't you tell me how beautiful she is?' Without waiting for an answer he walked out into the garden.

25

On the journey to the capital William told her about his ideas for the pond project. 'I was talking to Miguel and he knows where we can hire a mechanical digger. The pond needs to be at least four feet deep in the centre so we can have a floating island for the ducks. We can always have shallower areas round the sides where we can plant lilies and irises. I'll try to get a book on ponds when we're in B.A.'

'That's a good idea.' Sybil was thinking about meeting her city friends. She missed the Buenos Aires crowd, especially Ethel.

'It's great to be back in the city,' she peered eagerly out of the window as they reached the outskirts. Sybil thought back to her time on the estancia and she began to understand how Sophie felt when they were left for days, and sometimes weeks, in a house surrounded on all sides by the pampas. The magnificent sunsets were a fleeting delight. The gold and red colours were glorious to behold but they only detracted momentarily from the constant feeling of isolation.

Ethel arranged for them to stay with the Church family. Ma Church hugged Sybil when they met. 'You look well dear, come on in.' William went through to the garden where Mr. Church was weeding and hoeing one of the flowerbeds.

'Let's make some tea – the others will be back shortly. Ethel will be pleased to see you. She needs someone younger to answer her questions. How do you like living out in the wilds, dear?'

'It's not as bad as the estancia – though I did like the luxury there, the marvellous food and being able to ride and swim in the pool. It wasn't too bad for me because the children kept me busy but Sophie hated the place when she wasn't allowed to ride. It's different in San Juan because I have William and we're organising our home. But I do miss him when he goes away. I'm making friends but I feel awkward about inviting them round because we still have so much to do. It was strange during William's absence because I was speaking in Spanish all the time.'

At that moment William entered the kitchen. 'We'll soon be able to invite friends for dinner.' he looked anxiously at Sybil. Mrs. Church offered him a cup of tea and pointed at the chocolate cake on the table. Ethel was back early.

'I'm only working part time now. Nursing is a good career. One can always find employment.' Sybil was pleased to see her friend. They began planning the last-minute arrangements for the wedding. 'Shall we go to town tomorrow, Sybil? There are a few things I need to buy and you have to try your dress on this evening. The bridesmaids have been practising but you and Bobbie need to go through the rehearsal. Jack is so laid back that sometimes he frustrates me. He just sits there smoking his pipe and saying, *yes dear* and *no dear*. I suppose now Billy is here they'll be going out.'

When the men disappeared. Sybil and Ethel retreated to the patio. 'It is such a big step getting married. Ma Church has been wonderful but I do miss my own Mother. Financially it's out of the question for them to come. They still have the animals. Jack did say he didn't mind having the wedding in England but he has such a large family here. This is where we live so it seemed the right decision to stay in Buenos Aires.'

'Don't worry Ethel, I'm here now and I'm sure that one day you'll be able to visit Winchester. I'm lucky because the Railway pays for us to go home.'

'Did you have any doubts about getting married?' Ethel asked. She frowned and held her head in her hands. 'It's this thought about being tied to one person that worries me. We both want children and I'm sure he loves me but it's such a commitment. What did you feel like?'

'Being in love is the main factor, but I had William's mother to contend with. She didn't think I was good enough for her only son and I did have doubts for a while after our visit to Manchester. I felt inferior because I left school so early. I seem to have a chip on my shoulder about that. William has been in the Flying Corps and his life has been more exciting than mine. It's different for you because you have a nursing qualification. In fact, it's the opposite from us because Jack just works in an office and you're the one with the qualifications.'

'Hold on, Sybil, Jack hopes to be promoted and he'll have the chance to become manager.' Ethel was indignant.

'Well, I envy you because you can find a job anywhere. I suppose I can as well but it is so domestic just looking after children. I wanted to continue with my studies and perhaps try for University.'

'You never know, you may have the chance one day to start a new career.' Ethel was trying to give encouragement. 'Not in San Juan.' Sybil said sharply.

'I'm very happy with William. I just have to come to terms with him travelling up country and leaving me on my own.'

'We're going to Cordoba on our honeymoon for four days and then Jack wants to visit you. That's if you and Billy agree. According to Jack we're staying in a posh hotel in Cordoba and I think he wants to go up into the mountains with Billy when we come to San Juan. I heard them talking about tents and suitable clothing. So I don't expect they'll want to take us. It's a bit much when it's supposed to be my honeymoon!

'Shall we call Bobbie now so we can try on the dresses?'

Sybil tried to change the subject.

●●●

The wedding went as planned but it was all over too quickly for Sybil and the next day they were on the train back to San Juan. Strangely, she was pleased when she entered the front door. Everything was clean and tidy and she was surprised at the homeliness of their small house.

'It's lovely to be home,' William said, taking her hand. 'I do hope you are happy here,' he stared intently into her eyes.

'I'm happy when I'm with you,' she answered putting her arms round his neck.

William was home for a few days and he spent most of the time with Miguel who was driving the digger. It was noisy with a lot of shouting. The plan, drawn by William, was hanging on the wire netting of the chicken run so that both men could refer to it, but Miguel ignored it most of the time. This annoyed William who wanted the pond to have a natural shape, not just round or oval. Helga called in to make arrangements for their visit to the vineyard and Sybil took her down to watch the construction work. William came over when he saw her and was pleased when she asked to see the plan of the proposed pond.

'I can't persuade Miguel that I don't want straight lines or just a circle.'

'He's a practical man and it's easier to make squares or circles.' Helga pointed out. 'We have a lovely pond at the vineyard. It started out as a circle and then Dad tweaked it here and there until he had the shape he desired. You can talk to him about ponds when you and Sybil come over.'

'That sounds a good idea. Saturday is convenient for us, isn't it Sybil?'

'Is that the Manchurian way to spell depth?' Helga teased William about his spelling on his precious map.

'You're pulling my leg,' he smiled. 'You're right! I should have checked all the words. I hate to think what it will be like when you're matron at the hospital.' He walked off grinning to himself. Sybil and Helga laughed and retreated to the house to study the calendar.

On the following Friday, William was busy checking the tennis rackets. He asked Sybil to find the box of balls purchased during their visit to B.A. Sybil was surprised at his enthusiasm. He seemed to have forgotten that he detested all Germans. Perhaps he was growing out of his obsession? Helga collected them in one of the vineyard trucks and they were surprised to find that she was driving. The young man sitting beside her climbed out to meet them.

'This is my brother Carl. You can sit with me in the cab, Sybil.' The other two climbed up on the back and sat opposite to each other on the side seats. Carl was two years younger than his sister. His hair was slightly darker but his eyes were the same piercing blue. The journey took about three quarters of an hour and Sybil could just about hear the two men talking above the noise of the engine. They were discussing the state of the roads and Carl was pointing out several landmarks including large crosses on some of the hills and the occasional shrine with flowers surrounding a Virgin Mary.

'They're nearly all Catholics around here.' she heard Carl say. Sybil relaxed a bit because she thought William was enjoying himself and he was trying to please her by coming on the trip. Helga's mother greeted them at the front door of a rambling house partly built of stone with stained wood trimmings. There were flowers everywhere and the house looked down a steep valley where vines stood in perfect lines.

'Where's Father?' Helga asked.

'He's just popped in to see how Pablo is.' She turned to her guests.

'Pablo broke his leg a week or two ago and his wife is going mad with him at home. It is difficult for an active man to keep still when he's been told by the Doctor to take it easy. Why don't you walk down to meet your father?'

As they descended through the terraces, Sybil noticed that William was impressed.

'I don't really know about grapes but I've noticed some of the vines are growing with supports and others are more like bushes.'

'We grow two varieties of vines here and they're all at different stages of development. There's Father!' Carl pointed at a small figure climbing up the path. Helga waved and ran to meet him.

'We can sit here and wait. My sister is a bit of a Daddy's girl and he misses her now she's living in town.'

'Your parents must miss you when you're in Buenos Aires?' Sybil pointed out.

'Aren't you interested in the Vineyard?' William asked. It's a marvellous place and what a legacy.' Sybil thought about her back garden in Bath and a picture of William's Dad on his perfect lawn in Manchester flashed through her mind. They were mixing in different circles now even though they were German ones.

'I love the Vineyard but Father thinks I ought to have qualifications in basic engineering before starting full time here. He thinks I should see a bit of the world and that means living in the capital for a year or two. I'm interested in the railways. I like the thought of building a system that opens up the country. It means people can travel easily and companies can use them for moving their goods. Helga says you've flown in aeroplanes William? I'd really like to chat about that.'

Sybil's heart sank. She knew what William was like when he started talking about the war.

'If you're interested in flying you can come round to our house where I can show you my album of photographs from my flying days. But at the moment I have lots of questions about this place. For instance, who started the wine business in San Juan? I suppose it was the Spanish.'

'Wine production started in the sixteenth century when the Spanish settlers arrived and it was the Catholic priests who planted the first vines. The wines were used in their communion services.'

'I suspect they were also used for other reasons.' William grinned.

'The wines improved in quality when a French chap called Poujet arrived in the 1850s. He brought with him his expertise and new varieties. Now we can grow Cabernet Sauvignon, Merlot and Chardonnay depending on the height above sea level. San Juan is six hundred and fifty metres above sea level and the grape varieties are grown at heights suitable for each one.'

'It can't be just the height, the climate must play a big part?'

'Yes it does, the right temperature, the long hours of sunshine, low humidity, not much rain or violent winds and good soil conditions all play their part.'

'It's fascinating; I saw some vines growing in Switzerland and in Tenerife but not on this scale. I don't think we have them growing outside in England.'

'My grandmother was English, you know. I expect Helga told you. My grandparents left Germany before the last war. It caused controversy with the rest of the family.'

'Here they are!' Helga was walking arm in arm with a tall grey-haired man.

After lunch William was happy to stroll round the vineyard with Mr. Schroder. This was Sybil and William's first visit to a place like this and both were enjoying the adventure and the welcome they received. After coffee and relaxing on the patio Carl went off to prepare the tennis court.

'We need some exercise after that lunch, Mother. They've brought their tennis rackets.'

William and Sybil soon found that they were not in the same league as their friends. William and Helga were both competitive, so they were well suited to play together. Sybil couldn't help laughing when Helga screamed at William after he missed an easy shot.

'Throw the ball higher, for goodness sake!' she yelled when William was trying to serve. Carl, on the other hand, was quiet and patient. Sybil felt she was improving all the time. They all collapsed on the floor, laughing, at the end of the game when William managed an excellent smash hit. Even Carl couldn't return it.

Sybil felt completely happy on the way home.

26

Sybil's friendship with Helga blossomed. When William was away working she often stayed the night. There was no need to disrupt Catarina's routine by asking her to move into the house. On Thursdays, Sybil attended the meetings organised by the Railway Wives. 'We're having a garden fete to raise money for the children at the hospital'

'What are you going to do with the money?' William enquired.

'Helga says there's a need for toys and picture books. We can ask a carpenter to make small tables and chairs for the children to use.'

'Sounds a good project. I suppose Helga is organising it all. I hear she's been coaching you in readiness for our next tennis match. We are going to be busy with Ethel and Jack coming next week.'

On the evening of Ethel's arrival, William and Jack disappeared to make plans for their forthcoming hike into the mountains. They packed haversacks with their personal luggage and Miguel, who was joining them on the trip, was organising the hire of a mule to carry the heavy stuff including the tents and cooking equipment. The four friends stayed up late chatting, eating and drinking. Ethel and Sybil made their own plans including a visit to the Schroder's vineyard. Sybil sensed a certain irritation in her friend's attitude.

'What's the matter Ethel?'

'I wish we could go with the men, they always seem to have all the adventures.' Secretly, Sybil was pleased to have

Ethel to herself. 'It is hard trekking on some of the high paths. In fact sometimes it is necessary to make a new pathway. William did take me once but I twisted my ankle and he had to bring me back. I suppose he's told Jack about that disaster.'

'I'll let them off this time, but when we come again to stay, I shall insist that we are included in their plans.'

Helga dropped in to meet Ethel and Jack and she made everyone laugh when she started teasing William and giving them tips about surviving on the slopes. William always rose to the bait and Ethel joined in the teasing. Jack was used to banter and small talk. He sat quietly in the corner smoking his pipe.

'She's quite a spitfire,' he observed when Helga rushed away for her night duty at the hospital.

Ethel and Sybil's first outing nearly ended in disaster. Not having the use of a car, they decided to go on a horse and carriage trip into the centre of the town.

'We can go down the main avenue in the town centre and around the park.'

'We can look for a teahouse in the main street. I've never been there. We've been tied up with decorating and setting up the garden. We do all our shopping at the local stores.' Sybil felt anxious because she knew that Ethel was sometimes a daredevil and often took unnecessary risks. 'We shall have to be careful with our money. Miguel says that the pickpockets are everywhere in the markets.'

'You can take Billy's gun if you're scared,'

'You're joking, I'm likely to kill someone.'

'We'll dress sensibly and take our umbrellas. We can use them as parasols if it's hot and as weapons if we have to defend ourselves.' Ethel giggled and Sybil couldn't help joining in as they went to change into suitable clothes for their adventure.

They walked to the local shopping street where they could see three or four carriages waiting in line. The horses stood patiently like statues except for one that was eating from a rough-looking nosebag.

'We don't want to just take the first one, let's walk along and survey the situation. We need to check out the drivers.'

'Why? Sybil asked. It seems to me that we should take the first one in the queue.' Sybil thought that if she had to make a choice she would go for the best looking horse. Then to her dismay Ethel began bartering over the price. Obviously she was used to doing that in B.A.

It was a lively event and Sybil became nervous when the second driver in the line joined in the argument. There was the usual shouting and waving of arms and she blushed when she recognised quite a few Spanish swear words being exchanged between the two drivers.

'We'll take this one,' said Ethel pointing at the second horse and carriage. The first driver was furious and started waving his whip at the other driver and then at Ethel. The chosen horse moved forward out of the line. Ethel grabbed Sybil's arm and they climbed up into the carriage and sat gingerly on the plush leather seat.

'That doesn't seem fair to me.' Sybil was holding on tightly as they pulled away. 'That other one was first in the line.'

'Yes, I know that but he was charging nearly twice as much. This chap will be in trouble for undercutting the first driver, but we've managed to save on the trip.' Sybil didn't answer. She sat back quietly in the carriage.

It was partially covered in black canvas fitting tightly on the back and sides. The front was open and they had a good view ahead and if they leant forward they could see on both sides. At the rear was a small window made of a see-through material. A fringe along the top hung down blowing slightly in the breeze. The horse trotted gently along the road.

Sybil was just beginning to enjoy herself when a second carriage drew up beside them. They recognised the driver when he started shouting. Two rough-looking men were in his carriage and it was obvious that he was out for revenge.

Suddenly both carriages put on speed and a race was taking place.

'What fun! Hold on tight Sybil.' She held on but couldn't share Ethel's crazy enthusiasm. Their carriage began to draw ahead and when Sybil peered through the rear window she could see the poor horse straining at the bit trying to keep up. They were nearing the centre and people were scattering with fear and then ahead in the middle of the road were two policemen blowing their whistles and holding their arms above their heads.

The driver pulled in the rein and the horse reared up. Sybil and Ethel were thrown forward, slipping off the seat but still holding on to the handles on either side of the carriage. There was a mighty crash and as they tried to climb back on to the seat they could see the horse's head had crashed right through the window.

'There are three of us in here now,' Ethel laughed.

'It's not funny, just look at the poor thing.' Sybil gently touched the horse's nose. He was shaking in distress. But there was worse to come. The two thugs found their way round. One was attending the first driver who was lying in the road.

'He looks unconscious!' Sybil cried. The other one pulled the second driver off his seat and hit him with a violent punch. A nasty fight ensued with the two policemen joining in, trying to separate the two men.

'Come on, let's disappear from here.' Ethel slipped out of the carriage and helped Sybil. Then she started running and Sybil followed.

'What about paying?' Sybil called. She was frightened and confused so it was a relief to her when she heard her name.

'Senora Lawson?' It was Miguel's father, Rosario. 'Come this way.' He led Sybil and Ethel down a side street and into a dark bar. Sybil collapsed on a chair. She felt sick. Rosario ordered a brandy for each of them and Ethel was quieter now and sipped her drink in silence.

'My truck is near, so I shall take you home.' Rosario said in Spanish. 'First I shall check the scene of the accident.'

'He's bossy – I want to see what's happened.'

'For goodness sake Ethel, we're in enough trouble as it is. Just stay here and do what you're told for once.' There was an awkward silence between them. Sybil sipped her brandy and looked towards the door. She felt terrible and just couldn't understand Ethel's attitude.

'*Vamos* Senora, I've given the police your address. They will be in touch if they need your help.' They walked slowly down the narrow streets until they reached the garage where Rosario's truck was parked. They squeezed into the front seat and made for home.

'You look pale, Senora Lawson. Do you want to lie down on the bed?'

'No thank you, we'll be fine in a short while.

'I am sorry Sybil. I don't know what came over me.' A few tears were rolling down Ethel's cheeks.

'It isn't like you,' Sybil replied taking her friend's hand.

'The last few weeks have been hectic and our stay in Cordoba was a disaster. Then on top of it all Jack just goes off with Billy as if nothing has happened. In fact nothing did happen.'

Sybil felt awkward, she didn't want to pry into Ethel and Jack's private life.

'Let's have some tea, we can talk about things later if you wish.'

The next day Ethel was her old self again and Sybil was pleased to see her smiling.

'What shall we do today then? Shall we go to the cinema? I haven't been to the pictures for ages.' This seemed a good idea to Sybil as the local cinema was within walking distance. At least if they were sitting down watching a film nothing much could happen. They agreed to catch the matinee so they lunched early and strolled down to the small theatre. 'It looks like a love story.' Ethel bought the tickets.

'Are you on your own?' asked the man in the box office.

'There are two of us,' Sybil pointed out.

She thought it was strange that the usherette stared at them and rolled her eyes at the person selling tickets. They were shown to their seats and Ethel took some peppermints out of her bag and passed them to Sybil. They settled down to watch the film.

'It looks like Switzerland with those mountains and log cabins,' whispered Sybil. The scene then changed to the inside of the cabin with a young female sprawled on a bed. She was scantily dressed and that was when the hissing started. Two men sitting next to them started hissing and whistling and the rest of the audience was doing the same.

'Why are they looking at us?'

'I have no idea,' Ethel replied.

Then the lights went up and the usherette came running to their row.

'Senoras, this film is for men only. Please will you leave – we shall give you your money back.' The hissing changed to booing and arms with clenched fists were waved in their direction.

'Come on, let's go,' said Sybil who was thankful that Ethel just followed without adding more trouble to the scene.

Once outside, Ethel started laughing. 'I seem to be bringing you into trouble all the time. The ticket man didn't warn us. I suppose he thought we'd be invisible.'

'You've only been here a couple of days, and we've been in a pickle on both occasions. In a carriage accident and then thrown out of the cinema! Tomorrow we're going with Helga to the vineyard. I hope that visit will go smoothly.' It did and they had a restful day wandering round the garden and sitting in the shade chatting. Helga laughed at their exploits.

'I was there when they brought that poor driver in as an emergency. He was going on about two foreign women. I had no idea it was you two. Anyway, his injuries were superficial.' They were expecting William and Jack to be back the next day.

'Let's not tell them what happened. You know what a fuss they'll make about keeping safe.'

'I'll be glad when they're back.' Sybil felt weary with the drama of the last two days.

That evening they celebrated with bubbly wine. Helga joined them for dinner and afterwards they sat out on the newly constructed patio relaxing in the warm evening air. William took Sybil's hand and they smiled at each other. The peace was suddenly shattered. The bell rang and the front door was knocked loudly. William went to answer it and returned looking pale and worried.

'It's the police', he said. 'They want to talk to the two Senoras!'

27

William and Jack accompanied them to the local Police Station.

'I can't believe you're embroiled in such an incident.' William regained his colour but he looked angry.

'Ethel, was it you who started it all?' Jack asked.

'I only took the cheapest fare for the ride into town. I didn't know there was a law about choosing the first in the queue.' She used a defiant tone.

Sybil remained silent. She was embarrassed at being escorted by two burly policemen and William stamping along in a furious mood. When they arrived they sat in a small lobby as instructed. A tall distinguished-looking policeman entered the room. His uniform was neatly pressed and the row of medals attached to his coat caught the light of a lamp hanging in the centre of the room. A young woman followed him with a notebook. He asked Ethel to describe what happened and the girl took notes. He then turned to Sybil.

'Do you agree with this statement?'

'Yes, Sir.'

'Do you have anything to add?'

'No, Sir, that is exactly what happened.'

'I must apologise to you as visitors to San Juan. It is regrettable that you were involved in such a chaotic scene. You are now free to go.' Sybil blushed and held back when William grabbed her arm.

'Thank you,' said Sybil in a meek voice. 'Has the horse recovered? He was so frightened, poor thing.'

'Yes Senora, he just had a few cuts on his neck and he'll soon be back at work.'

'Come on, Sybil, let's go home.'

Ethel and Jack walked ahead, their voices were raised in conflict. Sybil held on to William's arm. He was calmer now but she felt deflated. She looked forward to her friend's visit and felt sorry that so much was going wrong. Ethel just didn't seem to be herself. There was something not quite right but she wasn't willing to reveal the problem.

'I think we shall try to go back to B.A.' Jack confided. 'Ethel is keen for us to find an apartment. She thinks we need a place of our own.' By the time they reached the house, Ethel had disappeared into the bedroom and the rest of them decided to call it a day.

Sybil's head was feeling strange and her legs and arms were aching. She thought it was just a reaction to all the drama. Next morning she still felt unwell.

'I've got a bit of a sore throat,' she told Ethel.

'Let me feel your head. You look flushed. Perhaps you're going down with something. I'll make you a dose of salts and then you can go back to bed.'

Sybil did as she was told. It was difficult to swallow the fizzy salts. But she did drink every drop. It was a relief to creep back into bed.

Jack was out in the garden with William where they were giving the final touches to the wooden arbour by the duck pond. Ethel busied herself packing the cases and chatting to Catarina.

'Help me quickly, I'm going to be sick,' Sybil called from the bedroom. 'Bring a bowl.' But they were too late. Sybil lost control and was violently sick all over the bedclothes and part of the rug on the floor next to the bed. Ethel and Catarina came rushing in with a bucket. The smell was vile and Sybil began to heave again. Ethel held her head and asked Catarina to bring a wet flannel from the bathroom. It seemed ages before Sybil's head fell back on the pillow.

'You'll have to get up,' said Ethel. 'Catarina needs to change the bedclothes.'

Sybil moved to the chair and sat shivering. Ethel covered her with a light blanket and went to the back door to call William.

'Billy, Sybil's not well. Can you come please? She looks quite grey. I think we need to call the doctor.'

William came rushing in, took one look at Sybil and yelled for Catarina to fetch Dr. Waisgluz who lived two doors away. He sat holding Sybil's hand, anxiety showing on his face.

'I'm all right. Ethel gave me a dose of salts. I just feel tired and I ache all over. My throat is terribly sore.'

When the doctor arrived he spent some time checking Sybil's throat and the glands in her neck.

'She needs to go to hospital. Put a few things together for her. I'll bring my car round.'

'What's the matter?' William asked.

'I'm not sure, but the symptoms could mean that she has Diphtheria. There are some cases around at the moment and I believe the isolation part of the hospital is in use. We need a second opinion. It is very catching and dangerous.'

William could hardly contain himself. 'What can I do?' He kept asking. Jack looked worried and didn't know what to say. Ethel, being a nurse, knew more about the disease. She warned Jack to keep away and she told Catarina to go home.

The doctor arrived and gently eased Sybil into the back seat.

'You cannot come', he told the others. You must stay here until I return.'

William didn't know what to think. He sat with his head in his hands for a while and then rushed into the bedroom.

'I'll fetch the Doctor's book, see what it says about

Diphtheria.'

'What book is that?' Ethel asked.

'It's "The Universal Home Doctor." It sounds terrible,' he read from the book:

'The incubation period is two to seven days. She must have caught it when we were away, Jack. Oh God, listen to this: *There is a case on record where a child coughed into the doctor's face while he was examining the throat, and the doctor died within twenty four hours from diphtheria. Germs may be picked up from articles of clothing, for although these germs thrive in human beings, they do not necessarily die when separated, but may go on living for months, until chance again allows them to enter another human being.'*

'We shall all have it and you've sent Catarina away and she changed the bedclothes,' said Jack. William was pacing up and down.

'Poor Sybil,' he kept saying. 'I can't lose her.' His eyes were filling with tears.

'Don't panic,' Ethel ordered. 'We don't even know for sure that it is Diphtheria.'

'It's the waiting,' even Jack was nervous.

'If I remember rightly – the disease can be cured if it's caught early. A membrane starts to grow at the back of the throat. Usually they take a sample of this and send it to a Bacteriologist to see if the germ of diphtheria is present, but in most cases they start the Antitoxin treatment immediately when a case is suspected. Time is of essence and the patient can die if he has to wait for treatment.' William was so agitated that he began to shout at Ethel.

'Don't tell me anymore, I'm going to the hospital. I can't leave Sybil on her own.' At that point there was a knock at the door.

'It's me,' said Helga. She was out of breath. A colleague told me about Sybil.

She rushed over and put her arms round William.

'They've put her in isolation and started the injections and she's responding well. It will take a bit of time before we know definitely. We need to disinfect this place. I've got the fumigating stuff in the car. Can you help me bring the bottles and buckets in please, Jack?'

'Sit down William - you can't do anything to help she's in good hands at the hospital.' Ethel moved to the kitchen.

'What if we catch it?' William held his throat as the others came in from the car carrying the equipment.

'You need to seek help immediately if you notice any of the symptoms: fever, aching limbs, sore throat and swollen glands.' They sat sipping their sweet tea whilst Helga planned the best way to fumigate the house.

'Clothes and all materials need to be washed and soaked in disinfectant. Then the furniture needs to be sponged down. It will be easier if we all work together. Where's Catarina? She needs to be told.'

'Ethel sent her home, Billy and I will go round to tell her.'

'It's best if she comes back to help us.' Helga explained. 'We need as many people as possible to use the disinfectant. I've had the antitoxin treatment on various occasions when it was thought that I had been in touch with the disease. I expect I'm immune by now and will be able to go back to the hospital and keep you in touch with what's happening.'

When Catarina returned, the five of them set to working together with Helga giving instructions. The curtains were taken down in all the rooms and any clothes used recently were bundled together. Anything that could be boiled was put in a separate pile. They felt exhausted and William was desperate.

'Thank you Helga, I'm so pleased that you're here to help but I do need to see Sybil. She will be thinking that I've deserted her, please may I come with you?'

'No William, you will have to be patient. If Sybil has the disease you will all have to be in quarantine for about seven days and nights. She's having the injections and they'll make her feel sleepy. I shall come in everyday with any news and bring you supplies.

'We wanted to return to B.A.,' said Jack. 'I'm supposed to be back at work next week.'

'You'll have to let them know. Your employers will not want you back until you're pronounced clear. I must go now.'

William escorted her to the door.

'Thanks again Helga,' he kissed her on the cheek. 'You're a brick,' he whispered.

•••

It was not long before Helga conveyed the news that the tests were positive. Sybil was diagnosed with a mild form of diphtheria. Her treatment was to continue until all signs of the disease had disappeared.

'I want to see her. Tell me how she's feeling,' William pleaded.

'She's holding her own but she is still in pain. She has to have her mouth washed out with boracic acid solution every few hours and ice poultices are being placed on her swollen glands.'

'How can she drink and eat?' Ethel asked.

'She can only have liquids, milk, beef juice and barley water. When her throat improves she will get ice cream and soups. She has a bit of a rash at the moment. Sleeping is difficult for she needs to stay on her side. Sybil wants to see you William even if you just look through the window. You'll have to wear a mask when you come to the hospital.'

'I'll come now. I'm desperate to see Sybil. His heart sank when he peered through the window. She looked so pale and small in the iron-framed bed. The room was empty, no carpets, curtains or furniture.

'The place is warm but it has to be kept well ventilated,' Helga explained.

'I feel so helpless . . . ' William turned away.

'She's waking up. Try to smile, she needs encouragement.'

William waved and pressed his gloved hands on the window. I love you, he mouthed.

Sybil gave him a sweet smile and she drew her pale hand from underneath the sheet and waved to him. Her eyes were heavy and closed almost immediately.

'Is she alright?' He took Helga's hand. 'Can't you do anything?'

'Everything is being done to make her comfortable. I'll take you home now.'

'I'll never forgive myself if she dies. It was me who thought we'd be better off without the girls on our mountaineering trip. She probably caught it at the cinema or on that silly coach trip.' Ethel and Jack were silent when they returned. William was blaming himself for Sybil's predicament.

28

The next seven days were the longest that Sybil could remember. It seemed more like a month. Helga was the only nurse she recognised, the ones that appeared at night were masked and well covered. The same doctor kept her informed about her illness and Helga brought news of William and the others. She vaguely remembered seeing William for an instance through the glass window of her room. That seemed a long time ago.

'How is William?' Sybil asked. 'He hasn't caught it?'

'No he would be in here if he had diphtheria. Ethel and Jack are going home this coming week.'

'What about William? Who will look after him?'

'I've been going round most evenings, helping with the cooking. Your tests are improving all the time. You're on soups and soft pastas and as soon as you have three or four clear nose and throat tests you'll be allowed to go home.'

'Thanks Helga, you've been a true friend. I can't wait to be back with William.'

'Don't be too excited - you will have a long period of convalescence ahead. You need to be monitored because the disease can damage your heart and other organs. Luckily for you your case has been a mild attack probably because you were diagnosed early.

Sybil knew she was feeling better because she became restless and was pleased that William had sent magazines for her to read. Whenever he had the chance he wrote letters and his correspondence cheered her. He kept her informed about the garden and the chickens:

'They are laying well and Catarina says she will make you an omelets when you come home. I also have a surprise for you when you're well enough to go out. At present I am keeping it a secret.

With all my love

William xxx

Sybil was allowed a small night table and she kept William's letters in the top drawer. Reading was pleasant but she soon tired and found her eyes closing. Her mind raced when she was permitted to sit on the side of the bed and stand for the first time, but her legs were weaker than she thought and she soon felt out of breath. Her times out of bed increased every day. At first she held on to the nurse but slowly she ventured out on her own. It was a delight when she was allowed out in the garden. Then William arrived and took her in his arms.

'Don't cry darling, I'm so glad you're better. They say you can come home soon.' Sybil clung to him.

'It's been awful,' she cried. 'If it hadn't been for Ethel giving me those salts I may have died.'

'How do you know that?' William asked.

'The doctor said that being sick had got rid of some of the toxins and cleared some of the membrane that was starting to form. That was just his opinion he told me.'

'Well, whatever, I'm glad you're on the mend. You will have to take it easy when you're home. They're being very good at work giving me time off when I need a break.'

Next morning William and Helga arrived to collect her. They brought clean clothes from home. The magazines were confiscated.

'The room will have to be fumigated, but I suppose you can take William's letters. Just put them in your clean bag.'

●●●

'It's a luxury for me to sleep in our bed again and to have you beside me.'

William was fussing about but secretly she was pleased to see that he was concerned about her.

'I've made a daily routine for you. It was partly Helga's idea.' He read from a sheet of lined paper:

Mornings – Breakfast in bed, rise at eleven, wash and dress. Short walk in the garden and sit outside in the shade, read or sew. All this if weather permits.

Lunch – at about half past one – this to be the main meal of the day.

Afternoons – siesta until three or four depending on how you feel Walk in the garden trying to increase the distance each day.

Evenings – A light snack, omelets, soup or sandwich.

Bed – early to start and later as your health improves. Rest is essential. Your body needs to heal and recuperate'

'I know who you've been talking to, you sound like a nurse.' Sybil smiled and stretched out her hand to him. He took it gently and pulled her towards him.

'I was so worried about you, darling. It was a nightmare. Ethel and Jack thought they were going to catch it. Then Jack let his boss know about being in quarantine. None of us could leave the house. Talk about hectic – I suppose we were lucky not to catch the disease. Helga was here to help disinfect the whole place.'

Sybil felt pampered by the attention and, as she sat quietly on the patio, she could hear the laughter coming from the kitchen. William and Helga were preparing lunch. She began to think about William and how easily he fell for any sort of praise. He tended to be deceived easily. I suppose it's because he lacked love when he was a child, she thought. It annoyed Sybil that he placed his boss on a pedestal and he also admired that chap Stephen whom he met on the ship coming to B.A. She found them pleasant enough - but they couldn't walk on water!

William came out carrying a glass of sherry. 'Helga says a small drop will not hurt you.' He handed Sybil the glass.

'We're bringing our drinks out in a minute.'

When they appeared William was beaming at the two fancy glasses that were decorated with pineapple wedges on their rims. He and Helga were laughing.

'She's been teaching me to mix cocktails. This is my present: a cocktail shaker and a recipe book. Helga says it's for my birthday.'

Sybil felt a strange twinge of fear, or was it anger.

'I thought you could make cocktails, William. I suppose you've had plenty of time to learn all sorts of things whilst I was in hospital.' There was a sarcastic tone in her voice. William stopped laughing and stared at Sybil.

'I'm sorry,' she mumbled. 'I'm feeling tired and just wish I could join in with the fun. I think I ought to go to bed.' They walked Sybil to her room.

'I'll bring you something on a tray.' Helga helped her into bed.

On her own again Sybil felt tears coming to her eyes. 'I'm just jealous. I don't like anyone becoming close to William.' Every day Sybil regained more of her strength and she became impatient when it was time to rest. Slowly she started taking over in the kitchen and Helga's visits became fewer. Catarina was to return after a long break in quarantine. Sybil felt that things were returning to normal.

'The doctor says I can start going out again and I'd like to go to the market,' she asked William.

'If he says you can go out I can give you your surprise present. So we'll go this afternoon for you to choose,' he clapped his hands together like a child.

'Where are we going then?' Sybil was intrigued and wondered if William was going to buy her a new coat for the winter.

'It won't be a surprise if I tell you. Wrap up warm. I don't want you to catch cold.'

Rosario came to collect them in a borrowed taxi. 'This is my cousin's car. He's doing well as a taxi driver. Many of the horse and cart drivers are saving their money to buy cars.'

'I'm sorry for the horses. What will happen to them?' Sybil asked.

'They're not that well looked after. The drivers only

think about money. Some are so thin that they wouldn't even make good steaks.' Rosario shook his head as he turned away.

'We don't eat horsemeat, do we Sybil?'

'No we don't. Let's change the subject, I don't like talking about this.' William took her hand and squeezed it.

They pulled up at a *Quinta* on the outskirts and walked through a gate that led to the ranch. A young woman came out to greet them. She wore a white starched pinafore. Her dark hair was drawn severely into a long plait that bounced from side to side as she ran to meet Rosario.

'This is my youngest daughter, Silvana.'

'Where are they then?' Rosario enquired.

'In the barn Papa, Senora Pereira is with them.' Sybil and William walked arm in arm.

'Is this my surprise?'

'Just wait and see.'

In the barn Sybil could hear gentle squeals coming from behind some bales of straw and as she peered round the corner she was delighted to see a large box holding a mother and her puppies. She detected a low growl coming from the box but she was allowed to proceed slowly towards the bitch and her babies.

'They're only five days old. Olga is a good mother protecting her litter. Senor will have to take his turn later. We only allow one person at a time. She has ten puppies and all are doing well.'

'Whatever is she doing?' Sybil asked. To her dismay the bitch was flinging the puppies across the box and licking them all over. Some looked soaking wet and were whimpering at being disturbed.

'They've just had a feed and some are so greedy that they fall asleep at the bar.'

'What does that mean?'

'We call it the milk bar,' she laughed. Olga is over-conscientious. Each puppy has to be washed clean after every meal whether they like it or not. With ten babies it's quite a task and soon the litter, including mother, will fall asleep.' William put his head round the corner but Olga barked loudly at him, so he disappeared again.

'You're a good, beautiful girl, Olga,' Mrs Pereira stroked the dog's head.

Sybil looked at the bitch with her pricked-up ears. 'She looks so intelligent and those appealing dark eyes could get round anyone.'

'Would you like one of the puppies?'

'Oh William, I'd love one. Could we have a bitch, then she could have puppies like Olga?'

'Hold on, love, that's rather drastic and I don't like the smell much. Let's just have a puppy dog this time.'

'You're right, William. I'm only just recovering from my illness.' Sybil was disappointed but she still felt tired on occasions.

'You have to be fit to breed animals. Rosario could bring you round each week to see their development. It's a thrill to see them open their eyes for the first time. They're born deaf you know? Their hearing is very acute when their ears open and they jump at any loud sounds and it's so funny when they find their individual voices and bark at each other.'

'I'd love that as long as Rosario doesn't mind bringing me here.'

'May we buy one of the dog puppies please?' William asked.

'Yes you can. The senora can choose the one she likes best.'

'That will be difficult. I like them all,' Sybil smiled at William.

'We had a terrier when I was a child. I'm not sure what breed this is. Are they police dogs?'

'They're Alsatians sometimes called wolfhounds. They originate from a place called Alsace on the borders of France and Germany. They were trained to protect sheep and nowadays they are used as guard dogs.'

'That's just what we need where we live,' William told the breeder.

'In Buenos Aires the police are training them to search for people and they have several duties when they become fully trained police dogs. The chief dog handler is coming from the city to see these puppies. They're looking for five to buy for their district. My husband and I are not sure if we want the puppies to go to B.A. We think family homes are better for them. They do need strict training and that makes some people change their minds. I'm sure that you and the senora will make excellent owners.'

The next few weeks were a joy for Sybil. She worked hard at her recovery plan and was now feeling stronger. Every week Rosario took her round to see the puppies. There was one little boy who kept coming to her. She was sure that he recognised her as soon as he heard her voice. William and Sybil went shopping for puppy items. They decided that he should sleep in the kitchen and they made room for his basket in a corner under a tabletop. They bought water and food bowls and a box full of toys. Senora Pereira gave them a food list and Sybil learned to prepare the meals for the puppies on her many visits to the barn. They also discussed names.

'They are so regal, perhaps we should call him King or Prince?' William suggested.

'That's a bit grand.' Sybil complained. 'I like short names like Sam or Ben.'

'Let's compromise then, what about Duke?'

'Yes, I quite like that, though I may call him Dukie.' The day came when they had to collect Duke.

'We'll take a blanket, just in case we need it, and some paper,' Sybil tried to hide her excitement.

'He really has grown. It's hard to believe that this big lump was one of those tiny puppies.'

Rosario lifted him up onto Sybil's lap and the puppy's legs hung over her knees and he kept trying to lick her face.

'Don't let him do that Sybil, you'll catch something else,' William frowned at her.

'You hold him then, he is strong.' Sybil giggled. 'He won't keep still.'

William pulled the puppy over and tried to contain him on his lap but the animal kept trying to get back to Sybil. Rosario was laughing.

'You will have to be strong, Senor,' he insisted.

'No Duke sit still,' William demanded. The puppy turned and stared at William and was quiet for a second. Sybil thought William knew the answer, but just as she was about to congratulate him the puppy turned and licked William on the nose.

'Ugh', he yelled. 'He's disgusting!'

'We're nearly home now,' Sybil, was in fits of laughter.

When he was loose in the garden Duke tore round the perimeter like a mad thing.

'We'll never catch him. He needs to have a small area in which to exercise. Senora Pereira said he would damage his legs if he's allowed to run wild.'

'It would help at night. We don't want to be searching for him all over the garden.'

'I'll make a temporary enclosure with some chicken wire. I think it's necessary to do it straight away. I don't know why we didn't think of it before.'

'We were too busy buying toys. Look at him now. He's found the chickens.' At this point Catarina came out with a bag of tit bits: small biscuits and pieces of cheese that she handed to Sybil.

'Duke come! ' she called rattling the paper bag. To her surprise, the puppy came galloping towards her and bumped into her legs.

'The lead, you must ask him to sit, Senora!' She held a piece of sausage above the dog's head and moved forward saying 'Sit.' Duke sat with his legs sprawled out in a most unsophisticated way. He liked the sausage and proceeded to jump at Catarina. She yelled at him and he strolled off looking for something else to do.

'He is going to be a handful,' thought Sybil. They managed to attract him into the kitchen whilst William worked on the temporary enclosure. 'It has to be strong.' Sybil told him. She prepared Duke's supper. He was still on four meals a day. This meal at half past four consisted of raw minced beef with biscuits. He wolfed it down in a few minutes flat and Sybil decided to walk him on his lead. On their return William lifted him up and gently put him in his basket. The excitement of coming to his new home had exhausted him and he fell asleep almost immediately.

He slept for over two hours and this allowed Sybil and William to enjoy their evening meal without being disturbed. 'He's so good. He loves it in his basket.' When he did eventually wake up, William took him out on the grass. He sniffed round his new enclosure and then trotted back into the kitchen. They both played with him sitting on the kitchen floor until he dozed off again with his head on Sybil's lap.

At about half past ten Duke was given his last meal of the day, a milky dish of porridge and then William took him out and put him back in his basket with a couple of biscuits.

'Let's go to bed, I'm tired out, it's like having another person in the house.'

They just managed to settle in their bed when a terrible shriek came from the kitchen followed by pathetic howling. Duke didn't like being on his own and he was making sure that everyone in the house could hear his plight.

29

Sybil woke the next day with pins and needles in her arm where it had hung down on the side of the bed consoling a distraught puppy. She looked down at him in his basket. He was curled in a tight circle. 'Poor baby, it was the first night without his mother.' William was not keen about having animals in the bedroom. She even considered sleeping in the kitchen next to the puppy's basket.

'You have to be strict with him and start as you mean to go on!' William insisted, turning over and shielding his ears under the blanket. After about an hour or more being strict with a defenceless puppy, William gave in and went to the kitchen. Sybil followed and was relieved to see him pick Duke up in his arms like a baby and march for the door. 'Bring his basket!' he yelled. 'I suppose if he's going to guard us he'd better sleep next to you in the bedroom.' Without ceremony he plonked the puppy down on Sybil's side of the bed and climbed back under the clothes.

•••

Sybil's life was full and happy. Duke became her constant companion during the day and he looked out for William in the evenings after work. He soon learned to live with the chickens, ducks and rabbits and Sybil was pleased that he was on hand to guard the house when William was away on his mountain trips. The gun had been relegated and forgotten until one night Sybil heard rustling and faint bumps coming from the sitting room. The bedroom door was kept closed. Duke was restricted from running all over the house. She stayed motionless but the odd noises continued. She nudged William who was so startled that he jumped straight out of bed.

'Where's my gun?' he whispered moving quietly over to the wardrobe. Sybil looked at Duke. He was lying on his back with his legs in the air. Sybil was frightened but she couldn't help seeing the funny side.

'It's out there where the burglar is,' she said trying to keep a straight face.

'Duke, go see . . .' William called. The dog rushed to the door barking and William let him out. He flew round the sitting room sniffing the ground and out into the kitchen. William grabbed his gun from the desk and he and Sybil followed. The back door was open and Duke disappeared into the dark night. A glass panel had been smashed in the door. Sybil picked up the torch and followed William. They could see a figure hanging on a branch of the eucalyptus tree and Duke was jumping and barking underneath. As Sybil shone the torch on the intruder, he threw himself over the fence and started running towards the road. Duke came bounding back carrying a shoe.

'Look Sybil, he nearly caught the burglar!'

'You good boy, Duke.' Sybil put her arms round the dog.

'I'll take the shoe down to the police station tomorrow and we ought to have that tree felled. It's too easy to climb.' Sybil kept her arms round Duke. He was panting heavily and she felt her own heart beating faster than usual. What if the burglar had been carrying a gun? Her pet may have been shot! She shivered at the thought. Duke pulled away and trotted over to William who rewarded him with a deserved biscuit.

•••

Helga's brother Carl finished his training in B.A. and returned to work on the family's vineyard. His ambition to be a surveyor was halted when his Dad's health deteriorated.

'What about your mother?' Sybil asked.

'I think she wants to return to Germany. She misses her family and she thinks that medical care is better in the homeland. She's probably right but Dad doesn't want to leave us behind. I think it would cheer them up if you and William could come over to see them more often. They miss the company of young folk.' The four friends arranged a tennis tournament inviting other young people from San Juan to join them. This was successful and the older folk enjoyed watching and organising the refreshments.

Life was beginning to change on all fronts. The work on the line and bridges in the Andes was nearly complete and the only work to be done in the future would be maintenance. William was offered a post in B.A.

'I don't think I can stick being inside all the time,' he told Sybil. 'There is an alternative though. You remember Stephen? He and I are considering starting our own business. He has been importing tractors and I am trying to sell them. I think I may have sold one to that farmer on the main road. Sybil listened quietly. She was not a fan of William's friend and she felt worried.

'There is such a demand for agricultural machinery. Just imagine what we could sell all over the country! You know what it's like on the estancias. Mechanical harvesters and other machines could boost their productivity. There is even a small rotavator that will fit between the vines. This would make life easier for people like the Schroders!'

'If a machine does the work, the villagers and people like Carlo will lose their jobs.'

'I know that,' William answered, 'but I don't see how you can stop progress. Things change and I suppose someone always has to suffer.' Sybil pictured in her mind old Carlo and his son Carlito. Generations of that family had worked in the vineyards. What would happen to the manual workers? William became obsessed with his new venture. Stephen was luring him on with promises of fame and fortune. He came round to the house most evenings and Sybil felt as if she was an outsider in her own home. They bent over sheets of figures and maps of different areas and the only time she was acknowledged was when she offered them tea or coffee. Later at night it became whisky or brandy.

'It's only a nightcap.' Sybil worried about William's liaison with Stephen and when she was alone with him she asked: 'How can you manage to do both jobs?'

'If we start to succeed I shall leave the railway,' he announced. Sybil held her breath.

'I thought you loved your work,' she murmured.

'I do, but this is a chance to make a fortune. You do understand Sybil?'

'Yes, but nothing is certain, the outcome might be the opposite and you'll be left without a job.' William went off in a huff.

'Come on Duke, let's go for a walk.'

After this altercation, Stephen and William met at the local bar and none of their plans were discussed at home. Often, William returned worse for wear late at night. Sybil's frustration increased and she decided to have a break and visit Ethel in B.A. She knew she could confide in her friend. After recounting all she knew about William's project she turned to Ethel.

'And on top of all this I think I may be pregnant!'

'Darling, that's wonderful,' she walked over and hugged Sybil.

'Think yourself lucky; Jack and I have been trying for a baby for ages!'

'You must have sorted out your problem then?' Sybil remembered how unhappy Ethel had been on their first visit after the wedding.

'Yes, we're fine now with our own apartment and the doctor says we're both fit and healthy. We just need to relax and wait. So was William pleased?'

'I haven't told him yet,' Sybil admitted. 'He's too tied up with this new company and he's out a lot and I wanted to make sure before I say anything.'

'You can see my doctor when you're here if you like. Dr. Elms is quite a sweetie.' Ethel arranged everything and that evening they talked more about William and his plans.

'The problem is that they are doing well. Stephen does the importing bit and William is good at the selling side. Stephen's father has been helping with contacts. We have managed to save quite a bit. William says we'll be able to afford our own property in a year or two. But we see so little of each other.' Sybil sighed.

'Perhaps you have to make that sacrifice if you want to be rich!'

'I was happy as we were before.'

The visit to the doctor was kept secret. Sybil was thrilled when her suspicion was confirmed. The baby was due in the summer. She promised to tell William when she arrived home. Ethel arranged a few outings and they went round to see the Church family for lunch one day. Mrs. Church hugged Sybil.

'Sybil, you look lovely. The mountain air must agree with you. I hear you have a dog now.'

'He's called Duke and he's a wonderful companion.' She enjoyed being back with her friends but the time went too quickly. William was pleased to see her. 'I've missed you darling. We seem to have sorted out the company. Stephen has a small office in San Juan and he hopes to open a second one in Mendoza. I shall have more time in the evenings and we can start going out again. I've missed our outings.'

'I have some news.' Sybil walked over to him. 'Let's sit here on the sofa. I'm going to have a baby!'

'What did you say?' William enquired, nervously clasping his hands.

'I'm pregnant and the baby should arrive in the summer.'

William leaned over and pulled Sybil into his arms. 'Are you sure? Did you know before you went away?'

'I had my suspicions and when I mentioned it to Ethel she arranged for me to see her doctor. He confirmed it and gave me a few tips. He also said I should contact my own doctor when I arrived home.' William kissed her tenderly. He was beaming at her. 'I wonder if it's a boy or a girl?'

'A healthy baby is all I want,'

'I suppose most Dads want a son.' William looked sheepish as he grinned at her.

'You have to accept what you're given.' Sybil was firm in her reply. 'We don't want to end up like the Crawfords. Poor Sophie only had boys and she desperately wanted a girl.'

'Perhaps one of each is the ideal!' William laughed. 'Now you'll have to take it easy, Sybil. No more digging in the garden and you ought to see the doctor as soon as possible.'

They ate together that evening and listened to some of their favourite records. Sybil felt happy again. In the back of her mind she still worried about the possibility of William leaving the railway. With the baby coming she felt more vulnerable than ever. Towards the end of the week, Sybil arranged to meet Helga for lunch. Ethel had warned her about facilities at provincial hospitals and she wanted to be reassured by her friend, who was now Assistant Matron, that everything would be safe at the San Juan local hospital.

'What wonderful news Sybil! Of course I'll be there for you. It's a shame your mother is such a long way away.'

'The doctor in B.A. said it would be a June baby. I'm really nervous. William is going to fuss so much, remember what he was like when I caught Diphtheria?'

'I think you ought to register with Dr. Waisgluz. He's only down the road and William will be pleased if he is looking after you.'

Sybil followed all the instructions. She was not sick in the mornings, it was in the evenings she felt rotten. Duke kept her company when she went to bed early. It was a relief when this stage of her pregnancy was over. Feeling the baby move for the first time was a delight. She couldn't wait to tell William. 'Look William, put your hand on my tummy, the baby is moving'. He did so and was thrilled and excited.

'He kicked me,' he laughed.

'It may not be a boy . . . I told you not to make your mind up.'

'A girl wouldn't kick like that. I've not made my mind up but I suppose I could teach a girl card tricks and she may play the piano like Mother.' Sybil fell silent. She certainly didn't want a girl like William's mother!

Her weekly visits to the doctor went well except for him insisting that she should wear an abdominal binder. It had buttons down the front and felt really uncomfortable. Helga told her not to wear it all the time if it felt so awful.

'I suppose it is to support your back' she tried to explain.

As the last weeks of May passed by William and Sybil checked through all the items they required for the baby.

'I love the cot you've made William. You are accomplished with your woodwork. It was diplomatic to paint it cream and I like the transfers of teddy bears and flowers.'

'Stephen liked it. He thought we could go in for selling cots, if I made them all!'

'That's all he thinks of,' Sybil replied. 'I'm tired now and my ankles are swollen again'.

'Go on then, off to bed. I'll ask Catarina to bring you some supper on a tray.'

Sybil lay on the bed feeling rather low. I wish my mother could be here. The baby is so quiet tonight.

30

During the last few weeks of her pregnancy Sybil felt lonely. Ethel was not coming up until after the birth and Helga was busy at the hospital. All the extra duties as assistant matron meant that she was unable to have time off in the evenings. When she did have free time she drove home to see her father. His health had deteriorated and the doctors in San Juan advised him to seek medical attention in the capital.

'My dad is so stubborn. He doesn't want to leave the vineyard and my mother just cries every time I see her.'

'What about Carl, can't he persuade him?'

'He has tried but he's out most of the day in the vineyard. That leaves mother on her own with Dad and the servants. He is a difficult patient and doesn't like being told what to do.'

Later on Sybil complained to William: 'Each day becomes longer and I feel so uncomfortable,' she grumbled.

'It must be awful. Have you written home? You may not have time when the baby arrives.' When she was alone again, Sybil sat at the desk that William had spent hours refurbishing. She placed her hands on the slats and rested them there for a while on the smooth wood. 'I'm so far away from my family,' she pondered. She tried to remember and conjure up Polly's face. She probably looks quite different now. Her sister always sent photos of the rest of the family but never one of herself.

Grace wants to be a teacher. She looks a serious young

girl in her photo. Millie's married and I missed the wedding. Jason is a father with one daughter. Sybil felt isolated, left out in the cold. She pulled herself together. I wanted to travel and here I am out in the wilds feeling sorry for myself. She turned the key and gently pushed. As if by magic the whole top bent and disappeared into the upper part of the desk. Sybil never tired of seeing this wonder of carpentry and design. Inside there were rows of small drawers and shelves. In the centre the wide shelf held the writing paper, sometimes blue but mostly white. On the flat surface was an exquisite piece of onyx in green and brown tones. It was carved into an oval shape with two inkwells, both with swivel lids. One held black ink and the other red. The larger well in the centre was designed for nibs and the nib holders lay in the four indentations. Sybil could see her holder sitting in the fourth row. William's writing pens were neatly stacked in the first three rows.

Sybil smiled to herself. William is so tidy! She remembered her father and his desk and how she was allowed to sit in his study when she was a child. Enough! She leant across the desk to take a sheet of white paper and with her favourite fine nib she began to write . . .

My dearest mother,

It is only a week or two before your eldest daughter becomes a mother herself and I can't help saying that I feel apprehensive and quite frightened. I do wish you were here! William has taken time off from work and is excited about becoming a father. He's very caring and will do anything to please me but it isn't the same as having my mother close by. There are so many things that I want to ask you and I know that this letter will take a month to reach Bath, so the baby will be here before you receive this note.

My friend Ethel has worried me somewhat. She tried to persuade me to have the baby in Buenos Aires because she feels that I am not receiving the attention that I need in San Juan. She says it is too provincial and that the hospital in B.A. has better facilities. There have been one or two instances where patients have had to be rushed to the capital for special treatment. On the other hand, women seem to be having babies all the time without any problems. I hope you can understand my dilemma.

Please tell Polly that I shall write as soon as I can with baby news. I hope Millie is happy in London. She did so want to travel the world. Best wishes to the boys,

I love you very much.

Your affectionate daughter,

Sybil

She reread the letter, folded it carefully and slowly put it in the envelope. She could feel tears prickling her eyes.

'Lunch is ready.' called William. Sybil struggled to rise from the chair. She peered at herself in the mirror. Even my face looks fat, she thought. Eating suddenly became unpleasant and as for sleeping: that was virtually impossible. Sybil tossed and turned. She was so uncomfortable – the lump seemed to be in the way all the time. Usually she ended sitting up in a chair or walking backwards and forwards in the sitting room. Duke seemed to understand her distress and paced up and down with her. His cold nose nuzzled her when she moaned to herself.

'There is not much room for the baby to kick. He or she is almost ready to come into the world.' Dr. Waisgluz explained. 'Do you have everything ready?'

'Yes, we've been ready for weeks,' William replied.

'I think to be on the safe side I shall send the Senora to the hospital. Matron is arranging a spare bed.' William could hardly contain himself.

'She is alright, isn't she?' he kept saying to the doctor. Sybil knew William would panic. She was feeling tired after so many sleepless nights. On reaching the hospital, she was pleased to find herself in a clean comfortable bed and fell asleep almost immediately.

Next morning she woke to find herself being examined by a young doctor. The stethoscope felt cold on her stomach. A discussion was taking place with matron and several other men in white coats.

'Is the baby all right?' asked Sybil. She could see William outside walking up and down.

'We are a little worried about the heartbeat. It seems faint but this may be due to the position of the baby. They do take up weird postures when they're about to be born.' William was allowed in to see her and Sybil held on to his hand.

'I'll never forgive myself if something happens to you,' he said grimly. 'I'm staying here all night. I'm not leaving you on your own.' Sybil's tiredness continued. She slept off and on. Then she suddenly woke up to find that she was wet. The sheet was a green colour and she began to feel sick. Suddenly the pains started and she was rushed to the delivery room. She could only remember being told to push. The pain was excruciating and she tried to do as she was told but a mask suddenly covered her face and she drifted away into a dark place. Eventually when she did wake up, there appeared to be a mist in the room. She was alone. 'Where am I?' she cried. A nurse came to her bed and offered her water. She took a sip. Her throat was so dry and the taste in her mouth was sour. The nurse rang the bell and in a few minutes the matron was at her side. 'Where is my baby?' Sybil cried.

'Calm now, calm – you are weak senora. I am very sorry I have bad news. Your baby boy did not survive the birth. We tried everything to resuscitate him but he was dead on arrival. We are not sure what happened. I am so sorry . . .Sybil felt blood rushing to her head. She thrashed her arms above the covers and began to scream.

'No, no!' she yelled. 'It can't be! Where is my husband?'

'He is sitting outside. It's been a terrible shock for him. Your friend Helga is with him. I'll ask him to come in to see you.'

William entered the room and Helga guided him to Sybil's side, then left. William looked grey and worn out.

His eyes were red from crying.

He sat on the chair by the bed and took Sybil's trembling hand.

'I've seen him,' he stuttered. 'A perfect little boy – I called him Henry.'

He covered his eyes with his hands and shook with emotion.

'I want to see him.' Sybil pushed William and tried to rise.

'You can't get up, Sybil. You've lost a lot of blood. They will bring him for you to hold.' A nurse came in carrying a baby wrapped in a shawl. Sybil could see his black curly hair. The nurse passed him to her and Sybil gently unfolded the shawl. His curls were just like William's, but his face and small body, though perfectly formed, were grey and cold. She covered him with the shawl held him tight to her body and wept. William put one arm round the baby and tried to hold Sybil with the other. They remained motionless in a world of sorrow.

31

As the light began to fade in the room the door opened and a person in a white coat entered and walked towards the bed. 'I am sorry I have to take the body to the mortuary. The padre will be here to talk to you.' William reluctantly passed his baby son to the man. Sybil clung to the little hand as long as possible.

'We don't need to speak to anyone,' William murmured. His head dropped down to his chest. Sybil turned away from him sobbing into the pillow.

'Why has this happened to us?' There was no answer.

The door opened again and a grey-haired man dressed in long black robes entered. He was tall but somehow he managed to bend over to take Sybil's hand. Then he reached for William's hand and with his cupped palms he held them together. He chanted in a sweet delicate voice that seemed to reach into Sybil's very soul. William remained calm and allowed his hand to stay captive. Somehow the poetry of the human voice captured the couple's melancholy.

A nurse arrived with tea and the Padre poured three cups, adding milk and sugar. He remained silent whilst they sipped their tea.

'Your dear son has to be buried, my friends. Do you have a Church?'

'No sir, Sybil and I do not go to church. We used to believe in God, but now I don't know what to believe.'

'There is a small church in the countryside near to my friend's vineyard. Perhaps we can bury Henry in view of the beautiful hills with the Andes in the background.' Sybil sobbed. 'Even if we go back to Buenos Aires, I think he should remain here where he was born.' William remained silent.

'That seems a good idea, Senor?' The pastor questioned.

'Yes, my wife can decide, I must have some fresh air.' He stood up and left the room.

Sybil's hands went up to her eyes and she began sobbing again.

'It is very hard for you, my child. You are weak and need to recover.' He held a small frame in his hand, it was a double picture and he arranged it on the night table next to Sybil. For a moment he placed his hand on her head and said a short prayer. She glanced at the picture frame and recognised the Virgin Mary with baby Jesus and on the right was Jesus on the cross. She pressed the handkerchief to her eyes.

'I am going to find your husband now and we shall arrange the funeral.'

Sybil stared at the two small paintings until they became imprinted in her mind and she quietly fell asleep.

On the day of the funeral Sybil was allowed to go with Helga. She was still weak from the birth. The church was in the centre of the village and some of the peones from the vineyard turned up to pay their respects. William and Carl carried the small white coffin. A wreath of blue flowers was placed on the lid. Sybil felt faint and Helga made her sit in one of the pews.

'Why has this happened to us?' she said out loud to Helga.

'I don't know my love,' she answered with tears in her eyes.

•••

Sybil remained in hospital for two more weeks. 'You must make an effort, Sybil,' Helga pleaded. 'William needs you.'

'He doesn't show it much,' Sybil whimpered. 'I haven't seen him since the funeral.'

'William's answer is to immerse himself in work but he's just as upset as you are and he spends most of his time in Mendoza working with Stephen.'

'I don't care if I recover or not. I feel there is nothing to go home for – I'm so miserable.'

'Well, you have to pull yourself together,' Helga roared in her matron-like voice. 'I'm fed up of checking all your animals. I'm playing with Duke. He misses you both. Then poor Catarina is trying her hardest to keep the chickens fed and tending your flowerbeds and then you have the cheek to say there is nothing left for you at home. You are lucky to have all those things.

'I hear the message! I will try to recover.'

'You can start by drinking your milk and eat your meals when they're brought to you.'

Sybil held out her hand to her friend, 'I am sorry, Helga.'

William came to the hospital when she was discharged. They decided to walk home slowly stopping to have a coffee at their local shop.

'We have to face everyone and hopefully people will be kind and soon forget what has happened to us.' He took her arm. Duke was in the garden eager to greet them as they came through the gate. Sybil cuddled him and Catarina was there with the kettle boiling. 'Welcome home Senora?'

Sybil was pleased to be home but things were not the same anymore. William was withdrawn. His bubbly personality and his enthusiasm for the future had ceased. Instead he was sombre and negative. One night he said: 'I shall never put you through anything like that again. We are not meant to be parents.'

Sybil could not believe this outburst, just when she herself was beginning to pick up the threads of her life again.

'I don't know what you mean William. Fate has delivered a blow but I don't see why we can't try again for a baby? Ethel has invited me down to B.A for a short holiday. She thinks it would be good for me to go to the seaside and she says she can arrange a visit to Mar del Plata for a week. Perhaps you'll feel differently when I come back?' William walked out of the house with Duke following him.

The break in B.A. and the few days at the seaside were a welcome tonic for Sybil. She looked up her old friends Robert and Evelyn. They invited her out to the theatre. Then she made the trip out to Hurlingham to see Sophie. Mr. Crawford was away on the estancia and Sybil learned that the Hurlingham house was a concession for his wife. She was able to spend time there whenever she liked. 'Sybil, how lovely to see you again! This is my new home. The children are away. Esme is still in Switzerland and the others are shipped to boarding school as soon as they're old enough. You know what Sam's like?'

'I suppose you see them in the holidays?' Sybil asked. She was taken aback by the marked difference in Sophie's appearance. Gone was the slim elegant figure dressed in the latest Parisian styles. In her place was a chubbier bohemian sort of character. She was wearing an artist's smock over a long black cotton skirt.

'Gustav persuaded me to take up oil painting again and Sam allowed him to set up a studio for me in the attic. You must come up and see my work when I've finished showing you the garden.'

They climbed the stairs to the studio and Sybil was astonished to see the number of paintings hanging on the wall.

'What do you think, do you like them?'

'I find it hard to believe that you have produced these works of art. I really like the paintings that you've done of the *peones* on the estancia. And the horse paintings are outstanding. I love the one of *Porota.* The cityscapes are just as good. You really are talented.'

'Gustav has sold quite a few for me. He takes them back to Switzerland when he goes home. He has a shop in *calle* Florida and I often go there to help him.'

On the way back to town on the train Sybil thought about William and hoped he was trying to return to some kind of normality. Sophie, with all her unhappiness, had managed to pull through and was enjoying life again. In Mar del Plata, Sybil walked with Ethel round the harbour where the fish were landed every day. There were sea lions near the fishing boats and on the rocks nearby. Each animal was trying to pick the best spot in which to stretch out and enjoy the sun. 'Let's try to go closer,' Ethel suggested. Some of the sea lions were crossing the road to sandy areas and drivers were hooting at them. It was chaotic for a time. Then a nasty whiff wafted across their path. It was 'a sort of fishy-come-flabby bodies' scent.

'Ugh, that's a vile smell,' said Sybil. 'I'm turning back.'

When they returned to B.A. Sybil spent the day with old Mrs. Church.

'You're like a second mother to me.' The old lady put her arms round her and drew her into the kitchen where they sat together at the table.

'How is Billy?' she asked.

'He seems to be well. He just works all the time.' Sybil could feel tears gathering as she tried to confide her thoughts to her dear friend.

'He doesn't want to try for any more children. He says he can't put me through all that again.' Mrs. Church stood up and came close to Sybil.

'He's devastated. It will take time for his heart to heal. All men want a son to carry on their line and William was so near to that dream. You will have to be patient, dear. He must feel that you've deserted him. You need to go back and give him hope and comfort.'

'I want to try for a baby. I shall be twenty nine soon and the longer we leave it the more difficult it becomes.'

'It will happen in good time, my dear.' Sybil felt happier that evening when Jack and Ethel took her to the ballet at the Colon theatre. The friendliness of the company and the drama of the music made Sybil relax and she felt that it was time she returned to William in San Juan.

The moment they went through the front door of Jack and Ethel's flat they knew something was wrong. Geoff, Paul and old Mr. Church were there. Paul, the youngest son drew close to Sybil. 'We have some bad news. I don't know how bad it is but there has been a serious earthquake in the Cuyo region.'

'Not in San Juan! ' Sybil cried. 'How do you know?' she almost screamed at Paul.

'We were messing about on our wireless sets and we heard the S.O.S. I think the centre is nearer to Mendoza.'

'I must go', she said rushing into the bedroom and pulling her case out from under the bed. 'I shouldn't have left him'.

'You can't go tonight – all trains have been cancelled.'

'How can I get there? Do you think Robert would drive me in his car?'

'No, dear,' said old Mr Church. 'You will have to wait. William will send a telegram if he's safe.'

'He may be in Mendoza at Stephen's office. I can't bear it. She crumpled down into a chair, her face distorted with grief. Ethel went to her side to comfort her.

'Billy is a survivor, I'm sure he'll be in touch as soon as he can. Come along I'll sit with you in your room.' Sybil could hear the men talking.

'It's centred east of Aconcagua. It could be anywhere in Cuyo. The scale is over seven. That means considerable damage if it struck a village or town.'

Ethel closed the bedroom door and Sybil lay on the bed. She tried to keep calm.

'William and I went to see Aconcagua. It is so majestic. I think he said it was nearly twenty three thousand feet high. You know what he's like with figures'. She turned away trying to hide her tears. The nightmare continued with Sybil drifting in and out of sleep. In the morning she woke with a terrible headache. Paul came round early.

'I've been twisting knobs and listening all night for news. There have been a few casualties out in the countryside but the main towns have only been shaken. The train service is starting again this afternoon. There is no news from William, but I expect it was just a tremor in San Juan.'

Sybil packed her belongings ready for her trip home. Jack arranged to accompany her to the station. The journey seemed to take longer than usual and other passengers like Sybil, were worried about their relations. No one seemed to know exactly where the most damage had occurred.

'Some think that over one hundred people have died,' said one man, mopping his brow with a handkerchief.'

'The Zond wind is hampering the rescue blowing dust everywhere'. Sybil knew what the wind was like – it was hot and dry and caused people to cough when it blew over fields and carried the fine dust into built-up-areas.

'San Juan was lucky, only a few tremors, I think,' said one lady holding a baby in her arms.

Sybil felt less nervous as her journey reached the final stages. 'William doesn't even know I've been worried sick about him.' She thought to herself.

When she reached home Duke nearly knocked her over in his enthusiasm. William came ambling to the door and Sybil flung herself at him.

'Thank God you're safe. It's been a nightmare waiting for news. I worried about the earthquake being in San Juan.'

'We did feel it here, the lights were affected and that one hanging from the ceiling started swinging about. Duke knew something was happening. He barked and howled for a while. I could hear other dogs doing the same.'

'I wish I hadn't left you now,' Sybil said clinging on to

William's neck. He gently lifted her up and carried her to the sofa.

'I'm sorry I was so angry and difficult before you left. The break has done me good because I've had time to think things through. Stephen and I have been making lots of money and, you're right, it doesn't make one happy. I wanted a child just as much as you and though Henry was cruelly snatched from us, I think we need to try again for a baby.'

'A family of our own is what we need'. Sybil snuggled up to William and held him tightly.

Part IV
1936-1949

32

'What are you doing, Sybil?' William asked when he came in from the garden. She was sitting with her legs up on the sofa.

'I'm reading through Polly's letters. I want to be up to date with what's happening back home. This one is about the jubilee last year:

Dearest Sybil,

We have been celebrating George V's silver jubilee. I helped to organise our street party for the children. It was a hot sunny day and everyone was smiling. The school piano was pushed out into the street and I and several other teachers and even some of the parents played tunes so that the children could sing and dance . . .

Mother helped with the cooking and I noticed that her small cakes and scones disappeared quickly. It is a shame that London is so far away because Millie wanted me to go up there for the celebrations.

The streets were full of cheering people and the Royal family appeared on the balcony of Buckingham Palace. There were some delightful photographs in the newspaper of the King's granddaughters, Princess Elizabeth and Princess Margaret. They waved to the crowds and Margaret made people laugh because she was so enthusiastic.

It has been a good summer all round because Fred Perry, our tennis star, won Wimbledon. I have been reading a lot and I was pleased to hear that a company called 'Penguin' has launched books as paperbacks. They will be on sale for sixpence.

I can't wait for your return next year. Mother knits every evening. She is so excited about the baby.

Look after yourself dear sister,
with love from Polly.'

'These letters are special,' said Sybil taking great care to fold the sheets and return them to the envelope.

'I enjoy listening to you reading the news. What is that list you have there?' William asked.

'I've looked through all the letters and made a note of items of interest, such as this bit about Mars bars. There were the hunger marches in 1932 and this company brought out a new chocolate bar. Polly said that Millie tried one in London. It wasn't just a plain bar of hard chocolate but a filling covered on the top with a soft layer of toffee and then encased by mouth watering milk chocolate.'

William laughed. 'Just as well we didn't have those bars here when you were raving about chocolate. What else is on the list?'

There's the bit about Marlene Dietrich, the German star: She wore trousers with a jacket and she looked like a man in a suit. Her tie was the same colour as her nail varnish. Everyone was shocked and most women were too scared to follow the trend.'

'How awful! I bet your Millie wants to have a go!'

'Then in 1934, do you remember we tried to listen to the King giving his Christmas message to the Empire? We managed to hear part of the speech on your new wireless but it kept fading and you were annoyed.'

'Didn't girls start wearing shorts at Wimbledon that year? Things are changing all the time. I'm not sure if it is for the better!'

'I'm really excited about our trip. I shall be able to meet all my nephews and nieces. Jason's children are grown up and Millie has two boys. Polly says that they're always in trouble and mother has to be very strict with them when they come to stay. Last time they were down in Gran's coalmine digging the coal and pretending to sell it by the bag. You can imagine the mess!'

'It will be great to see them all again,' William agreed.

●●●

William's new boss insisted that he should return to B.A. in June to help with the re-organisation of the drawing office. A rota was to be compiled for the maintenance of the track in the San Juan district. Stephen was becoming impatient.

'Why don't you leave?' he asked. 'You're very slow making your mind up.'

'Sybil isn't keen,' he explained. 'I don't want to upset her at present with the baby on the way. We're going to England in April and my boss wants me back in June. I shall be here in B.A. for three months, the baby is due in October so hopefully, if all goes well, we should be back here as a family for Christmas.'

His friend was disgruntled with his lack of commitment but William felt that Sybil and the baby were his main concern. His job should take second place.

●●●

Sybil and William made a pact about discussing the future.

'I don't want to tempt fate this time. Let's not collect lots of baby stuff. You can always dash out to buy things later.'

William agreed. 'I do want to decide what to do about Stephen. He's been pressing me about leaving the railway and working with him in Mendoza. I'm not sure that I want to do that now. My new boss appears to like me and he has plans for the offices.'

'It would be good to move back to Buenos Aires and perhaps live in one of the suburbs,' Sybil replied. She couldn't help thinking that facilities would be better for the baby in the city, especially the hospitals and schools, but she didn't mention this to William. She wanted him to make his own decision about his career.

The ship arrived in Harwich. They anchored in the river. Launches carried the passengers to the landing area and the luggage was taken to the Customs House. William fussed around looking for their trunk and Sybil stood with the cases. She was overjoyed when they walked out of the restricted area to find her brothers waiting.

'Hey Sybil, we're over here!' She hardly recognised Jerry and Chris. They both looked dashing in their flat caps and tweed jackets. Chris lifted Sybil off her feet and kissed her and passed her on to Jerry.

'You look wonderful, sis!' They turned to welcome William with handshakes and slaps on the back.

'Mother and Polly are preparing all sorts of feasts for your return.'

'Where's Jason?' Sybil asked.

'He couldn't have any time off and he's had a row with Mother. He and Jennie have moved to the other side of Bath. We don't see them that often.'

The three men discussed motorbikes and cars and Sybil found that she was dozing off with the rhythm of the wheels. She woke with a jolt when they stopped at the front door. Mother and Polly came running out to greet them. Smiles and tears showed their feelings of relief and happiness.

'Come on in, William. How lovely to see you both again! The boys will bring the luggage.' Mother held on to William's arm as they walked up the path to the front door. Sybil walked with Polly and felt as if she was going back in time. Her dear sister wore the same strict styles, tweed skirt, warm shirt and cardigan. At her neck she wore the opaque glass brooch that Sybil had given her for one of her birthdays. Inside the house nothing had changed. The heavy mahogany furniture and the comfortable upholstered armchairs were still there. The only new piece was the beautiful piano in the corner.

'It's French style,' her mother explained. Sybil admired the intricate carvings with the satin material in a misty pink as a background. The instrument stood out in the overcrowded room.

'That's mother's new piano. I'm allowed to play it at parties and I have to practise every day if I can.' Polly told them. Grace was similar in height to Polly and she wore the same style of clothes. How different it was in Buenos Aires where the women looked smart wearing the latest fashions. Sybil felt that she liked the homely clothes that her family wore. They look comfortable.

When she talked to William about this later, he said: 'I didn't notice they looked any different. You are a snob Sybil. Anyway, Buenos Aires is the capital. I expect London is just as fashionable.'

On occasions they went into town on the bus and Penny, Chris's young daughter, liked keeping them company.

'I see you're a learner, Uncle William?'

'What do you mean dear?'

'You have large capital Ls on your luggage'. William laughed.

'That's because our surname is Lawson,' he explained. 'It's a system they use on ships. All you have to do is search for cases and trunks under the letter L. If your surname is Smith you have to look under S.' William was impressed by the child's keen observation. He turned to the bus conductor who was waiting to take the fares.

'Two adults and one half to the Guildhall, please:' William passed a note to the man.

'Haven't you got the right money gov?' he moaned. Before William could answer, Penny called in a loud voice:

'Uncle William I must pay my own fare!' The five year old rummaged in her handbag for change.

'Thank you Miss! It always helps to have the right money.'

Sybil looked at William and laughed. 'If we have a girl, she'll probably boss you about.'

'I do hope you have a girl, Auntie Sybil. Auntie Millie and Uncle Jerry have boys and they're always fighting. We never see Uncle Jason – he has a girl but she's older than me.' The child looked dejected so Sybil put her arm round her.

'We shall have to see what we can do and you never know you may have your own sister one day.'

Sybil became Dr. Parker's patient. She visited him in his surgery every week and he advised her to have the baby in a nursing home.

'Here is a list of suitable places. If you can afford it I advise you to take a private room. The place at the top of the list is where I am the doctor on call. I know the staff and the matron are well organised and capable. Also the home is near to the main hospital if there should be any complications. You're a healthy young woman Sybil. I'm sure all will be fine.'

William decided that it would be wise to visit some of the homes on the list.

'I want you to have the best, Sybil!'

'I know you do, darling but I feel happy with Dr. Parker looking after me.'

Sybil became anxious when the end of May arrived and it was time for William to return to B.A. 'I do wish you could stay. You promise you'll be back in October?'

'I don't want to miss out on that occasion.' Sybil turned away clasping her hands together, but William turned her round and pulled her close to him.

'I know it's difficult to forget about the last time and sweet Henry. We have to move on and have faith in the future.

This time you have your mother and sisters with you. I shall be back in time.' He kissed her gently.

33

Even though she missed William, Sybil felt relaxed and happy. The whole family rallied round to keep her amused and entertained. William returned the first week in October. Dr Parker arranged for her to be admitted to the nursing home.

'It's almost as if you've waited for William to return before having the baby.' Mother smiled. Nancy was born at ten thirty weighing seven and half pounds. William was summoned immediately to see a perfect baby girl with tight black curls and a hearty cry. He held her in his arms smiling like a child. Tears of joy streamed down Sybil's face.

'We're a family at last!'

●●●

Mother and baby spent a week at the nursing home. When they were allowed home, flowers and presents awaited Sybil. There were even telegrams from Argentina from Ethel and other friends. But there was no time to relax. Nancy was a demanding baby with a good set of lungs.

'I wish I had my Al Jolson records. His singing might keep her quiet.' William complained.

'Bring her into the sitting room,' suggested Polly. 'I'll play the piano for her.'

'You're a genius!' William answered. 'I think she's trying to sing instead of crying.' Polly and Sybil laughed.

'I bet she's singing opera,' they chuckled.

The thought of opera reminded Sybil of William's

mother and father. They really ought to make time for a visit to Manchester.

'Can we manage a trip up to see your parents before we sail back to Argentina?' Sybil asked. 'Or perhaps it would be easier if they came here. There is so much to take for the baby.'

'I think that's out of the question. Dad has been poorly and it's a long journey. You know what mother's like?'

'Do we have to go back before Christmas?' Sybil asked.

'Perhaps we could leave it until the New Year . . . I've told Stephen that I'm remaining with the railway. I could try to ask for an extension to include Christmas.

'That would give us more time to arrange a visit up north.'

I haven't had time to give you the good news: I found a house for us in a place called Caseros. It's on the main line so we can reach town easily on the train.'

'What's the house like?' Sybil enquired feeling rather dubious. She remembered her disappointment when she saw their first home in San Juan.

'It's in a built-up area and instead of a garden it has a large tiled back yard and a roof space where you can hang clothes to dry. The previous tenants built a sitting area under a colourful tarpaulin and a brick cooking space for *asados*. You will miss the chickens and ducks but you'll have Nancy to keep you busy.'

'I'm sad we had to let Duke go, but I'm sure he'll be happy with Rosario. Perhaps we can have a smaller dog when Nancy starts to walk. I do want her to love animals.'

'Rosario is caring for the poultry and has agreed to find homes for them if the next tenants decide against keeping chickens.' Sybil felt sorry about not having a garden but she reflected that it may only be for a short while and decided to wait and see. After all, she was lucky to have a beautiful baby daughter. She felt confident that creating a loving home would be easy as long as the three of them were together.

A routine was soon established and Sybil was surprised at William's enthusiasm. Whenever possible he picked the baby up and nursed her on his lap. Penny, Chris's young daughter was keen to help. 'Her curls are very tight, they're like yours uncle William,' she said as she tried brushing the baby's hair.

'Be careful, don't pull too hard or she'll start crying.'

William sent a telegram to his boss asking if they could extend their stay to cover the Christmas holiday. To their surprise he cabled back with his congratulations and suggestion that they return to B.A. in the middle of January.

'That's great! We can spend Christmas here and visit Mum and Dad early in the New Year. I forgot that in Argentina they celebrate '*Los Tres Reyes*' on the 6th January.'

Celebrating Christmas with the family was a joy. Baby Nancy was the centre of attention. As she was born in October, she received a special locket with a small opal set in gold. It was from the whole family. Frank, Millie's husband purchased the opal separately and then he and Millie chose the design. Sybil hugged her sister.

'Thank you, darling. It is so beautiful. I'm sure Nancy will treasure it!'

'You are lucky having a girl. I feel jealous. We have two boys and Frank would love to have a daughter.'

'We have no choice. William was devastated last time but he's thrilled now we have a healthy baby.'

'I agree we're lucky to have two healthy sons.' Millie smiled and turned to join in the rumpus on the floor with the boys.

Sybil missed her brother Jason. The quarrel between mother and son was difficult for Sybil to understand. 'I want to go and see Jason and Jennifer, will you come with me please William?' she asked.

'Your mother is very serious and upset about the falling out. I can't see her moving an inch.'

'Well, I'd like to hear both sides of the story.'

'Mother is a real snob,' explained Jason. 'Jennifer wanted to move to this part of Bath so that we could have our own home and be near to her parents. We'd lived with Mother all those years and when the children arrived it became rather crowded. You'd think she'd be pleased that we wanted to move into our own home.'

'What did she say then?' Sybil asked.

'She wanted us to look for a house in her district and she blamed Jennifer for taking the children away from their grandmother.'

'That sounds unfair. Perhaps it's because of her age .

She feels everyone is leaving her.'

'She still has Polly and Grace at home and the two boys live quite near.' William pointed out.

'I'm hoping she'll come round in time. She refuses to talk to me when I call round but my sisters always make me welcome.'

'Perhaps you ought to take the children? ' Sybil suggested. Jason changed the subject.

'Now let me look at my new niece!' He took Nancy in his arms and called Jennifer. 'Just look, isn't she beautiful?' Jennifer came in with a pot of tea, placed it on the table and reached out for the baby.

'She's a darling – you both must be very proud.' Sybil noticed the smiles and tenderness between her brother and his wife and she felt relieved to see their happiness. Later William said: 'Mother just needs more time to recover from this separation. Jason is her first child and they went through a lot together. She must miss him.'

'What about your mother then, she must miss you?'

'My mother is quite different. I don't think she's the maternal sort. Look at you Sybil: Nancy is only a few weeks old and you're a natural mother, oozing maternal feelings!'

'You're not a bad Dad,' Sybil said taking Williams hands. 'We're so lucky, darling!' The trip to Manchester was arranged and Nancy was wrapped up warm in her new shawl.

'You need to take a rug. It's much colder up north and trains can be draughty, especially if people keep opening the windows.' She was proved right because it was snowing when they reached their destination. William's father was there to meet them. He looked much older and frail.

'Hello Dad, here's Sybil and this is your granddaughter Nancy.' The old man gently pulled the shawl back. A big smile appeared on his face.

'She's just like you, Will, but much prettier!' They were surprised when they reached the house and were ushered into the parlour where a fire was burning brightly. William's mother was all smiles. She kissed her son and turned to Sybil, giving her a quick kiss on the cheek.

'Are you holding the baby, Henry?'

'Yes I am. Come and see her, Rosie.' Nancy began to wake up. Her arms reached up in a stretch.

'She wants me to hold her.' Sybil felt nervous and stepped forward.

'Here you are, Rosie. Take her carefully.' The old lady held Nancy gently, staring intently into her face. Nancy stared back making little bubble sounds. Then William's mother amazed them all by kissing the baby on her forehead. She turned and handed Nancy to Sybil.

'She's not frightened of me. Now Will, tell me all about your life in Argentina. You don't write that often!' Sybil fed the baby and settled her in her pram. They sat down to a roast lunch followed by a delicious apple crumble.

'I can't believe this is my Mother,' William whispered as she went out of the room to find the Christmas presents.

'You can open this one Sybil.' She passed a large parcel to her, soft and over two feet long. 'Go on then, open it!' Sybil did as she was told. She tore the paper off and there were sighs of approval.

'It's a Teddy bear, gold fur with black glass eyes. Thank you so much, Mother'. Sybil was so pleased that she went over and kissed her mother-in- law.

'Now you open yours, William.' It was easy to see that his parcel held a book.

'It's *The Big Christmas Wonder Book* edited by John Crossland and J.Parrish, printed by Oldham Press, London.' Sybil took the book from William and read the inscription: *Manchester, England. To my Grandaughter Nancy Stella Rose. Xmas 1936, from her Grandad Lawson and Grandma Lawson.'*

'It truly is a wonder book. It says here that it includes over one hundred and fifty stories and poems by favourite children's authors.' Sybil thanked them again.

'I'm sure Nancy will treasure these gifts.'

On the way back to Bath on the train, William questioned his mother's change of attitude. 'There must be an ulterior motive: I can't believe she's changed that much.'

'She did seem to be pleased about everything. I was sorry to see your father looking so thin. Did he say anything to you about his health?'

'No, he just wanted me to promise that I would look after Mother when he died. I suppose he was trying to tell me something.'

'Oh William didn't you ask more when he said that?'

'No, I think Mother came in and he changed the subject.'

Sybil despaired of William on occasions like this. He never seemed to cotton on to serious matters.

'I don't know what we can do when we're half way round the world in Argentina.'

•••

Back home in Bath, William and Sybil started to plan their trip back to Buenos Aires. As usual William made lists for everything. 'Shall I make a list of people you want to visit before we leave?'

'Yes please. I want to see the doctor about Nancy's diet. Millie says I ought to stock up with tinned rice pudding and foods that I shall need when Nancy has to be weaned on to solids'.

'That sounds bleak' said William. 'I suppose she can't live on milk for the rest of her life.'

'She may need to have bottles if my milk dries up.'

'I don't want to know about that Sybil, just talk to your mother about it.' He made a quick exit to the garden. Sybil chuckled to herself. She knew exactly how to make him disappear when he became obsessed with his lists.

Polly came in carrying Nancy's present. 'Did you notice that in this book there is a colour souvenir of the coronation of King Edward VIII? It never took place. He abdicated last year. They must have published it before and this must be one of the early editions.'

'Let me have a look.' William took the book and studied the central pictures. 'It shows portraits of the seven previous kings called Edward. There's a double page showing the coronation procession and the king in the state coach, the fancy gold one.

'Well, it can't be real. They must be an artist's impression of the coronation that never was.' Polly explained.

'The book may be valuable one day – I expect they had to delete the pages once Edward left for France with Wallis.'

'The bear is a good present too,' Chris pointed out. 'He's a Merrythought toy, made in England. It says he's hygienic!' They all laughed. Sybil felt a twinge of sadness. This time, she loved being with her family and it was going to be harder to leave them. William worried her with talk of Hitler and the next war.

'Things are bad in Germany. Many people, especially Jews, are trying to leave the country. Hitler is shouting at rallies about the superior race. I'm glad we're going back to Argentina for Nancy's sake.' He never seemed to care how she felt about leaving her family behind. But that was just William and she was pleased that at least he was thinking about keeping their daughter safe.

34

The train drew into the station. 'Caseros! ' yelled the guard.

'I'll take Nancy. You organise the cases, William.' Sybil tried to be patient as she waited for the train to come to a standstill. She covered Nancy's face with the shawl. The hissing of the steam decreased and finally the carriage came to a sudden halt. A porter rushed to their aid and William handed the cases to him before clambering down the steps to the platform. He turned to help Sybil with the baby.

'We have a trunk in the luggage compartment. The name is Lawson.' William pointed to the rear of the train where the guard was throwing parcels and trunks out of the carriage. There were chickens in pens and even a cat in a basket placed on the ground. People were milling round to collect their belongings.

'I hope Nancy's trunk is safe!'

'You wanted to bring it with us, Sybil. I've put a strong lock on it. It should be secure. I told you the luggage is safer on the freight train.'

'I know, you're probably right.'

'Taxi!' yelled the porter as he pushed the trolley with the luggage.

Sybil held on to Nancy as she glanced out of the window. The ride was bumpy. 'Cobbles,' William explained. 'This is the main road but when we turn into the side streets the ride is smoother.'

'I like the trees, are they jacarandas?'

'I'm not sure, when I saw them before they were covered with bunches of blue flowers. I chose Caseros because of the avenues of trees and they make it seem as if we're still in the countryside.'

'I expect they're jacarandas. Sometimes when you stand under the flowering tree and look up at the sky, the flowers appear to have a purple tinge.

They turned the corner and came to a stop outside a small building. The pavement was wide with a colourful pattern. The bungalow looked like a house because it had a brick wall along the front of the flat roof. This made it appear taller.

'It looks like a balcony, but I suppose that's the roof garden.'

'The wall is wide and when I came to view the house the people had geraniums in boxes along the top.'

The front door opened and a young woman came out carrying a baby on her back.

'*Buenas tardes*,' she came forward to greet them.

'This is Senora Merlisa. Her husband is the landlord and they live next door. She doesn't speak English, only a few words.' Sybil went forward and peeped at her sleeping baby.

'She's called Negrita, mainly because of her black hair. She's three months old. My other children are grown up. This one was a mistake!'

Sybil allowed her to look at Nancy who was beginning to wake up.

'Oh Senora, she is *preciosa*!'

'Come on in Sybil.' William took the key and thanked the woman for the groceries.

'I bought some ice for the chest so you can store the baby food. My husband will be home soon so I must go. If you need anything please ask.'

When they were on their own William was excited about showing Sybil around their new home. 'I'll just give Nancy her bottle and then I can put her down.'

'She can come round to see the house and I have a special surprise!'

William was enthusiastic as usual. 'You couldn't help yourself could you?' Sybil grinned when she saw the wooden cradle that William had built.

'Jack painted it pink when he knew it was a girl and Ethel provided the sheets and lace quilt.'

'It's lovely, let's see if she fits.' Nancy kicked and started screaming.

'I told you she's hungry!'

The dining room extended across the width of the house and the kitchen was off to the right. 'These double doors in the dining room open on to the patio and can be left open in the summer. There are two bedrooms with adjoining doors so when Nancy is old enough she'll be able to have her own room. The sitting room is small but there is a fireplace in case of cold weather. We can also use the room as a study.'

'I love it William. It's so compact and the roof area is perfect for pot plants and we can have our own *asados* up there in the summer.' Sybil tried to hide her disappointment at the lack of a garden. She knew that they would be moving again in the future when Nancy was old enough to attend school.

Myrna, the lady next door was kind and helpful. 'Our babies are the same age. They will be able to play together.' William was not too keen on this idea.

'They're Italian you know. Their ways are so different. When I came to look round the house, she was just feeding the baby in front of everyone. I felt embarrassed, but her husband didn't seem to mind.'

'Don't be so stuffy, William. The women in San Juan used to feed their babies sitting on the pavement.'

'Well, I'm glad you're bottle-feeding now. I've got to start work again on Monday and I expect to be sent up to San Juan for a few days. I still have to keep an eye on the rails. They need to be maintained properly and I want to establish exactly what my duties are in the new job. I hate leaving so soon.'

'We shall be fine, won't we, Nancy? We shall miss Daddy though!'

Whilst William was away, Sybil learned a lot about babies from Myrna including all the little tricks about feeding, burping and keeping baby happy and clean. 'I feel safe with you next door,' Sybil confided.

'You must miss your family and English friends? I know a dear couple, Mr. and Mrs. Carter. They are English and live quite near and perhaps you would like to meet them? My husband did some building work for them and my sister goes once a week to clean their house.'

'I would like to meet them, Myrna. I want Nancy growing up listening to English as much as possible. She will pick up Spanish easily.'

Mr. and Mrs. Carter lived in an old style colonial house with an open veranda along the front. The basic structure of the extension was in black wrought iron with ornate columns. Baskets of flowers hung from hooks in the bays.

'Come in, dear! ' A voice called from the open door. A small figure emerged carrying a watering can. Her grey hair was tied back from her face and her eyes sparkled in the light. ' I'm Violet Carter. Bring the baby in and meet Arthur. He's probably still reading the paper.' Sybil took Nancy out of her pram and followed the small figure into a spacious hall. She opened one of the numerous doors and they entered a large sitting room. Mr. Carter was sitting by an open window that overlooked the back garden.

'This is the girl Myrna was telling us about, Arthur. She's English. What's your name dear?'

'Sybil, my surname's Lawson. William works on the railways and this is my daughter Nancy.'

'Come closer dear, let me see the baby?' Mr. Carter was sitting in a rocking chair, his legs covered by a rug. It squeaked as he rocked. His glasses were pushed to the end of his nose as he peered at Nancy. 'Typical Anglo- Saxon just like her mother,' he grunted, picked up his newspaper and went on reading. The maid came in carrying a tea tray. Mrs. Carter chatted continuously.

'I have two daughters and a son. Sonia is expecting a baby so we shall soon be grandparents.'

'God forbid!' came the voice from the rocking chair.

'Margaret is a secretary and Lewis is studying to be a doctor.' There was a loud bang in the hall.

'That's Pilkington again slamming his door. The old fool must be going deaf.'

'Don't be unkind, Arthur!' Nancy jumped when she heard the noise and started crying. Sybil tried to console her by holding her against her shoulder and patting her back.

'He's made the baby howl, pass her to me dear.' Sybil hesitated and Mrs. Carter said: 'He's alright, he's good with babies and children.' Mr. Carter stretched his arms out to take the baby and he sat her on his lap facing him. Sybil watched as Nancy screwed her eyes up and appeared to frown at the old man's face. He started rocking his chair and the baby relaxed. When he began to hum and whistle Sybil thought Nancy was trying to smile. William was sure that Nancy smiled at him but until now Sybil dismissed this and believed that the baby was just making funny faces.

When William was away she missed the company of Duke and wondered how he was doing living with Rosario. She told Myrna how she missed having a dog.

'Perhaps you can buy a small one. The girls would love to play with the animal but he will have to live with you. Eduardo hates dogs and will not have one in the house.' It was a surprise for William when he arrived home one evening and was introduced to Whiskers. 'Come and have a look on the patio! Sybil called.

'What have you and Mummy been up to?' he asked as they went through the kitchen.

'Doh,' said Nancy pointing at a bundle of white fur that

was whizzing round their legs.

'It's Whiskers.' She can't say his name yet.'

●●●

In the summer evenings William and Sybil took their chairs out on the front pavement. It was the custom for people to take the air in the early evening. The children played together. The older ones rode their bicycles in the road. It was a social time and, as it was a no through road, it was safe for children. As dusk fell, the fireflies appeared and William carried Nancy down to the railway line. Just before the end of the road there was a field where vegetables were grown and at night the whole area came alive with twinkling lights.

'Shall we catch one?' They often took a jar and it was easy to trap a firefly.

'Look Sybil, it's a small beetle. The light goes off and on and seems to come from underneath.'

'It's a shame to put them in a jar. I can let it go when Nancy falls asleep.'

William accompanied Sybil to the Carter's home and met the artist, Mr. Pilkington. Everyone called him Pilkington. He told people that he didn't have a past or a first name! 'He's a strange bird, good at cartoons and Violet likes his paintings.' William talked to Mr. Carter about the troubles in Germany. Sybil felt uneasy whenever the subject was discussed. She couldn't help thinking about her family back home. It was a relief to hear Mr. Carter warning William about the work that needed to be done in Buenos Aires.

'You're too old to go back if there is a war. There will be plenty to do here. I've heard that there are gangs causing trouble between the English and German communities.'

'I shall join up if I can even though Sybil is against it.' William whispered.

'You have a family to look after – they will never take you. My two youngest want to volunteer. Violet will try to stop them so that's going to be a disaster.' During the evening Sybil worried about William. 'What's the matter, darling? You look so serious all the time.'

'It's events back home. There is all this trouble with Germany and the Ambassador is warning all British citizens about the situation. They are calling for volunteers. War is imminent. If Germany invades Poland, Britain and France will declare war. It will not be safe to go back home and they certainly won't allow women and children to return.'

'Surely, you're too old to volunteer? Please don't go William.' Sybil could feel her heart beating rapidly. 'I can't go through all that again; we've got Nancy to worry about.'

35

Sybil was puzzled when William came home from work and went straight up to the roof garden without saying a word.

'William, Nancy is playing next door with Negrita if you wonder where she is?' There was no reply. Sybil climbed the stairs. She felt the warmth of the sun on her arms. It was the beginning of October and Nancy was nearly one.

'The Spring is my favourite season . . .' William was sitting, his elbows on the table, his face covered by his hands.

'What's the matter?'

'I just wanted a few minutes on my own. I've been to the Embassy today and Carter was right. I'm too old to fight for my country. My Dad always thought of me as a coward. My mates volunteered for the last war and I was drawing aeroplanes! Now it's too late to make amends and it's a shock when someone tells you that you're too old!' Sybil put her arm round his bent shoulders.

'I don't think you're too old, darling. You helped design the planes that played a part in our victory. I'm sure they'll find you important work to do here.' She kissed his cheek. 'I didn't want you to go. I have so many memories of loved ones leaving and never coming back. Then I had to watch the trauma of my brother fighting his way back to sanity. He never was the same again. I don't want anything like that to happen to you.' William stood up and took her in his arms.

'Perhaps the war will never start.' Sybil tried to be optimistic.

'Things have gone too far, darling. The Fascists in Italy are attacking the Jews. They will join Germany against the rest of Europe. There is even talk of Hitler invading Russia. They have found some interesting work for me to do, mainly raising money for the war effort. You and I can work together on that. We're experienced in organising fetes. You always have ingenious ideas – remember the cats at Helga's charity do?' They smiled at each other.

'I'll help whenever I can. You can do conjuring shows for children's parties. That ought to be worthwhile. Some of the women are planning knitting sessions, making warm jumpers and socks for the soldiers. The thought of trenches again makes me feel sick'

'I think planes will play a major part this time and there will be more bombing of towns and cities.' Sybil cringed thinking about her family. Polly had mentioned the plans to evacuate children from London.

'I'll go and collect Nancy. She will cheer us up.'

'Look Senora, they can nearly walk!' The babies were pulling themselves up on a stool and attempting to walk towards Myrna. They took a few steps and fell back on their bottoms. Sybil thought Nancy was about to cry but instead the two friends laughed as if it was part of a game.

'Arriba, arriba!' called Myrna and the girls crawled back to the stool and tried again.

'Daddy's upstairs, you can show him your new pets!' Nancy crawled up the stone steps, one at a time. She was cautious but learned quickly.

'Nails, da da nails!' William came to the top of the stairs and picked her up.

Sybil was pleased to see he was smiling again.

'What is she saying?'

'Snails – the chap at the market gave her a box with ten snails. We've put them in that glass tank you were keeping for fish.' Sybil laughed. William put his daughter down and held one of her hands. She pulled him towards the shady corner where the tank stood.

'Baby nail,' she pointed at a slimy creature crawling up the glass.

'Say sssssssnail, Nancy.' William repeated the word several times emphasising the long 's'. His patience impressed Sybil. By the end of the evening Nancy was pronouncing the word correctly. It was all a game to her even when she was splashing in her bath. They watched and cheered every time she said 'snail'. Sybil was so relieved that William was not leaving them to go to the war.

Sitting out on the pavement in the early evening was one of Sybil's favourite pass times. William was often late but she enjoyed Myrna's company.

'Negrita is walking well.' Sybil looked at the toddlers. They were watching the firefly. She put some grass and twigs in the jar. 'Shall we catch one for Negrita?'

They scurried around, Sybil with the butterfly net. As they walked slowly back to the chairs, each child was trying to carry a jar, Sybil noticed William standing by the front door. 'Come quickly Sybil. Can Myrna just look after the kids for a moment?' The tone of his voice frightened her.

'What's happened now?' He ushered her into the house and pulled her towards the bedroom. Nancy's cradle that had been put away in the spare room was in its old place on her side of the bed and there was something moving under the sheet.

'It's a baby, William! What's happening?' He stood shivering. A tear was trickling down his cheek. 'It's Helga's baby boy. She's dead!'

'What? Did she die having the baby? I thought you said she was going home with her parents.' The baby began to stir, making gurgling sounds.

'Have you any powder milk left? I expect he needs a feed. I'll go down to the Chemist to buy some. I'll explain everything when I come back.' He rushed out of the room and she heard the door slam. Sybil tiptoed over to the cradle and peered in at the child. He was tiny and his arms were waving. She wrapped the shawl round his fragile frame and picked him up. His fine downy hair was a silver blond and his eyes a dark blue.

'You're just like a cherub,' she said out loud.

'Are you alright Senora Sybil?' It was Myrna at the door. 'I saw Senor rushing out again.'

'Come in Myrna – William has gone to buy some milk for the baby. We are going to look after him for a while until we find out about his mother.'

'Nancy can come back with me if that would help?' Myrna said in her thoughtful way. 'I'll bring her back when it's time for bed.'

Sybil prepared a bottle whilst William held the baby.

'He's called Carl – she must have named him after her brother.' Sybil sat in her nursing chair and started feeding the baby.

'Now, tell me what happened?'

'I was in my office when a message came asking me to come to the lobby because a gentleman from San Juan was here to see me. I thought it was Carl but when I went down it was Rosario and his wife carrying the baby. They had a letter from Carl.

Dear Sybil and William,

Helga, my dearest sister, died a few weeks ago leaving a baby boy. Her last wish was for me to give the baby to you, William and Sybil, so that you can bring him up as an Englishman. This situation is very difficult for me. I am just preparing to leave for Germany to serve my country. My parents returned home some time ago because my father needed urgent medical attention. I have not heard from them since they left. They are oblivious to the fact that they have a grandson. My inclination was to ignore Helga's wishes and take the baby back to Germany when I go, but the thought of the forthcoming war and Rosario's anger at my decision made me change my mind. Helga wrote down her wishes in Spanish and gave it to Rosario. Apparently, he and his wife supported her during her pregnancy and

I didn't even know she was having a baby. She did not disclose the name of the father and Rosario swears he doesn't know.

I have rented out the hacienda and vineyard and hopefully I can return one day when the world is a more peaceful place. Helga is buried near to your dear Henry. That also was her wish. I am sure that you will take care of my nephew as if he were your own. You have always been true friends to my family. Rosario and his wife have agreed to bring the baby to Buenos Aires. I am leaving today to join the German navy. I hope that when the hostilities are over we can meet again. Baby Carl will be yours to cherish, as Helga wished. I agree entirely with her sentiments.

Your friend, Carl Schroder (dated December 1937)

'I can't believe this William . . . poor dear Helga.' She held the baby close to her heart and sobbed into his blanket.

'What are we going to do?'

'We'll just do what she asked.' Sybil did not hesitate. 'She has given us her son and we shall bring him up as our boy.'

'There are complications, Sybil – how do we explain to everyone that we suddenly have a son?'

'Myrna knows already. I've told her we're looking after him until we find his mother.'

'That's a lie Sybil. We know his mother is dead.' Sybil showed her frustration. She gently put Carl in the cradle and rocked it until he was asleep. William stood staring at her.

'We shall just say the mother is dead and we are adopting him. I intend to keep him William, so please check the law if you wish. In England people just look after orphan babies and the child takes the foster mother and father's name.'

Sybil began to organise the bedroom. Nancy was in a full size cot now. She arranged the furniture so that she could easily reach her daughter and the new baby.

'What are you doing?' William asked. 'I'm not sure that this is the right thing keeping someone else's baby!'

'We're keeping him tonight. Nancy has to become

accustomed to a new baby. You don't want her to be jealous do you?'

'No, but I can't get it round my head!' Sybil watched him rubbing his hands together in confusion.

'Let's just make some bottles up for the night and we can talk later when we've both had more time to think.' William stared at the small defenceless baby sleeping soundly in his new cradle.

They just finished preparing the bottles when Myrna came round carrying a tired Nancy. William took his daughter in his arms and Sybil thanked Myrna for feeding the two youngsters.

'I shall see you tomorrow. We are trying to decide what to do about the baby.'

'Baby! ' Nancy said.

'That's one word she can pronounce.' William carried the child into the bedroom. Sybil followed. Nancy looked at the sleeping Carl.

'Baby, my baby!' She clapped her hands in delight. Sybil felt the tears in her eyes and when she looked at William he was smiling with emotion.

'That gives us our answer. We have a daughter and a son. We can call him Charles. Carl told me once that Charles was his English name.'

They looked down at the baby. Nancy was nearly asleep holding on to her teddy. William held Sybil's hand and said:

'Goodnight Nancy and goodnight sweet Charlie.'

36

Next morning, Sybil made tea as usual. She felt tired because Charlie was fed several times in the night but now he was fast asleep with one small arm above his head. William just turned over, sighed and went back to sleep. She sat in the kitchen holding her mug of tea and thinking about William. Was he going to make a fuss about keeping the baby? He was so set in his ways and any thought of breaking the law sent him into a panic.

'Morning love,' he came into the kitchen all smiles. 'Have you made up plenty of bottles? It looks as if you'll need them after last night.'

'I didn't notice you offering to help?'

'You know how I feel – feeding is a mother's job.'

'Perhaps you could get Nancy up while I prepare the breakfast then?' There were squeals of laughter coming from the bedroom. They're bound to wake the baby, she thought. She decided to stay where she was and poured herself a second cup of tea.

'You'll be late for work, William,' Sybil called as she came out of the kitchen.

There he was holding Charlie on his lap and Nancy was trying to brush the baby's hair. He got up and handed Charlie to Sybil. 'I have a meeting this morning but perhaps I can make an excuse and have the day off. Can you manage on your own till I get back?'

'Myrna is coming in later and we're supposed to be going to the market. I shall just go on as normal.' When Myrna came she had a double pushchair for the two girls and Sybil prepared the old pram for the baby. A few of the locals noticed the new arrival but very little was said.

It was different when she went round to see the Carters. Violet Carter was inquisitive. 'Do you know his mother?' She asked. 'He's a beautiful baby, very fair-skinned'.

'His mother is dead. We want to adopt him. William is looking into the law and the adoption process.'

'Do be careful dear. You may be hurt if the father turns up.'

Sybil listened carefully to her friend, but Violet soon changed the subject to talk about her own children. 'They're breaking my heart by going to the war!'

Sybil took everything in her stride. William never mentioned adoption.

'It's great having Charlie! Nancy loves him. You're doing a good job, Sybil. She isn't jealous of her brother.'

•••

In 1939 Hitler marched into Poland and war was declared. William spent long hours away from home and Sybil was pleased to have the children. Ethel came over to stay whenever she had the chance. She travelled on her own by tram from Vicente Lopez. When William had to be away for a week, he encouraged Sybil to return with her friend.

'I'll feel happier if I know you're with Ethel and Jack. Argentina will not disclose what side they're on. Uruguay is staying neutral and I'm not happy about all the Germans in Buenos Aires.'

'William, we're miles away from Europe!'

'There's talk of the German navy stopping supplies to England and a lot of our food comes from South America.' Sybil suddenly understood what he was trying to say and she kept quiet.

'That Pilkington chap who lives with the Carters is being watched at the moment so I don't want you to go round there. Perhaps he has German connections.'

'I'll pack for the children and perhaps you can come over with us on the tram tomorrow?'

'Sorry, I have to go back tonight. Ethel knows the way. Just stay with them for a week or two.' Sybil clung to him as he said goodbye.

'Do keep safe William!'

Life in Vicente Lopez was different. Ethel and Jack lived in a charming bungalow. It was decorated with tiles on the outside. 'The builder came from Portugal.' Jack explained.'

'It's lovely and quiet here and you're near to the river.'

'You're so lucky, Sybil. You even have people giving you babies!' Sybil changed the subject when Ethel wanted to talk about Charlie.

'Shall we have a walk down to the river? Nancy could have a bucket and spade. I saw them for sale.' They strolled to the other side of the main road and made their way through the shacks selling beach toys – balls, big rings and even canoes. Some were selling food, fish, sausages and chunks of meat in bread and a variety of cakes and pastries. The tide was out and the beach extended along the coast.

'The river Plate is so wide that it looks like the sea.' Sybil remarked.

'What a shame the water is so muddy – if it were blue we could pretend to be at the seaside.' Nancy didn't mind and sat herself down to dig a hole. Ethel walked with her to the water's edge to fill her bucket and she was happy enough pouring water into the hole and sticking her toes in and out.

That evening when Jack returned from town he had some news about William and Paul Church. 'My brother Paul has been at the Embassy with William. Paul has taught himself a lot about wireless sets. I expect William wants to build a good machine so he can hear the news from England.'

'William has been fiddling about with short wave,

whatever that is?'

'The B.B.C. (I think it means British Broadcasting Corporation) transmits to the rest of the world on short wave. I'm not sure what it means either.' Jack picked up his pipe and retired to his seat in the corner. The canary in the cage began chirping and jumping from one perch to the other.

'Bird sings', Nancy said holding on to Jack's knee and looking up at him.

'Joey wants to come out of his cage. When you've had your tea we'll let him fly around the room.'

'We don't want him going under the sofa again,' called Ethel from the kitchen.

Sybil gave Charlie his bottle. The fresh air had tired him. He kept falling asleep.

'Don't go to sleep Charlie, you'll miss Joey flying in the sitting room.' Nancy was eating her banana sandwiches as fast as she could. 'I like honey with the bananas, Mummy.'

Jack closed the doors of the lounge. The bird flew round the room several times, perching occasionally on the top of the glass cabinet. Then it meandered down and stood on Jack's head. He was pecking at the hair and this made Jack call out: 'That tickles, Joey – stop at once!' Nancy ran over to Jack's chair mesmerized by the bird.

'My head, Joey, come on my head!' she cried bending her head down. Sybil and Ethel laughed.

'Joey has to know you before he will land on your head. You'll have to keep asking him and perhaps one day he will learn to like you.' Jack took the bird in his hand and allowed Nancy to touch him gently with one of her fingers before putting him back in his cage.

Sybil and the children stayed in Vicente Lopez for more than two weeks. Jack came home every evening with more disturbing news. 'There is a rumour going round that a large German battleship has been sighted in the Atlantic Ocean sailing towards Argentina. Paul's radio station has been broadcasting warnings. I haven't seen my brothers or

William for sometime now. That chap Robert, your friend, Sybil, has also disappeared. His wife and children have gone to Hurlingham to stay with the Crawfords. Mother thinks it's best for us to stay here or go back to your house in Caseros.' Sybil felt frightened.

'William wanted me to stay here – where do you think he is?'

'I have no idea but I suspect they're working for the British Embassy. We shall have to listen to the wireless. Dad lent me his set.' Sybil felt even more worried when Jack stayed at home. He set the wireless up in a corner of the room. Outside the aerial was attached to a mast. The three of them sat round the set for most of the day. Then on the 13th December an announcement that chilled them all came through the loudspeaker. 'The Admiral Graf Spe, a German pocket battleship has been spotted just off the estuary of Rio de la Plata. Witnesses at Punta del Este in Uruguay say that a battle is going on. There are two small ships and a larger one attacking the Graf Spe. People with binoculars say that the small ships are British.'

'Where is William? I wish he were here!'

'He'll be alright,' Ethel said. 'He has a family to look after'. The trouble with Jack's wireless was the same old thing. It kept fading and then went off altogether. The suspense mounted and Sybil found herself shivering with anxiety. Jack poured them a whisky each. 'Just sip it,' he warned.

'What if the Germans win out there? They may sail into Buenos Aires.' Jack stayed by the radio, day and night hoping for more news. It trickled out in small bulletins. 'There are three battle cruisers - the largest is HMS Exeter and two smaller ones. I think one is called HMS Ajax – I couldn't hear the name of the other one.'

'So are they winning?' Ethel was impatient. She wanted to go out with Sybil and the children but Jack told her it was safer to stay in the house.

'Apparently the Graf Spe has sunk quite a few

commercial vessels including the Doric Star. They believe that British sailors are on the battleship as prisoners of war.'

'Poor souls,' said Sybil. Our own ships are firing at them!'

'Exeter has been struck badly by torpedoes and has moved south towards the Falklands. The two smaller ships have continued to hit the Graf Spe but they too are retreating now. It doesn't look too good!'

'What will happen?' Sybil was frowning and fidgeting with anxiety.

'I'll go and prepare some food.' Ethel went into the kitchen.

'Billy can look after himself, Sybil. He's probably following the story at the Embassy.'

'He does get carried away sometimes. I think he wants to be a hero!'

The wireless came to life again: 'The Admiral Graf Spe has been seriously damaged by British ships and she is seeking refuge in Montevideo for repairs.'

'What was that about the Hague convention? It started to fade and I didn't catch the whole statement,' Ethel asked.

'Well, you are in the kitchen. It said that as Uruguay is neutral, the Graf Spe is only allowed to remain in the port for seventy-two hours. I don't see how they can repair everything in that time!'

'You go to bed with the children, Sybil. I'll stay up with Jack. We'll wake you if there is anything important.'

Next morning the news came: 'the battle ship has retreated to the estuary of the River Plate towards Montevideo. On arrival in port the wounded men were taken off to local hospitals. The dead were taken ashore and buried. All captives were released.'

'It must be difficult for the Captain. He's a long way from Germany and the ship may not be seaworthy. They do have to cross the Atlantic to find safety.'

'Oh Jack, you're not on their side?' Ethel could hardly believe her ears.

'I just feel sorry for the Captain. He has to make all those decisions. He can't be such a monster: he has released all the prisoners.'

Jack decided to travel into the city. When he returned Ethel asked him about his visit. 'They told me that I should have stayed at home with the girls and children. It is possible that the Graf Spe will make a dash for Buenos Aires where they can hang out for a while in safety.'

'What about your brothers and William?' Sybil looked drawn and tired after several restless nights.

'There is no news. I don't know what they're doing. Try to keep calm Sybil if you can. There is only one day left now. Crowds are gathering at Punta del Este to see the end of the battle.'

37

Sybil was lying wide-awake on the bed. She peeped over at Nancy and Charlie. They were both asleep so she tried to come to terms with her present situation. Here she was with the responsibility of caring for two small children with this cloud of confusion in her head. First, she was overjoyed at having a new baby and then came the doubts of whether it was right to keep him or not? Just when that seemed settled, William disappears and the possibility of a German invasion was looming!

She was thankful that she was here with Jack and Ethel, but she felt deserted. Ethel was not worried about the troubles - she saw it as an obstacle to her own plans.

'When can I go out again, Jack? I've already cancelled viewing two shops and I want Sybil to come with me next time.'

'I'm sorry, Ethel. I have so many things on my mind that I've forgotten about your project. Please tell me more about the plans?'

'I want to have my own business. I'm good at creating hats and I've decided to open a shop. I shall design special occasion hats for weddings and other celebrations. I need a small workshop behind the scenes. The hats can be displayed in the main part of the shop with other accessories such as jewellery, belts and silk flowers. The window has to be a picture to entice the customers to enter the shop.'

'It's a great idea,' Sybil agreed. 'Of course I'll come with you and perhaps you'll let me work with you sometimes?

Just at the moment I'm so worried about William. Why can't he be here with us like Jack is?' Sybil admired Ethel's determination. She carries on with her nursing and still has such exciting ideas for the future. Sybil felt inadequate – at one time she imagined herself as a career person then suddenly her path took a different direction. It is so unpredictable and frightening being married to William!

News came through on the 17th December that the Captain of the Graf Spe had ordered destruction of all sensitive equipment on board. A crowd gathered to watch from Punta del Este as the battleship limped out of the port to the outer roadstead. The people could see the charges being set and then a mighty cloud of smoke covered the final moments of the ill-fated ship. She was scuttled and sank in the muddy waters of the River Plate.

'What about the crew?' Ethel asked.

'Listen!' Jack snapped. The radio crackled to life: 'The Captain and crew were taken off by an Argentine tug. Others were left in Montevideo.' A few days later William turned up in Vicente Lopez. It was just as if he had come home from the office.

'Oh William, where have you been? Sybil clung to him as he picked Charlie and Nancy up in his arms.

'Paul and I went over to Montevideo in his boat. We saw it all from the headland and since we've been back we watched the crew being marched through the city. They were taken as prisoners. Some will stay in Buenos Aires and others are being moved to Rosario. I don't know all the details. Captain Langsdorff wanted to go down with his ship but he was prevented from doing that.'

'What happened to him then?' Jack wanted to know.

'He was questioned and then when he was left on his own he shot himself. He was found in his full dress uniform lying on the German flag.' The friends remained silent. Sybil with William's arm round her shoulder and Ethel moving over to take Jack's hand - almost in sympathy.

•••

'That boy is so lively that he needs to be with other children. Nancy starts full time school when she's seven. There's a good English school in Villa Devoto.' Sybil was trying to impress William. 'Villa Devoto is nearer to the city and has a large British community with a Church'.

'Just right for the children to go to Sunday school.' William added.

Sybil noticed an empty house in the same road as the kindergarten. 'I had a quick look through the fence. It has a lovely garden,' she told William. The building is on one floor.'

'It is a peculiar design,' William pointed out. 'I don't know why they build homes without halls. It's always necessary to go through one bedroom to reach the next!' In 1942 when Nancy was six the family moved from Caseros to Villa Devoto and the children were enrolled at the local kindergarten.

The kitchen needed alterations and William persuaded the landlord to agree to the changes. 'The garden is like a jungle!' William sighed.

'Yes I saw orange, fig and lemon trees. It will be good to have our own fruit.' Sybil smiled.

'Negrita will go to her local school. They look smart in their white aprons. Nancy will miss her friend, especially the cheese bit!'

'I don't think I've heard about that.'

'When the Montenari family have soup,' Sybil explained. 'They have a special dish with compartments for about six different grated cheeses. Nancy likes using the special spoon to put cheese in her soup. They use Parmesan cheese in all sorts of dishes.'

'I expect they use garlic in everything. ugh!' Sybil smiled to herself. Ethel told her about the health properties in garlic and she had been using it in small amounts for some time. William never noticed. Just before they moved Myrna was looking after the children. The weather was stormy and the lightning lit up the grey sky.

'Mummy, Mummy,' shrieked Nancy from the front door. 'Come and see, it's raining frogs!' Sybil ran out to see Charlie and Nancy running and jumping. They were both soaking wet, their hair plastered flat to their heads. Negrita was chanting and circling as if in a trance. The children were skipping and laughing as they tried to avoid stepping on hundreds of baby frogs. 'Look at those! They're being washed down the drain!' Nancy pointed. She was standing in the gutter where the excess water was flowing like a stream.

'Poor babies!' Charlie was frowning at the sad spectacle.

'I've only seen this once before. It's where the frogs have been drawn up into a cloud, probably from a near bye lake or marsh and dumped here in Caseros.' Myrna tried to explain. Sybil was as wet as the others and most of the neighbours were out watching this amazing phenomenon.

The move to Villa Devoto went to plan. Lola who worked for the neighbours was to be their new maid. Whiskers, was tied up on a rope because they didn't want him disappearing in the undergrowth.

'*Cuidado*, take care with the dog – you need to check for poisons. They were a funny couple who lived here.'

William did not like the sound of that. 'We shall have to keep the children safe until I can clear the garden.' The next three weekends William toiled in the jungle. He hired an elderly man to help with the digging. They burned the rubbish on enormous bonfires and among the items found hidden beneath the vegetation was a large roller made of stone with a wooden handle. Roquellio was given the job to walk up and down with the roller flattening the ground ready to be planted with special lawn seed.

Sybil liked the old man. 'He's a good worker,' she told William. After talking to him for a short while, she found out that he lived in a room by himself.

'My family stayed in Italy. I'm supposed to send for

them when I've earned enough money. All I can do is odd jobs and a bit of gardening.' Sybil wondered if he ever had a decent meal?

'I think he is younger than he looks. He probably spends his money on cheap wine. He does work well and we need some help with this garden.'

Can we afford to have him two days a week? I can include a lunch and perhaps I can find some of your old clothes. He looks so shabby. I don't know what he does in the winter. I'll keep that old mack for later in the autumn.'

Lola was not keen to share the kitchen table with Roquellio but in time they became civil to each other. There was always a big pot of stew cooking on Roquellio's day and Nancy often wanted to sit with them in the kitchen.

'I like dipping my bread in the juice like they do,' she said to Sybil.

'You can do that with us.' William told her. But he changed his mind when later she wanted to drink her tea out of a saucer. 'Nancy you need to do that in the kitchen with the servants. Just imagine what Mummy would say if you decided to pour your tea into a saucer when we're out in Buenos Aires. When Charlie is older we shall probably go to the 'Ideal' for tea. We can sit and listen to the music and sip our tea and if I remember rightly they have those long twisty sweets that they give to polite children.'

'I prefer to be in the kitchen with Lola and Roquellio. She puts her tea in the saucer because it is too hot and she blows on it to make it cool! She told me that she has to hurry her tea so that she can finish all the work that Senora Lawson gives her.'

William smiled at the explanation. He looked over at Sybil. 'I suppose your mother is a bit of a slave driver!'

'Go on out in the garden, you two. Will you check on Charlie please? He thinks he needs to climb every tree in the garden and he took Whiskers with him.'

When all the undergrowth had been cleared, Sybil had

to decide where to have a chicken run. Right in the far corner was a small building. It reminded her of San Juan, because she thought it was an outside toilet. Now it held a bale of straw and hanging on the walls were several garden implements such as an old fork and rake. At least in the main house they had an inside bathroom with, toilet, washbasin and a large bath. Sybil giggled when she remembered the first days of married life in their wood and tin home close to the Andes.

William and the children joined Sybil. 'If you could build a shelter on the side of the old toilet, it's an ideal spot. The run could cross the width of the garden.'

'I'll order some fencing to be delivered next week when Roquellio is here.'

'What are you doing Whiskers?'

'He's digging a hole – he's been doing it all morning. I think he's buried all his toys. He growls at me when I go to uncover any of his things!' Charlie told them.

'I suppose he couldn't dig in Caseros and he thinks this is a new game. We shall have to stop him because if I want a flower garden later on, he'll be digging in there!' Ethel, during one of her visits, showed Nancy how to stop the dog destroying the new lawn. 'Everyone needs to carry treats in their pocket when Whiskers goes out. As soon as he starts digging you must yell 'no', call him to you and give him a treat.'

'That's your job Nancy! He is your dog.' Sybil was surprised to see her daughter dedicate herself to this duty. She didn't give up and in time the dog learned to dig in the rough areas at the back of the garden.

'She's like you Sybil – she has a way with animals.'

The children enjoyed their mornings at the kindergarten until Nancy had a bad experience. She came home crying because the teacher told her to stand in the corner for spilling the ink.

'I didn't do it Mummy!' she sobbed.

'Who did it then?'

'It was that big boy called Cyril. He bullies everyone.' Charlie told them. He had his head down and was twisting his handkerchief. He avoided eye contact with Sybil.

'Why didn't you say something then? Poor Nancy had to take the blame!' Charlie made a quick exit with Whiskers into the garden.

One April evening William was home early. Sybil could tell straight away that something was wrong. 'Come and sit here,' he said in a solemn voice. 'I have some bad news. Bath has been bombed! Sybil felt faint. 'What can I do?'

'I'm going to try listening on our radio.' William went to his desk in the corner where he had his wireless set up. Sybil followed and they both sat together.

'Polly told us about the refugees arriving from London. They must have thought Bath was a safe place!' When the voice came through they sat completely numbed by the news. They could not remember the exact words only the horrendous facts: 'the city of Bath has been bombed on two consecutive nights. The centre has been razed to the ground. It is thought that over one thousand people have been killed. Bodies are still being dug out of the bombed sites. The famous Georgian Assembly rooms have been hit!'

38

'Why is Mummy locked in the bathroom?' Nancy was anxious.

'She wants to be on her own because we've had sad news from England. Bath where your Grandma and Auntie Polly live, has been bombed. It's a horrible war. Mummy is upset because we don't know if they're alive and safe!'

'I want them to be alive!' Charlie began sobbing. Sybil could hear all this and came out of the bathroom, her eyes red and swollen. William held her in his arms and the children clung to their parents in a tight huddle.

'We must say a prayer for your Grandma, Aunties and Uncles. I pray to God to keep them safe!' The children put their hands together.

'Shall we ask gentle Jesus to keep them safe?' Charlie looked up at William with smeared tears on his young face. Sybil could not believe that William was praying to God. 'Amen,' they said in unison.

It was nearly a month before a letter came from Bath:

It was a horror that I never want to go through again wrote Polly. *Mother and I were the only ones in the house. When the sirens went we crawled under the kitchen table. I made it as comfortable as possible with pillows and blankets, but Mother found it hard to relax. She wanted to sleep in her own bed and when it all happened again the following night she refused to stay in the kitchen. I sat with her in the bedroom. During the day I went out of the front door and heard about the damage in the centre of the city. The boys came round with supplies for us. They looked tired and dirty. They had worked all night helping with the rescue. Jason was acting like a madman pulling children from the debris and according to Chris his eyes were haunted like they were when he first came back after the sinking of his ship. I'm pleased to say that we are all safe, though traumatised. Mother has not been the same since the air raid. She is looking frail and her legs give her trouble. The doctor says that it's arthritis! I do wish this war would end so that you can come home to us.*

Sybil's reaction was one of anger - at first with herself and then with William for keeping her here far away from her family. She felt so helpless!

'It's no good blaming Billy. You married him and his work is here.' Ethel pointed out.'

'I was pleased when he was unable to volunteer for the war. I don't think he's been the same since. Remember how he was away all that time during the Graf Spe disaster? He is still secretive about his war work and stays away for a night or even days.'

'Really Sybil, your Billy is a wonderful husband! If you can't cope with the pressure, just do something drastic on your own. Go out and buy a new outfit, or a ridiculous hat from my shop or just go and have your hair cut off!'

'That's a good idea,' Sybil thought later. 'I'll go and have my hair cut off and I may even have one of those new fangled things . . . a perm!' That night she tossed and turned in bed. William was away again. She only ever had the ends of her hair trimmed. Now she felt it was time to make a sacrifice! Next morning when the children were at kindergarten, Sybil went to the local hairdresser. The salon was modern compared to the shop in Caseros.

'Senora, are you sure you want to cut your hair short? It's so lovely!'

'I have a few grey hairs and the colour has faded over the years.'

'If you are certain about having it cut, I can plait it for you before I start. Then when I cut, you can have the plait to keep. If wrapped in silk hair will last for years!

Sybil left the salon feeling conspicuous. Once outside she looked for a headscarf to hide her short curly hair. There were a few waves but the ends were now curling round her neck and her ears seemed to stick out in an abnormal way. She hurried home and started preparing lunch for the children.

'What is the matter Senora Sybil, why do you wear a headscarf in the kitchen?' Sybil undid the knot and with a certain amount of drama threw the scarf down on the floor. 'Oh Senora, what have you done? Your beautiful hair! What will Senor William say?' Sybil began to sob and Lola looked uncomfortable.

'It will be alright when we're used to the change.' Lola tried to be positive.

'I had to do something, I'm so tired of bad news from home.'

'Would you like me to collect Nancy and Charlie? Lola asked.

'Yes please, I'll have to be brave now and accept the consequences!'

Charlie ran in from school, hugged Whiskers and disappeared out in the garden.

'How were things today, Nancy?' Sybil enquired. Her daughter stood in the doorway staring.

'I didn't think that was you Mummy! Look at your curls – you look really pretty! Can I have my hair cut like that?'

'Come here, you darling girl. I'm so glad you like my new hairstyle. Let's see what Daddy says before we have your hair cut.' Charlie wandered in, followed by a panting dog. 'What's for lunch Mummy? Your hair looks funny!

The reaction so far wasn't as bad as Sybil thought, but somehow she needed to persuade Nancy to keep her hair long – or did she have to? Girls and women were always persuaded to keep their locks long and straight by their parents. It was almost a law. Perhaps it's time for a change?

'We can go to the hairdressers this afternoon, then we'll

both have short hair when Daddy comes home.'

'That's not possible because we need to make an appointment. But if you like, Nancy, I'll make you some ringlets like auntie Millie when she was young.'

'Yes, I'd like that but I also want my hair cut next week!' Sybil looked for an old pillowcase and tore strips of material for curlers.

After washing Nancy's hair Sybil towel dried it thoroughly before tackling the tricky part dividing the hair into manageable bunches and wrapping each one in a strip of material so that it hung down vertically. The curlers had to be left in as long as possible so they decided to take them out about half an hour before William's usual home coming time.

'Sybil, I'm home – I caught the earlier train!' She was in the bathroom putting a comb through her curls. Her head felt so light and she loved to see the curls bouncing back as the comb went through. Now she felt flustered. What was he going to say?

'I'm in here William, just close your eyes, I've got a surprise!' She came out and stood by the armchair with one hand on her hip imitating a model she had seen in a magazine. 'You can open, look now!'

William was speechless, his eyes widened in amazement. 'What have you done?'

'I'm modern now – I've had my hair cut short and permed. It feels wonderful!' At that moment Nancy came rushing in with her hair wrapped in strips of white material. 'You're not supposed to be home yet Daddy!'

'Good God, what has been happening to my girls? One has a mass of short curls and the other is covered in white bits. Where's Charlie? I hope he's normal.'

He began to laugh. 'I'm doing this because I don't want to cry!' he stuttered.

Sybil took Nancy to the bedroom and disentangled the homemade curlers. The ringlets were better than expected and Nancy loved them. She rushed to show William. 'You look like that film star, Shirley Temple!' He turned and winked at Sybil. That night when he held her in his arms he whispered: 'I loved your long hair. You were so beautiful when we first met, but I suppose it is still you under this mop.' He ruffled her hair gently. 'It will grow again! '

•••

Charlie was bright for his age so he was accepted at the English school almost a year earlier. This was convenient for Sybil when she had to collect them in the afternoon. Soon they were confident enough to walk the three squares on their own or with friends who lived in the same road. During the mornings the children were taught in Spanish and in their first years their exercise books were lovingly stuck together and covered. One Senorita was outstanding in her presentation. Nancy cherished her first year's book. 'Look at this, Mummy: my teacher has covered my exercise books in white parchment. The painting of palm trees, sea and sand are in watercolour.' Sybil made sure that the books containing the achievements of a year's work were kept safely on a new bookshelf.

'Do you like my '*palitos*' Daddy?'

'They do look perfectly straight, but I don't know why you spend time doing rows of lines?'

'I think it's supposed to help the child's hand control,' Sybil replied.

'It has worked – you can look at the end of the book where you can see the improvement. Nancy writes clearly.'

'I like numbers best, look at my book Daddy!' Charlie turned to the last pages to show William his sums.

'They certainly look neat and tidy.'

Sybil was busier when the children started full time school. She was forever making costumes for plays. Nancy, in particular, loved acting. She was in the nativity plays and was the 'Queen of Hearts' in 'Alice in Wonderland'. Charlie was chosen to be Aladdin and that was a challenge for Sybil. Ethel came to the rescue with a delightful Chinese hat. 'I wanted to be 'the genie!' Charlie informed them when he was trying on his costume.

'This is the star part,' Ethel pointed out. Luckily her friend was with her when the letter arrived from Bath. Sybil had hoped that the war would end in time for her to return to see her mother. But it was not to be:

Mother died peacefully in her sleep last weekend. We were all round her bed to say goodbye. Jason held her hand and told her that you wanted to be here with us but the war stopped you. Mother smiled when he said this, so I think she understood. Please do not grieve too much. She lived a long life caring for us all and her wish would be that you followed in her footsteps by cherishing your own dear family.

With much love from your sister, Polly.'

Sybil did grieve but mainly at night when she was in bed and about to go to sleep. She thought about Polly left on her own. Her sister had sacrificed her own life by staying at home to look after their Mother.

'Mother could be very demanding,' Sybil said to Ethel. 'As the oldest girl I experienced some of her sarcasm and unfair treatment. Polly must have been persecuted in the same fashion – she was brave to continue to the end.'

Ethel did not answer at once. Sybil suddenly remembered that her friend never saw her Mother again. They had saved the money for the fare but the war stopped Ethel and Jack from fulfilling their journey.

'The war has touched us all; few people have escaped the consequences.'

39

Sybil carefully carried a tray into the bedroom where William was working.

'How is it going?' she asked.

'It's taking longer than I thought. Building a dolls' house is so complicated. The four main rooms are fine, two up and two down. It's the stairs, doors and windows that cause a problem.'

'You know what Nancy is like? Everything has to be just right – it reminds me of someone! Charlie is quite easy in comparison. He will love his new train set.'

'Your friend Ethel doesn't help,' William complained. 'Nancy told me that Auntie Ethel is making velvet flowers and a felt lawn for the garden. So now I have to include a garden with a lawn and such things as a wishing well, lawnmower, trees and so on!'

'Ethel and Jack love the children. It is sad that they never had any of their own. I think your plan is perfect, William. The sliding doors at the back are ideal because Nancy can stand on a stool and open each room when she wants to play.

Are you going to stop for a break now and have your coffee?' They sat together on the end of the bed. William was working on the dolls' house project whenever he had a spare moment. He became so involved that he often took a day off from work when the children were at school. The dolls' house was hidden from view by a large sheet in the evenings. The children were unaware of the progress.

Sybil glanced out of the window. 'It looks as if we're

going to have a storm. It's so still and quiet. What are you doing, Whiskers?'

'He's sitting on my foot and keeps on scratching my leg with his paw – go off you silly dog!'

'Senora Sybil – come and see the lights in the sitting room.' Lola came rushing into the bedroom – '*un terremoto*' she cried. 'I think it's an earthquake!'

'Not in Buenos Aires!' William and Sybil rushed to the sitting room. The light fitting that hung on a chain in the middle of the room was swinging from side to side. William sat down in his wireless corner and switched everything on.

'It is an earthquake . . . Hold on! It's in the San Juan area. There is no clear picture of what's happening!'

Sybil suddenly felt cold. She remembered the last time an earthquake struck in the Cuyo district. At that time William was working in San Juan and she was on a visit to friends in the capital. She recalled her terror when she heard the news.

'Do you have friends there, Senora?' Lola enquired. 'It must be bad for the lights to move like that when we're so far away!'

'Senor William has many friends who work on the railway and I know some of the wives.' Her thoughts turned to the vineyard and the church in the village where her baby Henry and Helga were buried. The memories of the tennis tournaments organised by Helga and the lazy afternoons sitting under the trees in the Schroder's garden made Sybil smile. They were such happy times! The war had set their friends on opposite sides and she was suddenly overcome by the sadness of it all.

'The epicentre is near to San Juan and there are many casualties.' William broke into her thoughts. 'All trains have been cancelled and roads closed. What a disaster! We won't hear the full news for days or even weeks. I'll have to go to the office tomorrow – some of the bridges and tracks may have been destroyed.'

•••

It was not all bad news in 1944 because back in Europe the allies reached the German frontier and good news was arriving every day. It was the turning point when the Americans joined the battle. The Americans interned Germans, Japanese and Italians in camps just in case they turned out to be traitors. Some of these people who had lived all their lives in the U.S.A. were just whisked away. The same action was taken in England when hundreds of foreigners were imprisoned.

In 1945 Hitler killed himself in his bunker. The war was ending at last!

'The Americans have dropped an atom bomb on Japan.' William told Sybil.

'That's good isn't it?'

'No Sybil – thousands have been killed and those who have not died have been affected by radiation. They will die a long drawn-out painful death. It is horrific! Not only that, the whole area has been contaminated. All the vegetation has been scorched and the earth has lost its fertility. Paul says that the pictures coming from Japan cannot be shown in the newspapers because it looks as if everything has been burnt to a cinder - like the end of the world!'

'Don't, you're frightening me. Surely the Americans had to do something to end the war? Just imagine the poor Japanese children. It's not their fault! Let's not talk about it any more, it's making me feel sick.' Sybil tried to change the subject but William was being negative about everything.

'We shall be able to go home soon for a break,' she suggested.

'Things are not too good here. Juan Peron is making a name for himself. He's encouraged all the strikes and his aim is to nationalize the railways. He intends to carry out his threats next year. I feel like retiring – a lot of the English are going to leave and go home. My boss says we can have six months leave in 1947 if we can find a passage on a ship. I wonder if we ought to wait until 1949 – I can retire then?'

'No, William, let's go home when we have the chance. I want to see the family and it's good for the children to travel. We shall have to update our passports. What shall we do about Charlie?'

'You have Nancy on your passport so I shall put Charlie on mine. Carl never gave me a birth certificate; perhaps Rosario kept it. I shall have to ask him when I go up to San Juan. I do hope he and his family have survived the earthquake.' Sybil remembered how vulnerable their first home was. It was more like a shack than a properly constructed house. 'Thank God we live down here,' she murmured.

The disaster was greater than anyone in Buenos Aires could imagine. The number of casualties increased every day. Nine thousand one day, then over ten thousand the next minute – it was difficult to assess the numbers killed because they were still pulling survivors and bodies from under the debris. The news that saddened most people was the number of orphans. Babies and toddlers found sheltering under the bodies of their parents. Others were found under tables or staircases. It was difficult to describe the horror on their young faces. It showed in their eyes – a haunted lost expression!

During the same year of the earthquake Juan Peron met his future wife Eva Duarte. 'Look at this Sybil, he's forty-eight and his new girlfriend is only twenty four!'

'They make a glamorous couple and she wears lovely clothes.' Sybil turned the page. 'Did you see this? The government wants everyone to give up one week's wages for the San Juan appeal.'

'I don't mind doing that as long as the money goes to the needy and doesn't turn up in some greedy politician's bank account.' William was not too keen on the new wave of politicians emerging from the ranks of the military.

'The Peronistas are supposed to be fighting for the working class and when you come to think of it the railways are rather old and need a lot of money spent on them.'

'You are right Sybil - it has been a struggle keeping everything moving. We were not able to acquire new stock or spare parts during the war. The factories back home will have to re-tool after changing production for the war effort. It could be years before we receive the material we need.'

Sybil tried to be careful with her choice of words because she knew how sensitive William could be about his beloved railway.

'Seven of the railways are British and three are French. Just imagine how many people are employed – what will happen to them all when a military man is put in charge?'

'You can't jump to conclusions! They will probably keep the bosses on and, anyway, a lot of the railway people are Argentinos. They may be pleased with the change.'

'Whatever!' William shrugged and left the room.

Sybil felt guilty because she wanted to support her husband but at the same time she longed to return to England. She worried about being selfish with her constant desire to go back to Bath. William did not feel the same as her about family. 'My Father is dead and you know what my Mother is like? Her latest craze is spiritualism! She's not interested in us, only herself. Has she ever mentioned Charlie? No, not once, Mother doesn't even acknowledge his existence!' William had grown bitter about his Mother. 'I thought that as she grew older there would be a change but it hasn't happened.' Sybil recalled some of the acidic remarks that her mother-in-law made when they first married. In contrast, her own Mother seemed to be friendly with everyone and she was particularly fond of William. Sybil thought that fate has a strange idea of fairness when it came to death and who should go first.

In April 1945 President Roosevelt of the United States

died. It stunned the whole world! The war was virtually over but chaos reigned. Europe was in a state of destruction and communist ideas were buzzing everywhere. What would happen without Roosevelt and Churchill?

'It's the elections, today.' William told Sybil. 'I should stay in with the children and if you do go out be careful what you say!

'Are you going to work?' Sybil asked. 'There may be demonstrations in town!'

'No, I'm popping into the Embassy about Charlie's passport. Then I'm going to find out if I can arrange a passage on a ship for the four of us.' Sybil hugged him.

'Thank you, darling. I so want to go home! I'll write and tell Polly. When will it be?'

'Spring would be perfect, say March or April? It will depend on whether we can find a ship to take us. Robert and Evelyn are putting their names down for any kind of ship. They don't mind going on a cargo boat, though it may be more difficult for us with the children.'

●●●

Colonel Juan Peron became the president of Argentina in 1946 and during that same year he married Eva and she became the First Lady of the country. She soon became Evita, the darling and leader of the '*descamisados*'. (The men without shirts)

'We're going to the Circus!' Charlie announced as he rushed into the kitchen.

'The whole school is going. Parents are invited - please come Daddy!' Nancy pleaded.

'It's to celebrate the end of the war – I've managed to buy some flags to wave. You try and keep me away!' William laughed.

Charlie was more excited than Nancy when they heard the news about sailing to England. He was fascinated by ships and wanted to know about engine rooms and lifeboats. Nancy, on the other hand, worried about the people she was leaving behind especially Ethel. The two had strong ties. Nancy loved Ethel's shop where she was allowed to help wrapping jewellery for customers. 'She is never bored.' Ethel told Sybil. 'One of her favourite chores is making the *mate*. She even enjoys drinking it as long as she adds plenty of sugar.'

Then, there was Whiskers! He was nearly ten – a good age for a sweet mongrel. He had an ugly lump on his side and the Vet had warned Sybil to be prepared for the right time to say goodbye.

'Can't we take Whiskers with us? Nancy asked.

'He's old and not very well!' Charlie answered. 'Auntie Ethel will look after him when we're away.'

'I was asking, Daddy, not you Charlie!' Sybil heard the conversation and hoped William would tackle the subject sympathetically. She realised that Nancy was becoming anxious about her pet.

'Auntie Ethel has always had dogs of her own,' he stated. 'She'll know what to do if he is ill when we're away. The Vet will put Whiskers to sleep. He will not let him suffer!'

'You mean, he may die when we're away! I'm his mistress and I need to comfort him. I shall stay here!'

40

'I think it's better to ignore her.' Sybil told William. 'There's still time before we sail in March. When she sees us packing and discussing what we're going to do on the crossing and meeting the cousins and aunts – she'll change her mind.'

'I hope you're right. It was my mistake mentioning the Vet. Whiskers is well at the moment. He's a strong fellow but I hope he doesn't pine.'

'Don't mention it, William. The thought of her pet pining will just make her more determined to stay here.'

Preparations were extensive. 'I want to take everyone a present,' Sybil told her daughter. 'Auntie Polly said that children had not seen bananas during the war. Sweets and other foods such as cheese and butter are still rationed. I think I'll try to buy some of those tins of ham and salmon.'

'What about tins of fruit?' Nancy began to join in the conversation. 'We can't take fresh fruit. Dad says that the journey will take a whole month. Dried apricots are yummy. My cousins would like those and figs. Daddy told me that we are calling at some islands. The Canary Islands I think he said.'

'Yes, the one we are visiting is called Tenerife. You will see bananas growing there!'

Strangely enough Ethel was quiet and tearful. 'I shall miss you, Sybil. You are like a sister to me and, even though I know you're coming back, six months is a long time. Jack and I have decided to move in and look after your house. We thought Whiskers would be happier in his own environment. My friend Charlotte is looking after the shop and I can do odd sewing jobs here. Jack will enjoy looking after the chickens and doing some gardening.'

'Ethel, you know I want to return to England. William will not be happy when the railways are nationalized. He can retire in 1949 and we shall probably go home for good.'

'That's what worries me.' Ethel sniffed into her handkerchief. We are thinking of adopting a young girl. She's sixteen and both her parents died in the San Juan earthquake. No one seems to want the older children. Her parents were Jewish and that also goes against her. She's been helping in the shop. I've used one or two of her artistic ideas and they've gone down well with the customers. Jack is not too sure?'

'Well, you know what Jack is like? He's hardly adventurous with his plans!

If you like her and can offer a home you'll be doing some good. It must be awful in those orphanages! What's her name?'

'Olga, Teresa – her family moved to Argentina before the war. She has a brother but doesn't know if he is still alive. One day she is going to look for him.'

'That doesn't sound too good, with the atrocities that occurred in the war! I think she will be lucky to have you and Jack to guide and love her.'

●●●

The day came for their departure. Nancy put her arms round Whiskers.

'I'll soon be back, little boy. Auntie Ethel will look after you and she's bringing Kiki so you'll have a companion. Don't forget you're too old to play all day like she does – just take it easy.'

They went through the Customs and out to the quay where their ship was docked. 'It's called the St. Ina.' Charlie pointed. 'That's the way up that gangway. Look out Nancy, hold on tight!'

'You are bossy, Charlie. I can see where I have to go.'

'We're all in the same cabin, you children can be on the top bunks.' They dumped their cases and climbed the stairs to the deck. They could see Ethel and Jack waving to them. Nancy insisted on waving until the figures on the quay disappeared from view. 'Poor Whiskers, he will miss us,' she sighed.

There were only nine passengers on the ship so the Captain summoned them to the lounge. The furniture and wall panelling was dark oak. There was a reddish tinge on some of the tables. The passengers stood in a group.

'I'm Cecil and this is my wife Angela. That's my son Arthur. Your boy looks about the same age?' William shook hands with the man.

'Charlie's nine and Nancy is ten. This is my wife, Sybil.'

The other two passengers were women and they introduced themselves as Sylvia and Heidi – mother and daughter.

'Charlie is lucky, he has someone to play with.' Nancy whispered.

'I am older than you, but I could keep you company.' Heidi came over to shake hands with Nancy. 'I'm fifteen. I know I look grown up but I am a tomboy at heart! Can you swim?'

'I have been learning and Dad says I'll improve if the ship has a swimming pool.'

The Captain entered with two of his men. 'May I introduce you to my Chief Officer and Chief Engineer. These are the two most important members of the crew on my ship. One looks after the running of the bridge and organises the timetables for the crew and me. The Chief Engineer lives down in the bowels of the ship where he keeps the engines moving. There is one other indispensable member and that is the Chief Cook. You'll meet him this evening. He has an added challenge on this trip because it is the first time that the St. Ina has carried passengers. He's been studying his cookery book and I'm sure he'll come up with some interesting meals! The Chief Officer is here to tell you a story about the ship.' They saluted each other and the Captain excused himself. He was needed on the bridge.

'I will not keep you long as I'm sure you need to unpack and explore the decks. There are just a few rules. There are some 'no entry' signs that are there for your safety. The galley is out of bounds because it is essential for the cooks to work without interruption. Some will be preparing potatoes or other vegetables outside the galley and you are allowed to chat to them. The crew's quarters are out of bounds. The men need to relax in peace when they're off duty. The engine room is also out of bounds though I believe the Chief Engineer has offered to show passengers around if there is enough interest.'

'I'd like to see the engine room!' Charlie surprised everyone by putting his arm up and calling out as if he were still at school.

'Well done, young man! That's what we like to hear. I've been asked to give you a short history of the 'St. Ina'. Some of you may have heard – she was captured by the British Navy in the Bay of Biscay and handed over to our merchant company to be used as a cargo ship on the South American run. With the increased demand for passenger berths we were instructed to convert some of the cabins to take nine people. As you will see the ship is solidly built and the brass bells and handles are beautifully made. The Germans were known before the war for their excellent shipbuilding. Those of you interested in visiting the engine rooms will be surprised at the smoothness of the moveable parts. That is all now – if you need any information please contact me. I'm usually on deck and we shall meet everyday at meal times. Dinner is at half past seven. See you later!'

The journey proved to be one of excitement for the children. The crew enjoyed having the youngsters on board and created games for them to play. The pool was the usual kind made of a wooden frame covered by tarpaulin. Nancy and Heidi swam whenever they could and the boys became proficient at diving from a makeshift diving board. Just before lunchtime the girls watched the trainee cooks preparing the vegetables and often they were given miniature *empanadas* made with succulent beef and crunchy pastry. 'You won't feel like your lunch if you keep eating those!'

'Would you like one, Senora?' Sybil took one of the small pies. It melted in her mouth. 'I can see why you like them.' She grinned at the girls. There was one calamity during the voyage and that was William falling asleep in the sun. When he went to get up he found that he had enormous blisters on his knees and his legs were a bright red.

'You'll have to see the Doctor! It's no good moaning like that with the pain. He'll have to lance the blisters. They're like big boils hanging down on your legs!'

'Poor Daddy!' Nancy tried to console him. 'Mummy did tell us about the sun, it's dangerous falling asleep like that.' William spent the next few days in agony. It was difficult to find a comfortable position at night so he was deprived of sleep. It made him grumpy having to stay in his cabin. The lotion he was given to cool the skin turned white when it dried. 'I think it's called calamine.' Sybil told him to keep smearing it on the sore skin. The blisters were covered with gauze to stop any infection.

Crossing the Equator was fun for the children. Sybil and William felt as if they were old hands at this sort of thing. On the Canary Islands they bought more sweets and a large walking doll for one of the cousins.

'I suppose we have to give the doll away?' Nancy enquired. 'She is pretty with her golden hair and I've never seen a walking doll.'

'You are ten, Nancy, quite old for dolls!' Charlie had to have his say.

Uncles and Aunts and some of the older cousins were

at the docks. Sybil and Polly clung to each other, both sisters crying with joy!

'I thought at one time that I would never see you again!' Polly cried. 'It seemed that sorrow and heartache was here forever – what with the war and losing Mother. It was one thing after another!'

'We're back now and the war is over.' Sybil tried to calm the shaking body.

Millie was introducing the cousins to each other. 'You must be Nancy – I can tell because you look like your Mother! Charlie you're taller than I thought! She turned to the three cousins who were standing together and introduced them. My two boys are in London, you'll meet them later.' The children soon made friends.

'Auntie Polly says you are both going to attend St. Saviour's school during term time. Heather goes there so you will have one friend at least!'

Sybil was overcome by emotion – her sisters and their children gave her a great welcome. William was content talking about motorbikes and vegetable patches with Sybil's brothers. The journey back to Bath was one of complete happiness for all concerned.

The holiday came to an end too quickly. The children attended the local school. Nancy was in Auntie Polly's class and Charlie was in a lower form. I'd like to be in the same class as Nancy,' Charlie asked his Aunt.

'I've arranged for you to go in the third year because Mr. Garaway takes woodwork and your Father said you liked making things. Nancy will be doing craftwork, sewing and embroidery.'

'We like it at the school – I like doing handstands in the playground!' Both children settled well. They loved going for walks down the lanes and picking wild flowers. Each time they came back with bunches of bluebells.

'Nancy tries to pick every bluebell in the woods. She never wants to come home and she's always trying to persuade us to climb on the farmer's haystack.' Heather told her Mother. Sybil did not hesitate in telling everyone that she would be back for good in 1949. She knew William loved life in Argentina. It would be hard for him to leave the railways. Then there was Henry, their sweet son, asleep in that cemetery at the foot of the Andes?

41

Their return to Villa Devoto was not a happy occasion. Whiskers was ailing. He was in his bed most of the day. In order to help the children through the trauma of saying goodbye to Whiskers, Ethel had taken in a small rescue dog.

'Who's that? Charlie cried. A curly black bundle was whirling round his feet.

'He's lovely!' Nancy tried to catch the puppy as he jumped at her. She captured him and held him up for everyone to see before handing him over to Charlie.

'Where's Whiskers?' she asked, running into the kitchen. 'Oh Whiskers, you're not well!' Sybil felt for her daughter but there was nothing to be done. She could not understand why Ethel had kept the poor animal alive. 'What's the matter with him, Mummy?'

'He's old darling. The tumour is causing him pain. We shall have to say goodbye to him.' The whole family stood round the basket and Whiskers tried to lift his head. His tail wagged in greeting.

'I was going to take him to the Vet yesterday, but uncle Jack thought that you ought to see him, Nancy.' Ethel was holding the new puppy. 'You can share this new baby with me. He hasn't a name yet!'

'He'll never be like Whiskers!' Nancy knelt down by the basket, her arms trying to encircle the small animal. He had been her pet for as long as she could remember. Her body shook with sobs and Charlie joined her on the floor. He was crying but he managed to hug his sister. Sybil was just as devastated and William tried to console the family.

'I'm sad too,' he choked. 'But we have to do the right thing. I shall go to collect the Vet. If he puts him to sleep here, we could bury him in the garden and have a funeral for him. We don't want him to suffer any longer.'

Sybil was pleased that William had taken control. She felt fragile and unable to cope with the situation. Nancy began slowly to come to terms with her imminent loss. 'He's in such pain, even though Auntie has given him an aspirin.'

'He needs to go to heaven.' Charlie said to his sister. The two children collected flowers for the grave and they decided to sing 'All Things Bright and Beautiful'. William promised to carve a memorial stone.

At first Sybil was angry with Ethel for keeping the dog alive, but she concluded that Nancy and Charlie needed to learn how to face such tragedies. She felt that she was a coward at that crucial time, allowing William to take charge.

'I can understand why you kept Whiskers alive, but why did you buy a new puppy?' Sybil asked.

'The puppy is mine. I bought her as company for Kiki but, when Whisker's health deteriorated, I had the idea of sharing the puppy with Nancy and Charlie. He can stay here with you and I'll look after him when you go on holiday. I expect you'll go up to San Juan and perhaps Mar del Plata at sometime during the next two years. Then if you still plan to go home in 1949 I will take the dog back.'

Sybil explained to Nancy about Ethel's idea. 'I would like to keep him. What do you think about 'Bambi' as a name?'

'You were a real baby when we went to see that film. We had to leave the cinema because you were crying when Bambi's mother died!' Charlie groaned. 'We never saw the end of the film. We only know there was a happy ending because Dad bought us the book.'

'Nancy is sensitive,' Sybil explained.

'Dad told me that boys and men have to keep their emotions under control. I don't know exactly what he means. I do cry sometimes.'

'It's all right to cry . . . in a way it's better than hiding your feelings!'

•••

On the political side, Peron was acquiring power on all sides and in 1948 the British Railways became *Ferrocarriles Argentinos*. 'You should see them! The people are going mad. They believe that travel will be free and some have been using knives to slit the green leather seats in the first class carriages!'

'Can we go down to the bridge to see what's happening?' Charlie asked.

'Will you take us, William?' Sybil wanted to see for herself.

'I will, but you must promise to stay together.'

They walked down to the station and climbed the wooden bridge that crossed the train lines. A crowd was gathered on the station and some people were just watching from the bridge. 'I can hear a train coming!' Nancy held on to William's hand. The train arrived whistle blowing at full blast with people sitting on the engine frantically waving the Argentine flag. Others were sitting precariously on the steps and some even on the roof. All were cheering and waving as the train stopped at the station. Sybil looked over at William. His expression was one of sadness. It was the end of an era!

Sybil found herself trying to find buyers for their furniture. 'We had such fun buying all this stuff. It is a shame we can't take any of it home.'

'We thought we were great when we bought our sitting room furniture – no one had a black leather three piece suite with black velvet cushions!'

In the meantime Ethel and Jack went ahead and adopted Olga, the young Jewish girl. 'I'm so pleased for you Ethel. She is a clever girl and very attractive.'

'Olga works hard in the shop and she makes us laugh. Jack helps her to do the cooking at weekends and she comes up with some interesting recipes.' Sybil was delighted for her dear friends. She feared that she might never see Ethel again. The fares on the ships were well above their means and even William would find it hard to afford a trip back to Argentina once he retired.

After a short family conference William decided to sell Nancy's dolls' house so he took some photographs at different angles. He also made a drawing of the house in his usual meticulous fashion. He finished it by painting the drawing with his watercolour set.

'Guess what Sybil? Harrods want to buy the dolls' house. They've made me a good offer so I think I shall take it. I can frame the drawing so that Nancy can remember what it was like. A couple of weeks later William decided to take them to town for a special tea at the 'Ideal'. They walked down Calle Florida and when they came to Harrods . . . there was a surprise. 'Look everyone, there's my dolls' house!' Nancy ran to the window where a crowd was gathered to look at the scene. The house that William built was there in all its glory!

'It doesn't look the same. They've painted it a different colour.' Charlie told Nancy.

'I quite like it cream, it makes it look bigger.' The window dresser had made a delightful setting with all the dolls having a picnic. 'Look at that one on the swing! She's beautiful.' Nancy was impressed. 'It's a bit sad, Mummy, isn't it?

'Yes, darling but Daddy is taking a photo. You will always remember the fun you had with your dolls' house.' The house sold almost immediately.

This would be their last Christmas in Buenos Aires and Sybil decided to take the children shopping for presents.

'Let's go to Harrods to see Father Christmas?' Charlie pleaded.

'I thought you were too grown up for that sort of

thing.' Sybil laughed.

'I'd like to go, Mummy. The grotto looked really amazing in the Daily Herald!' Sybil agreed and they made their way towards the store. There were only a few people near the shops and Sybil had an eerie feeling when she saw the security men in their uniforms by the main entrance. Things had changed lately in the capital. There were occasions when people felt vulnerable. Crowds gathered at street corners to demonstrate or cheer for the President. She felt safer once inside the shop.

'I don't want to stay too long. Daddy will be worried if we're caught up in any trouble.' They stood in the queue and the children were right. The grotto was fantastic. At first they boarded an aeroplane that was supposed to fly them to the North Pole. As they sat in their seats the wings of the plane moved up and down. They appeared to be flying. Then when they arrived there was a walk through the snow and ice until they reached the igloo where Father Christmas was sitting with a pen and paper writing down what the children hoped to receive for Christmas.

'What did he say to you Charlie?' Nancy asked.

'He wanted to hear about my railway set. I asked if I could have some more carriages and a few cargo wagons.'

'I thought you were a long time. I asked for one of those dolls in the window, the one that looks like a baby. Mummy says you can feed them with a bottle.'

'Come on, we must hurry.' Sybil pushed them along. People around them were looking anxious and when they reached the main door the security men would not let them out. They were ushering frightened people into the store.

'We shall be closing and putting the shutters down in a minute. You will have to go through one of the back doors. It will be safer that way'

'Look at the fire!' Nancy shrieked. Sybil caught hold of the children and tried dragging them towards the back of the shop. She could see the crowd outside chanting and throwing wood onto a large bonfire. 'Viva Peron, Viva Peron' was the continuous chant. A mother pulling a small boy was the last to enter before the metal shutters came down with a ferocious bang.

'Quiero ver Peron! Quiero ver Peron!' the child was shouting as the mother tried to pull him away. 'He wants to see Peron,' someone yelled. Sybil saw the funny side of the situation when she was safely at home but at the time she was frightened. They were bundled out of the back door into a narrow alley and the Security man pointed to the left. 'You can catch a taxi up there or the underground is quite near. Sybil didn't fancy going underground and was relieved when a free taxi came along. 'You should not be out in this, Senora. They are expecting Peron to arrive at lunchtime and they say that Evita may be with him!'

William was not pleased when he heard about their adventure. 'I told you it could be dangerous in the middle of the town. To tell you the truth I shall be pleased when we sail home next year.' He hugged Sybil and held the children close.

•••

The time came to say goodbye. Sybil was amazed at the number of friends that turned up to see them leaving. Even the Crawfords were there. Sophie was wearing a long dress in vibrant colours. She was now designing fabrics for a well-known company. Mr. Crawford was wearing a cowboy hat and looked quite debonair. They both seemed content. 'I suppose they're doing their own thing now,' Sybil thought. Many of William's work people were there. Some had come from San Juan. Rosario and his son took pride of place. They appeared delighted to see Charlie but Sybil knew that Rosario had promised William to keep silent about the past.

There were two small people at the back of the crowd. An old man in William's old grey suit holding a bunch of carnations – it was Roquelio, the dear old gardener. Next to him was Lola, wearing one of Sybil's hats. They both had tears streaming down their faces. Sybil ran over and kissed them both. She had already said goodbye and arranged for a friend to take them on as maid and gardener. They were both elderly and were not expecting high wages. Just one good meal a day was all they hoped for! She had not expected to see them again and when she turned round holding the pink carnations she felt a sudden grief.

When it came to say farewell to Ethel, they clung together for what seemed ages, not wanting to part. William came at last to take her back to the children and she was shaking with emotion. 'You can't live in two places, Sybil. We've made our decision to go back to England.' The ship silently moved away from the quay. The gap became wider showing the brown waters of the River Plate. Then they could hear the engines. The family stood at the rails waving to their friends – for Sybil it was the end of her life in Argentina!

42

Polly invited them to stay at the old Lewisham home. It was not easy because there were only two bedrooms available. It was decided that Nancy would sleep on a large sofa in Polly's room, whilst Charlie was on a camp bed in the same room as Sybil and William. Sybil found that her sister was prone to hoarding bits of china and even chairs and small tables so it looked even more cluttered with all their cases and clothes.

'We won't be able to stay here long! Did you see your sister's face when Nancy flicked her shoes off and left them on the rug?'

'She's not used to children living here.'

'I shall start looking for a suitable house.'

Sybil enjoyed the company of her sisters. Grace lived quite near and the three of them met for tea whenever they had a chance. Her brothers came round at weekends and they were company for William.

'I would like to move out before I start work next month. It's good of Polly to have us here but I do feel restricted. She doesn't like me smoking my pipe and she fusses when I try to play the piano.'

'Shall we go and see that house again with the good views near Snowhill? I liked it.' After two weeks of house hunting, William was becoming frustrated. He liked to have everything under control. 'Sybil, you must make your mind up! Shall we agree on the house on the hill? The children have to go for their interviews at the schools soon.'

'Let's go ahead and put an offer in for the house.' Sybil agreed. 'We both like it and it's not too far from Larkhall. The bus stop is at the bottom of the hill. Convenient for us and the children.'

They moved in to Upper East Hayes and William immersed himself in planning the garden. He was determined to divide the garden into two levels. Both were designed to have lawns and flowerbeds. Sybil liked taking cuttings so every time she visited Polly she appeared with a variety of herb and shrub cuttings that she carefully planted in pots. 'This is going to be my herb garden . . . I have mint, sage, chives and parsley. I'm still looking for some thyme. I think Grace has some in her garden.'

William erected a flagpole on the top lawn and friends were amused when they saw the Argentine flag flying in a Bath suburb. 'What are you doing now with that steel tubing? Sybil asked.

'Chris salvaged this from one of his building sites. I'm going to build a kind of balustrade so we can lean over and look at your flowerbeds and I can imagine I'm on a ship looking out to sea! On clear warm nights we can sit here and look at Sham Castle and the lights of Bath.

'You are a clown, William! We always have to be different! '

Nancy and Charlie passed their entrance exams. Sybil shopped for uniforms. 'The boater suits Nancy, what do you think William?'

'My daughter looks good in anything! Charlie's cap is a bit too big but I suppose his head will grow to fit it!' Charlie lunged at his Dad and the two wrestled for a while on the floor.

William began his new post at the Admiralty. He was put in charge of sensitive drawings and he often made journeys to Portland in Dorset. 'It's beautiful down there by the sea.' He told Sybil. 'There are wooden holiday huts on Portland Bill and people use them at weekends and for holidays.

'Chris was talking about a family outing to Weymouth. If we go perhaps you can show me Portland, William?' Sybil and the children loved the beach at Weymouth.

'The sand is so clean.' Nancy was drawing a map in the sand. Charlie preferred to hunt for crabs and other small creatures at the rocky end of the beach.

'It's better than Vicente Lopez – that was just River Plate mud!'

The family were content in their new home. The children enjoyed their schools and made friends. Both were good at sport, Nancy with her hockey and netball and Charlie excelled at cricket in the summer. They swam every week in the warm mineral waters at the town baths. Sybil was happy now she was back with her family and William soon persuaded Sybil's brothers to join him at the local pub every Saturday. On some occasions they attended the music hall at the Palace Theatre. 'Could I come with you, Daddy?' Nancy asked.

'You can go,' Sybil answered, ' as long as Dad checks the programme in advance.' William forgot to do this on one occasion and Sybil was not pleased when Nancy and Charlie came home giggling.

'We saw Phyllis Dixey! Nancy blushed.

'She didn't have any clothes on! Charlie laughed. 'She was thinner than you Mum! Dad wanted to leave but Uncle stayed in his seat. He said that he wasn't going to waste his money! Anyway he thought it was art.' The two children started laughing again. That was the last time they attended the Palace! It was exciting when William came home from Portland and announced that he had put a deposit down on one of the holiday huts on the Bill. 'It's only two huts away from your brother's place. Shall we go down to see it at the week-end?'

'Please let's go, Mum! I want to learn about fishing rods and Uncle Chris said he would teach me.' Charlie was full of enthusiasm.

'We shall have to find some furniture if the four of us

are going to sleep in this small space.' Sybil wondered where she could buy some camp beds.

'They do have second hand sales in Weymouth. We may be able to pick something up there at a reasonable price. I can have a look when I'm down here for work.' William offered. Sybil decided to let William furnish the hut.

'I'm still looking for a decent suite for the sitting room and we need a few odd chairs for the bedrooms.'

'The house will look like your sister's home if you're not careful. I don't know if we can trust you at antique sales!' William nudged Nancy and smiled.

'Leave Mum alone! She likes going out with her sisters!' Charlie scolded.

•••

The years passed without any serious disruptions to their gentle existence but one day in 1956 the harmony was shattered when Sybil picked up the letter addressed to William. At that time she was fifty- eight years old and William sixty-two. They still had plans for the future. William wanted to retire when he reached sixty-five and they hoped to find a dream bungalow by the sea in Weymouth. The plan was completely forgotten on that fatal day.

The envelope looked very officious with the Royal Coat of Arms. That was Sybil's first impression when she took it to William who was still in bed. It was then that William was forced to divulge the first of his secrets. Sybil felt betrayed.

'Why did you keep all this to yourself?' She asked over and over again. 'I'm glad Nancy and Charlie are out. Perhaps you've told them and not me.'

'Of course, I haven't told them but I shall have to now.'

'I don't want to go back there – you will have to go on your own!'

'The children are invited. Nancy will be thrilled at the

chance to return to Argentina. We have to tell Charlie the truth about his mother. You are just as much to blame for that deception!'

Sybil felt trapped. William was right. She was the one who allowed things to slide because she always believed that Charlie was her own son. Sybil had developed a fantasy in her head that Charlie was a gift from her friend, Helga. He took the place of her lost son.

'Why do you think she committed suicide? It isn't the sort of thing a mother does.'

'She must have been very unhappy when her family went back to Germany. How are we going to tell Charlie now?'

'If we all go back to Argentina I can take him up to San Juan to see his Mother's grave and I can explain what happened. You will have to tell Nancy. It will be hard for her to accept that Charlie is not her true brother.'

'I can't go with you.' Sybil was in tears. 'I feel you've betrayed me keeping that secret for so long!'

Part V
1956

43

Carol and Frederic left the next day. Sybil was sorry to see them go because she enjoyed Carol's company. Frederic was rather overbearing but he made Nancy laugh and that was a bonus.

'We have two more days and Chichita is organising a boat trip to sail close to the glacier. She says that to see the enormity of the ice it's necessary to view it from a small boat.'

'Are you sure you want to do that? It sounds rather dangerous. We saw large chunks falling away when we were on the coach?'

'The other tour is to see the petrified forest. Perhaps you would prefer that Mum?' During dinner that night they decided on the second option. Sybil was trying to pluck up courage. She needed to tell Nancy the truth about her brother. She was sure that William would enlighten Charlie when they were in San Juan and he expected her to tell Nancy.

'I have something to tell you and I'm sorry that your Father and I have kept the secret for so long. It was wrong of us.'

'What are you talking about, Mummy?'

'It's about Charlie,' She paused. 'He is not your brother!'

'What! I don't believe it. What do you mean? Charlie has always been with us.'

'No, that's where you're mistaken. You were one year old when Daddy brought him to us in Caseros. In those days people often looked after children as a favour, sometimes they were adopted or just cared for, without any legal papers.'

'Where did he come from then? Was he an orphan from the earthquake?

'No, his mother was called Helga. She was my special friend when we lived in San Juan. Her parents were German and they owned a vineyard on the outskirts of the town. Your Dad and I had great times there with the family. Her brother was called Carl. It was a terrible tragedy . . . Helga killed herself!'

'How frightening!' Nancy cried. 'What did you do? Does Charlie know? Poor chap! He will be devastated. He's upset about Dad and you – and now he has to cope with this!'

'My priority at the time was to care for the baby, feed him and look after him as if he were my own. I thought Charlie was meant to take the place of my lost son.'

'Why did Helga do that?'

'We don't know because the war was about to start and Carl decided to join the navy. Helga wanted us to look after the baby and in her letter she requested that the boy should be brought up to be an English gentleman.'

'What happened to Carl then?'

'We never saw him again.' Daddy managed to put Charlie on his passport when we came back to England. He also went up to the Foreign Office to apply for a new passport for this trip. He was lucky to be given one.'

'Perhaps, they're looking for Charlie's father up in San Juan? And who is that Harry chap? Why did he go with them?'

'I haven't the faintest idea. I suppose Daddy's mates are sticking by him.'

'One could be Charlie's real father!' Nancy gasped. 'It's too awful to think about.'

'Tomorrow we are going on the trip to the forest. Let's try to enjoy ourselves. We shall hear all the news when we arrive back in Buenos Aires. I do hope Ethel will be there to support us. I'm tired of the quarrels.'

'Me too!' Nancy's voice quivered as she raised her hands to her face.

'It's not just Daddy's fault, you haven't been very straight with us either. I'm going to bed now.' She stood up and deliberately stalked out of the room.

Sybil felt some relief after telling Nancy about Charlie but there was still confusion about William's war secrets. Harry seemed to be a pleasant fellow but why had she not met him before? She asked the waiter to bring her a brandy to steady her nerves.

Nancy was subdued on their trip. She livened up a little when Chichita joked with her about the Petrified Forest. The coach dropped them about half a mile away and they walked through uneven terrain. Sometimes it was dry and the going was easy and then suddenly they came across a boggy area where moss covered the unstable ground. 'Please keep in single file. Antonio knows the way. We don't want any accidents.'

Sybil kept her head down concentrating on her footing until she heard the cries of delight. 'It's a lake in the distance.' They started walking on a ridge towards the water. The trunks of the bare trees on either side looked as if they were made of stone. 'It's because they've been under the ice.' There were two valleys ahead with separate glaciers. In the lake there were mounds of ice . . . large and small icebergs floating silently along. The sun was shining on the mountains and the lake looked magical with hues of blue and turquoise and a fine light grey mist in the distance. Nancy took Sybil's hand. 'This is nature in the raw – it is gigantic and so inspirational that it makes our problems insignificant!'

'You are right, Nancy. All this will still be here long after us. Love is the only way for us to solve our differences.' Sybil put her arm round her daughter and they strolled over to join the group.

●●●

Ethel was waiting for them at the hotel in Buenos Aires.

'Where's Uncle Jack? Nancy asked.

'He's at work this morning, but he's coming round later for dinner.'

'The receptionist said there was a letter for you, Sybil!'

'I don't recognise the writing.' Sybil prised open the envelope and started reading the letter. 'It's from Harry. He is back in B.A. and hopes to visit this evening.'

'What does he say?' Ethel asked.'

'Dear Sybil,

I have returned to the capital to fill you in about our visit to San Juan. As you can imagine, Charlie was shocked to hear about his birth mother and William wanted to stay with him for a while. They planned a trip up into the mountains William wanted to show him where he worked during the period that he lived in San Juan. I have been asked to escort you, Nancy and perhaps Ethel to San Juan to join them, as soon as possible. First, though, he wants me to explain to you about our involvement in secret work during the war. He hopes that my explanation may help you to understand how he was reluctant to enlighten you at the time. I shall come to the hotel at about half past seven and I'm inviting you, Nancy and your friends to come out with me to eat at a local restaurant.

Yours sincerely, Harry Blakey.

'It really is a mystery,' Ethel tapped Sybil's hand. 'Don't worry, Jack and I will come with you. It will be a relief to hear the truth.'

'How do we know it is the truth?' Sybil passed her hand over her forehead. 'Now you know why I feel betrayed! Why does William let this Harry chap do the explaining?'

'I suppose it's because he's upset about Charlie and don't forget you're partly to blame for that, Sybil. Billy is a sensitive person and you know what he's like about keeping rules and regulations. I expect he thought he was doing the right thing. You must give him a chance!'

That evening Harry was attentive to Sybil and Nancy. He helped them on with their coats and competed with the waiter when it came to pulling their chairs out at the table in the restaurant. They sat in a quiet corner and after ordering their meal; Harry began his story:

'William and I go back a long way. We met in Manchester at a local Magic Circle and for several years we kept in contact. We exchanged ideas about the latest tricks. The last I heard from him was when he joined the Flying Corps. In the meantime I was chosen to train as a secret agent and spent some time in Paris. It was a coincidence that I was sent to Argentina just before the war commenced. As you know there are many Germans in this country. It was my duty to investigate the rich families in the capital and other cities. My workload increased considerably just before hostilities began and I was allowed to take an assistant. You can imagine my surprise when William stood before me as one of the candidates. I knew he was the right man for the job!'

There was a short break when the food arrived. Sybil did not feel hungry.

'Why didn't I meet you before? '

'William told me about you, Sybil and the children. He was worried about withholding the truth from Charlie when he grew up. He told me how happy you were with your baby boy and admitted that he also loved having a son. He mentioned that he was devastated when you lost your first baby.

'So what did you actually do that was so secret?' Nancy asked with sarcasm in her voice.

'Our most important assignment was when the Graf Spe was in Montevideo. A group of six of us set off in a rowing craft. William was in charge of the boat and the other five, including me, were supposed to be dropped near the warship. We were all dressed in diving gear, even William, but he was not supposed to enter the water. My mates and I could speak fluent German and our job was to board the ship with the help of a double agent who was already on the Graf Spe. William dropped us as arranged and his orders were to return to base. Then he noticed that I was in trouble.' Harry paused for a while.

'The German divers guarded the ship in various spots and I had the bad luck to swim into one. As we were grappling with each other I could feel severe cramp in my leg. The German pushed me under and tried to drown me. At this stage William saw what was happening and, even though he was not armed, he turned the boat round and tried to save me. He used an oar to batter the enemy and then threw me a rope to catch. I felt like screaming with the pain in my leg but William managed to drag me on board. He then turned his attention to the German who was spluttering as he surfaced. William was about to hit him again over the head when he suddenly stopped. 'I know that man. He's called Carl Schroder and he's my son's uncle. I can't let him drown.' So that is how we ended up with two Englishmen and one German in a small boat. It was lucky for us that we were not seen in the bright searchlights! William gagged Carl with a large handkerchief and tied his hands behind his back. The poor man just sank down in the hollow of the boat. The cramp in my leg subsided, but I was exhausted after the fight. William was the hero! He saved both our lives.'

'That's why he was away for so long, Sybil,' Ethel muttered in a trance.

Sybil was speechless. William had been in so much danger and she was oblivious to the fact!

'So what happened to Carl? Did you just hand him over as a prisoner?'

'William wouldn't hear of it. 'He has been my friend for years,' he announced. 'It is not his fault that the war started.' William was in full control.

'You have two options Carl,' he whispered. 'Either we hand you over as a prisoner or we let you go free in

Uruguay and you disappear.'

'We never saw him again!' Sybil felt tears coming to her eyes. How brave William had been!

Nancy rested her head on her godmother's shoulder. 'Did you know about this, Auntie Ethel?'

'I knew about Charlie' I thought your parents would have told him when he was old enough to understand. As for your father – he was always difficult to fathom out. Your mother put it down to him being an only child, but I'm not so sure. One minute he could be a complete charmer, an extrovert with his conjuring and jokes. Other times he was obsessive about rules, laws and keeping everything in alphabetical order. When they first met your mother was the only one who was allowed to touch his gramophone records. Does he trust you with them now?'

'He's moved on to a cassette player now and he loves recording music, including us singing Christmas carols.'

'There was more to William's work.' Harry continued. He was given a list of names of people, mostly Germans who lived in the city. They needed to be under surveillance. He passed on valuable information to the secret service about their movements. Several of them were spies who were watching the comings and goings of British ships, especially merchant vessels carrying food supplies to England. In the end William was withdrawn from his duties after receiving threatening literature from the Nazis. He became nervous about the safety of his family and friends. I don't suppose he ever showed you the picture of the skull and bones he received with "Achtung!" written in large print?'

•••

'William knew about my work in San Juan. I was sent undercover to question the German families in the Cuyo district including the Schroders. I hid my identity by pretending to be interested in wine production and the possibility of exporting wines to the United States. We needed to find out if any of them were sending money back to Germany in support of the Nazi regime. It was our duty to sabotage or prevent this happening. The Schroders were planning to return to Germany because the old man was ill. The son and daughter wanted them to stay because of the dangers they might encounter in their homeland. The daughter held a responsible post as matron at the local hospital and she was determined to stay in Argentina.'

'We know all that because they were our friends!' Sybil confirmed.

'The son left to join the German navy and we know what happened to him. William allowed him to go free,' Harry pointed out. Sybil felt uneasy when Harry went on about Carl. It seemed as if he was blaming William for his escape.

Ethel came with them to San Juan and Sybil was pleased to have her support.

'What are you going to say to Daddy? Charlie may be angry with you!' Nancy was nervous as they drove to the airport.

'It is best to wait and see what the situation is when we arrive' Ethel was trying to keep everything calm. Rosario and his son were at the airport to meet them.

'Senor Lawson and Charlie are at the vineyard.' He informed them. Sybil and Nancy were in for a further surprise when they drove along the Schroder's drive to the old house. Sybil smiled, it looked just the same. When they arrived at the door a couple came out on the porch. 'It's Frederic and Carol.' Nancy cried. 'What are they doing here?'

'They're related to the Schroders,' Harry informed them. Carl and Helga are Frederic's cousins. Your son Charlie is related – what is he? A second cousin I suppose?'

'Where is Charlie?' Sybil asked.

'They've walked down to the church in the village.' Carol explained. 'The boy is agitated!'

'Let's go and meet them, Mummy!' Nancy pulled Sybil.

'Do you know the way?'

'I'm so frightened, darling. I love Daddy and Charlie so much!'

'Everything will be alright, Mummy, wait and see.'

The earth was dry on the path but the vines were being sprayed and the scent of the water on the earth drifted over to them. It felt as if it was beginning to rain. 'What a lovely spot . . . I can see why you were happy here.' Nancy went on walking ahead leaving Sybil to meander down at her own pace. She became slower and slower until she could see Charlie running up to meet her. He was smiling. She could feel her heart beating as he drew nearer.

'Mother!' he shouted. He reached her side and picked her up, whirling her round. 'You're very naughty, you and Dad not telling us the truth.' He kissed and hugged her. 'You'll always be my Mother, I love you to bits!' He rushed back down to fetch William and they sauntered up the hill together. Sybil noticed that both men took giant strides as they walked.

'Where's Nancy?'

'She's gone to see the graves. Helga is buried right next to Henry as if she is meant to be his guardian. I'll go and find her.' Charlie ran down the hill again.

William was silent.

'He's taken it well.' Sybil observed. William was still quiet.

'There is more Sybil, I think you'll find it difficult to forgive me.'

'Harry told me about the war.' She moved towards him but he backed away.

'I've learned more about Helga's death since I came up here. Carl was kept in the dark. She only told Rosario and his wife about the baby.'

'You told me all that when you first brought Charlie to Caseros.' She changed the subject. 'It's strange that we met Frederic and Carol when we were down in Patagonia. We enjoyed our trip and I told Nancy about Charlie when we were there. She was angry with me because she told me that you and I are bad as one another keeping secrets.' They sat together on one of the wooden seats. Sybil was tired climbing the steep slope.

'What's the matter, William? I thought you would be pleased to see me. I know about your war work – I never realised that you were so brave!'

'It wasn't bravery. At the time I just followed my instinct. It was a surprise to see Carl surface after I'd knocked him on the head. Harry wanted me to finish him off but I told him that I recognised this German and certainly couldn't kill him! It wasn't just because I knew Carl, I suddenly realised that I lacked the courage. I could not kill a fellow human being. My father was probably right – I am a coward!'

'What rubbish, William! I've never heard you talk like this before.' She took his hand but he pulled away and started climbing up the hill. Sybil followed at a slower pace. She couldn't understand William's attitude. Charlie and Nancy overtook her. 'Nancy is so impressed by Frederic. I think he's my cousin' Charlie whispered to Sybil as he passed. 'We're going to quiz him on where he lives in Germany?' Charlie was always an inquisitive child and now he was bound to enquire about his mother's background. The old folk may still be alive and she was sure that at the top of Charlie's agenda would be a search for his grandparents and his Uncle Carl. William was right when he said 'that things would never be the same!'

She strolled up the path feeling a lack of confidence in her future with William and the rest of the family.

'Carol has made tea!' She automatically sat by Ethel.

'What is it?' her friend asked.

'I'm not quite sure,' she answered. William didn't touch his tea. He moved towards the old orange tree. He looked over the wall to the paths below. Sybil followed him and touched his arm. He swirled round, took an envelope from his coat pocket and threw it at Sybil. 'Read that!' he cried.

He rushed to the house and disappeared inside.

Sybil picked up the envelope and stared at the writing. 'My son Charlie's birth certificate – if he ever requires the name of his father.'

Sybil could feel the blood rushing to her head. The others were staring at her from the tea table. The flap of the envelope was just tucked in so it was easy for her to open it and draw out the certificate. Her heartbeat increased as she unfolded the document.

Her eyes went straight to the top:

'Father – William Henry Lawson

Mother – Helga Galiena Schroder'

44

The certificate slipped from Sybil's fingers and drifted across the lawn. She turned and ran as fast as she could down the hill. As she turned the corner she looked back and saw Nancy retrieving the piece of paper from the grass. All those people having tea would soon know that William was Charlie's real father!

She remembered when she was ill with diphtheria how Helga had supported them both. Laughter from the kitchen and Helga's birthday gift for William had made her jealous. They seemed to have so much fun together making the cocktails. They were having an affair . . . it must have been going on for some time. William often went to San Juan. Charlie was approximately one year younger than Nancy. Months and dates made circles in her mind. Charlie must have been conceived when she was back home waiting for Nancy to be born. How awful!

The zigzag of the path made Sybil feel dizzy as she stumbled along. She pushed the wooden gate to the churchyard and limped round to the back where Helga and Henry were buried and fell to the ground by their graves.

'How could you do this to me? I thought you were my friend!' She shrieked. She sobbed into her hands . . . 'this is the end for me!' Sybil stayed there, her whole body shaking with anger and sorrow. A slight rustle and distant voices made her lift her head. William was standing near and further back, peering round the wall of the church, were her two children, Nancy and Charlie.

'Go on talk to her Dad – we can't leave her here.'

William approached and she allowed him to pull her up from the grass. She felt unsteady but was ready to face this man who, as far as she was concerned, had cheated on her. What story would he tell this time?

'We shall stay here for a while.' William called to the children and they disappeared from view.

'Sybil, I don't know how to explain! You will not believe me even when I tell you the truth. The story is too much for anyone to accept – even I can see that. If I were in your shoes I would turn my back and walk away. I only learned this week that I'm Charlie's father. I have never seen his birth certificate before. It was Harry who told me that the document existed. Carl has no idea that I fathered Helga's baby!' There was a long pause before William continued.

'Rosario was the one who held the certificate and kept it a secret because he feared that it would cause trouble between you and me. He told me that Helga had confided in him: 'William is my only love,' she explained to him. 'There is no happy ending to my story because he loves Sybil.' There was a further pause. Sybil felt fearful, as if she was in a dream. William remained silent for seconds that seemed like minutes before he continued: 'She knew that I was in love with you Sybil and that I would never leave you.' He looked pale and worried. 'Helga was devastated about her parents leaving and Carl's decision to join the navy. She felt that she was being deserted by everyone she loved!'

'So what happened?' Sybil sobbed.

'When I left you in Bath and returned to Buenos Aires, I had to negotiate the terms of my new job. I had to see Stephen about withdrawing from his business. That was when I went up to San Juan to tidy up my old office. In the evening I thought of calling on Helga to see how things were going for her. She was at the hospital so I went round there to say 'Hello'. She was finishing at eight and asked me to wait for her. We went to a new restaurant that had recently opened and I was looking forward to hearing news about her family. Instead I found that Helga had changed. She always was such a lively girl but that evening she seemed depressed – or what I would call morose!

We bought a bottle of wine and went back to her flat. The place looked untidy. She was not bothering to clear up. The sink was full of dirty dishes. It was so unlike her to live like that! She found a couple of glasses and as we drank she told me all about her fears for her parents and that she had begged Carl to stay to look after the vineyard but he refused. She said that many of their English friends were turning their backs on them. 'I think I'm being watched by the secret police,' she told me. There was a further pause as William rubbed his head and eyes.

'We drank quite a lot of wine because she had a stack in the flat and she suggested that I sleep there on the sofa. Somehow I ended up in bed with her! I do feel so ashamed! I have no excuses . . . The only good result is Charlie. I can't pretend not to be pleased that he is my real son!'

Sybil cringed at his words. 'It is hard to believe! You must have seen her lots of times without me knowing. I remember when I was ill you and she spent time together!'

'I did enjoy Helga's company. She was funny and clever – but I only deceived you once, Sybil. I can't remember much about that night but I can assure you that it was a one-off occurrence. I suppose things may have been different if I had met Helga before you. I'm not sure.'

'So you never thought of telling me about your liaison when I was in England. Nor did you say about your heroics on the River Plate or anything about Harry and your death threat! Do you think that was entirely fair?'

'In retrospect – no!' he agreed. 'At the time I concluded that the best way forward was to keep quiet. I was not lying to you! There was no way that I could foresee the future and this present nightmare.'

Sybil turned away, unable to express her feelings, and

commenced the long walk back to the Schroder's house. Nancy joined her, trying to hold her arm. They walked in silence. Charlie ran to his father. The other guests had dispersed and only Ethel remained.

'I need to leave here.' Sybil sobbed. Can we reserve a room at the local hotel?' Ethel took control.

'Yes, dear! We can talk there. Please let your Dad know?' she asked Nancy. Sybil glanced at her daughter – she was pale and distraught. 'Your mother needs some space for a while. She'll be fine in time. It's all a shock.' Ethel explained.

•••

Sybil spent two days and nights at the small hotel with only Ethel as company.

William and the children called several times but she asked Ethel to send them away. On the third day she joined her family on the train back to Buenos Aires.

'You can stay with me as long as you like Sybil. Jack and I can put you up!'

'Thanks Ethel, you are a dear friend but I have to return to England. Your words of advice come from a clear head. Mine is still confused. I need to make difficult decisions.' Nancy and Charlie tried hard to help but Sybil kept her own council. She was not ready to speak to William.

The return to England was a nightmare. William decided to stay in London with Charlie who was determined to arrange a trip to Germany. Rosario had told him that Carl was alive. 'I want to find my uncle and tell him the truth. My grandparents may still be alive!' William tried to advise him to wait for a while but to no avail. 'Frederic gave me their home address and I want to find them.'

Polly was there to meet Sybil and she was the bearer of more bad news. Whilst they were away Millie's husband had died of cancer. 'She's devastated and has rushed in to a job looking after an old lady. We've been out to see her but she is adamant about staying there. The house is about five miles from Bath and she only sees the other servants. One is a charwoman and the other is the gardener. She has left her family in London!'

'Everything seems to be going wrong. Wait till I tell you about William! You'll never believe it!' Polly listened to Sybil's story.

'Mother used to tell us when we were children to always tell the truth but she didn't explain that sometimes it is kinder to withhold information. It looks to me that William has done exactly that about his secret service work! I think you were both wrong in omitting to tell Charlie. As for his night with Helga . . .that must be difficult for you to swallow!'

'Yes it is!' Sybil ran crying to Polly who took her in her arms and held her whilst she sobbed. 'The thing is, Polly, that I would never have had the joy of caring for a baby boy if Helga had decided to live and perhaps fight against me for William?'

Sybil stood before her sister, her tear- stained face showing the agony she was feeling.

'It must be hard – I have two sisters in distress but you, Sybil, are the luckiest! William is still alive and has not deserted you. He knows that your family is here to support you and Nancy. He is trying to console your son and help him to find his new relations. The revelation has been a shock to Charlie! You are not the only one to suffer. As for Millie . . . she has lost the love of her life to a terrible disease. She has watched him disintegrate before her eyes!'

'Oh Polly, I am selfish. Nancy and I will go out to see her.'

Sybil hardly recognised Millie. Her hair was nearly grey and tied back severely in a bun. She had never seen her sister like this.

'Darling Millie!' she cried. The sisters embraced and Nancy waited her turn to kiss her aunt. Sybil realised that Polly was right. Millie needed to be with her family.

They sat in the enormous kitchen in the country house. 'There are some scones in the pantry. Will you bring them out, Nancy please?' She pointed to a door on the other side of the room.

'Why are you working here, Millie?' Sybil asked.

'I had to leave my surroundings. It was agony walking through the rooms of our home. The emptiness was frightening. I decided to come back to Bath but that seemed just as bad with everyone feeling sorry for me. I needed to do something useful. When I saw the advertisement for a live-in carer, I applied and here I am. Come up and see my rooms.'

The ancient house impressed Sybil. Millie showed them some of the main rooms on the way up. It was like going back to the past. It reminded her of some of the descriptions in Jane Austen's novels. The satins and brocades looked faded by the sun. 'We have to remember to close the shutters as the sun goes round. Albert usually does that but Mrs. Grayson wants me to check that he's complied with her orders. She is quite a stickler for rules and protocol!'

'Who is Albert?' Nancy asked.

'He's the gardener. I'll show you round the grounds, then I have to make Mrs. Grayson her tea. She likes sandwiches and one small scone or cake. It has to be just right!'

'I can help you with that,' Sybil said. In fact she thought it would be an ideal solution for her to have a similar post to help her to come to terms with her own problems. They followed Millie to the kitchen where Sybil helped to make some cucumber sandwiches and Nancy arranged a selection of cakes on the two-tier silver dish.

'I'll introduce you to Mrs. Grayson. She likes meeting people.'

The old lady was sitting in a large winged chair, her legs covered by a tartan blanket. Millie moved a side table with a white tablecloth and set a place with plate, knife and delicate cup and saucer.

'It's four o'clock Mrs. Grayson. Would you like to have your tea now?'

'Yes please, Millie. Will you help me to the table please – my legs are stiff this afternoon.'

'My sister and niece are here. Would you like to meet them? They've just returned from Argentina.'

'I'll have my tea first and then we can move over there where they can sit and talk to me. Argentina! That is far away. Did you make these sandwiches, Millie? They are cut just the way I like them.'

'My sister made those. She is used to making dainty sandwiches and she's a very good cook.'

'You're not bad yourself Millie. I enjoyed that chicken at lunchtime.'

Sybil and Nancy smiled at each other when they heard Mrs. Grayson. She had a very deep sophisticated voice. Nancy was happy to recount her visit to Calafate.

'I went to a finishing school in Switzerland when I was young and we went to see a glacier. One never forgets that kind of experience.'

When they were leaving, Millie pulled Sybil aside. I've been here for several months. I would like to go back to London to sort out some of my affairs. Would you be prepared to stand in for me when I go? She's quite vulnerable and has a weak heart. I don't want to upset her. She seems to like you, Sybil!'

'I'll have to talk it over with William. I think we are going to sell our house.'

'There's plenty of room here – it would be somewhere for you to stay whilst you decide what you and William are going to do. I don't think Mrs. Grayson would mind. She is no trouble!'

Sybil tried to take in Millie's offer. She knew that a new start was what she wanted and this was an opportunity to try for her independence. If they sold the house, William could go down to Portland and she, at last, may be able to achieve her own wishes for a well paid post. Her step lightened at the thought. She and Nancy walked briskly down the road to catch the bus back to Bath.

•••

Sybil found it difficult to talk to William about selling the house. It was, after all, the first home they purchased together. Somehow a place was different when you owned it. Rented places had been the norm until they settled in Bath. Now William was talking about buying a bungalow by the sea.

'Millie would like me to stand in for her when she takes a break. She still has to face selling the house in Croydon. The boys want her to go back home.'

'I can see that you want to help your sister but you don't know how long she'll be away. Are you sure you want to sell our house?'

'We talked about that long before this happened. You said at the time that you would like to move to Weymouth. I want to help Millie. It will give me a chance to earn some of my own money. I feel like having the time to think about our relationship. You have hurt me William and I'm finding it hard to just go on as if nothing has happened!'

'Where will I live?' William asked. He looked lost and dejected. Sybil had to be strong and not give in to his pleas.

'You can arrange to sell the house and there is plenty of room at Ardgay. You can also use the hut at Portland when you're down on the coast.'

'You do want to stay with me Sybil? Please say yes.'

'I've not decided. She bent her head to hide the tears that were forming. 'We shall have to wait and see. Nancy is starting college in London and we still don't know what Charlie intends to do. I don't know if he will ever forgive us. And what will happen when he finds Carl?'

'I'm worrying about that too. He said he would write when he finds his uncle. Apparently Frederic has promised to meet him in Germany so he won't be completely on his own.' William shook his head. 'He may even decide to go back to San Juan with Carl. He was impressed by the region and, who knows, Carl may invite him to work on the vineyard.'

'He is an adult so I suppose he has to make his own decisions, but I shall miss him and so will Nancy. It looks as if we are splitting up and each one of us will end living in a different place.'

Sybil rushed out into the garden looking for Polly. 'Are you sure you want to leave all this?' Polly pointed at the view and the garden. She was playing with Teddy, the Scottish terrier.

'The house is big and I'm starting to find the hills too steep. It will be better for us to have a bungalow. I'm going to look after Mrs Grayson when Millie goes back to London. I don't think William likes the idea but he'll have to put up with it!'

The arrangements were made and Sybil moved out. She started her employment at Ardgay and at first enjoyed the change. The other members of staff made her welcome and she found her work easy. She had plenty of time to think. Mrs Grayson was charming, alert and full of fun. Her only disability was her fading eyesight.

'They've said on the wireless that we're in the middle of a drought! Ask Albert to come and see me, please, when he's finished opening the shutters. I have thought of a way to economise on water.' Sybil settled the old lady in her favourite chair looking out over the garden. She found Albert and passed on the message. He was busy working in the vegetable patch.

'Oh no!' he groaned. 'What has she thought of this time?' Sybil laughed when she later found him walking down the back stairs with two buckets filled with water.

'What are you doing?'

'I told you she's mad – I have to carry the bath water down and use it to water the plants!'

'Surely we can think of something easier. If we had

some drainpipe we may be able to set up something from the bathroom window and let the water go down into a barrel. I'll ask my brothers.' It didn't take the boys long to set up a contraption that worked perfectly. Mrs. Grayson was delighted.

William was kept busy showing people round the house and he was pleased at the profit they made when eventually their home was sold. Most of the furniture was put in store and some of the larger pieces were sent to a saleroom. They kept the books because William wanted to make fitted bookcases for their new home. He came to Ardgay and left some of his belongings, mainly clothes. Soon he made friends with Albert and even persuaded him to visit the local pub. During the rest of the time he watched television and annoyed the maids in the kitchen.

'I'm bored here, without a workshop or shed and I feel I'm wasting my time. I've looked up the railway timetable and I'm leaving next Monday.' He turned and entered the bedroom. 'I'm going to pack a few things. Even if I find a bungalow it will take ages before the contracts are signed.' Sybil did not expect him to leave so soon. On the Saturday he caught the bus to Bath to let the others know that he was leaving. 'Chris said he would come with me. I think he only wants to go fishing.'

On Monday William was up early. After breakfast he was ready to go. 'I'm off now!' he called to Sybil. She was in the kitchen making him some ham sandwiches. Quickly she put them in a paper bag so that he could carry them easily.

'Here you are . . . I've made you a snack for lunch, just a few sandwiches!'

'Are they ham ones?' He asked as he put his hat and coat on and blew Sybil a kiss. He walked out of the front door without looking back.

45

On the train to Weymouth I began thinking about my life with Sybil. My mother warned me about married life. She never liked Sybil from the beginning but my Dad loved her. He thought I was lucky to find such a 'pearl'! Our wedding was perfect! Sybil's mother accepted me as a son and I loved being part of the family.

We had ups and downs in Argentina especially losing Henry. I wanted to be involved in the war and my time with Harry was dangerous and exciting. I just couldn't tell Sybil . . . it may have put her and the children in danger! Then there was Charlie – I was oblivious to the fact that I'd fathered a son. Helga never told me that she was pregnant' She must have thought the same as I did that it was an error of judgement under the influence of alcohol. I have admitted that I was wrong.

My only consolation is Charlie. He may be the reason that will keep Sybil and I together. She cannot deny the joy he brought to us and even Nancy loves him as her brother. I shall do my best to keep Sybil and I know she will be pleased if I find a bungalow for us. This time I shall give her every chance to choose!

●●●

I thought I was doing the right thing when I came to Ardgay. William had to be punished in some way. Polly warned me about seeking revenge. 'If you really love him you have to forgive.' I was amazed at Polly's advice.

'You have never been married, Polly. How do you know what I should do?'

Of course, she was right. Love for me is like an obsession especially where William is concerned. I felt lonely again when he was away selling the house. I kept wondering if he was eating properly.

When he came to Ardgay I could see he was bored. He likes being surrounded by people and having projects to do. He was away now finding us a new house! How many homes have we had in our life?

I watched him out of the window. He shook hands with Albert, picked up his case and walked slowly out of the gate. I could see him walking down the lane. He wore his favourite gabardine mack, unbuttoned because it was still warm. He carried his case in one hand and his paper bag with his sandwiches in the other. He must have known I was watching because he turned, set down his case, waved and blew me a kiss.

My heart skipped a beat and I waved briefly. 'Please hurry back William!' I opened the gold locket hanging round my neck, glanced at the miniature photograph of a smiling youth. Then, with my little finger, I gently touched the perfect black curl nestled on the other side. I tried to call after him: 'you and I have twin souls, William. We shall never be parted!'

The End.

Oh! Who can ever be tired of Bath?
Jane Austen
'Northanger Abbey 1818 Ch.10

About the Author

Phyllis Goodwin was born in Bath, Somerset. She lived the first twelve years in Argentina and returned to England in 1949 and continued her education in Bath and London. She travelled and worked in Spain and Portugal. She married and studied at Southampton University. She has two children and four grandchildren. Now a widow she lives on the Isle of Wight.

Also by Phyllis Goodwin:

'The Field Spaniel – Anecdotes and Observations'

'The Field Spaniel Book of Champions'

Coming Soon:

'Field Spaniel Tales'

For more information about her books please check out her Blog and Website at www.maydene.co.uk

To receive news of future books and articles sign up on her blog at www.maydene.co.uk/wpf

CRY FOR ME ARGENTINA

Printed in Great Britain
by Amazon

62672877R00201